BENIDORM VIRGINS

BENIDORM VIRGINS

JANITA FAULKNER

For my parents, Edward and Joan McCarthy
God bless you always x

ACKNOWLEDGEMENTS

I have so many people to thank for supporting and assisting me with writing this book. Firstly, I would like to thank my beautiful family, Nicola, Kate, Steven, Alex, Tom, Abby, Lea, Stuart, Jess, Isabelle, William and Leon for encouraging me to follow my dream of becoming a writer, and always being there for me, as I, will always be there for you.

Thank you to Jo Kirtley, for all your encouragement and motivation, as I strive to become a writer.

Thank you to two of my dearest friends Susan Stenton and Hazel Woods, for your continual assistance with reading draft after draft. Your honesty has been invaluable. That is after all, what true friends are for. I am truly grateful we met all those years ago at Ashton Telephone Exchange, where we worked as GPO Telephonists.

Thank you to all a Create Space for helping to bring my book to life.

Thank you to my own "Benidorm Virgins" who gave me such a fantastic hen party, many, many years ago in the wonderful and crazy town of Benidorm.

Thank you to you my readers for choosing to read my book .... without you, my dream would still be a dream.

And last but not least... Thank you to my amazing husband and soul mate David, for believing in me, we really are a wonderful team. "You and me always and forever." X

ONE

My mission before I went home from work that night—and yes, I chose to accept it—was to get *absolutely smashed*, I muttered to myself as I rushed out of the twelve-story glass building where I worked eight hours a day Monday to Friday.

It was raining again. No surprise there. It was, after all, Manchester city centre, the rain capital of the world.

I threw my red double-breasted Primark coat over my head in an attempt to protect myself from the rain—you know, the fine stuff that soaks you through—and began dodging the traffic as I dashed across Deansgate, as if on trials for the Olympic one-hundred-metre sprint.

I ran onto Bridge Street, down Southgate and dived straight into Mulligans bar to await the cavalry...my bessies, armed with tissues, TLC but no chocolates; I'm on a diet as per usual. Well, anything really, to save me from a night of self-destruction.

I caught a glimpse of myself in the mirror. *Shit*...I looked as though I'd been dragged out of the River Irwell. I shook myself like a dog to remove some of the rain that had stuck to my work clothes during the short journey to our favourite bar. I ran my right hand briskly through my hair and tried to make myself look a bit more presentable.

I quickly scanned the bar for my bessies, but the only faces I recognised were those of the staff. I smiled courteously as droplets of rainwater took it in turns to race down my face, whilst I politely ordered a bottle of house white, as I was a little short of cash at the moment. It wasn't the best, but it would do the job. I took a seat at a table by the door. With a quick twist of the lid, I opened the bottle; I do love these screw-top bottles. With the wine now settled right up to the brim of my large glass, my mission began.

In dribs and drabs, my bessies began to arrive—Libby, Jess, Sarah, Faith, and Sam. In that order. We've been friends for so long, we know the script by heart: if one of us is having a crisis, consume lots of alcohol, bitch, gossip, and talk complete and utter bollocks, and by the time we leave to go home, the problem will be solved or at least on track to be. In any case, we will have had a good catch-up.

Two of the gang were missing due to the life-or-death get-out clause. Frankie, who is a doctor, had to perform emergency surgery and would catch up later, and Chrissy was attending a funeral in her home country of France.

"Excuse me," I demanded, slurring out my words, tears sliding down my face. The remaining dregs of the bottle of house wine had now been consumed. "Will somebody please buy me another drink? All I have left in my purse is my megarider, a coin for a shopping trolley, and a couple of euros. I don't think they accept them in here."

"I'll go," Jess answered my plea. "Another wine, Ellie?"

"Yeah, please, sorry, Jess," I replied, looking up at her with Halloween-scary eyes. My waterproof mascara hadn't worked and had now reached my chin. Jess placed a caring hand on my shoulder before she turned in the direction of the bar.

"E'are, I'll get these," shouted Sam as she walked in. "Anybody else want anything?"

"No ta, Sam, just got 'em in," answered Sarah.

I had known it was going to happen soon—within six weeks, my solicitor had said—and today had just so happened to be that day.

Monday to Friday at a quarter to eight, without fail, I leave home to catch the eight o'clock bus into work. But oh no, today—because my washing machine decided to have a weak bladder moment and flood all over the kitchen floor—the time was more like eight fifteen.

As I was mopping the floor, I heard the rattle of the letterbox, followed by a thud on the carpet in the hall as the postman pushed through today's delivery: a subscription magazine I could no longer afford, an assortment of brown-and-white envelopes, and a pile of junk mail that went straight into the blue recycling bin so kindly provided by Tameside Council, which stood outside my house alongside the brown one, the grey one, and the green one. I didn't even realise the postman came so early. Why did I have to open the brown windowed envelope before I left the house? Well, probably because it was addressed to me, Mrs. Helen McDonald, that was why. And printed in the right-hand corner, next to where the envelope had been franked with a second-class postage mark, were the words MANCHESTER COUNTY COURT.

I knew the contents before they were revealed, but nevertheless, just to be certain, I ripped the envelope open. My decree whatsitsname was looking at me.

I wasn't sure why now, hours later, I was sitting in a pub in the middle of Manchester, crying on a Friday night after work and acting like a spoilt brat. I was finally divorced. I should have been happy. I was. It was what I wanted, after all. My emotions were all over the place. The tears, I suspected, were probably relief. I would have no more endless meetings with solicitors. No more arguing with Andy, my now-official ex-husband. I did have the reality of legally being classed as a single mother of two beautiful daughters, Roxanne, fourteen, and Isabelle, who'd be twelve the next week (a.k.a. Roxy and Izzy), and now they would be statistically classed as coming from a broken home.

Fifteen years ago, I, like most twenty-year-olds, was all grown up. I knew everything. Yeah, right! I was going to get married, and that was the end of it.

Andy and I met at Wright Robinson High School in Higher Openshaw, where we both attended, but we didn't start going out until I left. I was sixteen, an office junior at a solicitor's in Ashton. Andy was an eighteen-year-old apprentice mechanic at the Ford dealer in the same town, and I couldn't get enough of him. Like when you tried alcohol for the first time, and it made you feel all warm and giddy. You just couldn't wait to have it again.

There were a million reasons why he made me feel this way. We'd go out on a Saturday night to the pubs in Ashton town centre, and to end the night he always took me for a curry at the Indian in the precinct. I'd never been treated like that before. I thought I was lucky if I got a bag of chips from the chippy off the lads I went out with pre-Andy. Furthermore, he was dead fit, a good kisser, and he had a car. None of my friends were going out with a lad who had a car. It didn't even bother me that it was falling to bits, rust coloured with specks of the original blue paint dabbed here and there. He was also the first person I'd ever gone to second base with—on the backseat of that rust bucket, parked up in a car park in Daisy Nook Country park at two o'clock in the morning, alongside other cars that were bouncing away just like ours.

I think I did love him in the beginning. What did I know about love? But as the years passed by, I forgot who I was. I wasn't me anymore; I was part of we, my own identity merged into the life where I was now taken for granted. "Make us a brew, Ellie?" or "Get us a beer, Ellie?" or "Elle, did you iron my work pants?" Never a please, thank you, kiss my arse. Andy was a lazy bastard who had two speeds: slow and stop. It didn't take me long to work that out.

Oh, don't get me wrong. Life was great at first when we married. As a wedding present, our parents gave us the thousand-pound deposit we needed for a little two-up–two-down terraced house on Katherine Street, Ashton, to play house in. We had our friends round till the early hours of the morning, drinking and partying. We went food shopping at ASDA by the roundabout, to buy everything my mum told me I wasn't allowed to have because it was bad for me. Then reality set in. I fell pregnant with Roxy shortly after we married. It wasn't planned. That's when the arguing started, mainly because of money. We had none. Or I didn't. He did. I never knew I could cry so much. I couldn't ask for help off anybody because as far as the world knew, my life was perfect, or as perfect as it could be for a girl of twenty who was in love or thought she was. So first came Roxy, and then two years later, Izzy was born.

As the years passed by, I accepted my life for what it was: shit. I wished Andy would piss off and leave me and the girls. I wanted him to have an affair. I encouraged him to work away from home—even work late at the garage. I had to do something. All this bad energy was eating me alive. I couldn't just up and leave. What would I do for money? My salary wasn't that great. Where would we live? And those were just a few of the worrying thoughts buzzing around my head.

I attended a two-day motivational course at the Midland Hotel, St. Peter's Square. Work had made arrangements for any employees who wished to go. "You'll be inspired"—they sold it to us—"not only in your work lives, but in your personal ones, too." If I'm honest, at the time I wasn't really into all that motivational stuff. It was the words "two days out of the office, free buffet lunch" that sold it to me, so my name went down first on the list as it was reluctantly passed around the office.

I took a seat on a table at the back of the conference suite with Alice and Jane from accounts, Alan, the building manager, and Olive, the receptionist, and a gathering of people from companies across the Greater Manchester area I can only assume were also there because they thought it was a two-day skive away from work.

After the facilitators had made their long introductions, which were the most interesting parts of the course, we sat and watched endless presentations either delivered in person or on-screen of how to set and achieve goals, manage change, expand the mind to enable you to reach your full potential, and above all, be positive.

Whilst they were talking I kept looking around the room for anything sharp that I could use to slit my wrists. Now that would have been one hell of a positive move. Two-day skive or not, this was killing me. "Close your eyes, and visualise tasting the sourness of a lemon," one of the facilitators encouraged us. What was all that about? Maybe it was the frame of mind I was in—normally I'm not this negative—but I really didn't get the tasting-lemon thing.

Our group was at breaking point. That was when Alan suggested we play a few games like hangman, I spy, noughts and crosses, anything just to pass the time. We were giggling so much, I had visions of one of the facilitators throwing the whiteboard marker in our direction, hoping it would smack one of us in the head to shut our group up. When I was in high school, Mrs. Parker threw a chalk eraser that landed on Karen Paxmax and cut her eyebrow open. Karen went off to Manchester Royal for stitches, and the rest of us were put on detention.

As I looked around the room during the second day, I could see everybody else was now also contemplating doing away with themselves. I watched one girl continually pop what looked like pills into her mouth. They were probably sweets, but those will kill you if you eat too many—if you believe the story recently published in one of the Sunday supplements about what you can and can't eat. A bloke looked like he was trying to put himself out of his misery by eating himself alive, starting with his insides by repeatedly pulling things out of his nose and munching them in his mouth. Yuck. Another group had the same idea, but they started with their fingernails. My group had even stopped playing games; they weren't helping.

It was about three o'clock, and I could feel myself starting to nod off when I heard one of the guest speakers say, "Ladies and gentlemen, I would now like you to think about where you would like to be in five years' time and write it down in the expensive folder accompanying this course," to which he appended a *ha-ha*. I should have been taking notes in it since the course began yesterday, but mine was full of hangman, noughts and crosses, and doodles. I sat and stared for about a minute and then felt myself going into a cold sweat.

In five years' time, I was going to be five years older, and the only changes in my life would be that first, my hair would need colouring to hide the increasing grey, and second, my weight might go up. They do say the older you get, the harder it is to lose. That was it. My life may as well have just ended there and then. Then *pow*—the kind of *pow* you got in the old Batman television programmes—it was like I'd had a good bang on the head. I went home that night and told Andy I wanted a divorce. I didn't care about the worrying questions buzzing around in my head anymore. I just knew I had to do it.

Andy moved back in with his mum, Sheila, that same night and became the mummy's boy he always was. Sheila loved having him home and waited on him hand and foot. No wonder he was so flaming useless. It didn't take him long to start putting himself out there with the *ladies*. He was a good-looking bloke, midthirties, no commitments, so it was no surprise to me he wasn't short of women to date. Andy made a point of telling me, when he came to collect the girls, all about his conquests. "What you after?" I asked. "A scout badge for vagina collecting? I couldn't care less, I'm not interested." He asked about my sex life. I didn't answer, not that there was anything to tell. I was loving life, spending time with my girls.

I visited my parents to give them the breaking news and immediately had to be reminded of what they had told me fifteen years ago: I was too young, and Andy was a no-good waste of space. Not really what I wanted to hear, but yes, Mum, I know that now, even though I'll never admit it to you. Yes, you were right! Nobody actually said to my face, "I told you so! You were never right together. You were just so different." But behind my back, the old gossip vultures were having a field day.

"'Ere, Ellie." Sam passed me the drink I'd so rudely demanded.

"Ta." I managed a smile.

"I don't know why you're so upset, Ellie," Sam said.

"I remember when my divorce papers came through," Jess joined in.

"So do I. That was one hell of a party." Sarah smiled.

"One of the best days of my life." Jess lifted her glass up in the air as if we had just proposed a toast. "I know my ex is your brother, Ellie."

"I know, Jess, you don't have to say any more. Paul was a knob." I sniffed.

"Well, what's that matter with you, then? We should be celebrating. You know us, any excuse for a party and all that." Sam laughed.

"It's just that I keep thinking about things."

"Like what, for God's sake?" Sam asked.

"Like, say, if I apply for a job, or if the girls go to uni and I've got to fill their forms in, they'll want to know my marital status, and I'm going to have to tick the box printed *divorced*!" My crying turned to sobbing. "I never wanted to be a divorced person and have my kids come from a broken home."

"Oh, Ellie, love, don't worry about that, I never tick divorced on forms," Faith said. "If anybody wants to know my marital status, I always tick widow."

"Widow? You're not a widow." Libby looked shocked. "I didn't even know they had a box for widow."

"Well, some of them do," Faith explained. "And if any-body thinks for one minute I'm going to put I'm divorced on any paperwork...well, world, you can think again. The day I got divorced, that cheating bastard died, as far as I'm concerned, so I'm a widow. It's bad enough me knowing I'm divorced without the whole fucking world knowing I'm a failure."

"Oh my God, are people gonna think I'm a failure? I never thought of that," I exclaimed, my sobbing getting louder.

"You're not a failure, Ellie. Good choice of words, Faith!" Jess snapped as she leant over to comfort me.

"No...they're probably thinking, 'Lucky cow,'" Sam quipped.

"You're the best mum," Jess continued. "A fantastic friend, a wonderful person. It took a lot of courage to go through with this divorce, and it's over now."

"Oh, Ellie, I'm so sorry. I didn't mean…" Faith sighed. "It's just whenever I think of Pete, I get so angry."

"Everybody'll I think I'm a failure and wonder why I'm divorced. They'll be thinking was it my fault—did he have an affair, did I cheat on him, am I a rubbish wife. The list is endless." I stopped for a quick intake of breath. "Well, that's it… as of today, I'm telling you all now. I am *never* getting married again, *never* dating. I'm off men for good." I finished the rest of my wine as if I'd just been given a shot of tequila.

"Helen McDonald, will you pull yourself together?" Sam snapped. "What's got into ya? If ya carry on like this, you're having nothing more to drink, and I'm gonna give ya a slap."

"Are you gonna become a lesbian?" Libby asked. "I believe it's all the fashion these days."

"Libby, are you for real? You don't just become a lesbian. It's not like you wake up one morning and say, hey! I'm going to become a lesbian today. It's your genetic makeup, you stupid cow," Jess shouted, which attracted attention from other customers in the bar. She shot Libby one of her "shut up, you're not helping" looks. "And you call yourself a bloody teacher."

I interrupted. "No! I'm not going to become a lesbian. For a start, I can't stand the smell of tuna!" I giggled.

"What?" Libby yelped with a puzzled look on her face.

"I'll explain later," Sam replied, laughing.

"From now on it's just going to be me, the girls, and this." I leant over into my faithful Prada handbag, which was a gift for my thirtieth birthday from my bessies, pulled out a super-duper, top-of-the-range vibrator I'd purchased from Ann Summers on Market Street during my lunch break today, and plonked it in the middle of the table.

"So that's where ya went at dinner." Sam smiled. "Ya should have said. I'd have come with ya."

"Well, this is what's going to be putting a smile on my face from now on. Ya know, I've not had an orgasm or sex for eighteen months."

"Yes, it has been noted." Sam smirked.

"I've not." I picked up Jess's drink and took a slurp. "I've called him Ryan." The tears were now drying up. I wiped my face on my sleeve and began to giggle. The alcohol was well and truly in my blood system now. "Ryan's now my new best mate. We're going to have so much fun getting to know each other, aren't we, Ryan?" I stroked the box tenderly and leant in to give the vibrator a kiss. "I went to Boots as well and bought loads of different creams and stuff by Durex to help with the fun." I removed those items from my bag and dropped them on the table to join Ryan.

"And why've you called it Ryan? Pray…please do tell." Sarah sniggered.

"It looks a bit like Ryan Giggs: tall, firm, sculptured. Don't ya think?" I oozed.

Libby reached over and picked up one of the products to examine it. "Why do you want strawberry-flavoured penis gel? It's not like you're going to have to give Ryan a blow job. Could you imagine if they invented a vibrator you did give a blow job to? You could fill it with your favourite drink, and when it climaxed you got a shot of, you know, like vodka. I should think about inventing one. Bet I'd make a bomb."

"You really should have been born blond, Libby." Sam shook her head.

"Nobody I know who's got a father who is from India and a mother who was born in Manchester is born blond, Sam. I'm mixed race. We're all dark."

"No, I'm not going to give Ryan a blow job." I giggled.

"You'll be the only one who hasn't then, Ellie." Faith smirked.

"I just grabbed everything on the sex shelf." I took the lid off the strawberry-flavoured gel and squirted a bit on my finger. "Anybody wanna taste? It's really nice. I tried it before I put it in the basket. Wonder if it's got any calories."

"I'll check for you, Ellie, when I go to Weight Watchers on Monday and text you," Libby replied.

"She really is stupid." Jess sighed.

"Thought ya had no money," Sam said. "Haven't ya got a new washing machine to buy?"

"I needed cheering up."

"Don't know what you're complaining about, Ellie, I've lost my orgasm," Faith announced.

"What a stupid thing to say, Faith, you can't just lose your orgasm," Sarah said.

"Well, you tell me where it's gone, then, Miss Smarty-Pants, because for the love of God, I can't find it. It just up and went after I stopped seeing that Derek bloke, and no amount of self-pleasuring has located it. Lately, I've spent that much money on batteries for my Rabbit, I'm thinking of buying shares in Duracell. I was even thinking of booking myself in for a smear test, just to see if I still had any feelings down there."

"Derek probably nicked it at the same time he ran off with that five hundred quid that went missing from yours." Sam laughed. "Ya don't half pick 'em, Faith."

"Tell me about it." Faith sighed. "I don't even know why I'm that bothered, when a block of Dairy Milk usually did it for me after I kicked Pete out. Easily pleased."

"You, easily pleased? Yeah, right," Sarah said.

I took another gulp of Jess's wine, and the glass was empty. "Not sure if I need another drink or if I'm hungry. Any of ya fancy a curry? We could get a taxi down to the curry mile."

"I'll go," Faith said, examining my newly acquired products by removing them off the table and putting them back into my bag. "Wonder what this button does?"

"I'm going to ring a taxi to take us back to yours, Ellie. We'll have a girls' night and order a takeaway." Jess removed her mobile phone from her bag.

"I don't wanna go home until I am absolutely smashed. I still feel like shit." I spoke again like a spoilt brat as I picked up Sarah's drink and finished it. Yuck, it was soda water. I forgot, she wasn't drinking, with her being pregnant.

"Ellie, we can get smashed at yours and have a sleepover, can't we, girls?" Jess was now looking for support.

"Sounds like a plan. I don't fancy going home to an empty house. Pete's taking the kids to Blackpool this weekend," Faith said.

"Yeah! Good idea. Roxy and Izzy are staying at Andy's—that'll balls up his Friday-night shagging session. He's gonna have to play Dad."

"I'm not sure I can come. I'll have to check with Jim." Sarah sighed.

"I'll have to check with Jim," Faith mimicked.

Faith and Sam pulled me to my feet, and Sarah gathered my belongings, ignoring Faith's mimicking. Staggering and slurring, and just in case my bessies didn't hear me the first time, I announced, "And as I said...I'm telling you now. Men are off the menu for me forever. I mean it."

"Course ya do," Sam said, trying to steady me.

"I mean it! Men...arseholes, all of 'em, just use us." A group of men chatting by the bar caught my eye. "Arseholes!" I shouted. One put two fingers up at me. It could have been one; my eyes were now seeing double. The rest ignored me.

"I'll agree with you there, but not all men are bastards, Ellie. Some of them have been kind enough to *drop dead* already," Faith called out as she pulled me towards the door.

"Maybe it's you who should become a lesbian, Faith, if you hate men so much," Sarah said.

"The only female getting anywhere near my bush and flue is Professor Jackson, my gynaecologist, and even then

I'll be keeping a watchful eye on her—she bats for the same team," Faith answered.

"Ya don't believe me, do ya? I can hear it in your voices." My voice was getting louder, and I was beginning to attract more attention.

"And talking of bastards, I still can't believe our Sarah married that bastard Jim last month. And why did you marry him again, our Sarah? Because you love him. That's the biggest load of crap I've ever heard. You didn't have to get married to him just because you're pregnant."

"He's not that bad, and I do love him," Sarah replied. "And besides, I didn't want to have a baby without being married."

"You didn't even have a proper wedding or honeymoon. He's a dominating freak. It'll all end in tears, I'm telling you now," Faith continued. "If he threw a big, juicy T-bone steak into a river full of crocodiles and shouted he'd changed his mind, you'd dive in and try to retrieve it."

"Don't be ridiculous," Sarah snapped. "You know, Faith, over the years you've blamed your bad moods and bitchiness first on PMT and then the menopause. Have you ever thought that maybe you're just a complete and utter bitch?"

"Stop it, you two," Jess shouted.

"I'll show you. Men! Yuck," I slurred.

"We'll see," Sam said, dragging me through the door Jess opened for us.

I grabbed onto the hardwood doorframe, protesting, "I don't wanna go home yet. It's too early. I know—let's all run down Deansgate naked and see if we can get arrested."

"Let's not, Helen McDonald, and besides, you won't get arrested—you'll get sectioned under the Mental Health Act," Jess the solicitor advised.

"Aw, Jess, you spoilsport. I feel like doing something really silly." I giggled as Faith began peeling my fingers from the doorframe one at a time.

"We could call into Browns for champagne cocktails, we've not been in there for ages," Libby suggested.

"I'm trying to get her home, Libby," Jess replied. "Do you really want to do something mad, Ellie?" Jess turned to the others and whispered. They laughed.

"Yes. I really do, 'wanna make this a night to remember'." The Shalamar song came bursting out of my mouth, as if I were auditioning for *The X Factor*. I changed the word "gonna" into "wanna" because I'm clever like that. I should have been a singer-songwriter; I'm always coming up with my own words.

"Well, come on, then, it may sober you up as well," Jess answered, taking me by the hand.

It had stopped raining now, I noticed, as I stood outside Mulligans. The Manchester air hit me with full force as my body, supported by Jess and Sam, was marched along Deansgate, Spring Gardens, and York Street into what used to be Piccadilly Gardens—or it might still be called that—watched on by people who were now merging into the city centre for the start of their Friday night out. Whilst walking through town, I forgot I'd been moaning for the last two hours about not liking men anymore, and found myself shouting to passing groups of men, "I'm newly divorced, and if anybody wants my number, speak to one of my entourage."

We suddenly come to a stop at the fountains.

"We haven't done this for ages." Jess laughed. "Come on, it's gotta be done."

"It's gotta be done," Sam shouted as she pulled me in, closely followed by Jess, Faith, and Libby, all howling with laughter. Sarah, being pregnant, stood to the side, holding onto our belongings and smiling.

The dancing began, me spinning around and around with outstretched arms, intermittently being shot by jets of water piped from underneath the marble tiles we'd taken to dancing on. Faith singing, 'I'm gonna wash that man right out of my hair.' Not that she's got a man in her hair; she hasn't got a man, full stop.

The rest of us were singing Yomanda's 'You're Free to Do What You Want to Do,' at full volume. A group of lads in their midtwenties walked over, shouting, "Get your tits out for the boys." Encouraged by others, we all shouted, "It's gotta be done!" and duly obliged.

FIVE YEARS LATER...

TWO

The weekend was nearly over, and it was back to work tomorrow. I sighed. It's not as if I didn't like my job—I did. Well, sort of...well, I didn't hate it. Now there's the difference. I was a legal secretary at one of the biggest law firms in Manchester, smack bang in the middle of the city centre, close to some of the best shops, bars, and restaurants Manchester had to offer, which was probably one of the reasons why I never had any money in the bank and lived for the fifteenth of the month, every month: payday.

Sunday nights were pretty much the same for me, preparing for the week ahead. I'd gone and got myself into the habit of setting up camp in front of the TV in the living room for the arduous task of ironing clothes for the week ahead. I wasn't an organisational freak or anything like that. I loved my bed too much and struggled getting out of it in a morning. The first thing I did Monday to Friday when the alarm went off was hit the snooze button and grab an extra ten minutes. It just had to be done.

One of the ways I made the ironing easier, if you can call it that, was to put on a girly DVD and open a bottle of wine—not really fussed what kind, as long as it was wet and didn't taste like vinegar. The second way I could make ironing easier was to get another member of my household to do it, but as that never happened, it was always option one in this house.

Tonight I was watching *How to Lose a Guy in Ten Days* with the best eye candy and orgasm-thought-provoking material on screen, Matthew McConaughey. All my bessies knew I fancied him. Just hearing the slow drawl of his Southern American accent got my juices flowing downstairs, if you know what I mean.

Mr. McConaughey did make the ironing easier, not that I really paid attention to the film whilst I ran the iron up and down an assortment of shirts, skirts, and trousers. I slipped into autopilot and drifted off into my own little world, dreaming of what it would be like to be Mrs. Helen McConaughey...Bet I wouldn't be stood in the bloody living room on a Sunday night, doing his ironing. We'd have a housekeeper for that. My days would be spent making love beneath cloudless skies and drinking champagne. Matthew might even let some accidentally trickle onto my boobs and with gentle strokes of his tongue remove it, slowly taking his time, and then continue working his way around the rest of my body so it wouldn't feel left out. Heaven!

Aww, no... Shit! I was abruptly brought back to reality by the smell of burning. I'd gone and done it again, left the iron too long in one spot, this time on my new white shirt.

Now it had a lovely brown mark on it. Maybe I was getting a bit too carried away there with Mr. McConaughey.

Cupboard doors were being banged opened and closed in the kitchen by Darren, my boyfriend. What was he up to now? He must have been hungry. He's always hungry. He has the character of a Jack Russell, faithful, very loving. But he never sat still, and he was always up to mischief. When I wasn't expecting it, he'd pop up behind me, giving me a fright, usually by grabbing me in the most inappropriate places whether we were in the house or out in public. I can't imagine my Matthew would do that...not that I'd object, though!

The pop of a champagne cork ricocheting off the ceiling in the kitchen was a sound I'd recognise anywhere. Darren laughed.

"What ya doing?" I shouted as I removed my new shirt from the ironing board and threw it on the floor.

Darren came into the lounge carrying two champagne flutes and handed one to me. "E'are, madam. Champagne?" He spoke in a very bad French accent.

I gave him a puzzled look, not because he handed me a glass of champers and spoke to me in a daft French accent but because of the stupid expression on his face.

"Bee careful drinking zis," he continued in his silly accent. "Zerrre cud be somefin' at zee bottom."

"Darren, what are you going on about, and what's with the accent?" I took the glass from him. All I wanted to do was finish the ironing, have a long hot soak in a bath filled with Radox bubbles, finish my bottle of wine, and get into my super king-size bed with clean-smelling bedding. Oh! And get back to Mr. McConaughey. I don't want much.

He had the biggest grin spread across his face; A grin only used for when Manchester United get beat. Darren supported Manchester City, always has done. He has a tattoo of the club's emblem on his chest close to his heart—he loves them that much. He has a tattoo with my name on it, on his bum—right cheek to be exact. He had it done on a drunken weekend in Blackpool with his rugby mates after they'd played a game in Fleetwood. I dream about Mr. McConaughey, he dreams about Manchester City. Derby day can be quite intense in our house as I'm a Man U supporter.

I decided to knock the champagne back in one, just to get rid of him, as I heard him say, "Take your time."

Coughing and spluttering champagne everywhere, I screeched, "What ya tryin' to do, Darren, kill me?"

"I told ya to take your time." He laughed.

Panic began to flow through my body, as I looked at the understated gold solitaire diamond ring I'd nearly choked on, now lying in the palm of my hand. I was speechless, a rarity for me, but I knew what was going to happen.

The expression on Darren's face changed; he'd gone all serious on me. Darren was hardly ever serious. He struggled down onto his left knee—he'd hurt it playing rugby yesterday—and took my hands in his. Those big dark eyes were staring up at me (those eyes had initiated sex more often than I could remember). My heart was pumping faster, and I felt as though I was choking on the ring.

"Before you say anything, please, Ellie, just listen to me…" He cleared his throat with two little coughs. "I was tryin' to come up with some big speech about how much I love ya and why we should get married, but ya know me, I'm rubbish at that sort of stuff. But I love you, Helen McDonald, I really do. I don't want to say you're my partner or girlfriend anymore. I want to call you my wife. I want to shout out loud and tell the world you are my wife." He paused. "I know I promised I wouldn't ask you again for a while, but that was nearly a year ago. So please, Helen Kathryn McDonald, will you take me, Darren Michael Fletcher, to be your husband? Would you do me the honour of being my wife?"

"Oh, Darren." I sighed.

"Come on." He smiled. "You're never gonna find any-body else who'll love your cute little dimply bum like I do."

I smiled as I lifted my eyes to the ceiling. I do love him. He isn't perfect—find me a man who is, and I'll do a moonie in the middle of Ashton market—but he's kind, generous, and hardworking, and most of all, he loves me unconditionally, even them embarrassing stretch marks and sagging boobs I'd spent a fortune on buying creams for over the years, as I fell out of love with them a long time ago.

I'd lost count of the number of times he'd asked me to marry him since we moved in together, and I did know how much he wanted us to be married, but he'd never got me a ring before. He was gripping my hands so tight now they were turning blue.

I looked straight into Darren's eyes to offer my reply of no again with an explanation—but yes flew uncontrollably out of my mouth.

I froze. *What just happened?* I looked around the room and then at Darren. "Oh, sod it, why not? Yes, Mr. Fletcher, I'll marry you."

Darren stood up quickly and pulled me in close, kissing me all over the face with sloppy kisses like the excited Jack Russell he was.

"D'ya mean it Ellie?"

"Yes…Darren….Yes, I wanna marry you."

He punched the air. "I can't wait to call you Mrs. Fletcher. Mrs. Helen Fletcher, the wife, ma bitch."

"You're mad." I laughed. "And if anyone's ma bitch, it's you." I kissed him again. Ten minutes ago, I was dreaming about being Mrs. Helen McConaughey. How things can change. *You're forgiven now, Darren, for interrupting me and my Matthew.*

"Darren, put me down. You're squashing me." I giggled.

He gently released me back onto solid ground. Darren took hold of my left hand and placed the ring on the third finger. It was sticky, but I didn't care.

"It's beautiful, Darren. I love it."

"I know you don't like flashy jewellery, Ellie. If you want to change it and get a bigger one, I won't mind. Just say the word."

"Don't be daft. It's perfect."

"Right, celebration meal, then—I'm off to KFC for a boneless bucket. Why don't ya go and slip into something more comfortable for when I get back." Darren slapped me on the bottom as he walked into the hall.

"Like what, my old grey jogging bottoms and fake Uggs I wear when I'm gardening?" I yelled after him.

His keys jangled as he grabbed them off the hall table. "See ya in a bit and put some more champers on ice. Tonight's your lucky night, lady." The front door slammed behind him.

THREE

Had that just really happened? I was forty-one and felt as dizzy as a teenager who had just had her first proper snogging session.

I'd like to say Darren and I first met at some swanky hotel in Manchester, sipping champagne cocktails and eating fancy canapés off silver platters as our eyes met across a crowded room, a choir of angels in the background singing, "Love Is a Many-Splendored Thing" as birds circled above our heads like in the Disney films, but it didn't happen like that. Quite the opposite.

I'd been out celebrating my thirty-sixth birthday, and having lost my bessies somewhere on Canal Street in the Gay Village, I found myself in a drunken state, sat at the bus shelter outside Wetherspoons in Piccadilly waiting for the familiar colours of red, yellow, orange, and white of the Stagecoach all-night bus to Stalybridge. Darren was smoking, leaning against the bus shelter next to a JC Decaux advertising board promoting Matthew McConaughey's new film. *A sign*, I thought to myself. *How bloody lucky am I to be looking at the two fittest blokes on the planet at the same time?* And as it seems to, in most people after having consumed too much alcohol, a confidence not usually present suddenly reared its little head and said, "Get in there, girl, you're not getting any younger."

Doing as I'd been told, I heaved myself up, pulled my belt of a skirt down, and approached him with what I thought was the appearance of being sober. I ungracefully tripped on a broken paving flag and fell off my new sparkly, strappy shoes from Primark. I just thanked God I didn't have my Bridget Jones knickers on, as he got a right eyeful when my belt skirt managed to wrap itself around my waist as he grabbed hold of me. It couldn't have worked out better, and after thanking Darren for saving my life—a slight exaggeration—and apologising profusely for making a complete idiot of myself, I starting talking...well, sort of talking. I was just slurring, from what I remember or from what Darren told me.

When the bus arrived, he paid our fare, and we sat together at the back of the 216. When the bus reached my destination of Ashton bus station, he asked if he could walk me home, where we carried on our drunken conversation outside my little two-up–two-down house on Katherine Street, where I'd lived for sixteen years. With big, strong arms, he took hold of me and kissed me for the first time. My body was on fire, my head shouting, "Quick, dial 999 and request the fire service to cool the girl down, but don't send the men in uniform. That'll make things worse." On the other hand, my heart was saying, "Sod off and let the girl enjoy herself, and if you do come, make sure them uniforms are on."

He asked for my mobile phone, and I willingly passed it to him, watching him key his number in with an "I'm not telling you to, but I want you to ring me" voice. I did, and the rest is history. A year after we met, both our houses were put up for sale, and we bought a small three-bedroom detached cottage in Mossley, with a view of the Saddleworth moors.

I really do love him; that's never been in question. Just the mere mention of his name or a brush of his hand weakens me, even after nearly five years together. It's the marriage thing. It changes people and scares me. Getting divorced was the most painful thing I've ever had to go through. Not just for me, but for Roxy and Izzy. Not much changed at home, really, after the divorce, apart from we had less money. But we managed. I got to enjoy the taste of fish fingers and Aldi baked beans. I just added a bit of tomato sauce to give them more flavour, and I learnt there was so much you could do with an onion and a pack of mincemeat as well. I didn't want all that again.

Whilst married to Andy, I always classed myself as being a married single parent, like most women if they're honest, so in some ways it was easier not having him around. One less child to look after, I kept telling myself. Well, me and my girls survived, and I couldn't see any lasting effects of the divorce with Roxy and Izzy. In fact they probably see more of Andy now we don't live together. He's got to make the effort. Darren's great with the girls and took on the role of stepdad quickly, dropping them off at dancing class and Guides, and going food shopping—more than Andy used to do. He was always too tired when he got in from work, poor sod. "What am I?" I used to say. "Bloody bionic?"

"Yeah, but women were created different to men, multitasking and all that," Andy would reply, and I'd tell him to go fuck himself. He obviously thought I ran on the expensive long-lasting Duracell batteries, not knowing I ran on the cheap Poundland ones, and just to survive the day I had to force out every bit of energy I could and then crawl into bed at night to recharge so I could repeat the whole mundane shit again and again. Bill Murray in *Groundhog Day* thought he had problems. My whole fucking life was sodding *Groundhog Day*. Towards the end of our marriage Andy began to complain about the lack of sex in our relationship, only getting it once or twice a week. "Lucky you," I'd reply, "I've not had any for years, all I get are your sticky remains dribbling down my inner thighs." He didn't like that.

I'm so glad I put my name down for that motivational training course at work and decided that my life with Andy was over so I could start to live.

I grabbed my mobile phone off the fireplace to call Roxy and Izzy. No power—nothing new there, then. I looked at the house phone on the sideboard and spotted the handset wasn't attached. *Why doesn't anyone put it back on the stand when they've finished using it?* I screamed inside.

I rushed around the lounge like I was on some CBBC game show looking for hidden prizes, pulling cushions here, throwing them there. "Come here you," I said as if the handset could hear me, hiding in between the cushions on the sofa, like it was playing a game of hide-and-seek.

After a couple of rings, I heard Izzy's cheerful voice speaking to me. "Hiya, Mum."

"Hi, sweetheart, where are ya?"

"At Roxy's flat. Why? What's the matter?"

Roxy, who is twenty, now no longer lives at home. She is a student at Salford Uni, studying nursing. Her placement is at Hope Hospital, and as most students want the student lifestyle, she moved into student accommodation near the hospital.

"Nothing, I'm glad you're together. You OK?"

"Mum, I only left the house an hour ago. You OK?"

Izzy's eighteen and lives at home with me and Darren. When school finished, she didn't want to go to college. She opted to do an apprenticeship in travel and works at an independent travel agency in Ashton. Next year she is hoping to work in Spain or France as a travel rep.

"Yeah, couldn't be better. Look, I've got something to tell you." I couldn't hide the excitement. "Darren asked me to marry him, and I said yes."

"Aw, Roxy, Mum's finally said yes to Darren! They're getting married."

Excited screams came flooding down the phone. I moved it away from my ear to protect it from going deaf.

"Mum, that's great! About time—we haven't had a party for ages." Izzy giggled.

"Is that all you think about? Parties?" I started to laugh.

"Where is he? Can we talk to him?" asked Izzy.

"No can do, gone off to KFC to buy a bucket for a celebration meal. You know him, he loves his KFC."

"Can we be bridesmaids?" Roxy shouted in the background.

"Course you can. Big frilly dresses like them toilet-roll covers—you know, like what Jordan wore when she married Peter Andre." We all laughed.

I heard a rustling on the line and Roxy's voice was in my ear. "Don't think so, Mum. Want it to be a bit classier than that. Are ya gonna have a hen party? Where ya gonna go?"

"I've not thought about that yet. Can you believe I was in the middle of ironing when he proposed? Why, are you both coming?"

"Not a chance, you and ya friends make us and our friends look like angels," Roxy replied.

"What ya trying to say, Roxy?" I sniggered.

"I'm saying, Mother, you're all mental. You and your friends shouldn't be allowed out on your own. I think it's about time you started taking carers with you, and it should be a two-to-one ratio—two carers to one of you." Roxy laughed. "I just hope that when you're old and go into a nursing home, you're not put into the same one. I can imagine me and Izzy being called into the manager's office to get a telling-off because you're being naughty. Like the one you and Dad got off the head teacher at West End, because Izzy released all the birds in the aviary in the school hall? She'd watched Jasmine do it in *Aladdin*. Remember. It took Beryl, the school caretaker, weeks to catch them all."

I laughed at the memory. "Don't remind me. But she was right. That cage was far too small for all the birds in there. Anyway, I've told you I'm not going into a nursing home. That's why I had you two. I thought we'd discussed that already." I continued to laugh. "So does that mean you're not coming?"

"Got it in one," replied Roxy.

"I didn't think I'd be talking about this tonight. I suppose we could go to Blackpool for a hen party. We've always had some good nights out there. Or a spa weekend. I'm sure the girls'll come up with something."

"This is soooooo exciting," exclaimed Roxy.

"I've got to run. Darren'll be back soon, and we're having a carpet picnic, so tell Izzy not to rush home."

"Mum!" screeched Roxy. "Too much information!"

After reuniting the handset with its stand, I quickly tidied the ironing paraphernalia away and stuffed the clothes, even the ironed ones, into a cupboard under the stairs and rushed into the kitchen to grab the open bottle of Taittinger champagne from the fridge. I filled the ice bucket I pinched from Brannigans, Manchester, after a boozy night out, grabbed a blanket out of a cupboard in the lounge, and took a couple of glasses off the dresser. As soon as I'd thrown the blanket on the floor, neatened it out, and put the glasses and champagne to one end, I hurried upstairs to change.

I opened our bedroom door and looked at myself in the full-length mirror on the wardrobe. Not good—hair going greasy, scrunched up on top of my head, makeup worn off—but no time for a full makeover, and it wasn't like Darren had never seen me not looking my best before. I retouched my makeup and applied a thick layer of come-to-bed deep-red lipstick, let my hair down, added a bit of mousse to give myself a bedhead look and a quick squirt of hairspray to keep it in place. With a swift pull at my underwear drawer, I found a red-and-black basque, all lacy and racy, a suspender belt and red fishnet stockings purchased from an Ann Summers house party at Sam's. Not what I'd call comfy, but Darren would be happy. Maybe he should try wearing an outfit like this; then he'll know how I suffer just to make him happy.

Now that I thought about it, he did actually wear something similar when we went to watch the live *Rocky Horror* show at the opera house a couple of years back. Roxy and Izzy did his makeup, gave him a long blond wig to wear, and put false nails on him, painted black. After dressing himself in a black basque I got from a charity shop, a studded thong he had—I didn't ask where it had come from—stockings, suspenders, and knee-high black boots only zipped halfway up his legs because his calves were too muscular, he took himself into the lounge and downed a bottle of red wine for Dutch courage before we left the house. The top part of his basque was used to house cigarettes in one cup and a lighter in the other as he had no pockets in his outfit. The best part of the night was to watch him and his mate Marc squirm with all the attention they received from the transvestites and gay blokes who normally frequent the Gay Village. To my knowledge, they never dressed like that again.

After giving my lady bits a quick soap-and-water tickle in the bathroom and dressing, I covered myself in Dior's Miss Dior, my fragrance of the moment.

Time was pressing on, and Darren would be home soon. I rushed back downstairs, nearly tripping in my four-inch stilettos in the process. They're not the type of shoes I normally go out in, these were my dressing up shoes. I'd definitely end up in A and E with a broken something or other if I did try and go out in them. I struggled in three inch ones nowadays, especially when I'd had a drink.

Back in the lounge, I lay on the blanket, and positioned myself as provocatively as I could whilst wearing this basque. The bones were killing me, and it was a tad bit on the tight side. It's been a while since I dressed up wearing this basque, but I know Darren will enjoy it, it's his favourite. Think I might have to go on yet another diet, and get a few pounds off, before I wear it again. The things we do for love, hey! I gave my head a quick flick from side to side to position my hair sexily over my shoulders and gazed lovingly at my engagement ring, waiting for Darren to return.

I suddenly realised I hadn't put any music on—not that music would be required to create an atmosphere, but it wouldn't do it any harm. I quickly got up off the blanket and went over to the CD unit, where I picked out three of my favourite CDs. Barry White—can't beat a bit of the love god, a compilation of the greatest love songs, or so the CD says— a bit cheesy, but it set the scene, and *Simply Red* because I love the sound of Mick Hucknall's voice. After placing the CDs into the CD player and pressing play, I turned the music down low, lit a few IKEA vanilla-scented candles, switched off the lights, and threw myself back on the blanket. Phew…I didn't know if I was ready for a night of lovemaking or a glass of Horlicks and then bed. I was knackered.

The sound of a key in the lock was the sign I needed to get into position. I lifted up my upper body and leant onto my left elbow, with my left leg stretched out and right knee raised. I tossed my bed head back into a kind of statuesque pose. The front door opened and slammed closed. Darren dropped his keys back where he'd taken them from earlier, and his heavy footsteps on the wooden floor made their way closer to the lounge.

He stood, for a moment in the doorway, looking at me. I've seen that look on his face a thousand times. His eyes were undressing me. Not that he's got much to take off; I've done half the job for him. He placed the KFC bucket onto the sideboard.

"What ya doing lying on the floor half-naked, Mrs. Fletcher? You'll catch your death," he said, smirking.

"Shut it…Mr. Fletcher, and get over ere and show me why I'm marrying ya."

Walking slowly in my direction, kicking off his shoes—with KFC no longer on his mind—he knelt down beside me and placed a kiss gently on my lips. My body stirred as he wrapped me in his arms and pulled me close. Our tongues touched and shivers ran at Formula one speed up and down my spine.

Darren slowly unclipped my basque to expose my breasts and paused to admire them.

I sighed. I could breathe now, thank God, and he'd never know it was a sigh of relief because I was dying for him to get it off.

He gently caressed my breasts, taking hold of each one in turn so they felt equally loved. I arched my back in pleasure as he gently kissed and stimulated each nipple.

A gratified moan left my mouth. My hands quickly located the top of his jeans and began to unbuckle his belt and zipper as he gently placed me back onto the blanket. I watched as Darren removed all of his clothes to expose his strong muscular frame. He leant over and kissed me again on my mouth, whilst tracing his fingers slowly down my neck and along my sternum, passing my belly button and down into my pleasure zone, stopping to tease my clitoris with slow circular motions. I gasped and felt incredibly lucky he'd never needed a GPS to give him directions—his years of sexual experience never ceased to amaze. His fingers moved swiftly inside of me—I was ready, and he knew it. With his body positioned on top of mine, we were soon moulded together as one, moving to a synchronised rhythm with faster and shorter breaths. Pulses racing, heat radiating from our bodies. With every thrust, my head was screaming for him to go deeper and deeper inside of me. I went into my own world of pleasure until our bodies exploded in unison. We lay there for some time as we listened to our bodies recover.

As the evening moved along, we continued with our little picnic from KFC on the blanket, talking about anything and everything, laughing, drinking, and making love. I didn't give Monday another thought.

"You know what, Ellie?" Darren's arms are still around me, holding me close on the blanket.

"What, my love?" I exhaled and looked at him with adoring glassy eyes.

"I can't believe you kept making me have sex with you, and we let the KFC go cold." He grinned.

I reached out, grabbed a cushion off the settee and playfully whacked him over the head with it. "You could have always put it in the microwave to warm it up, but no, you were toooooo busy drizzling gravy onto my boobies and licking it off, you naughty boy."

He laughed. "Come on, pretty lady, I think I need to get you to bed. We've both got work in the morning, and you're drunk. God help you tomorrow."

"Don't you worry about me, I'll be fine." I was slurring. "Hey, when did all the candles go out?" The living room was now only lit by the low flames flickering through the artificial coals of the Velux gas fire.

"No idea, Ellie. Too busy shagging your brains out." He laughed, scooping me up in his arms.

"Onwards and upwards," I commanded as he carried me out of the living room and up to bed.

FOUR

I woke with a jolt, courtesy of my morning alarm. The Bangles were singing "Manic Monday" at the tops of their voices. Great, just what I wanted to hear. How could it be morning? I was sure I'd only just climbed into bed. Oh no, there it was, the pounding hangover headache, my punishment for having too much of a good time last night.

"Hit the snooze," Darren mumbled.

I dragged my arm from beneath the covers and pressed a button on the radio alarm. I might have pressed snooze, or I might have turned it off. Didn't know, didn't care.

I felt Darren's breath heavy against my neck. He lifted my hair to one side and gently kissed it. His left hand slowly moved down my naked body and stopped to caress my stomach. Then it headed on its journey south.

"What ya doing?" I slapped his hand.

"Thought we might have a bit of a replay, ya know, from last night before we get up for work."

"Ya can think again, my lad. The only thing I'm thinking about is what to write for my obituary in tonight's issue of the *Manchester Evening News*." I groaned. "I can't go into work today. I'm dying."

"Go on, Ellie, hair of the dog and all that."

"Sex is not a hangover cure, Darren."

"Works for me." Darren sharply removed his hand from my stomach. "Come on, then, you'll feel better once you've had a couple of paracetamol and a glass of water." Darren sounded ever so concerned, but I'm sure I could hear a snigger in his voice.

"I don't need a glass of water, I need a hose pipe forced down my throat, and ughh…my mouth is angin', you wouldn't want me to put this tongue in your mouth. Believe me, I don't even want to put it in my own mouth." I grabbed hold of my head.

"Don't be so dramatic. You're such a drama queen." Darren gave me a gentle nudge in the back.

"I'm not going in," I said, throwing the quilt over my head. Suddenly I got the urge to go to the loo. I was gonna be sick. Quickly throwing the quilt off my body, I dashed into the bathroom, closely followed by Darren.

"Good night, wasn't it?" He gently rubbed my back as I slumped on the floor with my head in the toilet bowl, bringing up the contents of last night's little feast. Such a caring guy!

I grabbed a handful of toilet paper from the roll to wipe my chin and pulled myself up. "I'm getting back in bed and ringing in sick. Why do you never get a hangover? I hate you sometimes."

"Years of practice, Ellie. You'll be OK once you've qualified...my little apprentice."

Darren always calls me his apprentice where drinking is concerned because I'm rubbish at it.

"You're not funny—you know I can't drink. You're supposed to look after me, you know, you being my mentor and all."

"I know, sorry, Ellie, but ya know how ya get when you've had a drink." He laughed.

I gave Darren a look to kill, flushed the toilet, and went back to bed to die. "Always thinking of yourself."

I put a pillow on my head, trying to drown out the noise of Darren's electric toothbrush. It sounded like a pneumatic drill. I wanted to tell him to turn it off, but my mouth wouldn't work. Then he had the nerve to have a shower, and that sounded like heavy rain dancing on top of a caravan roof at a Towyn campsite. I swore to God, if he started singing, I'd get out of bed and stab him with whatever I could get my hands on.

Me and hangovers are not the best of friends—never again, I told myself, but how many times had I said that? I never learn. But I meant it this time. I was getting that sick feeling again.

"I've put ya a glass of water on the side, and there's a packet of paracetamol. I'm off. I'll ring you later." Darren removed the pillow from my head and gave me a kiss. "Bye, Mrs. Fletcher." The bedroom door banged to a close behind him. I placed the pillow back over my head.

FIVE

I reached out of bed and fumbled around on the bedside cabinet for my mobile, knocking over the glass of water in the process, and after I located the number for my office, pressed the call button.

"Good morning, Baxter and Turnbull Solicitors, can I help you?"

"Hey, Sam, it's me," I croaked.

"Morning, babes, what's up?"

"I'm not coming in today. I need to talk to the bitch. I feel as though I've gone ten rounds with Ricky Hatton. In fact, I can still feel him punching me in the head with them bloody big boxing gloves."

"Lucky you." Sam laughed. "Don't mind a bit of a gingar."

The bitch is what we call our office manager, Brenda. Brenda, the bitchy witch. Childish, I know, but hey, she owns that nickname. Brenda looks so old. She's probably fifty-fiveish but dresses far too old for her age. Her hair is a mucky brown-grey colour and looks as though she cuts it herself using garden shears, having a basin as a template;

Brenda would be an ideal candidate for one of those makeover shows. We even think she has a moustache, but nobody's ever been brave enough to get close to her. Sam constantly makes sarcastic comments about her BO and sneakily squirts her with perfume or deodorant at every opportunity. We even buy her toiletries for birthdays and Christmas, but Brenda never seems to get the hint. Every company has a Brenda. She is a vindictive cow who has stabbed both Sam and me in the back so many times, I'm surprised we're still standing.

"I'm dying."

"Why, babes, what's the matter with ya?"

Sam and I have been friends ever since we sat next to each other on our first day of nursery school. I remember being ushered into the classroom, crying, by Mrs. Jones, my nursery teacher, and she sat me down beside Sam, who was also crying. Sam looked at me and said, "Hello, I'm Samantha. Will you be my friend?" and we've been friends ever since. We've shared everything over the years, from nits to our deepest, darkest secrets. There's nothing we don't know about each other. Sam is the sister I chose for myself.

Sam's five six, with long honey-coloured hair out of a bottle, chiselled cheekbones, and a body to die for, not like a typical forty-one-year-old. Sam is over the top when it comes to her body. Her stomach is as flat as a pancake, which is her reward for working out five mornings a week at the gym around the corner from our offices. She returns in the evenings for extra training sessions off her personal trainer in things other than weights, which Sam says is a far better way of working out; it keeps the pelvic floor muscles tight. About three years ago she had a boob job because she couldn't stand it that her boobs resembled a cocker spaniel's ears.

Sam is married to Martin, and they have two boys—Dale, fifteen, and Josh, eleven. She had them both by caesarean. She tried to convince me it was for medical reasons, but the real reason was she'd watched a video of childbirth at antenatal class and couldn't come to terms with the fact her vagina was going to be changing from the size of a drinking straw to that of a sewerage pipe in a matter of hours. She gave me a call when she got home, and I can still hear her screaming down the phone now. "No amount of exercise or surgery could ever put my flue back to its original size. How would I ever be able to have sex again? I'd never be able to grip a butternut squash, let alone a penis." I just cracked up on the floor in hysterics.

"I've got the worst hangover ever. Darren proposed to me last night, and I said yes. We got really drunk, had lots and lots of sex, and now I am paying the price."

"Bloody hell, Helen McDonald! Congratulations.... What happened to 'I'm never getting married again. All men are bastards'?"

"You're not funny, Sam, and thanks for reminding me…again."

"You gonna be coming in to work tomorrow walking like Tina Turner." She laughed. Sam always said if you ever wanted to do an impression of Tina Turner, walk around, like you've had too much sex, and you'd nail it.

"Sam, don't make me laugh."

"Go on then, babes, give me the details. Hen party, when and where? Wedding, when and where?"

"Please, Sam, will you stop making me laugh? I feel like shit. You just don't care, d'ya?"

"Course I do, Ellie, I'm dead happy for you." Her laugh was getting louder. "So go on. Hen party?"

"Sam, I've not thought about anything since I opened my eyes this morning, and thinking of a hen do with you, full of champagne and plastic willy straws, is the last thing on my mind. The way I feel at the moment, I should be laid out on a cold slab waiting for my own autopsy." I groaned.

"That's because you're such a lightweight. Told ya, ya should have started drinking younger, you'd be an expert by now. Don't think you'll ever learn, will ya. Anyway," Sam continued. "Why you ringing the bitch and not me?"

"I'm ringing in sick. I'll tell her I've got an upset stomach and the runs or something like that. Can you remember what I used last time I rang in sick, when I went off to the Trafford Centre looking for an outfit for Darren's work do?"

"You are pissed, Ellie. You're not in work today, idiot, you booked today off as a holiday because you wanted a long weekend. You said all you wanted to do on Monday was stay in bed, watch a bit of Jeremy Kyle to see how the other half live, realise your life's not as bad as you thought it was, read magazines, and eat shite."

"I'm not thinking straight." I moaned. "Oh God, Sam, why do I drink? You'd have thought after all these years and nights out I might be a little bit of a drinker. I'm not doing it anymore."

"Course you're not."

"Will ya stop laughing? You're doing my head in. I won't be eating anything today, not after what I've just thrown up. I might put the telly on later to watch Jezza and *This Morning* and then *Loose Women*. Wonder who's on today. Hope Colleen is."

"Stop feeling sorry for yourself. Hen party—where we going? It's got to be somewhere good. I've not been on a hen party for ages. Been to a few good divorce parties, though."

I never really had a hen party when I got married to Andy. I didn't have the money to spend on a hen party. I was too busy saving to buy bits and pieces for our house. About ten of my friends went over to Sam's parents house, the week before my wedding, played a few silly games and got wasted on cider and Cherry B. I've never drank cider since that night. I was so ill. Even to this day, if I smell cider I start to heave.

"Hen party.... that was the first thing Roxy said to me, not that Izzy and Roxy are coming. They think we're all mad, and to be honest, I don't blame them. Can we talk about this tomorrow? I feel like I'm gonna to throw up again."

I sensed Sam smiling down the phone. "What do you mean, can we talk about it tomorrow? Ellie, it's all we're gonna be talking about until we go. See you later, babes. Say congrats to Darren for me."

I pressed the red button on the handset, threw it on the bed, grabbed the quilt with both hands, and dragged it over my head.

SIX

After a good night's sleep and no sex, much to Darren's disappointment, I felt almost human again and ready for a day in the office with Sam to start making plans for our wedding.

"Morning, babes." Sam threw her arms around me, as I walked into the office and gave me a great big hug.

"Morning," I replied, oozing confidence.

"Go on, then, show us ya ring."

I lifted up my left hand.

"It's stunning, Ellie. He's not a bad catch, is he."

"I know, apart from all his farting and burping."

"How ya feeling now? Ya know, after your wild night of passion. I noticed ya can still walk with your legs together."

Sam makes me laugh. "Great, now I've slept my hangover off. I won't be doing that again in a hurry."

Sam had already made us both a brew. They were steaming nicely on our desks. Neither of us becomes fully functional until we've had at least two cups of tea each, and before I even thought about turning on my computer, I told Sam about the wedding plans Darren and I had discussed last night.

"We're hoping to get married on May twenty-fifth next year at St. Andrew's Church."

"On your birthday. Good idea."

"I thought I'd make it easy for Darren, you know, only have to remember one important date in the year, so hopefully he'll remember not just my birthday but our anniversaries as well." I laughed. "We're gonna have a big wedding, not like one of them *My Big Fat Gypsy Wedding* things, something traditional, especially with Darren never being married before. He's never even come close. I'm sure he had commitment issues. He's the male version of Julia Roberts in *Runaway Bride*. His previous girlfriends only had to mention the word marriage, and he was off like a shot."

"Or maybe he was waiting for that one special person that would make his cock stand to attention quicker than—"

I cut her short. "It's all about sex with you, isn't it, Sam."

"Not always." She paused. "OK, yeah, suppose it is."

"Anyway, we want Roxy and Izzy to be bridesmaids, and we'd love it if you, Chrissy, and Frankie would be, too."

"Wow! Me, a bridesmaid? I'd be honoured, Ellie. It's not like I've not done it before for ya, if ya know what I mean." She put her hand in front of her mouth and yawned, then giggled. I knew exactly what she meant. Sam was my maid of honour when I married Andy.

I got up from my desk, playfully nudged her in the arm, and gave her a hug. "Thank you."

"And now…for the most important decision you're going to have to make about this wedding." Sam did a little drumroll on her desk with the ends of two Bic biros. "Hen party?"

"I'd like to go somewhere with a bit of sun, just for a few days. What d'ya think?"

"What do I think? I've been thinking of nothing else since ya rang me. I was on the Internet most of yesterday. Well, actually all of yesterday. I didn't do any work. Good job the bitch was in meetings all day. Have ya seen the state of my desk?" It looked like a parcel bomb had exploded on it. "I should have worked my way through these audio tapes and got the letters out yesterday."

"I'll help."

"Knew ya would, babes." She smiled. "I was checking out Benidorm."

"Benidorm? Yeah, never been. Sounds good to me."

"If ya wanna get married in May, what about going in March? The weather's not too bad, have a look." Sam pointed to a chart on her computer showing the weather was anything from fourteen degrees to twenty-four degrees. I was just happy not to see a minus sign in front of any of the numbers. "Warm enough to sunbathe, so we can sit around the pool and look, as Craig Revel Horwood says, 'Fabulous, darling.' We could go on a Friday morning and come back on a Sunday night. So what d'ya think?"

"Fan-bloody-tastic! I'm up for that, and I'm sure the others will be, too. Yeah, let's do Benidorm."

I walked back around to my desk and switched on my computer. "I'll send an e-mail to the girls to let them all know about me and Darren getting engaged, that way they'll all find out at the same time."

"Already prepared one for ya," Sam said. "Saves time. I'll forward it to ya. Add your bits and send it out. Job's a good un."

"If only ya moved this fast when doing what you're paid to do, you'd never have anybody complaining about deadlines being missed, then."

"Priorities, babes, priorities."

To: BFFs
cc. Michelle Taylor
From: Ellie McDonald
Subject: Going to the chapel, and I'm gonna get married TO DARREN

Morning, ladies

Hope you're all OK.

I just wanted to let you all know, Darren proposed to me on Sunday night and I said YES!

I know…I said I was never going to get married again, but I've decided there's no point in waiting any longer for Mr. McConaughey to come along and sweep me off my feet, especially now that he's a dad. Fat chance of that happening now. So I've said yes to Darren. Also it's a good excuse to have a PAR…TAY…

We're planning to get married on my birthday next year at St. Andrew's Church.

I'm in work with Sam, and we've been talking about my hen party. Sam's done all the groundwork.

We were thinking of going to Benidorm in March. How does that suit you all? Friday till Sunday. Can you let me know what you think?

Text or e-mail me.

Speak to you soon

Love, Ellie. oh! and Sam xxx

It didn't take long for my iPhone 4 to start bleeping with message alerts.

Congrats, about time…I'm coming. I'll go off sick. Libby xxx

Libby's thirty-seven and a primary-school teacher at a school in Harpurhey, Manchester. Married to Barry—boring Barry, as we call him—and they have three children—Ben, fifteen, Michael, twelve, and Rachel, nine. Libby's always up for a laugh and is the most animated member of our group. Very dramatic, overexaggerates everything, and seems to wave her arms about a lot.

I'm very happy for you both. Would love to but can't commit at the moment. Congratulations, Sarah.

Sarah's thirty-nine and married to Jim. Even after five years we're still shocked that one day out of the blue, Sarah announced they were getting married, not inviting anybody, and going off to Gretna Green. He's very controlling, is our Jim, and didn't want the fuss. What Jim wants, Jim gets. They have a beautiful little five-year-old daughter called Maisy, whom Sarah dotes on. We know Sarah and Jim have problems, but she won't admit it. We just wish she would talk to us about whatever is bothering her.

Hope I'm not the last to answer, only just got out of surgery. Yes. Fantastic. Congrats. Speak to you later, F. x

Frankie's a thirty-six-year-old paediatric doctor at Tameside Hospital. Doctor Frankie, as all her patients and parents call her. She goes way above and beyond what is expected of her at work. She knows all the words to "Let It Go" from *Frozen* and can be heard singing it along with her patients on the wards. She doesn't sing it as good as Idina Menzel, but she gives it a damn good go. She can kick arse like a Power Ranger, and she even has to discipline herself sometimes as she gets so carried away with her patients.

Frankie and I adopted each other twelve years ago after her sister, Kat, who was one of our best friends, died of cervical cancer when she was twenty-nine. Frankie is five six, with long brown hair, or it could be bright red. I haven't seen her for a couple of weeks. She's a feisty lady and our karaoke queen, always up for a party and a giggle. Did I mention—she works hard and parties harder.

Faith's text immediately reminds me of the script from *When Harry Met Sally*:

YES! YES! YES! YES! YES! I'll do your chart and get back to you. Faith xxx

Faith's forty-seven, Sarah's older sibling, and a sister at Tameside Hospital, in men's surgical. Faith hasn't always been a nurse—she used to work for the dreaded Inland Revenue, but when the chance to take voluntary redundancy was offered, she revealed she had the calling to be a nurse, which amused everybody, I can tell you. Blood was a no-no, and so were moaning people. And if you had the urge to vomit, Faith would be off faster than the *B* of the bang. But when she came to meet us at the end of her first week of training on the old people's ward and announced she'd spent half the afternoon fishing around in a bucket of warm sick trying to retrieve a set of false teeth whilst throwing up in the toilet at the same time, we knew she'd make it as a nurse after that. She divorced her husband after the affair he was having with his secretary came to light about six years ago. Scott, age twenty-three, and Charleen, age twenty-two, are their offspring, named after the characters in the *Neighbours* soap, which was her favourite TV programme when Jason Donovan and Kylie Minogue were in it during the eighties. Charleen has just announced she's pregnant with baby number three, and after splitting with her boyfriend, she is in the process of moving back in with her mum, as she's finding it hard to cope on benefits and with her two other children, who are aged five and three. Faith has always been a bit weird—you know, shopping in Affleck's Palace, into the occult, horoscopes, and all that. We half expected her to call her children Hocus and Pocus. Thank God for

Neighbours, that's what I say. Faith recently split up from her boyfriend of eight months, some weirdo she met at a mind/body convention they were attending, so when she's not moping about and trying to work out how it all went wrong for her and the weirdo, she spends her time reading tarot cards and doing people's horoscopes, even if they don't want them done.

Sweetie, that's wonderful news. Congratulations x from Chrissy.

Chrissy is forty and divorced, and she will readily admit she uses men for sex, meaning she treats men the way they treat women: without feelings. She's been let down by men so many times in her life, she's given up on finding love. Chrissy has everything going for her: the perfect body and hair that wouldn't look out of place in a commercial featuring Davina McCall. And she is the boss—and by that I mean the *big* boss, the owner—of loads of different companies worldwide, with her base in Manchester. She is wadded.

Oh! That's the best news I've heard in ages. PARTY TIME. In Starbucks. See you in a bit. Jess x

Thirty-seven-year-old Jess is a bubbly character and my brother Paul's ex-wife. They divorced about ten years ago, after he went on a stag do to Ibiza and ran off with one of the cabin crew on Ryan Air. He and Jeremy now live in a flat in the centre of Manchester. It's probably my fault he's gay. I wanted a sister, and when he was little, I used to make him sit there for hours so I could put his curly blond hair in bunches and dress him up in my clothes. Jess is a solicitor and works here with Sam and me. She has a daughter called Alesha who's seventeen and studying for A levels at Ashton sixth form.

Jess has been having an affair with Alan, a professor at Manchester University, for the last two years. She bumped into him in a car park at Manchester Royal Infirmary. When I say she bumped into him, she did—she crashed into him reversing out of a parking space. They have been inseparable ever since.

First, thank you for telling me that you and my brother are getting married. A phone call would have been nicer. Second, are you being SERIOUS? BENIDORM is such a tacky place, full of common people. It's like Blackpool with sun. RING ME URGENTLY…Michelle

Michelle, or Mrs. Bucket—and we do pronounce it Bucket, not Bouquet—is Darren's sister. She's thirty-eight, but you'd never think it. She acts and dresses far too old for her age. The only thing I have in common with Michelle is Darren. I felt obliged to invite her along on my hen party, even though I know she doesn't like me or any of my friends. I have tried to get on with her, but she just turns her nose up at me all the time. I'm not good enough for her older brother—she told me the first time I met her. Describing her as a snob is an understatement. She thinks she's so much better than anybody else. Her husband, Nigel, works for HSBC and travels the world. They've got two children—Alister, seventeen, and Francesca, fifteen—and loads of money. As soon as Nigel started making his way up the corporate ladder they moved from Manchester to live in Alderley Edge. There's not sign of a Manchester accent now when you speak to Michelle. All those expensive elocution lessons really paid off. She really does need to loosen up. Sam says she needs a good seeing to. That should sort her out. Sam thinks sex is the answer to everything. I'm hoping she won't come to Benidorm. The others won't be happy I've invited her, but I'll worry about that later, depending on her answer.

I shouted out to Sam each time I received a message from the girls.

"E'are, Sam, have a look at this. I've just got a text from Mrs. Bucket." I tossed the phone over the desk to Sam.

She read it. "Ignore her, silly bitch." And she put two fingers up at the phone and tossed it back. "This is gonna be great, Ellie—we just need to work on Sarah."

"Why don't we call round to hers after work for a brew tomorrow?"

"She'll only let us go round if Jim's on lates. You know she'll come up with some kind of excuse if he's home," Sam answered. "I'll text her later."

"OK, but look at all this work on our desks—we need to get started on planning the hen party."

I looked at my desk, my work had built up, too. There were letters to be typed, filing to be done, telephone messages written on post-it-notes, stuck all over my computer screen to be returned. "Work so gets in the way of life," I sighed, as I sat back in my chair and picked up my cup of tea, which had now started to go cold. At the side of my computer I have three, six by four photographs on my desk, in silver frames, that always make me smile if I am having a bad day. I have a photo of Roxy and Izzy, faces beaming, posing with Micky and Minnie at Disneyland Paris, taking pride of place. My Mum and Dad paid for us all to go as a Christmas present when the girls were six and eight. It was the best family holiday we ever had together. There's a photo of me and Darren from our first holiday away together, in Turkey. I love this picture; it brings back so many happy memories. I'd just been presented with a bottle of champagne for winning a belly-dancing competition, and we took ourselves off to the beach to celebrate. We stayed up all night as I wanted to watch the sunrise. As we left to go back to our apartment, Darren asked an older couple on their early-morning walk to take the picture for us. Boy, do we look rough. One of my false eyelashes has come off, it looks like a caterpillar's crawling up my cheek, and I've got sand on my face from where I'd been lying on it.

The last photo on my desk is of me and my bessies on a night out in Walkabout, Manchester, ten years ago. I picked it up, my eyes drawn to Sarah. She looked so happy—her eyes smiling, there is so much life in them—she didn't have a care in the world before she met Jimmy. *What's happened to you, Sarah? I wish you'd tell us.*

"Oi." I hear, as a scrunched-up ball of paper hits me on the head.

"What ya do that for?"

"To wake you up, thought you'd gone into a coma for a minute."

I passed Sam the photo of our night out. "What happened to Sarah, Sam?"

"Jim, that's what happened. Look, I know you worry about her, but we can't do anything about Sarah for now. It'll all come out in the wash one day, and we'll be there to pick up the pieces, but hen-party planning's the priority for today, so snap out of it."

Both Sam and I have been on so many training courses about time management and prioritising, we may as well put into practice what we've learnt. Benidorm was a priority, so after a very brief discussion, we agreed to work like Trojans until lunch and then concentrate all our efforts on arranging my hen party for the rest of the day.

Sam went out to Boots to buy a meal deal for our lunch, and a cake each from Patisserie Valerie, as we didn't have time for a lunch break today. After spending three hours and nearly going blind looking on the Internet at hotels and reviews and checking out flights, we agreed on a hotel situated near the Old Town, wherever that is, called Hotel Guadalupe. We checked it out on Google Earth, and it looked like a pretty good location, with plenty of bars and clubs close by, and the beach only about five minutes' walk away—or ten minutes if you're drunk. We chose an early flight on a Friday morning, leaving at seven thirty from Manchester Airport to make the most of the weekend, and a return flight from Alicante at six on the Sunday night so we could all be back in work on the Monday. I had already made my mind up I was going to take the Monday off work because I knew I'd be wrecked. I felt exhausted just thinking about it.

I e-mailed the details to my bessies and waited for them to get back to me. I'd ring Michelle later to find out what she wanted to do. They say you can choose your friends, but you can't choose your family, and if it wasn't for Darren, I definitely wouldn't have Michelle as a member of my family *or* as a friend.

"We'll have to organise transfers from the airport to the hotel. Then a massive shopping trip to the Trafford Centre, and we're going to have to join Weight Watchers again—and more gym sessions. If ya think I am going to Benidorm looking like this, you are so mistaken," Sam said breathlessly.

"You've just eaten a cake for your lunch."

"My last supper…God, it was good."

"Samantha, there's nothing wrong with ya, and besides I've been barred from Weight Watchers for smashing the scales up the last time we went because Claire said I'd not lost any weight that week, and all I'd lived off was shitty ready meals and lettuce."

"Slimming World then," she suggested. "And it's cheaper, more money for shopping."

"OK, we'll try them." I shrugged.

"We need to come up with a name for us all to have on T-shirts, like when Martin and Darren go away with rugby. Ya know, a tour name. We could have something like The Girls Just Want to Have Fun Tour and plaster it across our chests."

"It's too long, and besides, not all of us have size thirty-four-double-D chests to have it plastered across, Samantha." I rolled my eyes. "No, we can do better than that. Oh! Look at the time, Sam. It's ten past five. Where's today gone? I don't want to be in this building a minute longer than I have to. I'll see you tomorrow."

I got up from my desk and gave my best friend a hug. "Thanks for today. It's been great. Same tomorrow?"

"You bet. Now let's get out of here before somebody sees us, and we ruin our reputation of not being dedicated to our work. The bitch may think we're working late after some kind of promotion." Sam laughed.

SEVEN

I could hear Shaun Ryder belting out, 'You're twisting my melons, man,' as I stood outside our house, rummaging through my bag, looking for my house key. I opened the front door, and a wonderful aroma greeted me. So did the view.

"Darren, I can hear your music halfway down the street. You deaf?" I shouted, laughing.

"Hi, Ellie, didn't hear ya come in. Oh baby, what a night have I got planned for you." He turned the Mondays down a couple of notches.

I couldn't help but smile. Darren stood by the cooker with his back to me, wearing his new Jamie Oliver striped apron. Nothing else. His cute little bum cheeks were peeping out at me, taking it in turns to play peak a boo, as he moved from side to side, dancing to the music, whilst stirring the food.

It's a rarity for Darren to arrive home from work before me, but when he does cooking helps him to de-stress. Unlike mine, his working hours are not set in stone and his job is extremely demanding. He and his friend Marc own a construction company based in Tameside that works on building projects up and down the country.

Darren is a brickie by trade, and Marc is a joiner. They started the business off small and built the company to a good size. They now have about ninety people working for them. Darren is forever asking me to leave Baxter and Turnbull's and go and work for them. I have considered it, especially when having a bad day, but I'd miss the buzz of being in Manchester and working alongside Sam.

"You've been a busy little bee, and what you're cooking smells delicious," I said as I threw my coat over the stand at the bottom of the stairs and kicked off my shoes. I walked into the kitchen, cheekily grabbed his bum, and placed a kiss on his cheek. "What we having?"

"You'll have to wait and see." He turned and kissed me gently on my mouth. "I've run the bath for you. Go get comfy, and I'll come and join you soon."

Is he for real? Bath…food…every woman's dream man, and he's in my kitchen, and I'm gonna marry him. I pinched myself. I flinched. Too hard. *Darren, hope you don't change after we get married,* I thought.

"This is lucky. Izzy texted earlier to say she's not coming home tonight."

"No luck involved. I paid her off. Twenty quid—a bargain."

I quickly made my way up to the bathroom and was excited to be greeted with a bath full of bubbles, varying sizes of glowing vanilla candles placed strategically around the room, and a bottle of white Zinfandel waiting patiently to be opened in my Brannigans ice bucket placed on the toilet seat. Very classy. Our bathroom is mirrors and tiles, creams and golds, really chic. We spend so much time in the bath putting the worlds to rights, drinking, and making love, it's a wonder we're not all shrivelled up.

"Are you in yet?" Darren shouted. "Don't worry about the wine, I'll open it when I come up."

"Gimme a minute, I've still got my clothes on. Or do you want me to get in fully clothed?"

"Naked, baby, naked."

I climbed in, wiggled down, and covered myself in the fluffy white bubbles. As I stretched out, water splashed over the side and onto the floor. I'd clean it up later. I lay in silence, watching the flames of the candles dancing on their own podiums. When Faith did a tarot-card reading shortly after Andy and I split up, she told me I was going to meet the man of my dreams within the next two years. Well, she was wrong—I never dreamt about somebody like Darren. I didn't know a man like Darren existed. I dreamt of one who picked his undies up off the floor, didn't pick at his toenails, and occasionally made me a brew. I'd have settled for that.

I was snapped out of my little trance by Darren's size tens making their way up the stairs. He entered the bathroom and threw his apron on the floor.

"Them boobies are looking mighty fine, Ellie, bobbing around in them bubbles." He bent over and gave them a quick wobble.

"My mate doesn't look too bad, either." I looked up at the penis that had been putting a smile on my face for nearly five years.

His erection started to build as he opened the wine and poured us both a glass. "You've still got it, girl." I smiled. I lifted a hand out of the water to take a glass from him as he climbed in to join me.

"So, we've gotta bit of time to kill until the food's ready. Any suggestions?" he asked cheekily.

I didn't answer, only smiled. I took a sip of wine. It was good. I lay back down in the water and arched my back to expose my bubble-covered breasts. Darren's hand danced steadily around my toes, slowly rubbing each one in turn. Mmm, so relaxing and such a turn-on.

I waited until he'd finished and knelt in the water, bubbles dripping slowly down my body. I relieved Darren of his glass and placed them both on the side of the bath. *I'm in charge tonight*, I thought. He could read the signs. He let me. I straddled him and placed a gentle kiss on his lips. They were so soft and moist against mine. He returned my kiss, our bodies screaming for each other as our tongues touched. I lived for his kisses. The kisses continued as we positioned ourselves so we could be as one. The rhythm began slowly, easing into a faster pace. Darren reached for my breasts with his mouth and teased my nipples. *Yes, Yes. Come on, baby*, my inner voice shouted at me. I moaned with pleasure as water splashed over the side of the bath, my body tensing as our intimate explosion took place. I collapsed into his arms, and they wrapped around me as if to tell me he would never let me go, and I didn't want him to. This was where I belonged.

Darren broke the silence. "Ellie, I'm gonna have to move…I don't wanna ruin your tea." He leant over the side of the bath, grabbed a towel, and climbed out.

He's not perfect. What man is? I love him, and he loves me. I felt all mushy just thinking about him. I never thought you had these sorts of feelings past your teenage years, or is it just the lucky ones who do. If so, I counted myself as one of the lucky ones.

"Ellie, move your arse," Darren shouted up the stairs. "You've got ten."

"Moving," I shouted back. I was so comfy lying in the bath daydreaming about us.

"Are you out?"

"Yes." I'm such a liar. I climbed out of the bath and took the fluffy white bath sheet that had been warming nicely on the towel rail. I wrapped it around my dripping body and made my way into our bedroom. After drying myself, I clipped up my hair, slipped on a red silk nightdress with a split up the side and went downstairs into the dining room.

Again, I was welcomed by candles glowing around the room, and a large bouquet of red roses, which had been placed on my chair, with a card telling me I have made him the happiest man alive. Barry White, the love god, was singing "Just the Way You Are." I don't think I could ever get sick of listening to Barry White.

Darren had replaced his apron with a pair of shorts and a T-shirt. Not the same effect as before, but I wasn't going to complain.

"Is madam ready for her first course?"

"I'm starving. What we having?"

"Tomato and basil soup, followed by mustard lamb and a selection of mixed vegetables, finishing off with brandy and cream profiteroles with extra chocolate poured over the top."

My mouth salivated. "That's two stone I'm putting on, Darren. Are you trying to fatten me up, so when I go on my hen party, nobody'll wanna run off with me?"

"Got it in one." He blew me a sarcastic kiss.

As we made our way through the courses, I told Darren all about my day and what Sam and I had been planning. I can't say he was surprised at how quickly we had arranged the hen party. He knows organising is something Sam is very good at. I told him about the text from Sarah and how worried I was about her. He told me not to interfere; it was none of our business. I didn't agree.

"I've not even thought about my stag do yet," he said, putting another profiterole into his mouth. "Have you contacted the church to make an appointment yet?"

"Sorry, haven't had time, been too busy organising the Benidorm trip." I laughed. "I'll get on to it tomorrow. If the bitch had caught us today, she'd have gone ballistic, but luckily she was out all day."

I told Darren about the text from Michelle, and he smirked.

"I still haven't called her. I'll do it tomorrow."

"Why've you picked Benidorm?"

"Well, none of us have been there before, it's only a couple of hours away, loads of nightclubs and bars, and it's warm enough to sunbathe." I remembered Darren telling me about the time he went to Benidorm about fifteen years ago, with a group of lads. He couldn't remember where he stayed or anything about the bars as they spent the whole time drunk, but he did remember getting banned from the hotel pool, once for skinny-dipping when they got back from a club late one night and once for having a dive-bombing competition one afternoon with his mates.

"Sam said we need to come up with a tour name like you and Martin do when you go away with rugby. We're going to have T-shirts printed."

"Chrissy and Sam could have Tits and Clits on Tour on theirs." Darren laughed.

I threw a bread roll in his direction.

"You bitch!"

I smiled.

"OK. I'll leave that to you and your hen-party coordinator." He laughed.

After we'd finished our meal, we headed into the lounge and snuggled up on the sofa with half a box of Lindor chocolates to watch a couple of prerecorded episodes of *Game of Thrones*.

Darren can't just sit and watch the television, he has a comment on anything and everything on TV. Even the *Game of Thrones*, can't escape his moaning, as it goes from scene to scene.

"Bollocks.... These girls are never virgins." Darren spoke as we watched the men and women cavorting in the brothel. "They sure don't act like virgins."

"They're not all virgins, Darren, just those younger ones." I pointed them out.

"I've only ever had sex with one virgin, and she never moved. It was like making love to a block of wood. Bet this lot have never been virgins."

I laughed. "Everybody's been a virgin at least once, Darren."

"Suppose..... Yeah, like you and your bessies going to Benidorm."

"Yeah, we're the Benidorm Virgins." I chuckled. "That's it: Benidorm Virgins."

"What?" Darren looked puzzled.

"Our tour name—Benidorm Virgins."

"Benidorm Virgins? To be called a virgin, ya've got to be one, and there's not a virgin between ya."

"You're so funny, Darren. Not! It's the first time for all of us. It's really catchy. We'll get it printed on the front of our T-shirts, and we'll look great and get loads of attention. Darren, it's gotta be done." I planted a big kiss on his lips. "You're brilliant."

Darren smiled. "Chrissy'll love that, her being called a virgin."

"Need to ring Sam." I jumped up off the sofa and ran off to get my mobile.

"Bang goes my night of passion," Darren shouted. "Once you two start talking, there's no shuttin' ya up."

"I won't be long, and besides, you've had it once already today. Some men would be grateful just for that."

"I'm not some men." He smiled.

EIGHT

"Like a virgin, ooh, touched for the very first time." Sam sang at the top of her voice as she danced into our office. "Like a vir-ir-ir-ir-gin, when your heart beats next to mine, ooh…ooh…Benidorm Virgins, I've been thinking about it since you rang last night. It's brill, Ellie, I love it. I can see it now, Benidorm Virgins in big white lettering plastered across the front of our T-shirts. That'll get some attention."

"That's what I said," I answered, smiling. "Darren can't stop laughing—he thinks we're mental. You know, he called you my hen-party coordinator."

"I can live with that." Sam laughed. "Normally it's something a lot worse."

I didn't tell Sam what Darren had suggested for a T-shirt name for her and Chrissy.

"Do ya think we're gonna get any work done today, Sam?"

"No chance, too much to organise. You're gonna have to contact the church, Ellie, sometime today, or you might end up with a hen party and no wedding."

"That might not be a bad thing." I replied smirking. "OK, if we get time. After I spoke to you last night, I tried to call Sarah but got no reply. I've asked Darren to have a word with Jim today."

"And say what?" Sam asked. "If Jim's not gonna get anything out of it, he won't let Sarah come. Bastard!"

"Well, I was thinking, if Darren told Jim about planning his stag do. You know, he always said if we ever got married, he'd go on an adventure weekend to Scotland or Wales. Jim's an adrenaline junkie; he'll want to go. I'll get Darren, in his own way, to convince Jim to let Sarah go, even to suggest it to her. You know Darren—he'll come up with something. He can talk his way into or out of anything."

"Well, we'll need to find out soon so we can book before the prices go up."

"Don't worry—when I book, I'll pay for Sarah. We can sort it out later with her. I don't want her to get any more stressed than she already is. Oh! I've just remembered—I've gotta ring Michelle. I can't put it off any longer."

"Good luck with that one. Remember, just keep smiling and nodding."

I heard Cindy Lauper singing, "Girls just wanna have fun." Our new mobile ringtone. We had downloaded it off iTunes that morning.

I looked at the screen. Michelle. I showed the phone to Sam, and she mouthed, "Fuck off." One of the senior partners, James Tranter, was about to leave our office, and she didn't want him to hear her use such foul language; he thought only sweetness came out of her lips—both sets of them. James had a thing for Sam. I wanted to tell him, "Take a ticket, James, join the queue." He didn't really need to come into our office, but he continually made excuses, asking for stamps, not that he used them, or to borrow coffee, not that he ever made a brew. He usually waited until the bitch was either out or away from her desk. He never stood a chance with Sam. She had made it one of her rules, not that she had many, but she never messed around with anybody she worked with, or if they were mingin'. James was both.

I answered as cheerfully as I could and put the call onto loudspeaker.

"Helen, about your e-mail. I'm shocked you didn't call yesterday. I'll be honest with you Helen, I expected you to ring immediately."

Michelle insisted on calling me Helen all the time. The only other person to call me Helen is my mum. She always said if she wanted me to be called Ellie, that's the name she'd have given me on my birth certificate.

"Ahh…"

"Do you really think Benidorm is a suitable place for somebody like you to go to for your hen party? I have heard so many bad things about it. You should hear what some of the girls with whom I met up with yesterday afternoon told me about the place. Not that I told them I have been invited to go, it was just general conversation. I'd die if anybody thought I'd associate myself with that place. Do you know, people actually have sex on the beach? And have you seen that TV show? I only watched one episode. It is so full of common northern people, transvestites, swingers, and drunken louts. I really do think you should reconsider. There are so many nice places you could go. Peckforton Castle, for example, has got excellent spa facilities, and the restaurant is lovely. Or Titanic Spa, Yorkshire, where they do a wonderful Elemis facial. Helen, you're just not the type of person who should be in Benidorm."

Sam and I were choking, trying not to laugh at this pompous, up-her-arse voice blasting down the phone at me. Sam pulled faces and stuck her tongue out at the phone, which made me want to laugh even more.

"Michelle, I'm…not sure what to say. We're all northern people, and we're nice."

"Some of you are."

"I'm sorry you feel that way, Michelle, but I'd like to go there, and all the girls want to go there, too."

"You mean that tart Chrissy and the other one, Sam."

I dived around the desk and clamped my hand over Sam's mouth.

"Michelle, I'm sorry, but that's where we're going. I would like you to come"—I was lying again—"if you want to come. You're more than welcome."

"Not by me." Sam's words were muffled; I still had my hand over her mouth.

I gave Sam a look that said, "If you promise not to speak, I'll take my hand away from your mouth." Her eyes agreed, so I released my grip and shuffled back around the desk.

"I'd like to book this afternoon, so just text me and let me know what ya wanna to do. I really need to get back to work now." I pressed the red button to end the call without giving her a chance to answer or say bye.

"Fucking bitch. Tart, am I?"

"She has got a point, though, Sam," I teased. "Anyway, forget her—research on clubs is the plan for this afternoon."

"Like strip clubs?" Sam teased back.

"Don't even think about strip clubs or gettin' me a male stripper, Sam, you know I can't stand 'em. All greased up, shaking their meat and two veg in your face, asking you to rub oil all over their body. Yuck! The only bloke gettin' that privilege is Darren."

"You know I'd never do that to ya, *Helen*. I know ya don't like 'em."

"I mean it, Samantha."

"No male strippers. Got it."

"Good, just so long as you have!"

By Friday lunchtime, everything was booked: the flights, hotel, airport transfers. Michelle texted to say she was coming but not happy about it. We would just have to try and lose her when we got to Benidorm, or even better, at Manchester Airport. I could send her to the wrong terminal—there are three, after all.

Cyndi Lauper was singing again. I looked at the screen. It was Sarah.

"Hiya, Sarah. How are you?"

"Great, Ellie. How are you?" She doesn't give me time to answer. "Have you booked Benidorm yet?"

"Yep, all done." The line went quiet. "Sarah, are you there?"

"Oh…yeah."

"Sarah, what's the matter?"

"It's just…I was wondering. Would it be possible for you to see if you could book an extra place for me?"

"You're kidding."

Sarah sounded subdued and hesitant. "It's just…Jim rang me a couple of hours ago. He told me about a conversation he'd had with Darren this morning and wanted to know why I hadn't said anything to him about you getting married or your hen party. I told him I'd forgotten all about it. He suggested that I go with you to Benidorm. He said he could do with a break from me."

I wanted to scream. He wanted a break from her? Sarah needed a break from him, the moron!

"I can't believe it, Ellie. D'ya think you could see if ya could book an extra place?" Sarah's voice was croaking as if she was on the verge of crying. "I was gonna ring you earlier, but Maisy's not been too good this morning, she's got a bit of an upset stomach. She's asleep now, so it's the first chance I've had to call."

"Sarah…" I wished she was in front of me so I could give her a big hug. "I've already booked for ya. I knew Darren'd come through for ya, and besides, how could I have a hen party without ya?" I wanted to cry.

"Oh, Ellie, thank you." There was excitement now in her voice.

"I got Darren to plant seeds, Sarah, and he did a really good job. Jim fell for it hook, line, and sinker. Jim's such a slimy bastard, Sarah, what ya still doin' with him?"

"Ellie, he's not that bad." Her voice reverted back to her normal quiet tone.

"Sarah, why ya always making excuses and sticking up for him? It drives us insane! Hopefully, by the time ya come back from Benidorm we'll have knocked some sense into ya."

The line goes quiet.

"Sarah! Sarah! You still there?"

"I'll let you get back to work. Thank you, Ellie. Speak to you soon."

"Hey, hey, you OK?"

"Fine, thanks, Ellie. Jim's just come in from work, he finishes early on a Friday."

"OK. No problem. Speak soon, right?"

I hear buzzing on the line to indicate the call has ended.

Sarah was a nervous wreck whenever Jim was around. I hated it. She never used to be like that, all meek and mild. She really did give as good as she got and used to be as wild as the rest of us, just like in the picture on my desk, smiling, boobs out. We never needed an excuse to get them out. It got to the point that if anybody wanted to take a picture, the boobs just came out, as if it were a law.

Thank God we'd stopped doing that now. Nowadays I only have to lift the hem of my skirt for somebody to have a good look at mine if I've not got my reinforced Wonderbra on.

It was as if she was empty inside. Before, Sarah would never go out of the house with her roots showing, but now she didn't even have roots; bet she'd not seen the inside of a hairdresser's for years. Her mousy hair, always tied up in a greasy ponytail, was now the hairstyle she wore. She never wore lipstick anymore either. Sarah of old would never even open the front door without putting her lipstick on first. Then there was the trouble with her wedding. They had just upped and gone to Gretna Green. Nobody got an invite, and as the years went by she had just seemed to go more and more into herself. She never came on our nights out anymore. She'd say she had nothing suitable to wear, couldn't get a babysitter, or Jim had arranged something for them. Yeah, right.

Occasionally she'd meet Sam and me for lunch in Manchester, but only when Jim was in work, and even them dates were now becoming few and far between. Sam reckoned they had money problems, and they were too embarrassed to say anything. I thought there was more to it, and so did Faith, but if we couldn't get her away from Jim and get her to talk, how were we ever going to find out what was wrong? I couldn't wait for Benidorm—hopefully we'd get the answers we were looking for.

"Hey. It's Saturday tomorrow. How d'ya fancy meeting up at Moon Under Water? Let's see if we can get a few of the others there. I've been thinking about having a fancy-dress theme one night. We can thrash out a few ideas." Sam spoke with yet another mischievous look in her eye.

"Like we need an excuse. It's a date. I'll text everybody. Shall we say oneish? Hopefully Sarah should be able to come. Ashton are playing away tomorrow, and Darren's picking Jim up, so she can get her mum to watch Maisy."

"That's if the bastard doesn't go out and lock her in the house again, like last time we arranged to go out. Mistake, was it?"

NINE

Sarah and I manoeuvred our way briskly through the hustle and bustle of shoppers on Deansgate and headed straight into Moon Under Water, excited at the thought of spending the afternoon with our best friends. As I thought, Sarah asked her mum, Joan, to watch Maisy so she could join us. I couldn't honestly remember the last time Sarah had come out on her own without Jim in tow to have some girly time. And we did plan to have some girly time, filling the afternoon with an array of gossip, booze, and if time allowed, a bit of shopping.

As we made our way through to the back of the bar, I spotted Sam's blond ponytail bobbing around as she rearranged the furniture with Faith in order to accommodate us all. They'd already pulled a couple of tables together and were placing the chairs around them. Faith and Sarah went off to the bar to order our first drinks of the day… Bacardi and Coke.

Chrissy and Libby, arms full of heaving shopping bags, squeezed their way through the lively bar, turning the heads of customers who'd already taken advantage of the two-for-one meal offers and cheap beer. I waved excitedly.

"Harvey Nichols is mad," Chrissy exclaimed as she approached. "You'd think they were giving all their merchandise away." She dropped her shopping bags down onto the floor. "Ellie, come here, sweetie, and give me a hug. Seems like an age since we last saw each other."

Chrissy enveloped me in a great big bear hug filled with so much love. I rested my head briefly against her long shining dark hair and breathed in her fragrance. Chrissy always smelt really good.

"Can't believe how packed it is in here as well," Libby remarked as she flung an arm around my shoulder and placed a kiss on my cheek. "Is there a football match on in Manchester today or something?"

"Libby," Sam laughed, "there are clues everywhere. The place is full of Man United football shirts. What d'ya think?"

"What've ya been buying?" Faith asked.

"Nothing special, just bits and bobs. Some Trish McEvoy makeup, a couple of tops by Julien McDonald, a dress by Stella McCartney. I forget the rest. You'll have to have a look through." Chrissy was well known at all the high-end retailers in Manchester. Sales assistants knew they'd make good commissions from sales to Chrissy and would fall over one another just to serve her.

Chrissy's bits and bobs would cost us mere mortals twelve months' salary to buy.

Money drips through Chrissy's fingers because she's got so much of it. Christina Elenor De Beaufai was born in France in 1974, the youngest of three children. Her family is wadded due to them being very much involved in the oil-and-gas industry. What Chrissy gets in her allowance from her trust fund every year, I will never make in my lifetime. That's unless her mum drops dead and I marry her dad instead of Darren.

Chrissy's parents travelled a lot with her dad's job, and when Chrissy was eight, the nanny was dismissed, and Chrissy was sent packing to a boarding school in Surrey. After boarding school, she moved back to France and five years later married Phillip, a boy she'd known most of her life, who now worked for her dad. She never really settled back in France, and with Phillip's job taking him around the world, it didn't matter where they lived, so Chrissy decided to move back to the familiar surroundings of Surrey and set up home there. Not that she spent much time there…she found it difficult to stay put anywhere. The longest she's ever settled in one place for more than five minutes is in Saddleworth, where she lives now in a beautiful old converted farmhouse, with her horses, dogs, and housekeepers, Mr. and Mrs. Thistlewaite. Her therapist, whom her parents spent a bomb on, blames her being unable to settle on being sent away to boarding school at such a young age. *I could have told them that for a fraction of the cost* I remember thinking when she first told us the story about her past life when we all went to stay in Blackpool for the weekend. We'd known her for about twelve months, so it came as quite a shock, to know we had a friend who was so wealthy.

Chrissy left her husband and filed for divorce eleven years ago. She knew he had problems keeping the zip up on his pants, especially when he worked in Asia, and boy, did he spend a lot of time in Asia, negotiating the building of oil rigs and other boring stuff. The working girls in those countries he visited seemed to put the men into some kind of trance, and with so much sex on offer, he found it hard to resist. She knew he was having sex when he was there, even saw pictures of him with some of the girls in the bars he frequented. Chrissy's size-ten knickers had more fabric on them than what the girls were wearing in the photos on his phone, she commented. But she'd passed caring by then as she'd already began to build up a life for herself and was now finding it hard to keep her own knickers on.

The final straw came when she walked into their summer house in the South of France and caught him with his pants down, literally. He had one of the house-maids pinned up against a wall, bonking her senseless, his head so glued to her breast he looked as though he was being breastfed. After packing a few things into her Jaguar XJ, she set off driving and ended up in the North of England, where she decided to stay. Not many people know Chrissy's background, and she prefers to keep it that way.

Sam introduced Chrissy to our little gang after they'd met at a gym in Ashton. Having a love of sex in common, they soon became great friends, and so did we.

"E'are, Chrissy, pass 'em 'ere, then," Faith said.

"Like you're gonna wear any of 'em," Sarah quipped. "Chrissy said she's been to Harvey Nic's, not Affleck's Palace or the Willow Wood Hospice shop."

"I like to look. What's got you, snappy knickers?" Faith snapped back as she started working her way through the bags of shopping.

"Anybody heard from Frankie and Jess?" Sam asked.

"Frankie's running late, something about an emergency at work this morning, and I've just had a text off Jess—she's gonna to be late. Alan's only just left to drive to Kent," I replied.

Alan, Jess's boyfriend, moved to Manchester from Kent about three years ago to head up some medical-research project at Manchester University. He drives back home at weekends to see his wife Stella and son Justin, but the trips are becoming less frequent, usually with the excuse of having to work. Alan constantly tells Jess he is going to divorce Stella but doesn't want to do it until his son finishes college, as he is studying A levels at the moment and doesn't want to distract him with pressures of a divorce. Alan loves Jess; you can see it a mile off. He hangs off her every word, and for her sake, I hope he does divorce his wife one day. Chrissy and Faith are always telling Jess he needs to grow a pair and stop messing her around, but Jess is having none of it. Alan is her soul mate and she is not going to give him up.

"I don't know why he bothers. It's gonna to take him at least five hours to get to Kent. It can take five hours just to cross that bloody bridge at Dartford. I know, I've been stuck in the traffic there on the drive down to Dover with Barry and the kids, and he'll be back again tomorrow," Libby said as she took a sip of Faith's Bacardi and Coke. "Ooh…that's good. I'll have one of them. My shout, the usual, is it?"

"Certainly is, sweetie," Chrissy replied on our behalf.

"He has got a wife, you know, Libby," Faith chirped.

"How can we forget, Faith? You keep reminding us," Libby replied, walking off in the direction of the bar, followed by Sarah.

"E'are, Sam," I whispered. "Have you seen those marks on Sarah's wrist? I noticed them as she put the drinks down on the table. I couldn't quite make out if they looked like burn marks, or if they were faded bruises. She pulled the cuff of her sleeve down, as she saw me looking in her direction."

"Will you stop panicking, Ellie," she whispered back. "She probably just caught it or something."

The Moon Under Water must be the biggest pub in Manchester. The building was a cinema when I was little, and I remember my mum bringing me here as a treat to watch all the Disney classics. In keeping with the character of the building, the designers incorporated a lot of the old cinema features when it was renovated in the early nineties. We always use this pub as a meeting point before we go shopping or on a night out. It has a great atmosphere and attracts people of all ages, not just for its cheap drinks, but for food as well. If ever we need a hangover fix when we stay over in Manchester city centre, this is where we come as they do the best breakfast ever.

As soon as everybody had arrived and the ritual of kissing and hugging had been performed, Sam and I talked about the arrangements we'd already made for Benidorm and our name, Benidorm Virgins. It went down great. With the excitement of the hen party, and since we hadn't all been together for ages, we were fighting for air space, as we had a lot of catching up to do.   I thought it was best not to invite Michelle. I didn't want her to ruin the afternoon, and if she found out she was going to have to wear a T-shirt with the words BENIDORM VIRGINS splattered across it, she'd probably have a coronary. I decided to fill her in nearer the time with the details.

"So who's up for a bit of fancy dress on the Saturday night?" Sam shouted above the noise of us all.

"What ya thinking?" Faith answered.

"What about St. Trinians?" Sam suggested.

"I'm too fat for suspenders and short skirts in public. I only dress like that in the bedroom for Alan." Jess grinned.

"Ooh, too much information, Jess," I replied, smiling.

"I've got an idea—old women," Sarah offered. "We could go to charity shops for our outfits, wear Nora Batty tights, and drag around shopping trolleys with booze in them."

"Most of us already do." Faith jumped in first. "I'd be wearing my own clothes."

"Speak for yourself, sweetie." Chrissy laughed.

"We can't wear anything too clingy. I've got to wear a TENA Lady. If I don't have one on when I'm dancing, people will think I'm doing a scene from *Singin' in the Rain*." Jess grimaced.

"What d'ya mean?" Libby asked.

"I'll be dancing around in a puddle of piss, only without an umbrella." Jess laughed. "You've got all this to come, Frankie, after you have children and your pelvic floor muscles go."

"Well, that won't be happening anytime soon," Frankie explained. "I've got to find a fella first, and besides, I won't be letting my pelvic floor muscles go. I'll use some of them love balls. You should try 'em, Jess."

Note to self—buy love balls. Don't want to be dancing around in a puddle of piss when I'm older. And don't stand too close to Jess when we're in Benidorm, just in case she forgets to wear a TENA Lady, and I end up dancing in her puddle of piss.

"Nuns," Faith said.

"Nuns? Are you joking?" Frankie screeched. "I'm not going out looking like a big fat stuffed penguin."

"Devils...We could wear PVC red catsuits," Libby suggested. "How sexy would that look? Definitely wouldn't be spending any money when we go out that night."

"Libby, you really need to engage your brain before you speak. Can you honestly see me wearing a PVC catsuit? I'm a size eighteen and five foot nothing. I'd look like

a skinned version of Fred the Red, the Man U mascot."
Sniggers went around the table. "And you can stop the
sniggering." Jess laughed.

"Policewomen then?" I shouted, as voices were getting quite high. "We could all wear that. It's just a white
shirt and black pants or a skirt."

Sam supported me. "Yeah…We can buy hats, truncheons, and handcuffs off the Internet. I like the sound of
that."

"They sell all that stuff in Claire's accessories," Sarah
added. "I've seen them in there when I've called in for
Maisy's hair bobbles and slides."

"Policewomen, yeah—oh, we could have some fun
with those handcuffs and truncheons." Frankie joined in.
"Maybe that would be one way for me to bag a man, I
could handcuff myself to him and throw the key in the
sea…Policewomen, I vote for policewomen."

"Frankie, the only reason you haven't got a man is
because you keep going for the wrong ones," Jess said.

Frankie is the only person I know on the planet who
was routing for Gaston to win Belle's affections in *Beauty
and the Beast*. She didn't care there was a moral to the
story—she wanted the one with the good body to win. She
can still be like that now. Hence the string of no-hopers
she keeps dating. She hasn't had a serious relationship for
around twelve months. She knows Mr. Right is out there.
It's just she can't seem to find him, but at the moment she
is happy with Mr. Right Now.

"I've got some handcuffs at home. Do you remember the police officer I shagged a few years back? He left them," Chrissy said.

"Why doesn't that surprise us?" I giggled.

"Hey, if it wasn't for him, we'd have never got a lift home in the back of his police van on Ellie's decree whatsit night five years ago, when we all went dancing in the fountains in Piccadilly. No bus would let us on, remember? I love Greater Manchester police." Sam laughed.

"Show of hands, then. Who votes for policewomen?" Chrissy asked.

We all raised our hands and agreed on a fancy-dress outfit: policewomen. Watch out, Benidorm! I predict a riot.

TEN

"Ellie, I nearly called to see if you and Sam wanted to meet up for lunch Thursday. I was off work…teacher-training day," Libby began.

"Teachers…you lot are never in work. No wonder we have so many problems with kids on the streets. They're never in school," Faith said.

"Oh, stop moaning, we put more than the hours in, Mrs. Misery Pants," Libby answered back. "We were gonna take Barry's mum's ashes to Blackpool."

"Aw, how is Barry now?" Sarah asked, ever so concerned.

Barry's mum had died suddenly of a heart attack about twelve months previous. Her ashes had sat on top of the fridge in Libby's kitchen since they collected them from the undertaker's because Barry couldn't decide what to do with them.

"He's OK. It's not as if he was close to her or anything," Libby answered. "I told Barry it gave me the creeps looking at that casket thing every time I walked in the kitchen, and I swear I could feel her eyes following me around the kitchen in that disapproving way she always had. She never liked me."

"Nutter," Sam mouthed in my direction. I stifled a laugh.

"I said, 'Barry, you've got to make your mind up what you're gonna do with them ashes,' and he said she always liked Blackpool, so he finally decided that that was where he was gonna take her and throw her off Central Pier. I said, 'It's a pity she's dead, I'd have loved to have done that to her when she was alive.' The old witch." Libby came up for air, took a gulp of her drink, and continued. "Anyway, we arranged to go on Thursday with it being a teacher-training day at school, but Debenhams were having one of their, you know, blue-cross days, and I didn't want to miss it. That's why I was gonna see if you wanted to meet up for lunch. So I took the ashes off the top of the fridge, went into the downstairs loo, opened the box thing, threw the ashes down the toilet, and flushed. Job's a good un…I figured she'd get to Blackpool eventually. All toilet waste ends up there, doesn't it?"

Wine flew in the air, courtesy of Jess and Sarah spurting it out of their mouths, missing Chrissy and Faith. I passed them each a tissue to wipe the drips from their chins. I thought they were going to choke.

"I can't believe you did that!" I gasped. I didn't know whether to laugh or cry. "What did Barry say?"

"What could he say? It was done." Libby took another sip of her drink. "Then I recycled the box in the brown bin. Come on, you'd have done the same thing. I don't get many days off during the week, and they hardly ever have those blue-cross sales on at weekends. I got some really great bargains, there was fifty percent off in some departments."

We were speechless. It was so typical of Libby, always doing things without thinking. Sarah broke the ice by offering to go to the bar to get another round in.

"I'm really looking forward to your hen party, Ellie. I've not been away for ages, and with all this wedding talk, I can't wait to start planning mine," Jess gushed.

"Hasn't Alan got to leave his wife first and get a divorce?" Faith scowled at Jess.

"He will…soon. Alan's just waiting for the right time."

"Wake up, Jess. It's not going to happen. He's just like all men. They stand at the altar, promise you the earth, and then shag anything with its legs open that walks past them," Faith said bitterly.

"Shut it, Faith. You don't know anything. And stop being the bloody victim and spoiling things for other people. Not all men are Pete," Jess snapped.

"You do need to move on, Faith. You have to get over Pete," Frankie agreed.

"I know, I'm sorry. You're right, it's not Alan's fault."

"Faith, why would you even want to be with Pete? He's nothing more than a fucking slimy bastard. He was sleeping with four women," Frankie said. "And it's not like he was anything special to look at."

"Five women."

"Five? I thought it was four," I said.

Faith continued. "No, I'm sure it was five. He was sleeping with me."

"Oh, yeah, I forgot about you."

"Yeah…so did he." Faith snorted. "Do you trust Darren, Ellie? Do you think Darren would ever cheat on you?"

"Are you mad, Faith? What a stupid question. Were you at the cooking sherry before you came out? Do you even realise your mouth has already started talking shit?" Sam retorted.

"I'm just asking. I'd hate to see you get hurt. I don't want you to—"

I interrupted. "Faith, I'd like to think Darren wouldn't cheat on me, but nothing's guaranteed. But…if he did, I know who it'd be for. Delia 'I'll teach you how to boil an egg properly' Smith." I chuckled. The wine was settling in nicely.

"Delia? She's a bit old for Darren, isn't she?" Jess said. "Alan would leave me for that newsreader on breakfast telly, Suzanne what's-her-name."

"Barry fancies her, too." Libby nodded.

"Darren loves his Delia. Food and football are his passion. Delia can cook, and she owns a football club. Every man's dream."

"She doesn't actually own Norwich, Ellie," Chrissy assured me. "Somebody who that ex shit of mine knows owns it."

"She's got more of a stake in a football club than I do." I laughed.

"But what's she like in the bedroom department?" Sam wanted to know. "Can she fuck as well as cook? She can't be good at everything."

"I've never seen anything in the papers about that, and you know I'm up to date with all the celebrity gossip. Pity really that the *News of the World* was caught out for phone hacking or we might have read about it in one of their Sunday supplements." Libby smirked.

"I'm going to the bar. Does anybody want any crisps or nuts?" Frankie asked as she stood up.

"Frankie, are you mad? How can you ask that?" Sam exclaimed. "We've only got four months before we go to Benidorm, and I'm already struggling to get down and touch my toes. Just get drinks. In fact, I'll help. It's all exercise."

I could see it was going to be hell with Sam for the next few months; she was already obsessed with exercise. I was going to be dragged to the gym with her either before or after work, and I didn't know what she was mithering about. Not able to touch her toes? She's so flexible she can bend down and perform oral sex on herself. I honestly believe that if God wanted me to exercise and touch my toes, he would have situated them somewhere around the belly-button mark.

"I'm going to the loo," Sarah said.

"Wait, I'll come with you," I shouted.

I linked my arm through hers as we made our way through the bar and up the winding staircase, that led to the toilets on the first floor.

"Are you OK, Sarah? You seem a bit quiet today."

"I'm fine, Ellie. Honest."

"We worry about you, Sarah. I worry about you."

"Don't be daft Ellie, there's nothing to worry about. I'm fine."

"How's Maisy doing? I'll have to come round to yours for a brew. It's been ages. She must be getting so big now."

"Maisy's doing really well, thanks. I'll show you some photos when we get back down." She smiled. "She's settled into nursery now and made some friends. Her best friend changes from day to day. Toby was Friday's best friend."

"What shift's Jim on next week? I could call over one night, get us a takeaway, bottle of white?"

"I can't do next week. Sorry, Ellie. I've got such a lot on. I'll let you know when's good, OK?"

"OK, but let's not leave it too long, shall we? I've been meaning to ask. What've you done to your arm? I noticed those marks earlier on your wrist."

"Oh, those." Sarah laughed nervously as she pulled at the sleeves of her jumper. "I caught myself getting some roast potatoes out of the oven on Wednesday. Maisy distracted me. I can be so careless sometimes." She bit her bottom lip.

"Me too, I know what you mean." *No, I don't...*

As we made our way down the stairs back into the bar, we could see a crowd had gathered around our table, and we'd only been gone for ten minutes. *Who's got her boobs out now?* I smiled to myself. Frankie'd asked a group of lads to join in with a game of word association. Each time you got the answer wrong, you had to knock back a shot. I could see this was going to get messy. Frankie waved to me. "I don't think I can be bothered going shopping now," she shouted above the noise.

"Pub crawl," Sam answered. "I'm like you, Fran."

"I agree. I'm all shopped out. Let's move on to another bar," Chrissy added.

Sarah and I watched as they finished off the game. Frankie won, as usual, and downed two shots just because she wanted to. I'm no good with shots. They don't agree with me. The last time I was on shots in Manchester, I ended up getting stuck up a lamppost outside a pole-dancing club on Deansgate, trying to show off to a group of men queuing outside. I managed to climb up OK but got dizzy when I got to the top. It was really embarrassing for me, clutching the lamppost for dear life, hearing Sam shouting across the road for a white knight to come and help a damsel in distress. And Sam being Sam, they quickly responded. They thought it was some kind of joke; Sam told them I did it all the time just to get attention. So I don't do shots anymore.

It doesn't matter how much Frankie drinks—it never seems to affect her. Frankie's job is so stressful; that's the reason she parties hard whenever she goes out. Her motto is "Live for today…fuck tomorrow." Always the optimist.

ELEVEN

We stayed on Deansgate, calling in at Living Room for a couple of drinks, then headed over to Corbiers, which is just off St. Ann's Square, for a couple more. Next we made our way along King Street to the All Bar One, but not before stopping in at Sam's Chop House, for yet another couple. We finally arrived at Browns Bar, another one of our favourite places in Manchester for cocktails. Sam disappeared hours ago, with one of the lads playing the drinking game we met in the Moon Under Water. I texted to say we'd meet her in All Bar One, but she didn't show, so I sent her another when we moved on to Browns. Chrissy rang her driver, to come and collect her shopping. He also took Libby's for her as well. Sarah left us as we were stood outside Living Room; Jim stopped off to collect her on his way home from playing rugby. Sarah appeared really embarrassed when his car screeched to a halt by the kerb just as we were about to walk into the bar. She was supposed to be getting a taxi home with me and Faith. Jimmy must have her tagged. Even we didn't know where we were going to be.

The Edwardian building, which houses Browns, used to be a prominent bank—it used to be called Athenaeum, which we could never pronounce, so we we're glad it changed its name—with its high ceilings, incredible nouveau art, and amazing wrought-iron work, is a complete contrast from Moon Under Water, with its cheap booze and football shirts. By day, the bar is light with people stopping in for a quick drink and a bit of lunch, but at night the lights are dimmed and it becomes sophisticated and classy. We've had many a good time in here, working our way through the cocktail menu, sitting around laughing and joking on the comfy black-leather seats, weighing up the talent, like so many other women. The men you get in here shop at places like All Saints, Armani, and Mr. Pink's on King Street and use expensive, "I'm after a shag" aftershave. Women in here have been known to go after the same piece of meat, which has been quite funny to watch, but if Chrissy and Sam were in the running, the other women didn't stand a chance.

"Ellie, I'm gonna have to sit down. I feel as if I'm walking on a bouncy castle, which must mean I'm pissed." Jess wobbled as we walked away from being served at the bar, carrying our Riveting Raspberry cocktails.

"Don't you spill that drink! It cost eight quid," I replied seriously.

"As if. I'll go down before I let this baby loose."

"Look, Faith and Frankie have got a table. Let's go over there."

"Do we have to?" Jess pleaded. "I'll give you two guesses what Faith's talking about. She got that pathetic look on her face. I'm sick of listening to her, Elle."

"Come on." I took a tight hold of her arm and navigated our way through the crowd of a busy Saturday night in Browns, accidentally-on-purpose knocking into suits holding bottles of beer on their boys' night out.

I felt a tug on my arm and turned to see Chrissy's perfectly manicured hand gripping my sleeve. "Ladies, don't look now—which means you will. Oh, go on, then—take a look at that fresh bit of meat standing by the door," she said excitedly. We turned towards the main entrance to see a young man in his late twenties looking right back at us. "If only you could feel his arse...God, it's firm. He must have used a shoe horn to squeeze into them pants tonight. It's going to be a struggle getting them off, but I'll give it a go. His cock looks like Linford Christie's in his Lycra running shorts."

"We've only just walked in, Chrissy. How on earth have you picked him up?"

"With style, sweetie, with style." She licked her top lip. "I'm just going to nip into the ladies', and then we're leaving."

Chrissy is just like sticky flypaper, oozing the three s's: sex, style, and sophistication. That's how she traps men for sex so quickly. She's a Venus flytrap, only in human form. After her divorce, she had a steady flow of lovers and broken hearts, until she made the decision, after a bottle of

Bombay Sapphire and tonic, that she was never going to fall in love ever again or miss out on an orgasm. She's the only woman I know who has an orgasm every time she has sex, and that's because she makes sure she does.

So after that decision-making night, for about six months, whenever she went to bed with a man, she'd get him all hot, instigate her pleasure first, and then up and go, leaving him deflated, like she'd been so many times. She wanted to start up a campaign for all women to do this with their partners, lovers, or husbands to see how they liked it, when they'd built themselves up for an orgasm and blip… nothing happened. "Take, take, take. That's all it is with men," she'd say. The man came, had a cigarette, smiled triumphantly as if he'd just secured those rare Wembley Cup final tickets, and then rolled over and fell asleep. She goes all the way now—she missed the feel of a man being inside her—but not until she's had her orgasm.

"I thought you were meeting up with that doctor bloke tonight," I said.

"I'm bored of him. Every time we have sex, I feel as if he's giving me a checkup down below. I thought he'd be a bit more adventurous, knowing what he knows about women's lower body parts. He's a gynaecologist, you know."

"Yeah, we know, he works at Tameside. Frankie knows him," Jess slurred.

"Oh yeah, I forgot. I've decided to stay in Manchester. I'll ring and book a suite at the Lowry from the cab. I'll call you tomorrow and give you all the details." Chrissy likes to give a blow-by-blow account of all her sexual conquests, and to our knowledge she's been in every sexual position known to the *Kama Sutra* and more. Sam said if ever Chrissy lost all her money and needed a job, she could always run away with the circus and become a contortionist.

"Say bye to everybody." Chrissy quickly put her arms around me and planted a kiss on both cheeks. She repeated the ritual with Jess.

Libby didn't move an inch from the bar after we got served, as two young men, whom I recognised to be footballers from Man United's first team, caught her attention when we walked into Browns. She introduced me as I walked by. They were on the way to Rosso's for a meal with friends. I was salivating so much I found it difficult to speak. The younger one of the two, with immaculate hair, olive skin, big dark eyes, and a white T-shirt clinging to his sculptured torso, was hanging on Libby's every word. I was hanging onto his voice. He was speaking with a smooth—very smooth—Italian accent. He could have been saying, "I've been shovelling shit all day down the sewers." It sounded orgasmic to me.

I hoped they were not expecting anything from Libby. You heard about footballers all the time, chatting up unsuspecting women, filling them with alcohol and drugs, and then going off to top-class hotels and having wild orgies, making women do things you may have only read about in a tacky magazine or watched on channel 4 (or is that just me wishfully thinking). Anyway, she never crosses the line, our Libby. She likes to go out, have a good time, and go home without spending any penny. She's a compulsive flirt, but the faithful type. They'd stand more chance with Sam. I'd have told her there were footballers about if I knew where she was.

When Jess and I finally arrived at our destination—the table—Frankie and Faith were deep in conversation, as Jess predicted, and we caught the middle of the same conversation we'd listened to for years. "Frankie, if only I knew the reason why Pete cheated on me, that would help. We were good in bed—"

I interrupted Faith, and Frankie smiled as if to say, *Thank fuck for that.* "Hi, do you know where Sam is?" I pulled a chair up to the table and sat down. "She came in just after us. I waved to her to get her attention. There's a couple of Man U players going spare over there."

"Sam's probably already going down, in the toilets," Frankie replied.

"Have you had too much to drink, Faith? You're talking about Pete again. Thought you were going to stop doing that. We're sick to death of you going on about him," Jess said acidly.

"Listen, Miss Not-so-perfect. It's women like you who end good marriages," Faith snapped.

"Faith, Pete was cheating on you with four other women, not just one. You're better off without him, anyway. Why is it whenever you have one too many, the subject always turns to Pete?" Jess retorted.

None of us could understand why or how Pete got four women—or five, including Faith—to have sex with him. It's not as if he was charming, good-looking, and smart, or had a platinum no-limit credit card, qualities women who were going to have an affair normally went for in a man. What was also baffling was that he was at it for two years, juggling those women about. I still don't know how he managed to remember their names. It took him ages to remember Darren's; he kept calling him Derran.

Faith only found out about the affairs when his secretary, Anna, telephoned to confess to her affair with Pete. She was angry she'd caught Pete cheating on her with three other women. Faith actually felt sorry for Anna until she remembered Pete was, in fact, her husband. Anna told Faith she and the other women had set him up to confront him that afternoon in a pub he used to take them all to that was a bit out of the way in Chadderton. It was a rough time for Faith, but that was seven years ago.

"I want a man. Don't want to be on my own." Faith sipped on her cocktail. "I can't seem to get a fella to stick around for more than five minutes."

"It's because you're boring. That's why you can't get a fella to stick around for more than five minutes. And besides, your marriage couldn't have been that good, or he would never have gone off in the first place—"

"Jess." I stopped her. "If you two can't play nice, then I think it's time we went home. What do you say?"

"I'm ready for my bed." Frankie yawned.

"Yeah, so am I. Sorry, Faith," Jess said and gave Faith a hug.

"Yeah, you're right, Jess, I know you are. I need to get over him. I will get over him. I'll do my cards tomorrow and start planning my future."

I looked at my watch, ten o'clock. Where had today gone? Well, they do say that time flies when you're having fun. Not bad for a one o'clock start. At the bar, the olive-skinned footballer was still engrossed with our Libby. The other one was talking to a giggling blond stick with no clothes on, not that I was jealous or anything. My head started to spin. I didn't fancy my chances of making it in one piece back through the crowd to her to let know we were leaving. I took my phone out of my faithful Prada bag and sent Libby a text, and she quickly replied: *bye xxx*.

Heading out the door, laughing and holding each other up, we waved and blew kisses in Libby's direction, and she sent a cheeky wink back.

"I should stay and help her, really," Frankie said, "but I can't be arsed. Let's go and get a kebab from Oldham Street before we get a taxi—it's gonna be porridge, salad, chicken, and fucking tuna for the next few months if Sam's got anything to do with it."

I sighed. This would be the last takeaway meal we'd have until we went to Benidorm.

TWELVE

On the day before the hen party of the year was due to commence, Sam and I decided to finish work at four, instead of the usual five o'clock, to buy any last bits we needed. Could it really have been four months since Darren proposed on that dreary Sunday evening? Not that we needed anything; it was just an excuse to get out of work early, away from the bitch with all her nagging and her smelly armpits. I told Darren I was going to be home late, so he went out straight from work to catch up with some friends and play pool.

There was no need to rush as all the shops were open late in Manchester. We stopped off at Mulligans for a decent bottle of white, not the usual house stuff; after all this was the pre-hen-party night. We chatted uninterrupted about anything and everything for an hour or so, totally unaware of the comings and goings around us, and then made the very difficult decision as to whether we should get another bottle of wine or go shopping. After much deliberation, we agreed to do the most sensible thing and go shopping, as we had an early start in the morning. We started by nipping into Kendals to do a bit of window shopping, stopping at the MAC, Chanel, and Dior counters and gathering samples along the way. Then we were on to Debenhams to do the same, only this time Sam purchased yet another bikini.

With time pressing on, I suddenly realised we'd had nothing to eat all day. I quickly walked over to the hot-dog stand outside Debenhams, followed by Sam, loudly protesting about high calorie content, which I ignored. I purchased a foot-long hot dog with onions and tomato sauce to share. "We've already started the drinking, we might as well start the bad eating," I said. Not a regrettable calorie had passed my lips, apart from a bit of alcohol, since having a kebab with the girls on our way home after the hen party–planning Saturday in November. Even at Christmas, I had sacrificed the pleasure of stuffing my mouth full of Cadbury's Celebrations or Quality Street. I must confess, though, I did hesitate at the After Eights but passed them all right on by to the person next to me in preparation for my hen-party weekend.

The taste of the hot dog made me feel all snug inside, like seeing an old friend and getting a great big hug, and with each bite not a trace of guilt jumped around in my mind. I'd survived four months of Slimming World and the gym, and with a new body of one and a half stone lighter, I deserved to enjoy this moment.

We walked arm in arm through the throng of late-night shoppers and Thursday-evening partygoers in the direction of Piccadilly to catch the bus home, laughing, chatting, and licking tomato sauce from our lips. We suddenly came to a halt outside Wetherspoons, and as if on automatic pilot, we both walked inside for a quick Cheeky Vimto before catching the bus and heading home.

Darren was already tucked up in bed when I arrived home at ten, the TV blaring out highlights of the last Derby game between Man City and Man United.

"You fucking blind bastard," he was shouting at the referee for upsetting his beloved football team as I walked into the room. I gave him a peck on the cheek.

"It's a recording," I reminded him.

"So what, cheating red bastard ref."

I'd hate to be a referee, with all the abuse they get. I chuckled to myself as I left Darren to his ranting and raving and headed into the bathroom to run myself a nice hot bubble bath.

Feeling all clean and fresh and slathered in Chanel No. 5 body lotion, I climbed into bed and wrapped myself around Darren.

"Get your bloody feet off me. They're freezing," Darren shouted as he attempted to release the grip I had around his body.

"Don't take it out on me because your beloved City got beat," I said, leaving my arms and legs firmly where I had originally placed them. "Don't be rotten, just let me get my feet warm. I'll make it worth your while."

He removed his left arm from under the quilt and draped it around my shoulders. He took hold of the remote with his other hand and switched the TV off. "Are you going to miss me, Elle?"

I hesitated.

"Hey, Missus. I'm talking to you."

"I know you are. I'm thinking." I giggled.

Darren playfully wrestled me over onto my back, pinned me down, and began to nuzzle at my neck. His face, in need of a shave, followed with the submissive tickling around my waist and under my arms.

"OK. OK. I'll miss you. I'll miss you. Stop tickling me."

"How much?"

"Millions!" I continued screaming with laughter, struggling to release myself from underneath his body. "Millions. Now get off me," I gasped as he released me, laughter still bubbling from my mouth.

Darren rolled onto his back, placing his hands behind his head, a very satisfied grin spread across his face. "How'm I gonna cope when you're in Benidorm, Ellie? Who's gonna make me a brew in the mornings?"

I quickly pounced onto his chest. He let out a heavy gasp of air. "Is that all you want me for, to be your slave?"

"In my dreams," he cheekily answered back.

I leant forward and kissed him tenderly on the lips. I kissed him again, only this time gently biting his lower lip. He returned the kiss with as much passion as when we first met, our tongues reaching out for each other.

With big strong hands, Darren gently rearranged my position, whilst slowly working his way down my body with kisses, stopping to take hold of one erect nipple in his moist mouth whilst caressing the other. I whimpered and moaned as two of his fingers unhurriedly moved in and out of me. The kisses continued across my stomach and between my legs, avoiding my clitoris. I begged him in my head not to stop. This teasing was becoming too much to bear. His tongue swept the top of my thighs and then he was pleasuring me. Gasping, I climaxed and arched my body high. He took a moment before he lifted his head, and when he did, he smiled as if very pleased with himself. As he moved his body on top of mine, I could see his penis throbbing in anticipation. I gasped again as he entered me without my body having time to rest. Our bodies were now moving as one, slow to start until the rhythm began to gather pace. My body screamed as I climaxed again, quickly followed by Darren. He collapsed on top of me, our hearts beating so fast, pounding against each other's chests until they recovered to their normal paces. He lay at the side of me and wrapped me in his arms.

"Night, Ellie McDonald. Love you."

"Love you, too." I took hold of his right hand, lifted it up to my mouth, and kissed it gently. Holding his hand, I drifted off to sleep.

THIRTEEN

I woke up to the sound of the Boo Radleys singing, "Wake up; it's a beautiful morning," the song I'd downloaded as my alarm for today. I let it play for a minute or so, excitement swashing around in my belly, thinking, *It is for me, can't speak for the rest of the world*. I fumbled around on the bedside cabinet until I came upon my mobile and cancelled the alarm. I hurriedly thrust my arm back underneath the quilt and wrapped it around Darren's firm, naked body and gave him a quick squeeze as I gently kissed his left shoulder. He began to stir. Exactly five minutes later, Key 103's night music rushed into the room. My second alarm, just in case I slept through the first one.

On any normal day, I struggled to get out of bed, but this wasn't a normal day. It was day one of my hen party. The day Sam and I had spent months planning, a three-day holiday with my bessies. I turned off the alarm and checked the clock, which shone 4:05 a.m. in bright red. I hurriedly threw the quilt off, bounced out of bed, and rushed into the bathroom to take a shower, removing the remains of last night's lovemaking from my body.

I'd already laid out my hair dryer, straighteners, makeup, and clothes in the box room before I went to bed last night, so as not to wake Darren until I was about to leave for the airport.

And now my hair was done, the finishing touches to my makeup complete. I dressed in a new pair of skinny jeans from George at ASDA and my red short-sleeved T-shirt with the words BENIDORM VIRGINS printed in white across the chest. I stopped and took a few minutes to scrutinize myself in the full-length mirror on my wardrobe. "Boobs still in the right place with a little help from my Wonderbra, a slight muffin top, but hey! We can't all look like Sam, and my bum's still way above my knees. All in all, Ellie McDonald, Mother Nature has been very kind to you. You're not in bad nick for a forty-one-year-old." I smiled as I turned from side to side.

I gently woke Darren. "Five-minute call, lover."

"OK," he mumbled back. "Ellie, you got money? Credit card? Passport? I'm not driving back home once I've set off to the airport." Darren yawned, probably having flashbacks to a holiday we had a couple of years back. As we approached the departure terminal, I realised I'd forgotten the passports. Luckily for us, the flight had been delayed until the evening, something to do with striking French air-traffic controllers. That was the one time I was thankful for a strike. Darren wasn't a happy bunny driving us back home, but as I said to him then, it was just as much his fault as mine because he could have checked and not left everything to me as per usual.

"Yes," I answered, checking the contents of my bag one more time, just to be sure.

Darren picked up the bright-pink suitcase I'd packed, unpacked, and packed again, and carried it out to our car, complaining about the weight—did I really need everything in it?

"Three days you're going for, Ellie, three bloody days." His voice echoed around Marlborough Avenue. Apart from us and a couple of squabbling cats chasing each other around the front gardens, Marlborough Avenue continued to sleep.

I stood beside the car for a moment to let the cool morning breeze touch my skin. It felt refreshing. In a few hours' time, it would be hot, hot, hot all the way for me and my bessies. I took one last look at the house and climbed into the passenger side, and Darren reversed off the drive to begin the journey to collect Chrissy and Sarah.

It looked like Blackpool illuminations as we approached Sarah's house; every room at the front of their four-bedroom detached had lights switched on. Darren pulled up outside their manicured lawn and cut the engine. Jim opened the front door.

"Alright, mate?" Darren asked. "Bit early for you, init?"

"Yeah, mate, wanted to give Sarah a quick last-minute pep talk. Ya know what I mean, Darren?"

"No, I don't, mate." He sounded puzzled.

"Can't have her thinking she can get up to anything this weekend. Wanted her to know her place." Jimmy laughed.

"Sick, insecure, silly little man," I said under my breath. I waved as Sarah came into view, pulling her suitcase, a nervous smile etched on her face.

"Gonna help her with her suitcase, Jimmy?" Darren asked.

"Big girl is our Sarah, aren't you, love? She can manage."

Darren climbed out of the car and relieved Sarah of her case, whilst she quickly hopped into the backseat and let out a sigh.

"Sarah," Jimmy shouted, far too loud for that time of the morning.

"What, Jimmy?"

"Just remember what I said. OK, Sarah?"

"Sure, Jimmy."

Darren climbed back into the car. "What the fuck was that all about, Sarah?"

"Oh nothing, Darren. He's just messing about. You know Jimmy."

Darren looked at me for an answer. I just shrugged and pulled an 'I've not got a bloody clue what that show was all about' expression on my face.

"See you tomorrow for poker night, Darren. Make sure you've got plenty of money on ya. I can feel this is gonna be a lucky weekend for me with no nagging wife or whinging kid to bother me."

"In your dreams, mate. Just don't bring your car keys, or I'm gonna be taking your Jag off you." Darren laughed.

"This is gonna be the 'fall of Jimmy' weekend. See ya, mate."

With no traffic on the roads, the drive to Chrissy's took fifteen minutes less than the usual thirty, and then we were on our way to Manchester Airport giggling like teenagers, much to Mr. Grumpy's annoyance.

"Tadaaa!" I dived into my Prada handbag, which has been compared by many to Mary Poppins's carpetbag. Holds everything, and pulled out three coldish bottles of Budweiser and quickly removed the tops with a bottle opener on my key ring. I leant over into the back and hand them to the girls.

"Thanks, Elle." Chrissy took a big mouthful of beer. "You'll have to give me the number of your driver. I'll definitely use him again if he looks after all his customers like this."

Darren muttered something inaudible to the human ear, probably something like, "Wish you'd all just shut the fuck up."

"You have a driver," I reminded her. "You should get him to carry a cold box of beers in the boot for you at all times."

"I'd arrive everywhere pissed if I did that, Ellie." She laughed.

Sarah took a polite sip of her drink and held the bottle in her lap. "I'm so nervous about this weekend, Ellie—leaving Maisy, my stomach's doing somersaults. I've never left her before."

"She'll be fine, and it's not as if Jimmy's looking after her. She's going to your mum's in a couple of hours, and she's gonna get spoilt rotten. Now get drinking, lady, it's gotta be done…and that's an order," I commanded like an army sergeant major, a big smile splattered across my face.

"Yes, sir." Sarah saluted me, the smile returning.

"And what about me?" Mr. Grumpy piped up.

"You're driving, and you know what I think about drinking and driving. And besides, it's too early. You've got work in three hours."

"Give us a swig then." He snatched the bottle out of my hand and took a quick swig before I could snatch it back. "And it's never too early for a drink."

I had been surprised when Darren offered to drive us to the airport at this ungodly hour. The only time we see four o'clock is when we're on our way home from a night out. He likes to be quiet first thing in the car, drink his Venti Starbucks Americano, and catch up with the latest sports news on *Talk Sport*. Bore…ring. That's what was on the radio as we were chattering away.

No, no, we can't have this, it's driving me mad. I removed some of Darren's CDs from the glove compartment. We needed something a bit more lively than all this sports nonsense. It was party time. I picked out an eighties compilation, much to Darren's annoyance, and we began to happily sing along to Mel and Kim, Spandau Ballet, Duran Duran, Yazz, and many more on the forty-minute journey. He could listen to *Talk Sport* and catch up on all the gossip about what Man City were up to on the drive home, I told him.

"Darren, we need to get into the lane for terminal two," I said as we left the M56 on to the slip road for the airport.

"OK, OK. Don't panic," he snapped and stayed on the inside lane.

We took our place in the queue with other vehicles and slowly made our way towards the drop-off zone.

"There's a parking spot." I impatiently waved my hand to the left. "Quick."

"Will you stop panicking? You don't leave for two hours, and besides nobody can get past me to pinch the parking spot," Mr. Grumpy snapped again. Bet he wished he'd never offered to drive us to the airport now.

"Sorry, I am just so excited," I replied. This eighties CD was so gonna get flung out of the car window as he drove off. I didn't think he'd ever want to hear them songs again, although we all sang "Love Shack" by the B52s really well—harmonies and everything.

"You'd never have guessed," he replied sarcastically.

We pulled in, and Darren turned off the engine. I quickly opened the door and climbed out of the car. Car fumes and cold air hit me in the face, and it was so noisy, with the sound of car engines and people talking. This place was buzzing, and so was my stomach. I took a deep breath and tried to contain my feelings so I didn't wind Darren up any more with my overexcitement.

"Right, have a great time and behave ya'selves. Don't wanna be watching ya on the ten o'clock news over the weekend," Darren said. "Tonight's headlines: Benidorm Virgins create havoc, blah, blah, blah. Tits and arses everywhere, blah, blah, blah."

We laughed and continued to behave like a group of excited teenagers going on our first school trip, only this time Mum and Dad weren't there to wave me off; it was the man I have agreed to spend the rest of my life with.

"If I don't make the headlines this weekend, sweetie, I'll know I'm losing it and I'll give up for good," Chrissy replied.

"I wouldn't expect anything else from you, Chrissy." Darren gave her an affectionate wink. He'd stopped being grumpy now we'd got out of the car.

"Flipping heck, Chrissy," Sarah gasped as she looked at the three cases Darren had unloaded from the car for her. "We're only going for the weekend! How much stuff do you need for a weekend? You've got enough gear here to last a fortnight."

"You have to be prepared for everything, sweetie. Were you never a Girl Guide? 'Be prepared' was their motto. I adopted it and found it suited me very well."

"I'd have thought 'If it's living, it's gotta be shagged' would have been a better motto for you." I chuckled.

"You, a Girl Guide? Never!" Darren exclaimed.

"I most certainly was." She smirked. "I attended the most boring all-girl convent school on the planet, and it was the only time we were allowed to socialise with the opposite sex—at the local Scout and Guide group. Probably the best education I had. You know, the first time I ever had sex outside was when we went to camp in the Lake District. We were there to do part of our Duke of Edinburgh silver award. I can still remember it like it was yesterday, being pinned up against a tree in the rain, listening to the sound of a rushing river. I thought it was great. Well, I was only fifteen at the time. It was with Peter somebody or other. He's in politics now—or was that the other Peter? I forget. Anyway, the things I learnt to do with a bit of string and a piece of wood on that camping trip before I got my hands on handcuffs and vibrators." Chrissy raised an eyebrow. "I really enjoyed being a Girl Guide. Would recommend it to anybody."

"You never cease to amaze, Chrissy." Darren shook his head, laughing.

My Girl Guide group was nothing like that; it was all beetle drives and making things out of papier mâché stuck on blown-up balloons. Bet Chrissy's group stuck papier mâché onto cucumbers and made giant dildos. The Scout group that was attached to our Guide group didn't have one decent lad there. They were angin'. I wouldn't have had sex with any one of them, even if my life depended on it.

Screaming laughter nudged me from my thoughts. I turned to see Faith and Sam running towards us, waving, dragging their suitcases on wheels behind them. And well, it looked like Frankie, only this Frankie's skin tone was a lot darker than when we last saw each other a few days ago.

"Frankie! Is that you, Frankie?" I stifled a giggle as she approached us. "What's happened?"

"Don't ask." Faith laughed. "Frankie's been the recipient of our jokes for the last thirty minutes whilst we were in the taxi."

"She overdid it with the Fake Bake. She used the wrong one," Sam answered. "She's been getting darker and darker all the way down here in the taxi, and by the time we get to passport control, she's gonna have to prove her ethnicity. Gonna get your minge out, aren't you, girl?"

"Shut it, Barbie. I don't look that bad, do I, Ellie?" Frankie asked as she kissed me on the cheek.

"Well, at first I thought it was Sinitta running towards us, but as I didn't see Simon Cowell at the side of her—"

"Stop it," Frankie exclaimed. "Really, is it that bad?"

It's a good job she can laugh at herself. We're not the kind of people who can let an opportunity like this go by without ripping her to pieces about it; it's just too funny.

Jess and Libby arrived shortly afterwards and joined in with the hugging and kissing. Only one person missing now—Michelle, my lovely future sister-in-law. I could only hope she'd changed her mind and decided not to come.

We made our way towards one of the automated glass-fronted entrances of the departure building, chatting along, suitcases in tow, oblivious to anything else going on around us, and waited there for Michelle. We stood there proudly showing off our T-shirts and enjoying the attention we received from passersby. Libby took out her cigarettes and offered them to Chrissy, Faith, and Frankie, who took the opportunity to have a last Silk Cut before we had to go inside. The way they were carrying on, you'd have thought they were about to do the "dead man walking" scenario and were never going to have a cigarette again, with all their moaning about not being able to have another one until they get to Spain.

"Don't look now. It's approaching from the right, and she's got a face like a smacked arse. And can you bloody believe it? She's wearing a camel overcoat. We're going to Spain, not the bloody Outer Hebrides," Frankie whispered just loud enough for us to hear.

We turned to watch Michelle walk slowly towards us with little pinhead steps, carrying a Louis Vuitton tote bag on her shoulder, a matching case on wheels by her side. I hadn't spoken to Michelle much during the last few months. We were stunned she actually wanted to come with us. I told her about the arrangements and T-shirts we were going to be wearing on the phone last week whilst I was in work. Sam and I were in hysterics as her voice changed pitch, going higher and higher as if somebody was pulling her knickers tighter and tighter up the crack of her bum.

She had telephoned Darren as soon as her call to me ended and asked him if he could get me to change my mind and go somewhere more respectable and dump the

T-shirts and fancy dress. She had a reputation to keep, she reminded him, and was so embarrassed about going to Benidorm she couldn't tell any of her friends where she was going. As far as her friends were concerned, she'd be spending the weekend in a swanky five-star hotel in Marbella, and hoped none of the photographs from the weekend made their way onto her Facebook page. This only made us fall about laughing all the more.

"Can't she walk any slower?" Sam moaned. "A snail moves faster."

"I don't think she'll like the attention we're attracting," Sarah said cautiously.

"I'm afraid this is how it's gonna be, and she's gonna to have to get used to it," Frankie replied quickly and stubbed out her cigarette on the wall.

Michelle always liked to make a grand entrance. In her world, she's the centre of attention, with being chairwoman of her Parish group, discussing home watch and the parish council, and arranging charity events and all that. She was accepted pretty quickly by the Cheshire wives when she moved to Alderley Edge, probably because being so plain and boring, she posed no threat to them.

All my bessies are a bit like Jekyll and Hyde—not in a bad way, but we've got two personalities, one for our normal lives, when we're mums, wives, employees, et cetera, and one for when we're together. When we are just us! This weekend the hair will be down, the wine will be flowing, and the high spirits will be out, because by Sunday night, things will be back to normal. None of us will ever grow old gracefully. We're gonna fight growing old all the way, some with a bit more determination than others. When Kat died, Frankie's sister, we all agreed we'd live life to the full and never waste a minute of it. We haven't always managed it that way, but most of the time we've tried. Life's short, we learnt the hard way; Kat would have loved to be here today. She loved life. It may have only been a short life, but there was never a dull moment. She packed a lot into those twenty-nine years. She might not have been here in body, but in spirit she was. She always is.

"Why did you invite her, again?" Frankie asked.

"You know why, because she's Darren's sister." I felt a bit awkward.

"Don't worry, Frankie, leave her to me. I eat people like her for breakfast. Hi, Michelle, isn't this just great?" Chrissy said assertively, a scheming look in her eye.

"Good morning, Helen, ladies," Michelle replied, a greeting that sounded more like my headmistress addressing the morning assembly. I felt like replying, "Good morning, Mrs. Barber. Good morning everybody."

"Come on, girls, let's get this party started. Selfie time." Frankie pulled out a selfie stick and attached it to her rose gold iPhone 6s.

"You've got a selfie stick? How childish!" Michelle gasped.

Chrissy linked her arm quickly through Michelle's and pulled her in close to have her picture taken. Three or four clicks later we began to make our way into the departure building, smiling and giggling, Michelle looking around to see if she knew anybody.

"Hey! What about me?" We turned to see Darren still standing by the car in the drop-off zone. "Hey, haven't you forgotten something?"

I didn't even realise he was still there. I'd completely forgotten about him or to say bye.

"Darren, I'm so sorry, I got caught up in the moment," I shouted as I ran across the road and threw my arms around his neck. We kissed, a full-on French kiss. Part of me didn't want to let go of him, but the other part of me was shouting, *Get off him—there's a bottle of Bud with your name on it in the bar for you!*

"Put him down, Ellie. You're only going for a couple of days," Sam shouted.

"I've got to go, Darren."

"I know. Have a great time. Take care. Love you, Mrs. F."

"Love you, too, Mr. Fletcher." I kissed him again on the lips and ran off to rejoin the others.

FOURTEEN

Checking in went smoothly, with nobody going over the allocated baggage allowance for a change, and once I was satisfied Frankie wasn't seated anywhere near Michelle on the plane, we joined the queue for the security checks.

All around me people were moaning and groaning about the time it was taking to get through security. I, on the other hand, couldn't have cared less. I hate flying, and I don't really want to die by the hand of terrorists, so if security asked me to walk naked on hot coals just to prove I had nothing to hide, I would.

"Do we really look like terrorists?" Sarah spoke quietly.

"I'd rather they do this than take any chances. You know me, Sarah," I whispered back, taking off my shoes and everything else I was asked to remove and putting it all in the grey tray being handed to me, trying desperately to avoid eye contact with the security people, just in case they pulled me out as one of the random checks, as I always seem to have a "Yes, it's me, I'm the guilty one" look on my face.

"Does this need to be removed from my bag, or can I leave it in?" Chrissy shouted as she removed a boxed, newly purchased Rampant Rabbit from her bag and held it up in the air. "It's battery operated, the same as my iPad, and you told us we had to remove that from our hand luggage."

The unimpressed security officer told her to leave it out.

Libby, Jess, and I couldn't help but watch Chrissy making eye contact with one of the security officers, whom we'd named "the Rippler" because of the way the muscles in his arms were rippling through his shirtsleeves; he must have spent all of his spare time working out at the gym. Our Chrissy likes a man with a well-toned body.

Chrissy purposely left the slim metal belt from her black leather miniskirt on to ensure the security alarm would go off as she walked through the metal detector. As the alarm sounded, Chrissy was taken to one side by one of the female officers, much to her disappointment.

She smiled sarcastically. "I'd normally expect at least the offer of a drink before I let anybody run their hands all over my body, but for you, I'll make an exception, sweetie." The woman's hands went between her cleavage, tracing the outline of her bra, then inside her waistband, making sure she wasn't carrying anything dangerous. The blank expression on the security officer's face didn't falter, nor did she say anything. She'd probably heard remarks like that a thousand times before. We sniggered quietly with the immature schoolgirl behaviour we'd now adopted. The Rippler stared straight at her; she winked, ran the tip of her tongue seductively across her top lip, and gently gave the bottom one a couple of quick bites. He was hooked. Once her first frisking of the day had taken place, she was asked to move on and collect her hand luggage. As Chrissy slowly walked by the Rippler, she skilfully slipped one of her business cards into his right breast pocket and carried on walking without looking back. Chrissy carries business cards everywhere with her, never one to miss an opportunity. The Rippler's eyes were glued to her rear as it wiggled from side to side.

The rest of us passed through security without any problems. I sighed with relief.

I always find it strange at the airport. One minute you're going through all the intensity and stress of check-in and security, where smiles and personality have been sucked out of airport staff during induction and job training. Then as if by magic, you're transported through a door to won-derland, the departure area. It's relaxed and full of excite-ment, with people laughing and chatting away in the bars and cafés whilst others try to find a bargain in duty-free, although it's not as good as it used to be, or in WHSmith, buying books and magazines to read on their holidays and overpriced sweets they'd never dream of buying in the world on the other side of security. I usually head to Boots for a meal deal to take on the plane with me, but not today; I think I may just be on liquids for the foresee-able future.

"Anyone for a coffee?" Michelle asked.

"You've got to be joking," Frankie answered. "Coffee? Are you for real? I'm off to the bar. Who's joining me?"

Bit of a daft question really. Who ever got a party started by drinking coffee, unless it was laced with navy rum and had a big dollop of whipped cream on top?

"For goodness sake, you're alcoholics, the lot of you," Michelle said.

"Beg to differ, Michelle." Frankie laughed. "Alcoholics go to meetings. We're binge drinkers. We go to parties, and that's where we're going right now."

Chrissy took Michelle by the arm and walked her through the maze of duty-free and in the direction of the bars before she had time to realise what was going on. I couldn't see Chrissy being a carer to Michelle for the whole of the weekend. It would cramp her style. I thought we should start taking bets on how long it was gonna last.

Jess spotted a table in the Spinning Jenny bar next to a group of men in rugby shirts and rushed over to claim it. We quickly followed, pulled over some more chairs, and dumped our bags on the floor.

"You can't be that cold, Sarah. Take your cardi off. You look like an old woman." Frankie said.

"Oh, I'll take it off later, Frankie. I'm still a bit cold, not as tough as you lot."

"Who you calling, rasta girl?" Sam laughed. "You've no right to call anybody. The only thing you're missing are dreadlocks and a spliff hanging out of the corner of your mouth. You're getting darker, I swear. Still can't believe the woman on check-in thought you looked like your passport photo, and you didn't get carted off to be checked out properly…if you know what I mean."

"Very funny!" Frankie laughed. "I need a drink."

Faith was placed in charge of the kitty. She was the most sensible member of the group, which didn't say much for the rest of us, but more important, she could be trusted not to blow it all in one go like Frankie—or if you're dizzy Libby, lose the money. We handed over forty quid each for starters.

Faith, Frankie, and I took our place in the queue at the bar. For six thirty in the morning, it was a pretty large queue. In front of us was a group of lads in their twenties wearing England football shirts, waiting to be served.

"Hope they're off to Benidorm. Wouldn't mind a piece of him in the number seven shirt," Frankie said, loud enough for him to hear. Number seven turned his head in our direction, and Frankie gave him a cheeky smile.

"Not a bad specimen, even if I say so myself. Hey, number seven, you into carrots?"

"Don't mind em," he replied.

"There you go Frankie, you're in." Faith laughed.

"Very funny, Faith."

"Ladies, what can I get you?" asked the young bartender, who was far too chirpy for this time of the morning.

"Morning, Tom," Faith replied. His name was printed on a badge hanging from a lanyard around his neck. "Nine cold bottles of Corona, please, with limes."

"Looks like you're in for a good time, where ya off?" Tom asked.

"Benidorm. Clue's on the T-shirt, Tom." Frankie smiled and pointed to me. "Hen party."

He laughed. "Duh…so it is. Well, lovin' the name, Benidorm Virgins. Not had any virgins pass through here in ages." He laughed again. "Don't think you'll be virgins for long, though—you're already beginning to get plenty of attention."

"That's the idea," Frankie replied, grinning."If there's one thing I'm going to Benidorm for, it's to lose my virginity."

I struggled to remove the open bottles from the bar as Faith handed over the money and grabbed a handful of straws. Frankie was no help whatsoever. She grabbed her own drink and went off to find number seven.

The atmosphere in the bar was lively with people getting their holidays off to a good start by consuming a variety of alcoholic beverages and eating the traditional fry-up as if it was going to be their last decent meal until they returned to the UK. There were a couple of other hen parties, loads of stag parties, a few families with children bouncing around excitedly, and lovey-dovey couples staring affectionately into each other's eyes. We didn't give in to temptation with the fry-up, concentrating on a more liquid kind of breakfast, although I could feel the draw of Burger King. The only time I ever have one is when I come to the airport; it's one of mine and Darren's holiday traditions. I decided I might nip in there later, even if it was only for a quick sniff. I didn't want to be seen to be letting the side down by eating food. "Eatin's cheatin'," we always say.

"This is great," Sarah said, sipping her Corona through a straw. "Who'd have thought I'd be sitting in a bar at seven o'clock in the morning and drinking a bottle of Corona—and it's my second drink of the morning." She let out a giddy little laugh. "I'm so glad Jim let me come. You know, this is the first time he's ever had to get Maisy up and ready for nursery."

"Jim let you come. Jim let you come. Don't get me started about Jim, our Sarah. I did your horoscope for ya last night." Faith reached into her bag and pulled out a crumpled A4 piece of paper and passed it to Sarah. "Say good-bye to your old life, the new one's just around the corner. It's looking good. Look…" Sarah looked at the crumpled piece of paper. "And I've brought my tarot cards—they're in my bag, so I'll read them later for you as well."

Sarah's eyes moistened as she looked at the paper. She quickly blinked. "Ya know I don't believe in all this mumbo-jumbo, Faith, and will ya stop going on about Jim? There's nothing wrong with him. Leave him alone; we're happy. I'll drink to having a great weekend away with my bessies, though."

I don't think any of us believed a word she said about Jim. I smiled across the table at her, and she softly smiled back.

Jess scraped the bottom of her stool as she stood and lifted her bottle in the air. "I'd like to make a toast. Benidorm, I hope you're ready for us because we're on our way." We raised our bottles in the air, clinking them against one another. "Cheers!"

Chrissy was on the prowl again, this time catching the eye of a man, probably in his early fifties, six foot, with striking silver-grey hair. He stood with a group of rowdy men at the far end of the bar dressed in multicoloured Hawaiian shirts, cheering on one of their group to down a pint of something. She smiled at him, and he took this as a signal to come over and join us.

"Hello, ladies…Mike. You look like you're all you up to no good. Where you off?"

"Benidorm," Chrissy casually replied.

"Can nobody read around here?" Frankie pointed at her T-shirt.

"Snap…and what lovely breasts you have." Mike smiled. "We're on a stag do. Dave, the lad in the orange Hawaiian shirt over there knocking the cocktail back, he's the unlucky one. We're hoping to give him a good send-off."

"Well, I believe Benidorm's the place to do it." Frankie downed her Corona and read the cocktail menu, not really paying Mike any more attention.

"Looks like you've already started," Libby said.

"Those shirts are a bit loud for me this time of the morning," Chrissy answered as she rested her chin in the palm of her hand. "I prefer something a bit more…calming." The word came out very provocatively. "At least until I've got a few more of these inside me." She lifted her bottle in the air and moved ever so slightly on her stool, revealing the top of her newly spray-tanned thigh slowly creeping out of her black miniskirt. Mike caught a sneaky peek. Jess and I looked at each other across the table, giggled, and shook our heads. *She's at it again.* Tiny droplets of sweat began to appear on Mike's forehead. He coughed to clear his throat.

"Well, OK…let's see if I can help. Can I get you another?"

"I'm nipping to the loo. Who's coming?" Jess interrupted.

"Me," answered Libby. "Wanna have a look at the duty-free. Oh, and we can pick up the magazines from Smith's."

"Chrissy…nice to meet you, Mike." She placed her bottle on the table and passed him her right hand. Mike politely shook it. "Sure, why not?" Chrissy pulled at the hem of her skirt as she stood. "So where are you all from? Anywhere we may have heard of?"

"Stockport, we're all with the Cheshire fire service." He looked towards his friends, who were now watching him.

When she heard the word Cheshire, Michelle lifted her eyes from the *Cheshire Life* magazine she was engrossed in. *Snob,* I thought.

Chrissy gave a little cough, a sign of approval. "Firemen, that's why the toned body. Interesting. So you're used to handling hoses? That's funny…me, too," she teased. "Wonder what position yours is in right now? Inflated or deflated?"

Chrissy hesitated, leant into Mike, and placed a manicured hand on his crotch "Mmmmm…inflated…it would be a shame to waste it."

"You offering?" Mike answered back jokingly.

"This is going to be fun," I whispered to Sam.

Chrissy looked around. "OK, follow me."

"Are you being serious?"

"I never joke about inflated hoses, Mike." She took him by the hand and led the way, whispering in his ear. They both started to laugh.

"Dear God, he said he was a Cheshire fireman," Michelle exclaimed.

Her comment fell on deaf ears.

"She's wasted no time. You could see in her eyes she was well ready to pounce," Frankie said. "Sam, you're gonna have to wake up, or Chrissy'll be one up on ya."

"She can have him. I've got my eye on his mate, the one in the orange shirt," Sam answered teasingly.

"Do you reckon she learnt her pickup techniques at Guides, Ellie?" Sarah laughed. Alcohol was now taking hold of her, and she began to relax.

"No, she's just a slut," Michelle announced. "He's a Cheshire fireman, for God's sake."

We all laughed. We didn't bite. We'd already had the conversation about Mrs. Bucket Michelle coming to Benidorm, and we'd agreed to ignore any negative or rude comments that found their way out of her mouth over the weekend. Sam said if in doubt, just smile, and then go and punch a wall.

"Where's she going?" Frankie exclaimed.

"Dunno. Let's follow her," I said. "Come on."

Chrissy had a head start on us, so Frankie and I had a bit of running to do. I felt as if we were doing undercover surveillance work for MI5 as we both hid behind the Bacardi stand, offering two bottles for twenty-two pounds, then the Chanel one, just so Chrissy didn't catch us following her. They ended up outside the prayer room.

"She's not taking him in there, is she?" I said, blushing.

"Nobody ever goes in there unless there's been a plane crash, and we haven't had one of them for a while," Frankie replied.

"Ha! This is so funny. Frankie, look at his face. He's following her like a little puppy dog. Chrissy flytrap is out again. He's not going to know what's hit him." I giggled. "And he wanted to give Dave a good send-off. Bet he can't believe his luck."

"It's gotta be done, Ellie." Frankie laughed.

We watched as Chrissy led Mike into the prayer room, then we turned and made our way back to report to the others, taking time to stop off in duty-free, having a good squirt of perfumes and collecting samples of anything we could get our hands on. By the time we got back to the Spinning Jenny and rejoined the others, we smelt pretty darn good.

FIFTEEN

Whilst we'd been away on our undercover mission, more people had come into the bar. I couldn't see a spare table. By the look of it, it was mainly groups of men and women on hen and stag parties. Faith had bought more drinks for everybody. We were now on cocktails, Faith's choice: sex on the beach. She should be so lucky. Faith would take sex anywhere; she was that desperate for a man.

"I've heard you've taken up golf, Frankie. Is it true? Never saw you as a golfer." Jess asked.

"Since when did you start playing golf?" Sam took a gulp of her cocktail.

"Yeah, about a months ago. The golf's not too good, but at least I'm guaranteed to hold a hard shaft in my hand twice a week." Frankie sniggered. "I've not had sex for ages."

"That's cos you're being fussy," Libby said.

"What you talking about? Fussy, I've not had any offers to be fussy about," she replied. "I only joined the golf club because one of the consultants at work told me they were full of divorced men, but I've yet to find one, and even if there were any, and I ran around the green naked with a seven iron up my arse, they wouldn't notice me. All they're interested in is that little white ball and who plays off what. God, men can be so pathetic."

"If men spent that much time and attention on our clitorises as they do on that little white ball, then we'd have the best sex ever," Libby remarked.

"Are you saying boring Barry spends too much time at Brookdale Golf Club, Libby?" Sam asked.

"I'm saying sometimes I wish I were a little white ball, that's all," she replied.

Ooooo, that was strange—Libby had never criticised Barry before for spending too much time up at Brookdale. In fact she encouraged him to go and play golf, saying he was spending too much time at home and kept getting under her feet. Now me, on the other hand—if Darren spent every hour of any day that had spare sunlight in it, playing golf, he'd soon know about it. I'd take myself up there, and I'd ram a seven iron up his arse. No man will ever take me for granted again. I could feel myself getting wound up just thinking about it.

But Libby, she never gets stressed or wound up, and she never loses her temper. She's the most laid-back person in our group. Probably that's why she's a good and patient primary-school teacher, and I'm an unorganised, stress-head legal secretary. No, normally everything just goes over her dizzy little head. It doesn't even waste time creeping in one ear, digesting in her brain, and then escaping out the other. I, on the other hand, only have to hear the word deadline and the panic attacks start taking over my body.

"Where've you been?" Frankie asked Chrissy as she came back to join us, like we didn't know.

"To the prayer room." She took a big gulp of her drink. "Needed that…mouth's a bit dry."

"Since when did you start going into the prayer room before you go on a flight?" I said.

"Since I fancied getting it off with that fireman." Chrissy laughed. "I came to the very quick conclusion as I took him in hand, if that hose was going to explode, it might as well explode in me. Besides there have been a few flying incidents lately, so I killed two birds with one stone. I did shout 'God' a couple of times."

"Have you got no self-respect?" Michelle lifted her eyes again from her *Cheshire Life* magazine as she shook her head in a disapproving way.

"Where are there firemen? And since when? Nobody told me," Jess gushed. "I love men in uniform, especially firemen—all of them big, strong, firm muscles. I've always wanted a fireman's lift. Do you think one of them would give me one?"

"By the sound of it, Chrissy's already had one." Faith snorted.

"You're disgusting," Michelle continued.

"Maybe if you relaxed a little more, you wouldn't be such an—" Sam stopped midsentence as I gave her one of my looks.

"Well, go on then, give us the goss," Faith said.

"Later. I'll be back in a min. Need to tidy up a bit," Chrissy answered as she headed in the direction of the ladies'.

"I'm off to the bar for fresh supplies. Sam, Ellie, come and give me a hand." Faith stood and picked up some of the kitty from the centre of the table. "Don't let Michelle get to you," Faith said to Sam as we walked towards the bar.

"I'm going to kill her, Faith," Sam growled. Then she paused. "I know, I'll do what I keep telling everybody else to do. Keep smiling and then go and look for a wall that's not already been punched by one of us." A sarcastic smile swept across her face as she linked her arms through Faith's and mine until we reached the bar.

The conversation between us all continued to flow, just like the alcohol, with lots of giggling and laughing. But when the girls started talking about what they wanted to do over the weekend, I could feel my body start to well up in a hot sweat. I liked Jess's idea of chilling around the pool and going to the spa much more than Frankie's pouring vodka down my throat for the whole three days. Don't know why she doesn't get drunk. I wish I could bottle her secret and sell it; I'd make a mint.

Sam and Chrissy set up a bet to see who would have the most sex whilst we were away. Chrissy reminded Sam she was already one up.

Jess offered to pay for her and Faith to go to any mind, body, and soul event anywhere in the world, if she didn't talk about Pete, her ex-husband, starting from then. Jess knew it was not going to happen, but she thought it would be worth a try.

Sarah's topic of conversation was Maisy. She'd been out of the adult world for so long, she'd forgotten how to communicate and be herself. I decided I was going to take her for a massage tomorrow, give her a bit of pampering. She would love it, I knew. I'll ask her later.

We left Michelle alone to digest her *Cheshire Life* magazine. The only person she made the slightest bit of polite conversation with was Sarah, who Michelle probably thought was only decent one of the group. *Sorry, Sarah, but I think I may be asking if I can put Michelle next to you on the plane, to give Chrissy a break.*

Frankie was now chief photographer and took every opportunity to get out her selfie stick and take photos of anything and everything she could get her hands on, and that included number seven.

"Ellie," Libby said. "I...I've got something to...tell you, and you're not gonna like it. None of you are."

"Why? What's the matter with ya?" I asked. "Don't tell me ya know something bad about Darren."

"No, no, for God's sake, no...Darren's the best bloke ever." Libby's voice faltered. "I'm...not coming with you to Benidorm. I've got a bit of a confession."

You could've heard a pin drop. Well, only around our table, you could.

"What d'ya mean, you're not coming? You're here."

"Ellie, I'm sorry. I'm not." Her voice trailed off as she looked at the floor. She inhaled quickly, lifted her head, and continued to speak. "Do you remember when we were out in November organising your hen party, and we went into Browns and we met some players from Man United?"

"Yes," I said hesitantly, waiting for what was to come next.

"The lad I was talking to…"

"The little Italian one?" Chrissy teased.

"Believe me, Chrissy, he's no little Italian, and he could give that stallion on Holt Farm, up at Harts Head Pike, a run for his money."

Well, pick them jaws up from off the floor—where'd this come from?

"Do you mean Marco D'Acampo?" Frankie gasped.

"Yes. I've been meeting up with him since then, at least once, maybe twice a week. It's nothing serious, just a bit of fun. He's wanted to take me away for a weekend for ages."

"I was gonna come over and give you a hand, you jammy cow. He's only a baby. What do you do, breast-feed him? You're old enough to be his mother." Frankie laughed.

"He likes older, more experienced women, and believe me, I do much more than breast-feed him." Libby blushed.

I'm gobsmacked. Libby has never cheated on boring, obese, golf-playing, TV-remote-hogger Barry, and she's kept this to herself since November. It's bloody March now.

"I never get the opportunity to get away overnight, and I'm really sorry. His family have a villa not far from Alicante Airport, and he's injured, so he can't play. He flew out yesterday, and he's sending a car to collect me from the airport."

Faith struggled to take in what Libby said. "What about our plans for the weekend? I can't believe you didn't say anything before."

"What about your husband?" Michelle asked archly, as if on cue.

"This has got nothing to do with Barry, and I'll make it up to you Faith, Ellie, everybody. Please say you don't mind. It's only happened over the last few days."

I didn't know what to think. We've always told one another everything—well, not everything, but most things—and this was definitely one of those things we would have told. A bloody twenty-six-year-old footballer, playing for the best football team in the world, and my friend has been getting jiggy with him for four months. No wonder she's been acting strange, shopping more online, and getting things delivered to my house. I just thought she got her shopping delivered to our house because they were less likely to get pinched if they were left in our porch. No, she was hiding stuff from boring Barry.

Frankie broke the ice. "You go, girl." She patted her on the shoulder. "Not every day you get an offer like that. If it was offered me, I'd be off like a shot. Sorry, Ellie, but I'm gagging for it. A Rampant Rabbit can't replace the real thing."

"Libby, it's OK. I'm just a bit shocked. I can't believe you've kept something like this to yourself for so long."

"I've wanted to tell you for ages, but it just never seemed to be the right moment."

"Believe me, Libby, there was always a right moment for that bit of gossip. You've been off having sex with one of the fittest players—no, probably the fittest player—in the premier league, and you've kept that to yourself. I could have sold that story to any of the papers and got myself at least another boob job and a fortnight in the Maldives with Martin, five stars. Has he got any mates?" Sam laughed.

"He's been getting tickets for Barry to go and watch United," Libby said.

"You are kidding, Libby. Where on earth does Barry think you're getting the tickets from?" Jess asked.

"I told him I've got a friend who works at United. He'd die if he found out. It's not like I'm planning to leave Barry. It's just sex, a bit of fun." She didn't sound very convincing. "I don't know what happened. One minute we were talking at the end of the bar in Browns, next we were bouncing around in a suite at the Lowry. In fact, we nearly bumped into you, Chrissy, and that bloke you were with. I've never had sex like it in my life. I never even realised sex with Barry was so stale. I can't give Marco up—he's like a drug."

"Barry's not going to find out from us, is he, Michelle?" Chrissy looked her straight in the eye.

Michelle stood up, snatched her bag off the table, and walked off in the direction of Starbucks.

I walked over to Libby and put my arms around her. "It's no problem, go and enjoy yourself."

"Thanks, Ellie. I really am sorry I didn't say anything before." Libby hugged me back.

Hope I've got no more surprises to come this weekend. Don't think I can take any more.

Sarah pointed to the departure board. "Our flight is boarding at gate 208. This is so exciting. I've waited years for this weekend. Come on, move." Sarah jumped up, grabbed her bag, and headed off excitedly in the direction of the gate.

"Need a hand with your bags, Chrissy?" Mike shouted.

"No, thank you, sweetie. I wouldn't want you to be getting the wrong idea."

"Anybody seen Michelle?" I asked.

"Mrs. Bucket is approaching from the left. Quick, run," Frankie said in a rasta voice.

"Chrissy," I shouted. "Grab Michelle."

SIXTEEN

Boarding had already begun as we approached the gate, and them little butterflies had returned and started to flap around my stomach in a nervous, excited kind of way. I located my seat, near the back of the plane. We always go for the back of the plane when we go away; it takes us back to our old school trips, when we always headed for the back of the coach. It wasn't cool to sit at the front; only the nice kids sat there. I securely fastened my seat belt. The firemen from Stockport were a couple rows in front of us, a group of lads from a rugby club in Oldham behind. There was also a group of girls from Liverpool to the right of us, with their hair in rollers and wearing PJs from Primark. Roxy and Izzy have ones with similar designs. This was definitely the recipe for a fun flight.

As the plane began to taxi down the runway, I spotted the airport pub out of the window to the left, with its beer garden, where I had stood so many times with Roxy and Izzy when they were little, drinking lemonade and munching away on packets of Walkers prawn cocktail crisps, watching the planes take off and land and dreaming about where we'd go if we could have afforded to go on one.

The cabin crew began to give a demonstration of what to do in an emergency. I watched, taking everything in. *Emergency exit, mine's behind me, already clocked that one before I sat down. Tie lifebelt here, blow whistle, yes, got that.* I read my leaflet, as advised, checked under my seat, just to make sure my life jacket was there, and read the leaflet again, just to be certain I'd taken everything in.

"Helen, what on earth are you reading that for? You know if we crash, you're not going to survive," Michelle said. "They say the only reason you have to bend forward and put your head in your hands when the plane is making an emergency landing is because when you crash, you will break your neck on impact and die instantly, but they will be able to identify you because of your dental records. That is, if you have a dentist."

"You never cease to amaze, Michelle—such a spreader of happy cheer. Oh, and for the record that's not true, Ellie. Don't listen to her," Frankie snapped.

"Frankie, leave it," I said. *Oh God, does Michelle think I don't go to the dentist? What's wrong with my teeth? Is Frankie just saying that to make me feel better?*

I tried to ignore her little outburst and said my prayers, asking that the plane wouldn't crash. I just hoped that he—I mean God—could hear me. Then I was good to go.

The engines got louder as the plane moved faster along the runway, and we were up. No going back now. To help with ear pressure, I chewed like mad on a piece of chewy I took out of my jeans pocket. Others started clapping and cheering. *I want a drink. I need a drink.* How long would it be before the cabin crew brought the drinks trolley down the aisle?

The captain introduced himself and the crew, and the announcement he made helped me relax my breathing a little. "We're in for a pleasant flight…" I didn't hear the rest of his speech. I released the grip on the arms of my seat and got some colour back into my knuckles. Chrissy pressed the overhead call button.

"Yes, madam, can I help you?" Alison, a member of the cabin crew, kindly asked.

"Do you have any champagne on board?"

"Yes, but only half-size bottles."

"Any good?" Libby looked up from the duty-free magazine.

Alison laughed. "Not the best, but drinkable."

"Since when have you been fussy, Libby? Nine bottles and nine glasses please," Chrissy said. "My treat."

"You lot are gonna to be hammered before you even get to Benidorm," Mike shouted.

"That's the plan," Jess shouted back.

Libby handed out the glasses as Chrissy passed around the bottles of champagne. We all popped our corks, laughing as we poured our champers. I smiled to myself as I looked around at my smiling friends.

"I'd like to make a toast," Chrissy announced whilst standing. "Raise your glasses, ladies. Here's to a fabulous weekend of sex, sun, and fun. Cheers, everybody."

"Cheers." We shouted back and clinked glasses. Michelle made an effort to raise her glass and gave me a sarcastic smile.

"We'll drink to that," a lad from the rugby club yelped. "Cheers!" they shouted and held up bottles of Stella they'd retrieved from their bags.

Sarah happily agreed to swap places with Chrissy and was chatting to Michelle about Maisy. I hoped Sarah could keep her occupied for the rest of the flight and that Michelle kept her mouth firmly closed, or Frankie would throw her off the plane, probably using the emergency exit located behind my row. I pressed the overhead button to call a member of the cabin crew again and ask for more drinks. The drinks trolley began to make its way down the aisle. This time, vodka and lemonade times eight. Michelle wanted a coffee. She might have a bit of an addiction to coffee. She had one earlier in Starbucks when she went skulking off.

"I'm having that lad in the orange shirt in the toilet before we land," Sam said confidently.

"You can have him." Chrissy smirked. "I'm after him in the rugby shirt over there, the one with lots of hair. Just imagine, Sam, running your fingers through it, then clamping onto it during midthrusting."

Sam demonstrated, holding on to the headrest of the seat in front whilst thrusting her hips forwards and backwards.

"Do you two never stop?" Faith quipped, not even bothering to lift her head up from this week's *OK* magazine, which featured Kerry Katona on the front telling why she was never going to do drugs again.

"You know us, Faith—very competitive," Chrissy replied.

"Hey, Mike. Who's your mate again in the orange shirt?" Sam shouted.

"You know who it is." Chrissy nudged her. "Dave. It's his stag do."

"Oh yeah, I forgot. It's OK, Mike, Chrissy's just told me. I know a great way to get his stag do off to a memorable start. I could give him an early wedding present."

"I can hear ya, ya know. I'm not deaf," Dave responded. "Why, what ya thinking, blondie?"

"How about me and you joining the mile-high club—never done it on a trip to Benidorm before."

"Sam, he's angin'," Frankie whispered.

Dave rose from his seat, walked up the aisle slowly, and stopped at Sam. "Come on, then, or are you all talk?"

Sam stood up. "I never say anything I don't mean." She smoothed her black H & M above-the-knee skirt down, made her way up the aisle, and disappeared into the toilet.

Passengers turned to watch as Dave followed her in. The click of a lock was heard, and a sign was lit to alert passengers the toilet was engaged, as if they didn't know.

"I can't believe the flight attendants are letting them get away with that. This is really embarrassing. Dear God, can't Sam keep the noise down? People are going to think I'm like that, being with you lot," Michelle said, forcing herself as far down into her seat as she could get.

"Nobody will ever think that, Michelle. They only have to take one look at you to know you're a frigid, miserable cow," Frankie replied.

"Just ignore it, Michelle—read your *Good Housekeeping*," I said.

"It's *Cheshire Life* actually, and I can't, they are making too much noise." She put her Roberto Cavalli sunglasses on, as if trying to disguise herself.

"Well, there ain't a lot of room in there," Chrissy replied sarcastically.

"Oh, and you'd know all about that as well, wouldn't you?" Michelle took the scarf from around her neck and tied it around her head like some fifties icon.

"No, actually, I have never had sex on a commercial airline that doesn't have a private, first-class cabin. Maybe I might give it a go with one of these rugby lads when Sam's finished."

"Hey, can I volunteer?" a dark-haired rugby player shouted up, to loud cheers from his mates.

The noise stopped, the lock clicked open, and Sam and Dave walked out to the sound of clapping as they made their way back to their seats. Dave smiled and nodded his head, clearly feeling very proud of himself. Not only for being a part of the mile-high club, but because he'd pulled Sam. Mike told us his mates had been taking bets on who'd pull her first. If Dave had been a peacock, his feathers would have been all fanned out and waving around for all the world to see. Sam smiled.

She took her place back in the aisle seat next to me and leant across towards Chrissy, who was sat by the window. "One all…This bet is on, baby."

"Bring it on, Sam, nothing like a bit of competition."

"Well, go on then, Sam, dish the dirt," Jess whispered.

"Nothing to tell. I bet one of the seven dwarfs has got a frigging bigger one than him. I'm glad it's not me who's supposed to be spending the rest of my life with him," Sam remarked. "Bet his wife to be will be shagging anything she can lay her hands on, on her hen party."

"Well, you were making plenty of noise in there," Faith commented.

"Kept banging my bloody head on the light on top of the mirror. It's bloody killing me." Sam laughed, rubbing the back of her head. "Anyway, what happened with you and the fireman in the chapel, Chrissy, or you keeping it quiet?"

"Yeah, it was good, I suppose. I've had better sex in a morning, but he was gagging for it. Bet he's not done it for ages," Chrissy whispered, with Mike only being a couple of rows in front of us. "He tried to take me from behind over one of the chairs before putting on a condom. I had to stop him. 'Hold it, tiger,' I said, or something like that."

"Hold it, tiger'?" Frankie laughed. "Chrissy, nobody says that. It sounds as daft as Hugh Grant in *Notting Hill* when he kept saying, 'Upsidaisy,' as he tried to climb over that garden wall when he was trying to impress Julia Roberts."

"Never mind that, Frankie. Mike apologised, bless him, and then went at it like a bloody Kango hammer after I put the condom on him. Oh! And he had great finger action. Apart from that, it was pretty regular. He asked if he could see me again. I told him no. Shame, really, he seemed kind of sweet."

"Why don't you see him again?" I asked.

"Don't start again, Ellie. I don't want to get involved, remember?"

"You're never gonna meet anybody serious if you don't start dropping your guard."

"Have you not noticed the gold band on the third finger of his left hand? I'm not even going there. Who's for another drink?"

"My sex life is shite at the moment." Frankie knelt up on the seat in front and turned to me as she spoke.

"You have mentioned it once or twice, Frankie." Faith sighed. "Have you ever thought a man could do you under the Trades Description Act?"

"What d'ya mean, Trades Description Act?" Frankie exclaimed.

"Mmmm, where do I start? Well, you wear hair extensions, false eyelashes, fake tan—and you can't even get that bloody right—chicken fillets stuffed down your already padded Wonderbra, pull-you-in knickers, false nails. A bloke goes to bed with one woman and wakes up with another."

"Two for the price of one…bargain." Frankie laughed.

"That's the problem. You've got to start being yourself, and one day Mr. Right'll come along, instead of the stream of no-hopers you collect. You need to be yourself."

"Since when have you started giving advice on how to get a man?" Sam asked. "You should be more like me—take no advice, give no advice."

"It's just an observation," Faith replied.

"I don't know. I like getting dressed up every once in a while. Oh, forget it. I'm sick of looking. I'm gonna do what Ellie did. She went off blokes, and when she wasn't looking, Darren—the knight in a shining red Audi A5—turned up."

"And I've not looked back since. No more self-induced orgasms for me." I sniggered. "I've not even seen Ryan Giggs for ages."

"You had an affair with Ryan Giggs?" Michelle screeched.

"No." Jess laughed. "Ryan Giggs is the name of her vibrator."

"That's all I've had for years, on and off," Faith remarked, "and I can't even begin to tell you the amount of times I faked an orgasm. Believe me, Meg Ryan's got nothing on me. In fact my sex life with Pete got to be so boring, I stopped lying there thinking of England and started thinking of more exotic places like Bali or Thailand, for example, just to pass the time. I'd count to twenty, make a withering noise, and repeat until he finished. Luckily, he never lasted too long. I still can't believe he cheated on me with four other women. How much sperm can one man have?"

"Oh, no, Faith, we're not getting onto that subject again," Jess squealed.

Faith stopped speaking.

"Why do we do fake orgasms?" Chrissy screeched, causing passengers around us to stop talking. "I never do it anymore, haven't done it for years. It should be illegal."

"Hear, hear," the girls from Liverpool said in unison. There was shock and horror on the faces of the men seated close to us.

"It's either because we've had enough and want them to get off, or because they're shite in bed, and we don't want to hurt their feelings," Sam replied.

"But hey, they don't care about us, so why should we care about them? If you have to fake an orgasm, you shouldn't allow the cock you're faking an orgasm with anywhere near your genitalia. It's such a waste of time and effort on your part. You should go and find one that really does work for you," Chrissy gasped.

I quickly looked around again at the faces of all the men sitting close by. They looked completely oblivious. Did they really not know women faked orgasms? Surely they couldn't think they made us climax during every sex session. I wanted to shout, "It takes more than forty-five seconds to make us climax." I stifled a giggle. Chrissy has given this little orgasm rant before, and whilst we do agree with her, we all still occasionally fake orgasms. But we'd never tell Chrissy, or she'd just get on her box again.

"Ellie, d'ya think I'm horrible, not coming?" Libby sighed.

"Libby, I don't mind, honest. We can do something again, when we get home. Don't worry about it." I smiled reassuringly at my friend.

"It's just…I know how you feel, Faith, about people, you know, messing around, cheating on their partners, but everybody's circumstances are different. Pete was a bit of an exception—he was messing about with loads of women."

"Like I need reminding."

"It's just you always say people don't think about the consequences when they start playing with fire. I think that's why I couldn't bring myself to tell anybody about me."

"And have you thought about the consequences, Libby?" Faith asked. "He's a top-class footballer. It could make the papers."

"That's not gonna happen. We're always careful; he reserves a room at the Lowry or somewhere out of town, and I meet him there. We never go together. I'm not going to leave Barry, if that's what you think, but ever since I met Marco, I feel alive. I really do. I want to spend time with him, and I know I'm not going to get a chance like this again."

"Well, go on, then. Tell all. We know you're dying to." Sam rubbed her hands together.

"Where do I start? He's got a body to die for. I've never seen a body like that close up. It's a bit like a younger version of those David Beckham adverts for his underwear, but I get to touch it, instead of drooling at it in a magazine, and he knows so much about pleasuring a woman. They do say Italians make the best lovers—I read that in the *Daily Mail* a few weeks ago. They did a poll of the best European lovers, and the Italians won."

"Well, it wouldn't be the British. I've slept with most of them, and they're not up to much." Sam giggled.

"I've never had sex like it before. I had to buy a book from Ann Summers to update my bedroom skills, and if anybody checked the history on my laptop, they'd think I had a sex problem. I've been looking up, well, everything. That's why I started going to the gym—so I could keep up with Marco. Sex with Barry is pretty regular...boring, in fact."

"You're funny, Libby." Sam smiled.

"I've never been as adventurous as you, Sam. Maybe I should have come and talked to you. Can we meet up when we get back, so you can give me some pointers?"

"Sure, why not? I'll give you pointers. May as well put my years of experience to good use, but don't be asking me for advice with Barry. You know I don't get involved."

"And why are you not asking me for advice, Libby?" Chrissy asked.

"Yeah, please, Chrissy, you as well," Libby replied.

"Libby, sweetheart…have fun and stop worrying about it. It's OK," I reassured her.

It felt like we'd only been in the air for five minutes when the pilot announced he'd started our descent into Alicante Airport. We'd been talking, drinking, and laughing nonstop since we got on the plane. Occasionally Michelle looked up from her magazine and joined in, but not for long. Jess was smashed. I hadn't a clue what she'd been drinking. Jess and I are not big drinkers, so it doesn't take much to send us over the edge. She spent most of the flight sat on Steve's knee—he was one of the firemen—rubbing his biceps up and down. If she asked him one more time to show her his hose, I might have killed her.

When the seat-belt sign went on, we managed to get her back into her seat before a member of the cabin crew approached to check we were all buckled up.

And just as at takeoff, I unwrapped a piece of chewy, popped it into my mouth, and began chewing to try to control the pressure in my ears. I took a firm grip of the armrests as the plane descended. My ears took it in turn to release the air pressure. It was so painful. The wheels screamed as they touched down on the tarmac. Clapping and cheering took place all around the plane, but I was clapping and cheering the loudest. I even gave out a couple of whoop-whoops.

"Thank you, God," I shouted, and boy, did I mean it. My bessies just laughed at me.

The prescripted announcement of "No smoking until you're out of the terminal building, take your belongings, thank you for flying with blah, blah, blah" came on. The purser could have been talking Japanese. I wasn't listening again. I just wanted off this plane, now I was here.

As I stood at the door to exit the plane, the hot and humid air crept up, and them butterflies were back in my stomach. The last time I had a feeling like this was over a year ago when me and Darren went to Tenerife for a week.

Steve was recruited by Sarah and Faith to help get Jess off the plane and into the coach waiting to transfer us to the airport terminal building. She continued stroking his biceps, telling him she'd love a fireman's lift—like he needed reminding as that was the main topic of conversation between them on the plane—so he promised he'd give her one if she behaved herself and got through passport control without any issues. I'm not sure what he meant by giving her one, either a fireman's lift or a good seeing to, but as long as it shut her up, I really didn't care. She promised she would and kept looking at him the whole time, her left index finger on her lips, indicating she was going to keep quiet.

We retrieved our bags from the carousel and said good-bye to our new friends the firemen, the girls from Liverpool, and the lads from the rugby club. I pointed my bessies in the direction of the exit and informed them our transfer to Benidorm would be right outside the arrivals terminal waiting for us with my name in the front window, as the travel company had advised. I turned on my mobile and texted Darren to let him know I'd arrived OK. I didn't tell him I was half-cut, and the next drink was going to send me to the nearest table to start dancing around with my knickers in the air, singing a bad version of Madonna's "Like a Virgin."

Frankie walked out of the airport first; she needed a smoke. Faith and Chrissy weren't far behind her.

"What the frig?" Frankie squealed.

"What's the matter?" Sarah said, running towards her.

Parked outside the arrivals terminal was a white limousine with the name MCDONALD in the front windscreen for all the world to see, and standing beside it was a muscular, blond haired, half dressed young man, wearing a white collar, black bow tie and black trousers, holding a tray of champagne.

"I've not ordered this," I managed to say. "There must have been a mix-up. I ordered a luxury minibus and I definitely didn't order a muscular, orgasmic Greek God, I'd have remembered for sure if I had."

"No mix-up. I ordered it." Chrissy walked over and gave me a hug. "If we're doing this, sweetie, we're doing it in style. It's not every day one of your BFFs has a hen party."

"Wow…thanks, Chrissy. I don't know what to say. Anything else gonna happen this weekend I need to know about?"

"Always say you never know," Sam piped up.

Faith, Chrissy, Frankie, and Libby puffed away happily on their Silk Cuts, whilst drinking their champagne. Sarah and I took our cases over to the driver. We climbed in and sat on the comfy red leather seats and then started bouncing up and down excitedly, trying not to spill our drinks. A deep-pile black carpet covered the floor. This was frigging amazing. There were lots of little cupboards and drawers dotted around, and we spent a few minutes opening and closing them to see what they held. The last time I remembered being this excited about having a good nosey around was when I was little. When we visited my mum's friends, I always made the excuse that I wanted the toilet, and then I'd disappear for ages, having a nosey around the different rooms of their houses. The biggest cupboard in the limousine had four bottles of Perrier-Jouet Belle Epoque champagne on ice waiting for us. Perfect. It must have cost Chrissy a bomb.

"He's here. He's here. There's Marco," Libby shouted.

Sarah and I quickly climbed back out of the limo.

"Oh my God. Oh my God. Girls, have a fantastic time. Ellie, I'll make it up to you, I promise." Libby started fiddling about with something at each side of her waistband and out popped her thong.

"What you doing?" Faith screeched.

"What does it look like? Starting as I mean to go on." Libby threw her lacy thong at Michelle. "Put them in your bag for me, I'll get them off you on Sunday."

"I'm not touching them." Michelle gasped and dropped them on the floor.

Marco D'Acampo pulled up alongside in an orange F-TYPE Jag with the roof down. This was all so surreal. I was used to seeing Marco D'Acampo running up and down the pitch at Old Trafford or being interviewed on TV, not picking my friend up at Alicante Airport. Was this really the same Marco? His six-foot frame climbed out of the car and kissed Libby on her left cheek. I could feel my knees weaken. I wondered if he was gonna walk along the line and give us all a peck on the cheek. He looked delicious, good enough to eat. Would I have spent the weekend with him if it had been on offer to me? I didn't waste time thinking about it, as the opportunity was never going to happen, and I'd got Darren, not boring Barry. He took her case and placed it in the boot of the car. Good job she only had a small case; he'd have struggled to get any-thing else in there. The boot was so tiny. An F-TYPE Jag would be no good for an ASDA weekly shop. You wouldn't even be able to get a twenty-four multipack of toilet rolls in there. Why was I thinking such rubbish? He was wear-ing navy chino shorts and a white vest top, showing off his sculpted biceps and dark olive skin. He wore navy boat shoes. He was tall. Wow! Was he tall. And drop-dead gor-geous. Libby jumped into the passenger seat, waving to us all. I wondered if he noticed we were all standing there looking like gorps. Sam was making funny noises. I think she may have just had her first orgasm in Spain. The one in the air was over France. Marco waved, and we blew kisses in return.

"Make sure you're back here for four on Sunday afternoon," Faith yelled.

I didn't think Libby heard Faith. As soon as they drove off, Libby's head disappeared into Marco's lap. I hoped the car was an automatic. Marco would have to concentrate very hard on his driving if Libby was getting her tonsils tickled. They'd not even got out of the car park. She was gonna be raw by Sunday night.

"And then there were eight, soon to be seven, hopefully." Frankie chuckled and looked at Michelle. "Well, come on, then. What we waiting for? Let's get some pictures taken with this lovely young man and then driver, lets get going to Benidorm."

The driver started up the engine after loading our bags into a small white van that was going to accompany us on our journey. He informed us in broken English, with a very nice hint of a Spanish accent, it was going to take around forty-five minutes to reach our destination. He said to sit back, relax, and open the champagne, which we didn't need telling twice.

"This is the life," Sam said. "Hey, it's got two sunroofs. Wonder if we can open them. I've always wanted to stick my head out of the sunroof whilst driving along in a limo."

"I thought you'd done that loads of times." Sarah giggled.

"No, she normally has her head out of the window either shouting to blokes or being sick, and it's usually me who ends up cleaning up after her." Jess laughed.

Sarah asked the driver if he could open the sunroofs. He readily obliged. Sam pulled herself up, champagne flute in her left hand, and popped out quicker than her boobs on a Friday night out in Manchester. Sarah followed, then me. Chrissy and Frankie popped out of the front one, waving their glasses. With the wind blowing in our hair and the sun blazing down on us, we sang along to "We Are Family" by Sister Sledge, which was one of the songs Faith had playing on her iPod. About a month ago we had all received an e-mail from her asking for our favourite songs as she wanted to compile a playlist to accompany us on our weekend. We tried to talk her out of putting "I Will Survive," her anthem, on the playlist, but she was having none of it. She told us that song had got her through her breakup with Pete, not that it worked.

Singing, dancing, and drinking continued on the whole journey into Benidorm. Frankie continued being the photographer and clicked away for most of the journey. Our driver, David, was a lot more patient than Mr. Grumpy had been that morning when he drove us to the airport. He even joined in with a few of the songs. Sarah screamed as we passed the Terra Mitica theme park on our left and pleaded with us to go, but it didn't look open, and we told her we wouldn't have time. Passersby waved to us, and car horns beeped. Yes, everybody knew the Benidorm Virgins had arrived.

SEVENTEEN

Sam was the first to spot Hotel Guadalupe, which was going to be our residence for the next three days. We slid back into the limo all windswept and slightly worse for wear after finishing off the champagne. We gathered up all our belongings. Jess quickly placed an unopened bottle of Bombay Sapphire into Faith's tote bag, and Frankie grabbed the Smirnoff vodka bottle and put that into hers.

The limo came to a halt, the engine switched off, and the chauffer climbed out. He walked around the car and opened the door I was leaning against. I slithered out and landed on all fours, to my bessies' laughter. As I scrambled around on the floor, trying to get myself together, a soft Irish accent said, "Excellent timing, my lady, your knight in shorts and T-shirt awaits." Accompanying that orgasmic Irish accent was an outstretched sun-kissed hand for me to take.

I looked up and held his gaze—maybe a little too long. If I had ever wanted a knight to come and rescue me, I couldn't have dreamt up a better one. I thought I had died and gone to heaven. I was being helped to my feet by a six-foot, sun-kissed, dark-haired thirtysomething Gerard

Butler lookalike with the best accent in the world, wearing knee-length black shorts and a T-shirt advertising Guinness.

"You OK, love, or do you always make an entrance like that?"

Blushing, I replied, "Ahh…I'm fine." I was slightly embarrassed and scared to have another look.

"I'm Jerry, and I own the bar across from the hotel—the Irish one." I looked across to where he was pointing and noticed the large green shamrock identifying the bar. "I thought I'd have a wander over and see who was in the limousine. Glad I did."

My eyes met his. *Wow, I have died.* The rest of the girls climbed out of the limo, stretching and having a good look around at the new surroundings.

"It'd be grand to see you later, ladies, if you fancy calling in for a drink. We have two-for-one offers on all day long."

"Well, Jerry, you may just see us later." I giggled like some love-struck teenager gushing at meeting her favourite boy-band member. "Oh, and it's Helen…Ellie. Thanks for the lift."

"You will be seeing us later, Jerry," Frankie shouted up. "You can count on it."

"Nice to meet you, Helen…Ellie, ladies." He smiled as he walked away in the direction of his bar, my eyes hot on his heels.

"Hey, how come you get the bloke with the Irish accent?" Sam asked.

"I obviously fall more gracefully than you." I continued to giggle. "Did you get a load of that? Fit or what?"

"He's not bad, I suppose," Sam said mischievously.

"Jealousy, Samantha, will get you nowhere." I laughed.

We retrieved our bags from David, our driver and thanked him for the excellent journey into Benidorm, before staggering up the steps to the entrance of our hotel, pulling our suitcases behind us. The champagne in the limo and the encounter with Jerry had tipped me well over the edge. I hoped there were no tables in the reception, because the way I was feeling the bra would be off, and I'd be dancing on top of them.

We were welcomed to the hotel by the concierge, who wore a badge informing us his name was Miguel. He opened the floor-to-ceiling glass door and pointed us in the direction of the reception desk, where an array of staff were waiting to greet us.

The hotel lobby was furnished with large-cushioned sofas in neutral tones, and a variety of green plants that complemented the decor of modern paintings and statues. It was extremely busy, with housekeeping staff going about their daily duties and guests reading newspapers and magazines, playing cards, relaxing, and drinking coffee. *Michelle'll fit right in here*, I thought. Other guests walked through, carrying towels and beach bags, no doubt on their way to spend the day sunbathing around one of the hotel's advertised three pools. Nobody under the age of sixty-five stood out as we approached the reception desk.

I looked to the far side of the reception and spotted, lined in neat rows, the dreaded mobility scooters for hire we'd heard so much about.

Two hotel porters relieved us of our bags, and after we checked in, they escorted us to our rooms, which were on the fourth floor.

We arrived at room 402 first. Sam and I shared this room. Libby should have been in with us, but she's probably lying around Marco's family's pool right now, resting her vagina after having mad sex and sipping cocktails with little umbrellas in. Room 404 was occupied by Jess and Faith. Chrissy agreed to share a room with Michelle, and they were in room 406. Sarah and Frankie took room 408.

Our room was nice and airy, with white walls and a couple of modern-art pictures screwed strategically to them (I hope they didn't think we were going to pinch them, just because we come from Manchester), three single beds dressed with white duvet covers and purple cushions, and a table and two chairs set next to the sliding glass doors leading out onto the balcony. The bathroom had a full-size bath and a separate shower unit, which I was relieved about because once Sam gets in the bath, there's no getting her out of it. Complimentary toiletries were on display around the sink unit, and stacked on shelving above the toilet and bidet were fluffy white towels for each of us.

We spent a minute or so opening and closing doors and drawers in the room to see what, if anything, was in them. I found the hair dryer, not that we needed it. We always brought our own and extension lead because they always have the plugs located miles away from the mirrors in hotels. Sam went onto the balcony to check out the view, and I went to the loo and tided myself up a bit before we went off to meet the others. We didn't spend too much time in the room. We didn't want to waste a single minute. We needed to get out and explore, and the first point of call was the Irish bar to check out Jerry—I mean, to have another drink.

It was pretty quiet as we walked into the bar. Background music softly played as early customers were filling up for the day with their full-English accompanied by pints of lager. The smell of bacon and eggs is one of the best smells in the world. I could feel my mouth salivating. It had been ages since anything that juicy had passed my lips. Jerry came into view juggling three plates of food. He smiled. My stomach did a quick somersault.

Jerry's bar wasn't the typical sort of place we usually frequented when we went away together, unless Sam and Chrissy were on the hunt for sex, because it was a sports bar. They knew they were almost guaranteed a quickie in the ladies' with all the testosterone-fit-to-busting men drinking in there, especially if there was an important football or rugby game being fought out on the big screen. There must have been at least ten giant televisions dotted about the bar, without any sound on, showing anything and everything sport related—football, rugby, dog racing, horse racing. You name it and it was being advertised and shown in this bar. Jerry was a Man United supporter, that was obvious: the place was covered with Man United memorabilia, posters, signed footballs, programmes from games gone by. Displayed on the walls in glass cases, alongside their photographs, were signed football shirts by Wayne Rooney, Bobby Charlton, and Stevie Coppell, just a few of the greatest footballers ever to play in the Theatre of Dreams. Looking up at the ceiling, I noticed scarves and flags from across the years pinned up there. Taking pride of place behind the bar was a signed eight-by-ten picture of Georgie Best in a gold frame: my personal footballing hero. How I loved Georgie Best. Now that was one man who was pure sex on legs.

"Hello again, ladies, what can I get ya?" Jerry smiled, and his perfect teeth glowed against the background of his perfect tan.

Sam stared at him with her luscious red lips parted. She stuck her fake breasts out farther than normal and began waving her honey-coloured hair around as if she were waving the Union Jack. She looked a right blond bimbo. In fact, if Sarah hadn't grabbed hold of her, she'd have probably just ripped her knickers off there and then and let him take her over the bar. We couldn't take our eyes off Sam. This man had really got to her.

"Would it be wrong if we ordered coffee?" Faith sighed. "I think I need a break."

"Are you kidding, Faith?" Frankie choked and looked around. "Coffee! Get with Michelle, coffee girl. Some party person you are. I'll have a Bud, Jerry, and a bit of the Irish accent attached to your body if you don't mind. No point in beating about the bush, we're only here till Sunday."

Faith glared in Frankie's direction, then began to laugh. "OK, get me a Bud again. How many days have we got till we go home? I'm never gonna survive—you know that, don't ya?"

"Faith, it's gotta be done…Buds all around, barman," Frankie proclaimed.

Sarah giggled. "I'm already smashed. I've a lot of catching up to do."

"Good on ya, Sarah." Sam slapped her on the back, laughing. "Glad you're back with the programme."

"Glad you're back with the programme, Sarah," I agreed.

"Apart from me, bartender. Please could you make mine a latte? Do you do that sort of thing in here?" Michelle gave Jerry one of her funny faces.

"Yes, madam, we do," Jerry replied. "We also wash our hands after taking a piss."

Michelle's jaw dropped. Her expression was priceless.

"Nice one, Jerry." Frankie laughed.

I really did regret inviting Michelle. She didn't like my friends. She didn't even like me; she's never made any secret of that, but I thought she should have made just a tiny bit of an effort. She really was no different from anybody else. Her roots were the same as ours. Born in Manchester, went to Fairfield High School for Girls, didn't do particularly well in her exams, married her longtime boyfriend, Nigel, who went to Audenshaw and then Sheffield Uni. He got a good job in a bank, he started making good money, and they moved to Alderley Edge, where the rich and famous of the north live. Not that I've got anything against anybody who lives there; it's a nice place. Me, Jess, and Sam have spent many a Saturday afternoon going around their charity shops, looking for a bargain, and weighing up the talent in the bars. Michelle thought and acted as though she was better than us, her roots now well and truly forgotten. By then I was thinking it might be me who punched her, future sister-in-law or not, and not Frankie.

"Take a seat, ladies and latte woman, and I'll bring them over." Jerry winked at me.

I blushed. Why did I keep blushing?

"Who does he think he is?" Michelle fumed.

"Only the fittest bloke in the bar. Now please, Michelle, shut the fuck up," Frankie growled. "Or I'll shut it for ya."

"That's enough," Faith said. "Are we going to keep this up all weekend?"

Michelle glared at Frankie, took a deep breath, and marched off in the direction of the ladies' again.

"Sorry, Ellie, I've tried. I really have," Frankie said. "I can't even get a civil word out of her. What is her problem?"

"You have kind of jumped down her throat a bit, Frankie," Sarah commented.

Frankie sighed. "I know. I can't help it. She rubs me up the wrong way."

"I'll have a word with her. Don't worry, Frankie, I'll sort her out," Chrissy assured us.

Jerry brushed his arm against my shoulder as he placed the drinks down on the table. I exhaled loudly. He smiled.

"What's got you, Elle?" Sam said.

"Nothing. Couldn't get my breath."

"I'll be having some of that Jerry before we go home. In fact, it's a good job I've got some knickers on now, or when I got up from here, I'd be leaving a slug trail. I'm tingling just thinking about him." Sam shivered and took a good gulp from her bottle.

"He's not bad, seen better," I replied, looking down at the ground.

"Not bad? Are you blind, Ellie?" Frankie said.

God, I wish I were.

"She doesn't need to look at other men now, do you, Ellie? Not now you've got your Darren," Jess kindly reminded me.

"Darren…Darren who?" I joked. "Yeah, you're right, Jess—don't need to look no more, nope, no more, nope." *Shut your eyes, girl, and drink your drink.*

As usual when we're together, we were fighting for airspace, laughing and chatting away, reminiscing about the things we've done in the past, the men who've been and gone, the games we've played on nights out. When we went out later, Jess suggested that we play "Who can snog the oldest bloke?" and we all had to put ten euros in as the prize money. Sam flatly refused to join in, reminding us that when we played it the last time we were out in Liverpool, the old guy's teeth fell into her mouth, and she nearly choked. It was funny. She was open for suggestions for other ideas, though.

Faith nominated herself to be entertainment coordinator for the weekend. Since her divorce from Pete, she only ever seems happy when she's bossing people around or organising stuff, which I'm OK with. I'm useless at organising stuff. Only one little problem—Sarah and Michelle were the only people listening to her as she kept trying to tell us what she had planned for the weekend. Jess kept going on about changing her TENA Lady, as she hadn't laughed that much in ages. She must be TENA's best customer. Chrissy and Sam were busy eyeing up the talent and still discussing who was going to get the most sex over the weekend, Sam reminding Chrissy the scores were level as she'd done nothing with the bloke in the rugby shirt on the plane. Frankie started on tequila shots and roped two lads in the bar to join her. I sneaked outside whilst nobody was looking to have five minutes and get some fresh air.

I spotted Jerry as I walked out into the sun, leaning against a lamppost, sucking away at a cigarette, talking to a guy. He smiled in my direction, nodded to the guy, and walked over.

"Hello, Helen...Ellie." That Irish accent again. Oh God...

"Hi, Jerry," I nervously replied. "Ellie's fine." *What's wrong with me?*

"Ellie—pretty name for a pretty girl." Every time he spoke, I felt as if he was putting me under some hypnotic trance. "So what you in Benidorm for, Ellie?"

"A hen party," I replied, unable to look him in the eye.

"Who's the unlucky girl?" He laughed.

"That's not a very nice thing to say." I playfully nudged his arm. "It's my hen party." I felt almost embarrassed to admit that to him, noting the electric shocks running around my body when I touched his skin.

"That's a pity. I thought I might have had a chance with you. I thought I could feel a bit of…sexual chemistry between us." He winked, and we both laughed, me nervously.

"I hadn't noticed," I lied. "Never been that good with science subjects, but you never know—I'm not married yet." *Where'd that just come from?* I stopped flirting when I met Darren; I never felt the need to once we got together.

"You know where I am twenty-four-seven—I'm in this place. It's my own little piece of County Cork I brought to Benidorm with me four years ago."

He was adorable. Totally shaggable. He did look like a young Gerard Butler. Fresh morning stubble made him look even sexier. My heart was racing. Why was I even contemplating what he was saying to me? I love Darren. I'd been totally faithful to Darren ever since we met in Manchester nearly five years ago. I'd never even looked at another man, apart from Mr. McConaughey, and he didn't really count because he's not real. Or rather, he is real, but the chances of meeting him are very slim, and as much as I love Darren, if I ever got the chance for Mr. McConaughey to drag me away somewhere for a quickie, there'd be no stopping me…

What was going on with me? I was blaming something: the drink and the heat from the sun. But Jerry's accent, his shaggy brown hair you could grab hold of during wild sex…his big, deep, dark eyes I could quite easily dive into…I needed some of that latte Michelle was drinking. Help! I needed to get away and quick before I did or said something I would regret.

"I…best go and see what the others are up to. I can't leave them alone for five minutes, or they'll have the place in an uproar."

"They're big girls." He laughed. "I'm sure they can look after themselves."

"No…no, you don't know them. Sorry."

"Well, you know where I am." Jerry threw the sexiest smile in my direction.

I smiled in return and wondered how I would manage to walk back into the bar with legs that felt as if all the bones had been removed.

Jerry followed me back into the bar.

Faith was getting everybody to drink up as I walked back to our table. She'd decided we needed to go for a walk around Benidorm, take in some of the sights, enjoy the sun, and most of all have something to eat, as nothing but alcohol had passed our lips since meeting at Manchester Airport. As we left, the girls waved and told

Jerry we'd return. I smiled at him and started to blush…
again.

We entered the street and were immediately attacked
by two old gents who were racing by on mobility scooters.
We quickly jumped back against the wall of the bar, just in
time to let them go by without any of us being casualties.

"Watch where you're going, you old git," Faith shouted.

One of the old guys turned and gave her the finger.

"Cheeky bastard," she retorted. "Hope you never end
up on my ward to have your prostate checked out, mate.
I'll ram my finger so far up your chocolate tea-towel holder
it'll pop out of your mouth."

"I've heard about these kamikaze scooters in
Benidorm. Half the people driving them can't even see,
their legs have stopped working, or they have arthritis.
Their reflexes are so slow they can't even use the brakes."
Sarah laughed.

"Well, if one of them comes near me again, I'm gonna
slash the tyres," Faith snapped. "Then they'll have to get
off and crawl. They're bloody lethal."

This had to be the epicentre for mobility scooters.
They were everywhere. One pushed past us again.

"Get off the pavement and onto the road—preferably
in front of a truck," Frankie screamed. "I'd rather take my
chances with the cars. It's safer." She began walking on the
road. We quickly joined her.

It wasn't long before we spotted the beach. It was
really busy, with the usual array of cafés and bars spreading

themselves all along the front. We waved to acknowledge a few of the lads from Oldham rugby club in a bar having breakfast. They waved back. We stood for a few minutes looking at the sand sculptures being created whilst we were being smothered in the heat of Benidorm.

The sea, a Man City blue colour, looked inviting, but that was one invitation I wouldn't be taking up. The thought of swimming in the sea filled me with fear. I never go in. I didn't really like the sea when I was growing up, even when we went on our family Maynes coach holidays to Devon or Cornwall. My dad couldn't do or say anything to persuade me to go in. Me and my mum would sit in our striped deck-chairs, with the windbreak we'd hired for the day around us, watching my dad and our Paul swim and splash around for ages. Occasionally I went to fill my bucket up with water to be used to fill the moat around the sand castles I'd build with our Paul, or maybe take a quick paddle, or go for a wee. My mum would tell me go and sit on the water's edge; then nobody would know I was having a wee. I still do that now when I'm on holiday, if I'm desperate. That was it though. But then I saw something that put me off the sea forever…The film *Jaws*. Knowing me, on the one occasion I did decide to go in, I'd get eaten by Jaws. You'd never catch me going on a cruise holiday for the same reason.

"Can we go on the beach?" Sarah said, running off like an excited child.

"Course you can, Sarah, anything you want," Sam shouted to her.

Sarah led the way. I commented to Sam how happy and relaxed Sarah looked. It was the first time we'd seen her like this in ages.

"Let's have a photo taken," Sarah suggested. "I'll ask that old guy to take one for us." She pointed to a man sitting on a deck chair reading the *Sun* newspaper.

"Err... Excuse me, sorry to bother you. Hi I'm Sarah," she smiled. "Would you mind taking a photo of us, please?"

"Course I will, Sarah. Alf, Alf's the name. How do you work it? I'm no good with these new mobile phones—give me an old thirty-five mil any day."

Sarah passed him her iPhone and gave him a quick tutorial. "And if you want to zoom in or out, just press this one at the side."

"Or if you can't do that, do what I do—stretch your arms out in front of you to zoom in closer or pull them back to zoom out," Faith shouted, laughing.

"OK, love." Alf smiled. "I'll probably do what your friend suggests, Sarah love."

We all gathered together, and click, the photo was taken. And then, as if on cue, like a chorus of squealing banshees, we shouted, "Just one more, one more..." I was beginning to feel sorry for him, poor old Alf. He was having his daily chilling session, probably having a good old read of the sports pages, and not even of his own accord, he had been turned into David Bloody Bailey, just to make us happy. It ended up turning into a full-on photo session, taking pictures of us posing with our arms in the air, hugging one another, or blowing kisses. Even Michelle smiled on a few. The shots Chrissy asked Jerry to put into her coffees may have started to loosen her up bit. I don't really agree with spiking people's drinks, but in this case, something had to be done just to get her to relax.

We got quite a bit of attention whilst we were on the beach with all the noise we were making. Everybody loved our T-shirts. Sally and Jayne, a couple of the girls from Liverpool we met on the plane, came onto the beach to join in with us before heading off to meet their friends outside the Red lion.

"Excuse me, girls." We turned to see a man in his late sixties or early seventies shouting in our direction. "Would you mind if I have a photo taken with you? I've never been with one virgin, let alone eight."

"Course you can, darling," Frankie cooed to him.

With walking sticks in both hands, he walked quickly onto the beach to join us.

"Ignore him, girls," the lady with him called. "It's his age."

He got himself snuggled up in the middle of us, cheekily wrapped his arms around Sarah's and Jess's waists, and gave each of them a quick squeeze. Chrissy and Faith each gave him a kiss on the cheek, and the rest of us posed around him. I assumed the woman was his wife. She took the photo.

"What you going on about, anyway, George? I was a virgin when we met and even when we married!" she shouted back once the picture had been taken.

"That's what you told me, Betty, but I know different." He laughed as he made his way back to the promenade. "You were the local bike, everybody said."

The lady hit him over the head with her handbag. "You cheeky bugger, George, I never was. Not that I didn't have my chances. I could have had anybody I wanted." She pulled at his shirt, trying to drag him away. "Sorry, girls, he needs his pills. You can tell he's not right in the head, he's wearing socks with his sandals, and that's a sure sign of madness." She was laughing now.

"We're staying at Hotel Guadalupe, room four-oh-six, if you want to come over later, George, for a drink," Frankie teased.

"OK, love too. I'll have to try and dump the old ball and chain first. I'll slip something in her tea later. Bye, girls, nice to meet you."

"No matter what the age, they're all mad here. We'll fit right in," Sam shouted over our laughter.

"Thanks, Alf. I think I need to take this lot for something to eat." Faith smiled.

"Are you being serious about having something to eat, Faith?" Jess asked. "Eatin's cheatin."

"Jess, you can't even stand up. You can't keep this up for three days. You'll be dead," Faith replied. "We'll stop off at one of café bars and grab a pizza, and then I've got a nice little surprise for us all."

"What you got planned, Missus?" Frankie sounded intrigued.

"Was gonna ask the same thing," I said. "A male stripper best not be involved."

"Get in there." Frankie punched the air.

"Would I do that to you?" Faith smiled. "Now stop asking me. Come on—food. We've got a busy afternoon ahead of us."

"Sounds very mysterious—wonder where we're going," Chrissy said.

"If it's anything to do with you, Faith, it's going to be something sensible, like a spa or a yoga meditation session…I just wanna get pissed and look for a good shag," Frankie said, linking her arm through Chrissy's.

"If you can't get a shag here, there's no hope for you. I bet even Faith could get one here." Chrissy laughed.

"I wish." Faith tutted.

"Maybe if you didn't dress like a sixties throwback, in your long flowery skirts and patchwork waistcoats, you'd stand a chance," Sam joined in. "Your daft hippie gear went out when? Oh yeah, in the sixties."

"Stop picking on her," Jess slurred. "If it wasn't for Faith, the Willow Wood Hospice shop in Ashton town centre would shut down."

"That's right." Faith nodded. "Now shift yourselves."

EIGHTEEN

We excitedly left an English bar, which was owned by a welcoming couple in their fifties, Ian and Claire from Bristol, who have lived in Beindorm for the last ten years. Our stomachs were now full of pizza, and fizzy lemonade and lime cordial. Faith refused to use any of the kitty to buy any alcohol. She said we needed a break. To be honest, I was glad of a nonalcoholic drink. We stumbled along behind Faith, who was navigating the streets of Benidorm, following directions off the piece of paper she was carrying. She still hadn't told us where we were going.

Benidorm really did remind me of Blackpool. If only there were a tower, they could have been twins. But hey! I've always loved Blackpool. I've spent many a good weekend there, so I wasn't going to complain. The streets were lined with the obligatory tacky gift shops selling everything from fridge magnets and castanets to jewellery that would either break in thirty seconds or send your skin green in a few hours. Between the gift shops were bars offering happy hours and cafés selling roast-beef dinners and fish and chips, giving the impression they catered for the Brits. Occasionally we came upon a tapas bar.

As we walked the streets of Benidorm, we heard cheering and spotted Mike, Steve, Dave, and the rest of the firemen. They invited us into the bar to join them, but we had to decline due to the fact we were on some kind of mission to only Faith knew where.

We finally came to an abrupt halt outside a nightclub called Max's that specialised in cocktails, if the unlit neon light outside was anything to go by. Faith rechecked the details on the paper she was holding and then led us downstairs to the entrance of the cocktail lounge. The sign on the door read CLOSED. Undeterred, Faith twisted the handle and walked in, we followed, intrigued.

The bar gave the impression it was closed. The lighting was sparse, and you could've heard a pin drop if Jess hadn't been moaning about her knees killing her from all the walking we'd been doing. Sam suggested she get a mobility scooter and join the rest of the oldies. Jess stopped moaning.

We made our way across the dance floor in the direction of the bar and noticed a table had been set up in the middle of the room with an assortment of bottles containing alcoholic drinks, some familiar some not. There were glasses, cocktail shakers, little paper umbrellas, and loads of sliced fruit. A tall, olive-skinned young man appeared from a doorway to the left.

"Joseph?" Faith asked.

"Hola. Faith?" he replied, greeting her with kisses—first on her right cheek, then the left, then the right again. Or was it the other way around?

"Ladies, may I introduce Joseph. He's going to be teaching us how to make cocktails," Faith explained.

"Hola, ladies, welcome to my club."

"Hola to you, too, Joseph," Frankie replied in a seductive voice.

Cocktail making—that was different. No wonder Faith wanted us to eat before we came. We began giggling again like teenagers. *Did I just see Michelle smile?*

"This is going to be interesting," Chrissy said, slowly running a finger along the table. "And how do you know Joseph, Faith?"

"His sister Maria's a nurse on my ward. When I told her we were coming to Benidorm for a hen party, she contacted Joseph and helped me to arrange this. I thought it'd be fun—you know, something different for us to do."

"Anything's better than sitting in a room for an hour, chanting with our legs in the lotus position." Sam smirked.

"It's great, Faith, thanks," I said as I walked over to give her a hug. We could always rely on Faith to look after us. If it was up to Sam, we'd have been in a strip club by now with her on the front row weighing up which greased-up bloke she was gonna be having next.

"I am so glad we had something to eat," Jess said. "I must admit I do feel a bit better. At least I can focus now."

"You're the best mum in the world." Frankie threw her arms around Faith to give her a hug. "Love ya."

"Come, ladies, gather around the tables." Joseph waved his arms. "I am going to demonstrate some cocktails and moves for you. Then you have got the next hour and a half to make and try your own."

"I'll come if you give me a minute." Frankie giggled. "If you're lucky, Joseph, I'll try some of my own moves on you."

"I look forward to seeing them, señorita."

"This is going to get messy," Faith said excitedly.

I felt a hand on my arm. It was Michelle. "Helen, is this really necessary? Haven't you all had enough to drink? It's only three o'clock, and you're all having trouble standing as it is."

"Michelle, please." I hesitated. "Look, if you wanna sit this out, do it, but Faith's gone to a lot of trouble to organise this, so don't try to spoil it." I felt sick to my stomach, wondering what she was going to do next. I turned to rejoin the others.

"Wonder what moves Joseph is gonna be showing us. I know what moves I'd like him to be showing me." Frankie demonstrated by gyrating her hips.

Michelle shook her head and moved to the opposite end of the table, next to Sarah.

Joseph threw bottles up in the air like a juggler in the circus, pouring the contents into a silver shaker. Taking ice from an ice bucket, he dropped it into the shaker. He mischievously took out another piece, walked over to Frankie, and put it down her cleavage. She screamed and tried frantically to get it out. Joseph placed the lid on the shaker and began to shake—not only the mixture, but his body. He was making a cocktail, and it looked more like a mild sex show, much to everybody's enjoyment. Frankie still looked flustered from the ice episode. Out of the corner of my eye, I saw Michelle staring at me; I turned away. She was not gonna get to me. Frankie also noticed Michelle, and I could see her going in for the kill. I rushed over to Frankie and grabbed her by the arm.

"Leave it, Frankie. It'll sort itself out," I said. "She thinks we've already had too much to drink and wanted us to leave. I told her we're not, but obviously she's not taking the hint."

"If she doesn't buck up soon, Ellie, I mean it, I'm having her. She's driving us all mad and putting a right dampener on things," Frankie replied.

"Ignore her. That's what I'm trying to do. Look! Joseph is shaking his butt in our direction."

"You're too nice, Ellie, but for your sake, I will."

"Ellie, Joseph has made this one for us. He's called it the Benidorm Virgins." Sam laughed. "You can have first taste. He said one of these, and you'll never need to use a vibrator ever again."

"I get the picture—pass it over, then." I leant across the table and took the drink off Joseph. "What's in it, Joseph? Sorry, I wasn't paying attention."

"This one is a secret of the bar. Lots of men buy it for the women they bring into the bar they want to have sex with. I've never had any complaints so far. Go taste, it will definitely wake up your...loins."

"I don't want my loins waking up. Maybe this drink is for you, Frankie." I giggled.

"Don't you be worrying about me, Helen McDonald, mine are already awake." She winked at Joseph.

"It's gotta be done," I shouted.

"It's gotta be done." The girls encouraged me.

I lifted the glass to my mouth, knocking it back in one go. "Wow! Shit, that was *good.*"

"Joseph you're gonna have to make me one of them. My loins need waking up. I need all the help I can get," Faith squealed.

"For you, Faith, anything. Señoritas, you can all have a go to make your own cocktails. You have recipe cards all around the table. You can also come up with your own cocktails. You will all be made to feel very welcome if you come into the bar tonight. We make the most amazing bespoke cocktails."

"Bespoke cocktails? What's a bespoke cocktail?" Sam asked.

"You tell our bar staff what flavours you like, and they'll make you a cocktail using only those flavours," Joseph replied.

"D'ya mean like chocolate-covered strawberries or apple pie and custard?" Jess asked.

"If that's what you like, give it a try. You won't be disappointed."

"Eating and drinking at the same time—how could anybody be disappointed? I'm coming back here tonight," Jess said.

"If you need any help, just shout out. I'll go and put some music on." Joseph walked in the direction of the stage.

"I'm good at music. Do you need any help, Joseph?" Frankie asked.

"Sure, OK, you can help me pick out some music." He held out his hand and Frankie took it.

I bet this place was buzzing at night. It had a good vibe about it. *Maybe we should come back tonight*, I thought. I'd suggest it later. Michelle walked over to the table, picked up a card, and started to make a cocktail. I smiled, trying to keep the peace.

"They're taking their time choosing some music." Jess took a sip of the cocktail she'd made and looked over towards the DJ booth. "I'm going over to see what the problem is."

Before I could grab her, she was off. I neglected to say I'd seen Joseph pull Frankie to the floor as they went into the DJ booth. I quickly followed.

"Yes. Yes, go on. Harder. Harder!" Frankie's cries could be heard now all around the room. "Oh my God. Yes, yes."

I giggled. "Jess." I grabbed her arm.

"I know, I know. I realise now." She chuckled and leant over the front of the DJ deck and saw Joseph lying on top of Frankie on the floor. "Am I to assume we've got to pick out our own music, Joseph?"

"Sod off, Jess. We're busy," Frankie said.

The hour and a half of making cocktails flew by. Not only was the floor covered in booze, so were we. We ended up having a bit of a drinks fight. If it weren't for us wearing bras, we'd look like we'd just taken part in a Miss Wet T-shirt competition. Guess who'd win—Sam, with Frankie coming a close second. They're the only two whose boobs were still where they're supposed to be. Not like the rest of us. Most of our boobs had already passed Watford and were now heading towards Brighton. We left Max's bar and after calling in a supermarket for essential supplies—booze, cigs, crisps and chocolate—we flagged down taxis to take us back to the hotel to get cleaned up for our first night in Benidorm.

NINETEEN

After we arrived back at the hotel, we all disappeared in different directions. Sam and I went to bed for couple of hours to recharge our batteries, but not before downing a couple of paracetamols each with a pint of water, and having showers to remove all the sticky cocktail concoctions that had been thrown over us. Faith and Jess went to check out the spa facilities so Faith could write a review for her blog, *You Gotta Have Faith!* It's all about promoting anything to do with the mind, body, and soul of the mature woman. She updates it every day. Frankie wanted to check out the bar before going for a lie-down and dragged Sarah with her. Chrissy and Michelle went for coffee.

I woke with a banging head. The paracetamol tablets hadn't worked. I threw back the covers and climbed out of bed. What a sight stared back at me from the mirror. "You looked an awful lot better this morning, girl," I said out loud. Sam was dueting with Kylie Minogue whilst lying in the bath. I could smell Fenjel wafting in the air, her favourite bath oil. I noticed a glass and a bottle of white wine were missing from the dressing table. She was going to be in there for at least an hour.

"Sam, I'm nipping to see Frankie, back in a bit," I shouted to her as I walked out of the room.

I knocked on their door a couple of times. "Frankie, Sarah, it's me. You awake?"

The door slowly opened.

"God, you look rough, Frankie."

"Have you looked in the mirror? Get in before somebody sees us." She pulled me by the arm into her room.

"Have you brought any quick tan? I've forgot to bring mine, and my legs look like milk bottles."

"Are you taking the piss, Ellie? I now look as dark as a Chinese farm worker."

"No, I'm being serious." I pointed at my legs.

"Yeah, I've got some. It's in the bathroom. I'll get it for you. Let me just have a wee." Frankie twisted the handle of the bathroom door. It was locked. "Sarah, why've you locked the door? Quick, open up—I need the loo."

There was no answer.

"Sarah, I'm bursting," Frankie shouted again. "Open up."

"No...sorry, I can't move, these bubbles have got me pinned down, and if I move, I may spill my drink. Do you know how long it's been since I've had a bath without any interruptions?"

"Damn...back in a min." Frankie ran out of the room, wearing just her knickers and wrapping her arms across her chest to cover her boobs.

"You OK in there, Sarah?" I shouted through the door. "Had a good day?"

"Absolutely fantastic, Ellie. Enjoying having a bit of me time."

"Not a problem. Enjoy," I replied.

I sat on the edge of the bed and waited for Frankie to return. There were clothes flung all around the room. If somebody who didn't know us walked in, they'd think we'd been turned over. We'd been there less than a day. What was the place gonna look like by Sunday afternoon when we checked out? As I waited for Frankie to return, I heard screaming laughter coming from Faith and Jess's room. I jumped up from off the bed and rushed into the corridor to see what all the noise was about, crashing into Frankie, who was rushing out of their door.

"What's going on?" I said.

"You've gotta come and see this. I was just coming to get ya." Frankie had tears in her eyes. "Jess is stuck in her spandex thingy. We can't pull it up or down."

"Pull it at the back, Faith!"

"I can't pull it anymore. I'm gonna wet myself," Faith cried. "We've been like this for nearly fifteen minutes."

"You look like you're halfway through skinning a rabbit, Faith." I was crying now. "I thought you didn't care what you looked like, Jess."

"I think she looks more like a Morrisons sausage that's burst under the grill," Faith replied.

"Cheeky cow." Jess laughed. "Ellie, I normally don't care what I look like, but the dress I've got for tonight's a bit too tight, so I bought this thing without trying it on, to make it easier for me to get in to. Now I'm stuck."

"I need the loo." Faith stood and slipped into the bathroom.

"Don't just stand there, Ellie, help me. I'm going to be pissing myself in a minute."

I couldn't move. I crossed my legs because I knew any minute now my bladder was gonna go.

"Have you tried talc?" I asked.

"Have you not watched *Friends*, Ellie? Did you not see the Ross episode where he got stuck trying to pull his leather pants back up when he'd been to the toilet?" Jess explained.

"Good point," I replied.

"What about if we all take hold of a different part and pull down at the same time?" Frankie said.

We positioned ourselves around Jess and each grabbed hold of a part of the spandex body shaper.

"Right, after three. One…two…"

"Is it we pull on three, or one, two, three, then pull?" Frankie asked.

"One, two, three, then pull," I replied and started the count again. "One…two…three…*pull!*"

Urine trickled down Jess's left leg.

"Off!" I shouted.

Jess fell onto the bed whilst the rest of us collapsed on the floor shrieking, trying to catch our breaths. Chrissy and

Michelle came into the room. They didn't need to ask what was going on; it was obvious.

"That's going in the bin." Jess picked up the body shaper as if she'd just caught a mouse and threw it into the bin. "And I'm going to finish pissing on the loo." She marched off into the bathroom.

"You two ready?" I asked. "Want to come to ours for a drink?"

"No, we'll meet you in the bar," Chrissy replied. "We're going to have a wander around the hotel to see what it has to offer in the form of fresh meat. I haven't seen anybody who's not potentially Zimmer-frame material in the hotel yet."

Michelle's eyes looked a bit brighter as Chrissy escorted her out of the room. The drink must have got to her.

An hour later, Sam and I found the girls in the hotel restaurant. It was an all-you-can-eat buffet. Jess waved us over. Whenever Jess and Alan eat out, they always go to the all-you-can-eat buffets in Manchester, from the Chinese buffet to the Indian one. And she wondered why she couldn't fit into any of her clothes.

"Jess, I need to move. You look like a pig at a trough." Sam gagged. "Don't you ever come up for air? Chrissy, swap places with me. I can't watch her eat."

"No, sit at the end of the table," Chrissy replied.

"It's disgusting the amount of food that goes into your mouth, Jess. You're putting me off." Sam flipped.

"Shush…leave me alone, twig. You're just bloody jealous because I eat what I want," Jess said, teasing Sam with a piece of beef dripping in gravy on the end of her fork before putting into her mouth.

Jess is the only person I know who couldn't care less about her weight or what she eats. We may give her a bit of grief about it, but it's just banter, and she's probably right about it being a bit of jealousy because we are always calorie counting. But she can look after herself. Gives as good as she gets. If Jess sees a cake she wants, she'll just buy it and eat it. The rest of us, if we see a cake we want, we um and ahh about it for ten minutes, then drag ourselves away, kicking and screaming in our heads, feeling guilty we spent so much time umming and ahhing about it. Sometimes I wish I were more like Jess and not so obsessed with what I can and can't eat.

"It is tempting, though, all this food," I said.

"I know, but it's for everybody, not just Jess," Sam replied.

Only Frankie didn't take part in the eating; she was sat at the table drinking a glass of Torres red wine and holding onto the bottle like it was her new best friend.

The restaurant was full to capacity. I made my way along the buffet table, plate in hand, knowing I should have stopped at the salad and cold meat sections, but the cheeses they had on offer were delicious. It would have been rude to just pass them by. Cheese is my weakness. I'd rather sit and eat a pound slab of Cheshire crumbly, with fresh crusty bread spread with thick lashings of Lurpak, than a box of Milk Tray any day. They had on offer lots of savoury foods: pies, lamb chops, pork chops, sausages, gammon, beef, and chicken. In the middle of the buffet was the biggest selection of puddings and cakes I had ever seen in my life. Just as quickly as the food was taken by hotel guests, the restaurant staff replaced it.

We all ate our fair share, a lot more than we normally did, but once we got started, it was hard to stop. We had dieted for four months, and some of them puddings were delicious. I felt fit to burst and hoped it might sober me up a bit, ready for another drinking session. Faith had to drag jess away, or she'd have had us sat in the dining room all night.

The dining room was quiet by the time we left. Most of the guests had already made their way into the Casablanca Ballroom on the first floor to play bingo with Sonia and wait for the evening's entertainment to begin. An Elvis tribute, the poster in reception advertised, was performing tonight. Tomorrow it would be a Robbie Williams tribute, plus a quiz around the pool in the afternoon at two o'clock. In the evening it was karaoke with Sonia and bingo promptly starting at 8:30 p.m. She was a busy one, that Sonia. I couldn't contain myself…

TWENTY

Our first port of call after we left the hotel was the Irish bar, but we only stayed for one drink as Jerry wasn't in. He was probably off chatting a girl up somewhere—not that I was bothered or anything, but I had enjoyed a steamy dream about him earlier. I hadn't mentioned that to anybody, but it was my suggestion we call in his bar first for a drink.

Since I'd met him that morning, he'd been constantly on my mind, which I felt pretty bad about, as I hadn't really given Darren a second thought—not even messaged him since the airport, not even a quick hello.

The streets were busier than they had been earlier, I noticed. We followed the same route as we had that afternoon. The bars and restaurants were all lit up with flashing neon signs, with staff standing outside trying to entice tourists in with offers of free shots and great menus. Most had some kind of live music on, or at least a quiz; you'd never get bored at night here. Mobility scooters still attacked us from all angles—with Frankie and Faith still threatening to slash their tyres—just not as many as earlier. They were still like irritating wasps at a picnic. If only we could put out a bit of jam on a jar lid to get them to hover around, then they'd leave us alone. Or we could use a huge mobility-scooter swatter to swat them away. Probably the missing drivers were all back at their hotels playing bingo and watching the evening entertainment with their own hotel's version of Sonia.

Jess pointed to a bar advertising Sticky Vicky. "In here," she shouted and headed in first. The bar was a bit dated. The chairs and tables could have done with a bit of scrubbing, as could the floor. My feet kept sticking to it. There was a comedian on stage halfway through his act.

"Come on in, girls—come on, don't be shy. We won't bite, will we?" He paused.

Everybody in the bar turned in our direction and looked at us.

"This lot can't bite ya, can ya? You've all forgotten your bloody teeth, haven't ya." The room filled with laughter. "It's nice to have some young bodies in here. Well, get in, girls, don't be scared. You'll get no problems out of this lot—they're all either dead or on the verge." He pointed to the customers scattered around the bar. He shouted to a young woman behind the bar: "Get 'em some drinks and bolt the door before they try to leave. It's so nice to welcome you all in here tonight. You look fantastic…and your perfume, the aroma, you all smell so good." He started to sniff at the air. "I get sick of seeing all this polyester, and normally at this time of year the only smell you get in here is embalming fluid.

Look how old the people are in here. Look at them two over there." The comedian pointed to an elderly couple to the left of the stage. "They've been here for days—I think somebody really could do with checking if they're still alive. But in saying that, even if they're dead, we should just leave 'em where they are—they make the bar look full."

"We're not as old as your bloody act, Bobby!" one of the customers shouted back.

We continued laughing as the young girl carried a tray of shots towards us. We each took one. The girls knocked them back. I quickly turned around, slyly poured mine onto the already soaked carpet, then lifted the glass to my mouth and threw my head back as if I'd just drank it. They all shuddered. By the looks on their faces, I could tell it was horrible. Bet it tasted worse than the medicine our mums gave us when we were little.

"What brings you to Benidorm, girls?" the comedian asked.

"A hen party and the promise of loads of sex," Sam shouted to him on our behalf.

"If it's sex I promised you, I never go back on a promise. I'll see you later." He winked. "Hen party? Who's the lucky girl?"

All fingers pointed at me.

"Come on, come up here, love. Let's have a quick chat with you."

Oh no…I hate being the centre of attention. Now, Chrissy, Frankie, and Sam would have no problems with being called onto the stage. My bessies were all clapping and shouting, "Ellie…Ellie…Ellie…" I caught sight of Michelle in the corner of my eye; she looked really embarrassed. *She's embarrassed? She should try being me for the next ten minutes or so.* My whole body went rigid with nerves. I thought I'd had enough alcohol, but obviously not. I climbed onto the stage, helped by the comedian, who looked like he'd had his fair share of groupies in his heyday. Now he reminded me of a dirty old man, with long hair covering his bald patch and a badly faded flowery short-sleeved shirt. I cringed as he tried to kiss me on my lips, and I turned just in time for it to be planted on my cheek.

"So what's your name, and where do you come from? I feel like Cilla Black, God rest her soul, on *Blind Date*. Do you remember that show, or are you too young?"

"No, I do remember it. My name's Helen, ahh…Ellie, and I'm from Manchester." The girls cheered and banged on the table, as did some of the other customers in the bar.

"Well, it's very nice to meet you, Ellie. I'm Bobby. Are you enjoying the sun, Ellie? You don't get a lot in Manchester, do you?" And he winked. "Sun, that is."

"Not really." I giggled, embarrassed.

"So who's this fella you're marrying? You are marrying a man, aren't you? You're not one of them lesbians, are you?"

"No." I continued to giggle like some kind of idiot. "Men all the way. Not that I've got anything against lesbians, but Darren's my fella."

"Well, you never know nowadays. Has he got a big, you know, man part? Does he keep you satisfied? Because if you're not sure, we could go to my dressing room and have a bit of jiggy-jiggy. Then you'll have something to compare it with and know if you are making the right decision."

My bessies were screaming with laughter. I wanted to die just at the thought. *Yuck.* The other customers in there were as old as my gran. It was embarrassing. I knew I shouldn't have stopped drinking earlier.

"He's fine. He keeps me happy. He knows what he's doing."

"Glad to hear it, Ellie." Bobby gave a dirty little laugh. "I'm delighted you've come into our bar for a little drinkie-poo. And to stop you from leaving me with all these coffin dodgers, you and the girls can have another drink on me."

Bobby shouted to the young girl behind the bar again. "Sophie, can you get Ellie a bottle of our best champagne? Not that cheap shit we sell to this lot, the nice stuff that we sell for five euros." The place was in an uproar with laughter.

Sophie walked over to the stage and handed Bobby the bottle of champagne. "Here you go, love," he said. "Enjoy your time in Benidorm. I want to wish you and your Darren all the best." He gave me another kiss on the cheek and passed me the champagne.

"Thank you," I managed to say and climbed down from the stage. That wasn't too bad.

"Get that open, and I'll get the glasses," Faith said.

"Hey, Sticky Vicky's on here in an hour. We're staying, aren't we?" Jess asked.

"Yeah, we're staying," replied Frankie. "I've heard she's got a flue as big as the Mersey tunnel."

"Never," Faith said.

"Have you never heard of her, Faith? She does a sort of magic act. Razor blades and even lightbulbs are pulled out." Frankie laughed.

"What you do you mean by a flue?" Michelle asked.

"A huge vagina—stuffs all sorts up it, pulls all sorts out of it," Jess replied.

"Sounds revolting. We're not watching that, Helen, surely?" Michelle said, a septic look spread across her face.

"We most certainly are." Frankie's patience had faded; so had some of the others'. "You know where the door is, Michelle."

"I'm sick of you talking to me like that all the time, Frankie," Michelle answered.

"And I'm sick of looking at your smacked-arse face," Frankie said. "I for one have had enough of your moaning, groaning, stupid facial expressions, and put-down comments you keep coming out with."

"Michelle, outside now," Chrissy shouted, and grabbed her by the arm, forcing her out of the bar. I followed.

Chrissy escorted her over to one of the wooden bench tables and slammed her down in a chair. "Michelle, sweetie, this may seem a strange question, but why did you come to Benidorm?"

"Because Helen asked me."

"No, Michelle, why have you come? For the love of God, we have tried to be patient with you, ignored all your ridiculous comments and remarks. All you've done since we met this morning at the airport is moan, groan, pull faces, and make everything awkward and embarrassing," Chrissy said.

"Me, embarrassing? Have you not seen how you're all behaving? You're the embarrassing ones."

Frankie yelled behind us, and I turned around and noticed she was being closely followed by Faith and Sam, who were frantically pulling at her top, trying to stop her.

"You think you are so perfect and the rest of us are, well, nothing," Frankie started. "I save children's lives every day. It's a bloody stressful job, and my release is to party. I party hard, and if you don't like it, well, piss off, but don't try to spoil our weekend. What do you do with your life? *Fuck all*...Oh sorry, you run your kids to school, go to the hairdressers—not that you can tell, unless you really are going for the Worzel Gummidge look—and do lunches with the ladies." Frankie was erupting like a volcano. "Go back to Alicante Airport and get back on a plane to your perfect little house, your perfect little children, and your perfect little husband." Faith grabbed hold of Frankie as she lunged at Michelle.

Michelle banged her hands on the table as she stood up and began shouting hysterically. "Oh! Oh! Perfect husband, have I? Perfect husband! Is that what you think? You know nothing." Tears began to flow uncontrollably down her cheeks.

We were frozen to the spot—I didn't know where to look as the tears flowed and flowed. Now it was Michelle who was attracting attention from passersby with her yelling.

Michelle slumped back into her seat and put her head down in her hands down. "My *per-fect* little husband, as you say, has been having an affair for the last two years." She looked up towards Frankie, her eyes full of anger. "My *per-fect* little life is not so *per-fect*, it's total crap. It's so crap, I feel like walking back down to the beach and into the sea and walking until I drown. Is this the sign of a *per-fect* life? I would say not. So you see Frankie, whatever you say or do is not going to affect me one tiny bit. If you want to hit me, well, go right ahead. Be my guest." Michelle paused. "Part of me would give anything to be like all of you. Seeing you together—your friendship—has made me realise what I've got, a big fat nothing. Yes! Maybe I'm jealous of your relationship. It's something I've never had. You're always having a laugh…not a care in the world. I've driven all my friends away because of problems at home. I'm so embarrassed and ashamed I've let things get this bad. I hate my life. I want to die."

"Oh, no! This is too heavy for me, Michelle," Frankie screeched. "Why'd you decide to bring all this shit up now? Couldn't you have stayed back in Cheshire and kept it to yourself? Just because your life's crap doesn't mean you've got to spoil it for the rest of us."

"Don't be horrible, Frankie, it's not like you." Faith walked over to Michelle and sat beside her. "I know what it's like to have your husband have an affair on you. It's horrible. When Pete, my husband—"

"And don't you fucking start on about Pete again. Oh! I've had enough of this. I'm going back into the bar. I'm not having anything spoil this weekend for Ellie, and if you think anything of her, Michelle, you'll get off your bony little arse and do the same." Frankie turned and walked back into the bar, followed by Sam and Sarah.

"I know we don't know one another very well, Michelle, and Frankie's probably right about you bringing all this up now, but if you want to talk about it, we won't mind, will we, girls?" Faith offered Michelle a tissue and looked first at Chrissy, then me. We looked at one another and sat down. Chrissy signalled for a waiter and ordered two bottles of decent white wine and four glasses. This, we knew, might take some time.

Chrissy poured Michelle a large glass of wine and made her drink it, then another. Faith and I shared the remainder of the bottle. Chrissy opened the other bottle for herself.

I whispered to Chrissy, "Why are you sitting here?"

"I have not got a fucking clue. Get drinking."

"It's all because of sex." Michelle blew her nose. "Nigel said he has urges, needs, and I was doing nothing about them. Our rows are always about sex. I don't like it, never have. I've never even had an orgasm."

Chrissy started choking on her wine. I slapped her on the back. I can read her like a book—she was dying to ask how, why, but she kept quiet and carried on drinking, listening with eyes as big as chocolate hobnobs. I hoped this wasn't going to take all night. It was beginning to get a bit nippy.

"Nigel, on one of his usual business trips in London around two years ago, met this woman in her midthirties. Apparently, she approached him in the hotel bar. Not the prettiest, he said. Well, he would say that, wouldn't he." Michelle sniffed and blew her nose again. "They started talking, he bought her a couple of glasses of champagne, she suggested they go up to his room for a nightcap, and they had sex. Every time after that when he went to London, they'd meet up for sex. He said he was desperate. Not long after, he started taking her away for weekends. He's even paid for her to come up to Manchester. He doesn't like to be seen out with her, so they usually stay in the hotel room. He said it's a bit like having a moped—everybody wants one, but nobody wants to be seen riding one." She sniffed again.

"How do you know all this?" Faith asked empathically.

Chrissy and I let out a little snigger.

"Have you really never had an orgasm?" Chrissy was unable to contain herself any longer. "Even nuns have orgasms. I heard them at it when I was at boarding school." Faith punched her in the arm. "What, Faith? I'm only asking. I can't believe you've never had an orgasm. Have you never even given yourself one, you poor girl? Don't you even own and electric toothbrush?"

"Chrissy!" exclaimed Faith.

"He had no choice," said Michelle. "I got a call from her about a year ago, she told me everything. I think she expected me to eject Nigel from our home there and then, but I didn't. Her plan is to run off into the sunset holding hands. She's left her husband and daughter and moved into a one-bedroom flat that Nigel helps to pay for because her salary as a receptionist at a private dentist's doesn't cover the costs," she growled. "Nigel constantly tells me he loves me and doesn't want to leave. I believe him."

"You idiot," Chrissy said.

"He's trying to end the affair, Chrissy, but every time he tries, she gets drunk and rings Nigel all night long, threatening to kill herself, which I have to listen to. He gives in and ends up going to London to see her. He says he wishes he could turn the clock back. She rings me all the time, threatening me and threatening to ring Nigel's boss, ruin his career. I've told him if she doesn't stop, I am going to call the police. I still love Nigel, and I understand why he's been having sex with her. She's called Alice, by the way. He probably thought he was in Wonderland when he first met her, and he was smiling like a Cheshire cat. Now he's in a nightmare, and so am I."

Faith commiserated. "She's definitely a bit of a bunny boiler. What do you want?"

"I don't want Nigel to leave me, but I hate sex. Always have. The sea looks the best option."

"This Alice woman doesn't want Nigel—it's the money she's after, the lifestyle," said Chrissy. "That's easily solved. Leave her to me. And if sex is your problem, I can help you there as well." Chrissy sounded excited. "That's my field of expertise. But for tonight, can we get back on track? It's not that I don't care, sweetie, I do, but we are here for a hen party, not a counselling sitting. I promise you that tomorrow you're going to learn all about sex, and you're going to have an orgasm that's going to take you to the moon and back. I'm willing to help you get your marriage back, and in exchange, you are going to walk back into that bar, apologise to Frankie, and enjoy yourself. We don't hold grudges; life's too short. Do we have a deal, Michelle?" Chrissy handed her a clean tissue.

Michelle blew her nose and sighed. "Yes, please, I'd like to start again. I really am sorry. Thank you for listening."

"Come on, Michelle, I'll look after you, and we can have a good talk about it all later." Faith smiled as she led Michelle back into the bar. I could she was getting all excited. Somebody new she could talk to about Pete.

I sat outside the bar and watched them all walk away. Wow, who'd have guessed it! Mr. and Mrs. Perfect weren't Mr. and Mrs. Perfect after all. Darren and Michelle weren't that close, but if he knew, he'd put Nigel into intensive care for hurting his sister. I hoped it would get sorted out soon. I didn't think I wanted Darren on GBH charges. I gave it a minute and followed them inside.

TWENTY-ONE

Bobby's act had finished, and the karaoke was in full swing as I walked back into the bar. Frankie and Sam were already on stage singing Shania Twain's "Man! I Feel Like a Woman." Jess and Sarah, acting as their backing dancers, did two steps to the right, clicked fingers, two steps to the left, clicked fingers, and repeated. Believe me, it was not a routine that had been choreographed by Arleen Phillips, more like Mr. Blobby. They tried to keep in time with each other, but due to the amount of alcohol they'd both consumed, it proved quite difficult. A few doo-wops were also thrown in for good measure, not that any Shania Twain song I knew had room for doo-wops. Looking at my friends, you wouldn't think that twenty minutes ago World War III had been about to break out.

As their song finished, and before Jess could claim the mike as her own to sing her signature song, "Big Spender," the door to the bar opened, and in walked a group of old women. I did a double-take. It was the Cheshire firemen in drag. They looked awful, yet at the same time absolutely fantastic. Not sure who their stylist was, but it was no Gok Wan. The charity shops in Stockport must've been rubbing their hands together when this lot walked in, see-ing pound signs before their eyes. Mike nodded his head to acknowledge Chrissy and then the rest of us. He was sporting a blond bob wig, with a red bow on the top, a flowery off the shoulder maxi dress and carried a yellow handbag. His dress sense, just like the rest of the firemen was terrible.

Jess launched into her song as gracefully as she could, stepping off the stage to embark on a tour around the bar, taking time to stop and kiss a bald man on the head and sit on the knees of two others. Watching her gyrate her sixteen-stone backside into some old guy's lap was just the funniest thing. There were some very happy pension-ers in there.

I caught sight of Michelle walking towards me on the dance floor. I turned to look at her as she placed a hand on my shoulder. "Helen, I am so sorry for everything that's happened today—actually, ever since you and Darren got together. I know you're the best thing that's ever hap-pened to him. He has never been happier."

I felt a little bit guilty that a fit Irish man had been on my mind all day, and when I thought of him, them excited butterflies started flapping around in my belly. "Yeah, we make a great team."

"Can we start again? You know, be friends? I'll do whatever it takes to make it up to you." She wrapped her arms around me, and I enveloped her in mine. She looked so vulnerable.

"All I ever wanted was for us to be friends, Michelle."

"I've made things so hard for you, I know."

"Fresh start, hey!"

"Thank you, Helen, you really are one in a million."

Frankie was heading in our direction, her pistols already out, but before she had a chance to speak, Michelle was apologising to her.

Jess finished singing to rapturous applause, took her bow whilst blowing kisses to anyone and everyone, and left the stage.

The DJ called Frankie's name. This time she sang "Girls Just Wanna Have Fun" by Cyndi Lauper—our theme song. She headed back towards the stage, and we followed to sing and dance along with her. Faith wanted to sing her beloved "I Will Survive" by Gloria Gaynor, but we persuaded her otherwise. We'd had to listen to her belting out this song for the last six years. Enough was enough. At least now she had fresh ears with Michelle; she could go off and bore her with the tales of Pete.

Mike waved Chrissy over to join him at the bar, and after a bit of encouragement from us, she finally gave in. The remaining cross-dressing firemen came over and joined us, bringing with them a bottle of shots. Hey, and they weren't bad little movers.

"Ladies, gentlemen," Bobby announced. "I'd like you all now to take your seats and welcome onto the floor the highlight of the evening—the one, the only Sticky Vicky."

Sticky Vicky was welcomed onto the stage with clapping, cheering, and whistling. There she was, this woman we'd heard so much about, stark naked, wearing only a smile and a green ribbon in her long dark hair.

"D'ya reckon she's the original one? Can't tell how old she is from here," Sam said.

"How old do you reckon she is?" Frankie said, clapping along to the music.

"I've no idea, but look at her figure," Faith shouted above the noise.

"Are they flags she's pulling out of her flue?" Jess asked, climbing onto a chair to get a better look. "Oh no, they are!" She started to giggle.

"It must be dead handy having her as a friend when you're doing a car boot and your hubby's got the car. You could stick all your stuff up her flue, carry a table, and walk to the car boot. Then drag all your stuff out her flue and put it on your table," Faith said.

"That sounds revolting." I chuckled.

I caught Chrissy and Mike walking out the bar. As I turned back in the direction of the stage, Sticky Vicky started pulling razor blades out of her vagina and asking a man to slice some paper with one. "That can't be possible. How does she do it? That's making me cringe."

"I don't know, and I don't care," Frankie shouted. "But I do know one thing—I won't be trying that anytime soon. I've got better things to do with my flue. Could you imagine one quick slip?" Frankie pulled her legs tight shut.

"It doesn't bear thinking about." Faith giggled. "I know I don't use mine much, but I don't want to make it redundant."

The act ended as it had started, to rapturous applause. Sarah never took her eyes off the dance floor all the time Sticky Vicky performed, and I didn't think I had seen her that happy in years.

"Did she really just do all that, the dirty cow?" Sam exclaimed. "Her vagina must be as saggy as a bin bag. Bet her husband feels like he's drowning having sex, putting his cock into that big black hole. He'll have nothing to grip the sides."

"Unless he's got a big one." Sarah giggled.

"She's got a cracking figure, though. Did you get a look at her stomach? Really good for her age," Jess said.

"I know, but why would anybody want to do that for a job?" I said, laughing. "And more's the point, how did she know that she'd got a talent for stuffing things up there, pulling 'em out, and making a show out of it?"

"That's something else Chrissy can do if she ever runs out of money, isn't it, Chrissy?" Jess looked around. "Where's Chrissy?"

"I saw her going off with Mike about ten minutes ago," I replied.

"Faith, we need more drinks," Frankie said. "Are you coming to the bar with me?"

"Yeah, no problem. Same again, everybody?" Faith asked.

"Why not?" Sam answered. "I'll come and give you a hand."

The DJ was going full on, and his music attracted more and more groups of people into the bar. The dance floor was fit to bursting as we all danced around, waving our arms in the air, singing along to songs from the seventies, eighties, and nineties. A group of lads from Newcastle on a stag do joined us. They were all dressed in Baywatch red swimsuits, with fake boobs, and long blond wigs. Not one of them had the figure of a model. They were hilarious. A couple more groups of girls came in, one group was from Liverpool, and they were in Benidorm to celebrate a thirtieth birthday and the other group were on a hen party from Ireland dressed as red devils, in PVC outfits. Not one of them looked like a skinned version of Fred the Red, the Man U mascot. They all looked pretty hot, and they seemed to enjoy the attention they received from the other people in the bar.

The lads from the fire service became our new best friends and didn't want to leave us. Steve and Frankie hit it off by playing drinking games and having dance-offs. Dave, the stag, spent most of the night sniffing around Sam, hoping for a repeat performance from earlier on the plane. She was having none of it; one of the Geordie boys caught her eye, and it wasn't long before they headed into the ladies' toilets, only to rejoin us twenty minutes later. He must have been good—she's never normally away for more than ten minutes.

"Are we moving on?" Faith asked.

"If you want to, but everybody seems to be enjoying themselves here," I replied.

"Have you seen Michelle?" Sarah pointed.

I turned to see Michelle dancing on a table with one of the Geordies, with the biggest smile I have ever seen on her face.

"Looks like her getting all that off her chest has given her a new lease on life. I'm gonna make sure I'm there for Chrissy's sex class tomorrow. Can't wait. Not that I need any tips or anything," I said.

"It's probably those shots earlier that helped as well," Jess reminded us. "I knew she'd be OK once she loosened up."

"So what's going on with Mrs. Bucket and her Nigel?" Sam asked, not really showing interest.

"He's been having an affair," Faith answered.

"I know that bit...what with, a frigging Muppet? Who'd be that desperate to shag him?" Sam scoffed.

"He's got sexual urges, apparently," Faith continued.

"Him? I thought he was more the type to get an urge to try and track down the elusive bus number or chase around looking for rare stamps. He's angin', a right anorak. I wouldn't touch him with a ten-foot—no, strike that—a twenty-foot barge pole," Sam said.

"Do you know, Michelle has never had an orgasm." I giggled, sipping on a vodka and Coke.

"This is too much. Is that possible? Everybody has had an orgasm...Oh, come on, let's keep dancing." Sam laughed.

"I clocked you coming out of the toilet earlier, Sam, with that Geordie."

"Fit or what?" Sam gushed. "Ellie, why have we never been to Newcastle? I might see him again before we go home, and I think a night out in Newcastle needs arranging when we get back. If all blokes are like that, we could make it a regular hangout."

"Oh no, what's Frankie up to now?" exclaimed Faith.

Frankie and Steve were in the centre of the dance floor, having a competition to see who could do the splits whilst trying to balance a pint of lager on their head. Steve had removed the long black wig he had been wearing and pulled his pink dress around his waist, revealing his black boxers, to enable him to try and do the splits. *Frankie's got to win*, I thought. *All them years of gymnastics at Medlock sports centre when she was younger.* A cheer went up. Steve collapsed on the floor, laughing, covered in lager. Frankie removed the pint off her head and downed it in one, then fell on top of him.

"Them two have been getting close, don't you think, Ellie?" Faith said. "Do you know anything about him?"

"No, but it's only a bit of fun," I replied.

"Nonetheless, I'm gonna check him out. I just want her to meet a nice bloke for once." DCI Faith headed off the dance floor in the direction of the firemen to start her investigation.

"Can I try your wig on?" Sarah asked Phil, one of the firemen. "I've always fancied being a redhead."

He took it off and passed it to her.

She turned towards a mirror at the side of the stage and placed it onto her head. "What d'ya think?"

"Fantastic, it really suits you. Maybe you should become a redhead," Jess said excitedly. "Where'd you get it from, Phil?"

"Age Concern in Cheadle."

"You mean it's off real people?" Jess cried.

"It's not a scalp off a dead person, Jess, it's a wig." Sarah laughed. "Just because Libby isn't here, you don't have to start talking like her."

"Wonder what she's up to."

"She can't be having a better time than us," Sarah replied.

"I haven't given Libby a thought. I'm too busy having a good time myself," I said.

"Can I keep your wig on, Phil?"

"Sure, if I can have a dance."

"Course Sarah will dance with—won't you, Sarah?" Jess pushed her towards him.

"Yeah…OK," Sarah shyly answered.

Our first night in Benidorm had been a great success, apart from the Michelle and Frankie incident earlier. I hadn't a clue what the time was, but slow dances were now being played. People were beginning to pair up. Sam was playing tonsil tennis with another one of the Geordies as they smooched around to Frankie Goes to Hollywood's "Power of Love," and the way his hands were massaging her buttocks, it wasn't going to be long before they would be heading off so he could show her his power of love. Jess and I tried to do a proper ballroom-dancing-style waltz whilst singing at the top of our voices. She was trying her best to lead me, the way we'd been taught at Donahey's dance centre when we were in our teens, but we gave up. There was no room. The other customers in the bar were getting a little fed up with us bumping into them.

My head started getting fuzzy, and I knew that was my cue. I needed to go back to the hotel; I needed to go to bed. Michelle, Sarah, and Jess left with me. Frankie had already done a disappearing act with Steve, and Faith said she'd come back with Sam and carried on drinking with the lads from Newcastle.

We staggered arm in arm back to the hotel, chatting and giggling, agreeing and then disagreeing if we were going in the right direction, as everywhere looked the same. After all, at three—or it could have been four—in the morning, one tree looked exactly the same as another tree. We stopped a couple of people to ask if they knew our hotel, but they didn't even know what planet they were on. Jess spotted Jerry's Irish bar, and I suggested we call in for a nightcap, sort of hoping Jerry would be in there. He was. He served us all Baileys on ice, and pulled up a stool and sat beside us, chatting along, asking about our night, looking like he was taking a real interest as he sat there, with his legs slightly apart and his arms resting on his knees.

I found it really difficult not to stare at him. I was blushing. I knew he was watching me. His dark-brown eyes were undressing me. I could feel it. My nipples started to go hard. I knew I was really attracted to Jerry, but why? Why now, after all this time of being with Darren? I studied Jerry when he wasn't looking in my direction. He had a cute dimple in his left cheek when he smiled, and there was a confidence in him, probably because he knew how attractive he was. I was trying to convince myself God was probably testing me to make sure I was doing the right thing by getting married to Darren. I finished off my drink and encouraged the others to do the same. I had to get out of the bar before I said or did something I'd regret in the morning.

Jerry stood as we did and placed a kiss on our cheeks in turn as we walked out of the bar. I was last in line, my heart beating so fast, I'm sure he could see it bouncing harder and harder in my chest. He caught my lip as he pulled away. I swear I was going to explode. I grabbed hold of Jess's hand to steady myself and walked out that bar as fast I could.

Jess and Sarah wanted yet another nightcap when we arrived back at the hotel and headed into the bar. Michelle was wrecked. I offered to take her to her room, more for my benefit than hers. I didn't want anything to happen to her, with her not being used to drinking. Once she was settled in bed, I hugged her and went back to join the others downstairs. By the time I arrived back in reception, Jess and Sarah had already made themselves comfy on the sofas, recapping the night's events and drinking Irish coffees. I kicked off my stilettos and sat down beside Jess, taking her coffee off her and having a big slup. That was good. That was very good. I licked off the cream moustache that had attached itself to my top lip. I had to order one for myself. I waved over one of one the bar staff and ordered myself an Irish coffee, only I wanted mine to have a double shot of coffee, hoping it might help to stop me getting a hangover in the morning. It probably wouldn't, but it was worth a try. I was laughing along with the girls as we reminisced about Jess's spandex incident this afternoon, when I caught sight of Chrissy rushing through the revolving door of our hotel, carrying her shoes.

"Hey, where've you been?" I enquired.

"With Mike…back at his room," she replied. "I need to wash my hands, which way to the toilets"

"Are you getting too old now that you can't hold it. If you need one of my TENA's you only have to ask," Jess slurred.

"Don't be silly Jess, I'll have surgery first. No I need to wash my hands, had to give a taxi driver a hand job. I've left my purse at Mike's hotel, so I couldn't pay for the taxi. So I offered him a hand job and after I explained what I meant he said yes."

"You never did," Sarah gasped.

"You should have come in the hotel and got the money off us," I offered.

"No it's okay. It didn't take long," Chrissy replied. "Where's Michelle?"

"I've just put her to bed—she's smashed. She'd been dancing on the tables with some Geordies we met after you left, they were on a stag do. It was really funny. She's fallen head over heels in love with the Geordie accent. She kept singing about 'a little fishy on a little dishy, when the boat comes in.' She said she remembers a programme when she was little about Newcastle. You wouldn't recognise her," I answered

"She's like a different person Chrissy. She's even dropped that dodgy accent she's been using. She talks like us now," Sarah giggled. "She's had a great night, but oh, is she gonna suffer in the morning."

"I've got something that will sort her out, don't worry about that. Where are the others?"

"Faith and Sam stayed with the Geordies. Frankie was with one of the firemen," said Sarah, and then she burped. "Sorry."

"I'm off up to bed, I'll wash my hands up in my room, I'm shattered. See you in the morning."

"We'll come up with you." Jess linked her arm through Chrissy's, and we headed over to the lifts.

TWENTY-TWO

I woke to see the sun peering into our room through a slight opening in the curtains. It was shouting happily, "Good morning!" and I was wailing, "Sod off and go back to bed!"

Sam's bed was empty. The whole of my head was being pounded—not only by Ricky Hatton now, Amir Khan had joined in. I stretched across to the bedside cabinet and grabbed a packet of paracetamols and a bottle of water. I quickly deposited two tablets into my mouth to begin the recovery process of a heavy night on the beer. I sighed at the thought of doing it all again today and then at tonight's fancy dress. I picked up my iPhone. *Is that it? Eight o' bloody clock?* I thought it would have been at least ten. A repulsive aroma filled the room. *What the...*

"Sam," I called out. "Sam, you in the bathroom?"

"Yeah!"

"Is that you? I mean the smell."

"My bloody stomach. Had summat that's not agreed with me."

"You could've shut the door."

"What, and die of fume inhalation?" She laughed. "I couldn't do anything, Ellie. I just dived in here. Jesus...it's pebble dashing everywhere."

"Sam, that's too much information for this time of the morning, thank you very much."

I couldn't stay there or it was gonna be me who'd die of fume inhalation. I grabbed a towel off the floor, picked up Faith's *OK* magazine, and threw it into the bathroom. "Read why Kerry Katona's not going to do drugs anymore. That'll take your mind off filling the toilet bowl."

"I don't fucking like Kerry Katona. You're getting me mixed up with Libby," I heard her shout as the door to our room shut behind me.

After knocking repeatedly on Faith's door to beg for a caffeine fix and getting no reply, I knocked on Chrissy's. Michelle opened it. Her eyes were red and wet. She'd been crying.

"Hey, Michelle, I was just...Hey, what's up?"

I closed the door behind me as I followed Michelle into the room she was sharing with Chrissy and watched as she sat herself down on the edge of her bed. I stifled a snigger when I saw Chrissy's fully clothed body sprawled facedown on her bed, feet hanging off the edge, murmuring.

Michelle buried her face in her hands, shaking her head. I cautiously sat down beside her on the unmade duvet ruffled up on her bed, putting my arms around her shoulders.

"You OK?" Chrissy mumbled.

Michelle's crying became heavier. Chrissy slid off her bed, dragging the duvet with her as she landed on her knees. She slowly picked herself up off the floor, staggered over, and joined us on the bed.

"Come on, sweetie, you had a good night, didn't you?" Chrissy took hold of Michelle as she sobbed hard into Chrissy shoulder.

"I'm so sorry." Michelle sniffed. "I'm so ashamed. I've managed to cut myself off from everyone. I've no husband, no friends. My life is such a mess. I just don't know what to do anymore."

"It's OK." I placed my hand gently on her shoulder.

Chrissy stroked Michelle's hair. "That's just the drink talking...How's your head?"

"Dreadful. It's never ever been this bad."

Chrissy released Michelle and walked into the bathroom, soon returning with four tablets. She handed two tablets to Michelle with a bottle of the hotel's complimentary still water. She popped the other two into her mouth and swallowed them without water, like an expert.

"Don't ask, just take. These will cure anything in an hour. I get them from my doctor on St. John Street."

Without question, Michelle did as Chrissy instructed.

"First, you have nothing to be sorry for. And second, you've got us, and now we know the reason why you have been a total bitch—sorry, but you have—we're all going to help. Look, you said you were sorry last night, and that's the end of it, OK? I was told you were dancing on tables and chatting up Geordies." Chrissy smirked.

"Oh God, I forgot. Oh! I'm so sorry."

"Stop saying you're sorry. You know, you could do a lot more to help yourself, Michelle. You're thirty-eight years old, going on sixty. You are one person in desperate need of a full makeover. Your hair is more than a bit wild," Chrissy commented, running her fingers through it and looking at her eyebrows. "Have you ever plucked these? And do you wax your pubic hairs? What about your glasses—have you never thought of wearing contacts?"

"I...sometimes!" Michelle exclaimed. "I've got contact lenses with me."

"I think you need to start wearing them. Michelle, without sounding too harsh, I'm surprised Nigel wants to go anywhere near you and your bush. Are you sure not having sex is the only reason Nigel doesn't come near you?" Chrissy asked.

"I'm a mess, aren't I?" Michelle answered in despair.

"Look, nothing is irreparable. You're one very lucky lady. You're going to be working with the best—me—and I am, I must say, a creative artist. Let's go for a walk before breakfast, get some fresh air, have a chat, grab a coffee. What do you say?"

"That would be good. Thanks," Michelle replied.

"You joining us, Ellie?" Chrissy asked.

"No, thanks. I only knocked to borrow some coffee."

"Knock yourself out, it's over there." Chrissy pointed to Michelle's Louis Vuitton travel bag sitting by the window.

There was a knock at the bedroom door. Frankie stood there in just her knickers and bra, giggling, still very drunk from last night. "Morning." She waltzed in. "Hey, what happened to you last night, Chrissy? You pole dancing again with the fireman?"

"Sure was. You met any more blokes who like messing around with things coloured orange?"

"Funny." Frankie laughed.

"Hey, we're going for a walk before breakfast. Coming?" Chrissy asked.

"Yeah, I'll come, everybody else is dead." She yawned. "It might wake me up."

"Ten minutes."

I fumbled about in Michelle's bag for the coffee. Nescafé decaf. I could have done with some of the proper stuff, but beggars can't be choosers, as the saying goes, and headed back to my room.

"Sam…you still in there?"

"Yeah! Ellie, I couldn't tell you if I was having a shit or a piss. It's coming out of everywhere."

"Why do you insist on telling me everything, Sam?"

"Wonder what would happen if we ever grew up."

"Not sure I want to find out just yet." I walked over to the kettle and flicked in on.

"Is that why you're playing with fire with Jerry?"

"Excuse me?" I headed towards the bathroom." I don't know what ya mean," I continued, standing in the doorway to the bathroom and covering my nose and mouth with my towel.

"Don't give me that. I know you went back to the Irish bar last night. Do you think I'm stupid? I've known you too long. You're acting around him the way you used to act when you first got with Darren."

"I am not." I stamped my feet like a spoilt child.

"Okay, you're not, but I suggest ya take a long hard look at what's going on when you're in Jerry's company. Maybe you can't see it, so to make it easy, I'll point it out for you."

I walked off sulking into the bedroom, sat on the bed, grabbed hold of a pillow, and held it to my chest like some kind of security blanket. "Sam."

"What!"

"Do ya think I'm making the right decision—ya know, marrying Darren?"

"Are ya being serious, Ellie? I can't answer that, but shouldn't you have done all this soul-searching crap before you agreed to marry Darren?"

"Is it really that obvious the way Jerry's making me feel?"

"Yes. Ellie, apart from lying spread-eagle on a table in his bar with your knickers around one of your ankles, you couldn't be making it any more obvious. Or...it could just be the wine and the sun that's making you act funny, but I very much doubt it."

I never thought I'd be getting married again, and here I was on my hen party. When I think how against marriage I was after my divorce…I can still remember some of the pain, but it had started to fade now, a bit like childbirth. You say you're never going to go through labour again, but most of us do because we forget the pain after that sweet little bundle of joy is placed in our arms. I just hoped this marriage wasn't gonna be like the onset of labour. When it starts, you remember the pain, and you suddenly change your mind, but it's too late to go back. No, it wouldn't be—*I love Darren and he loves me*. This time it was different. I knew it. But why was my head so full of Jerry?

Shit. I walked out onto the balcony to get some air, hoping it might clear my head. What was I going to do? Sam said I couldn't spend the weekend talking to Darren, and she had already told him before we came away that I was being banned from having my mobile. But the problem was I hadn't wanted to text him or talk to him.

I leant on the rail surrounding our balcony and looked at one of the hotel's three pools. I smiled. It wasn't just Germans who got up early to put their towels on the cream-coloured plastic loungers, not unless they'd started buying Union Jack towels. It was already busy down there. I made polite conversation with a couple smoking on the next balcony, who introduced themselves as Geoff and Andrea from Moston. Desperate to talk to somebody other than each other, they must have seen me as fresh meat. They told me they'd come here for four weeks every March and October for the last ten years since they both took early retirement from the post office. There's nowhere better in the world than Benidorm, Andrea enthused, and she knew; both of them had been everywhere for their holidays. Somehow I can't see Benidorm beating the likes of Thailand or the Maldives, not that I've been yet. Geoff told me he'd worked as a postman for over forty years; he could tell me some stories about what goes on there. *Bet you could, and I bet you got a good pension as well,* I thought. Fancy working at the same place for forty years. I'd only been at Baxter and Turnbull for seven years, and it was driving me insane—Sam, too—we had to get out of that place.

I politely excused myself. I wasn't really in the mood to hear about what they did in their spare time or look at pictures of their grandkids. My head was going dizzy thinking about Darren and Jerry, or maybe it was the hangover settling in.

"Let's get ready and go for breakfast. Too much thinking in a morning hurts my head, but if something is going on, it's my subconscious that's doing it. I love Darren. Now move, sore arse or not. Lecture time over." I threw a pillow at Sam. "Oh, and where did you end up last night?"

"Stayed with some bloke I picked up, got in about sixish."

"But you were with the Geordie lad when we left the bar."

"Oh, I did him, on the way back. I've never had sex with a bloke in a swimming costume before," Sam sniggered. "Then I got chatting to another bloke outside a bar and went with him for a walk on the beach."

"What happened to Faith?"

"A couple of the firemen walked her back."

"I'll go next door and see what Jess and Faith are up to. You've got a ten-minute warning."

Jess opened the door. "Come in."

"Jess, are ya gonna make us a brew, pretty please? I don't think I'll be able to move until I've had one," Faith shouted.

"Course she will—won't you, Jess?" I replied. "It was great last night, Faith, wasn't it? How the hell are we going to top that tonight? Did you notice Chrissy had sand on her shoes when she came in last night?"

"No shit, Sherlock." Jess laughed.

"I'm just saying. She likes this Mike. I can just tell because she doesn't really take to blokes she has sex with."

"I'll put the kettle on, and then I'm getting in the shower before breakfast. I'm starving. Do you mind if I get in first?" Jess asked.

"Fine by me, but how can you be starving? You never stop eating," Faith remarked.

"I love my food, and besides, Alan likes having something to chew on. He can't be doing with girls who are nothing but skin and bone. Bones are for dogs, meat is for men—that's what he always says."

"I'm not going down for breakfast. Don't think I can stomach anything," Faith said, slowly making her way back under the covers.

"Here you go, Faith. I'll leave it on the side for you." Jess placed the coffee on the bedside table.

"Thanks, love."

"Have a shower after breakfast. Please, Jess. We won't care that you stink." I laughed.

"Come on then, get a move on. See you later, Faith. Can we bring you anything back?"

"No thanks. See you later."

We stopped off to collect Sarah and Sam on the way to the lift.

TWENTY-THREE

The restaurant was just as full as it had been the night before. Everyone was getting fuelled up for the day with plates full of eggs, bacon, sausages—everything that the dieting club I paid five pounds a week for said I couldn't have. According to the club, most of these people would shortly be making a pit stop at the nearest hospital with blocked arteries.

Chrissy and Michelle were already tucking into the all-you-can-eat breakfast when we arrived. We gave our room numbers to the waiter and went to join them.

"Excuse me, how does this breakfast thing work?" Frankie asked a waiter, who was collecting plates guests had now finished with and loading them onto a trolley.

"It is buffet service, señora." The waiter's voice was soft, and he blushed.

"It's señorita, actually."

"Pardon, señorita. You help yourself to whatever you like, as much as you want."

"What, anything?" Frankie winked at the young waiter.

"Sí." He continued loading the plates onto his trolley, trying not to make eye contact. His face still very red, he then headed off in the direction of the kitchen.

"What're you asking him that for? You know how it works," Sarah said. "Did you see how he changed colour when you spoke to him?"

"Wanted to talk to him. He kept staring at me." Frankie stood and walked over to the buffet table, only to quickly return carrying two bottles of champagne.

"Where've you got them from?" Jess asked.

"Off the buffet table. The waiter said you can take anything."

Sarah gasped. "Isn't that just part of the display? You can't take the champagne, Frankie. Put it back."

"I can't put 'em back now, somebody will see me. Who wants some?"

We're not people to refuse a glass of bubbly, no matter what time of day it is. Even Michelle, who looked like death, said she'd have one. She really was trying, bless her. Frankie popped the corks, and the champagne began to flow. We all looked very classy drinking it out of coffee cups.

"Would it be OK to have some fresh orange with mine?" Michelle asked.

"Course you can. I'll get you some," Sarah said.

Low supermarket music, as I call it, was playing in the background as I watched the same people getting up and down to restock their empty plates. After a while it started to make my stomach churn. Just like last night, as soon as the food was taken off the buffet tables, it was replaced by more. If I ever heard of *The Biggest Loser* wanting candidates for their show, I'd point them in the direction of the Hotel Guadalupe, Benidorm. They'd be spoilt for choices of contestants.

"Can anybody hear that buzzing noise, or is it just me?" Sam said.

Everybody went quiet. "Oh! It's my phone," Chrissy said. "I put it on vibrate last night."

"Thank God for that. I thought I was starting with tinnitus." Sam rubbed her ear.

"Does everything you have vibrate?" Jess asked.

"Now that would be telling." Chrissy looked down at her phone and turned it off.

"So what happened with Mike last night?" Frankie asked.

"I think he's got a look of George Clooney, with his salt-and-pepper hair, big shoulders, rugged look," Jess enthused.

"You think everybody with salt-and-pepper hair looks like George Clooney." Frankie laughed. "You even think Alan looks like him."

"He does," Jess affectionately replied.

"Since when has George Clooney had a belly that hangs over his forty-inch waist?" Sam exclaimed.

"I mean Alan's face looks like George, not his body."

"I'll lend you my glasses next time you're with him. I think yours are a bit rose-tinted." Sam sighed.

"So are you going to see Mike again?" I asked.

"If I bump into him, I might."

"Is he married?" Jess asked.

"He's got a ring on, but I don't talk about personal stuff. You know me."

"Well, Chrissy, it's a bit hard to talk with your mouth full, if you know what I mean." Sam winked.

"You'd know all about that, wouldn't you, Sam?" Chrissy smirked back.

After breakfast we all opted to do our own thing for the rest of the morning. Sam had already booked herself into the hotel spa for a rejuvenating facial and body-balancing massage to ward off any signs of aging on her face and body after our night of heavy drinking. Faith went along, too. As she put it, it was probably the only chance she was gonna get to have anybody rub oily hands all over her body whilst she was in Benidorm. I suggested to Sarah we could join them, an early birthday present for her off me, but she declined, shrugging. She said it wasn't really her thing now. All that pampering stuff was a waste of money.

I can't lie. I was a bit disappointed by her reaction. In the years before Maisy was born, we'd always made a date at least once every couple of months, just the two of us, to go to have a good body massage and facial. Even when we were both skint, that didn't stop us. We'd merely book into the local college and let ourselves be used as guinea pigs for the beauty students.

Chrissy and Michelle spent the rest of the morning together, Chrissy spearheading the first day of the "Let's get Michelle a life" campaign. First on the agenda was an appointment with the hotel beautician for an urgently needed eyebrow plucking—the hairy caterpillar on top of her eyes was doing absolutely nothing for her—followed by a leg and bikini wax to make her look a lot less like a gorilla. Chrissy promised to take Michelle to see her stylist at Toni and Guy's in Manchester for a complete restyle of her long frizzy hair when they got home, followed by appointments at Harvey Nics and Kendals with their stylists to buy a complete new wardrobe. But for tonight, Chrissy was going to be styling Michelle's hair and dressing her appropriately for our fancy-dress night out.

Michelle did confess over breakfast that she hadn't brought anything for the fancy dress. She had been planning to give it a miss, pretending to be sick. The remainder of the virgins, me included, decided to spend the rest of the morning around the pool making sure enough sunrays had covered our bodies before the Robbie Williams tribute act and quiz started at two. We did think about hanging around for that. I bet it'd be a laugh joining in, waving our arms around in the air to the countless Robbie songs we'd all spent so many nights dancing away to in Manchester clubs. But we still had Benidorm to explore.

Out of the five pieces of swimwear I'd packed, three bikinis and two swimsuits to be exact, I chose the tangerine two-piece from Debenhams to wear. I spread a nice even layer of Nivea suntan lotion all over my body, draped a matching sarong around my waist, and went to Jess's room meet the others before going to the pool.

Sarah was chuckling away to herself as I walked in. "Jess, I don't mean to be rude, but you're not goin' out like that, are ya?"

"Why, what's wrong with me? Don't I look right in this tankini or something? The sales assistant in Selfridges at the Trafford Centre, where I bought it from, said I looked OK." Jess admired herself in the full-length mirror as she spoke, pulling at the top to hide her muffin top.

"I was in Kendals once with Roxy and Izzy when a lady with out-of-control ginger hair was trying on a midlength bright-yellow chiffon dress. She looked like a bloody pineapple. I nearly wet myself listening to the store assistant going on and on, telling her how wonderful she looked, how it really suited her colouring and complexion. Once me and the girls composed ourselves, I interrupted and told her she looked bloody ridiculous and not to buy it. Shop assistants will tell you anything, Jess, to get a sale." I giggled. "But it's not the case this time, Jess, honest. I think you may have forgotten something."

"What, then?" Jess cried out.

"Look south, Jess—looks like your bush is in desperate need of a pruning. Ooh, and I never knew you weren't a natural blonde," Frankie teased. "Do I spy a bit of ginger?"

Jess looked down. "Oh my God, bikini wax. I've been so busy lately, I'd completely forgotten."

"Don't worry, Jess, I've brought some hair remover," Sarah said, laughing.

"You've got that much pubic hair, Jess, if you straightened it, I bet it'd be nearly at your knees," Frankie continued.

"Get the hair remover, Sarah," Jess screeched. "And I was never a ginger, Frankie. Strawberry blond, my mum always called my hair."

"I'll be back in a min, Jess—it's in my bathroom." Sarah giggled as she headed out of the room.

"Ellie, let's go and grab us some beds before they get snatched up. We'll meet you down by the pool, Jess." Frankie took hold of my arm and pulled me out of the bedroom.

"OK, we'll be down soon," Jess replied.

"Hey, why the quick exit?" I asked as we walked towards the lift.

"Wanted to talk to you."

"Intriguing. OK, shoot."

Geoff and Andrea, whom I'd met this morning on the balcony, were just getting in the lift, and we shouted for them to hold it for us. They talked nonstop about how they were going to set themselves up around the pool early to get good seats for the Robbie tribute starting at two. Andrea confessed to being a big Take That fan. Howard Donald was her favourite because he had the most sculpted body and looked like he'd be the best in bed. She couldn't see Gary Barlow being too good—he looked too nice and polite. I didn't really think women in their seventies thought much about sex—quite refreshing to know. Geoff said it was all in her head; she'd never have the energy. Andrea said she couldn't wait to have a toy boy who lasted for more than thirty seconds and didn't have to use Viagra. We didn't know where to look. Frankie was egging Andrea on, not that she needed any encouragement. We said bye to them both when we arrived at the ground floor and continued with our conversation as we made our way through reception in the direction of the pool.

"What do you think of Steve?"

"Steve who?"

"Fireman Steve, friend of that Mike bloke who Chrissy's getting jiggy with."

"I don't know, not really spoken to him properly. Why?"

"I went back with him last night, to his hotel. Elle, it was the best sex I've had in ages."

"Maybe he has a thing for Oompa Loompas, you being all orange and that."

"Very funny, Elle. It's fading now, anyway."

"Well, considering you've only been having sex with a vibrator for the last two months, anything has got to be better than that." I laughed.

"No, I had sex with the new male nurse on our ward when I was on nights last month. I must have forgot to tell you. Anyway, I'm meeting Steve again later tonight. I said I'd text him and tell him where to meet me. You don't mind, do ya?"

"Do I heckers Frankie. It might be even better tonight when he sees you all dressed up like a policewoman. You know how the uniform services like to stick together."

I ordered four skinny lattes from the waiter when we arrived at the pool. Sarah and Jess took ages to find us, as they didn't know which of the three pools we'd set up camp in. Once settled, we began our chilling-out morning, and when we saw how many magazines Libby had bought from WHSmith, we knew we had more than enough to keep us busy. We were able to keep up with all the latest celebrity gossip and news from the reality shows we're addicted to.

Made in Chelsea makes me laugh. Even with all their money, they still moan and groan like us paupers, only they talk posher. Frankie prefers *TOWIE*; I think it's all that fake tan she likes. Jess watches them all. It's her escape from all the legal twaddle she has to endure each day at work. There were a couple of magazines about the soaps. Coming from up north we were all *Corrie* and *Emmerdale* fans.

"You're a bit covered up for sunbathing, Sarah. I thought it was only the Chinese who covered up at the first sign of the sun," Frankie commented.

"I'm not too keen on the sun. I'll read for a bit and then nip over the road to have a look around the shops and see if I can get Maisy something."

"Aren't you bit warm with a cardi on?" I said.

"No, not really. Don't you think it's a bit nippy?" Sarah answered, pulling her cardigan tightly around her body.

"You're kidding, right? Sarah, it's roasting. I'm going in for a swim to give me a bit of a kick-start and see if I can get this fake tan to fade a bit more." Frankie leapt up and jumped into the pool, letting out a wimpy yelp as she landed in the water.

Apart from me, none of the other girls had mentioned Frankie's fake tan for a while. The joke had probably faded now, a bit like her fake tan.

I got myself all comfy on my lounger and began making my way through the pile of magazines. An article in *Now* magazine caught my eye. "Hey, listen to this," I blurted out. "Marco D'Acampo, the twenty-six-year-old Manchester United and Italian international, is rumoured to be having an affair with a married member of the cast of one of our country's most popular soaps. He was spotted recently with a dark-haired mystery woman leaving the Lowry Hotel, Manchester. Remember, you heard it here first. Watch this space!' They've even got a picture of him outside the Lowry with her, but you can't see her face."

"Libby's got a look of her from *Emmerdale*. You know the one I mean, the one married to David—Natalie or Natasha—don't you think? Bet they think it's her," Sarah said.

"I think she looks more like the girl who plays her sister," I answered.

"If only they knew where twenty-six-year-old Marco was right now," Jess said. "I've not given Libby a second thought since yesterday. Wonder what she's up to?"

"The way she was talking on the plane yesterday, bet she's getting flung around Marco's family's villa like a rag doll, lucky lady." I smirked. "Still can't get over how she never told anybody about her and Marco. How the hell do you keep something like that a secret from your bessies?"

"Guess we all have our little secrets," Jess said.

"Why, what's yours?" I asked.

"You know mine, and it's not even a secret. Me and Alan and the fact I want to get married to him, even though I say I'm not bothered. Just wish it'd happen soon. He has promised me, though, that the day he proposes, he'll whisk me away to the Maldives for a week."

"Do you think it'll ever happen, Jess? It's been how long now? Three years?" I asked.

"I can only live in hope. Not sure I can keep going on like this, though, always coming in second. First bloke I fell in love with and married turned out to be gay, and the second one is married. His son leaves college the end of this year, and he said he'll tell his wife about us and get a divorce then. Glad your Faith's not around, Sarah. She'd be giving me a right ear-bashing now, Mrs. I-can't-stand-women-who-have-affairs."

"Oh…ignore her, she's always the victim," Sarah replied.

"What about it, Sarah—you got any secrets?" I asked.

"Me, secrets? Don't be ridiculous. No." She blushed.

Jess gasped. "It's in *Woman* magazine as well about Marco seeing somebody off the TV. Hope they don't find out who he's really seeing. Could you imagine what'd happen if the truth got out? We need to warn Libby. Remind me at the airport tomorrow."

I began to flick through the other magazines to see if there were any more stories about Marco when Frankie ran towards us.

"What've you been told about running by the pool?" I spoke mockingly as if disciplining Roxy and Izzy running around Ashton baths.

"Have you seen a copy of the *Sun*?" Frankie asked.

"What on earth are you doing reading the *Sun*?" Jess asked.

"I've not been reading it, you idiot. Look—the front page. I've just grabbed it off the table over there." She tossed it in my face.

I quickly scanned the headline and looked at the picture. "That's me waving."

"Yes, and Chrissy, and me, too, taken outside Alicante Airport yesterday."

Jess snatched the paper out of my hand and read the headline: D'Acampo, D'Acamping in Spain. They had pictures of him driving away in his orange Jaguar with Libby in the car. Luckily only the back of her head was in the picture, but nonetheless, it was Libby.

"Nobody'll know it's her, and besides, no one ever believes what's in the papers." I tried to sound convincing.

"No, it's just a bloody coincidence we're in the picture as well, and we're all waving," Frankie exclaimed.

The reporter was asking for people to call him at his news desk with any information on who Marco's dark-haired companion could be and what Marco was doing in Spain.

"Well, we can't do anything about it now," Jess said. "I'm getting my head down for a while. Think the hangover is finally kicking in."

Frankie and Jess stretched out on their sun loungers and, after making themselves comfy, quickly fell asleep to make up for their lost hours. Sarah went off to have a wander around the shops and look for a present for Maisy. I ordered myself another skinny latte, only this time with a shot of Bailey's in it, and sat back on my lounger to watch the world go by from under last season's floppy hat from Primark and from behind my French Connection sunglasses, which are so heavily tinted, nobody can see you spying. And oh! What sights I spied!

I chuckled at some of the old guys wandering around the pool wearing Speedos with their scrawny legs and bellies hanging over the waistbands. One guy who'd just passed me by could do with a new pair. The elastic had gone from the top of one of his legs, and his meat was hanging out. I childishly wanted to nudge Frankie and Jess and shout, "Cop a load of that!" but stopped myself now that I'm a grown-up. *Should I go over and tell him?* I considered it, but that might have been even more embarrassing. I decided to do nothing and continued to watch him until he sat himself down on a lounger at the far side of the pool and ordered a beer.

I did, however, question men's dress of a certain age. Do they honestly not know what they look like in Speedos? I should set up one of them e-petitions for Parliament to make it a law that the male species are only allowed to wear Speedos until they leave primary school or as long as they have a body like Marco D'Acampo. And don't even get me started on socks and sandals. Who came up with that fashion statement? Is that one written somewhere in one of Saga's handbook? "Now you have reached pension age, you must, at all times during hot weather, wear socks and open-toed sandals." I childishly laughed to myself.

Around the pool, groups of women sat in their little cliques chatting, knitting, reading, et cetera. I would've loved to be a fly buzzing around them all, listening to today's topic of conversation. Bet they were saying, "Cor…he's fit, him, you know, in them blue Speedos with that lovely beer belly hanging over. Wouldn't mind a load of that." Until they spotted all that he had to offer popping out of his Speedos and changed their minds, saying, "You can have him. I want one who can still look after himself." I chuckled to myself again.

I love people-watching. We spend hours on Deansgate doing just that on Saturday afternoons in summer. Never mind in another twenty-five years that'll be me and my bessies sitting around gassing. I might even give the knitting a go.

I started to feel sleepy and closed my eyes. My mind began to drift off to the weeks previous to my hen party and the plans Darren and I had made for our wedding. We attended an appointment with the minister at St. Andrew's Church, and everything was booked for two o'clock on the twenty-fifth of May. Darren and I visited loads of wedding venues in and around the greater Manchester area. Some of them had fancy sculptured gardens, Michelin-star restaurants. We even had a look around Man City's stadium. Darren refused to go and look at Old Trafford, so that wasn't even a contender as a wedding venue, but nothing grabbed us. And the cost! It's not that we don't like spending money. We do, it's just we hate getting ripped off. It's like the price of holidays going up when it's the end of a school term. You mention the word "wedding," and the prices at venues quadruple. What's that about? We want everybody to remember our wedding as a great wedding, not one where our friends have to go into debt just to have a good time.

In the end, after a meeting with the chairman at Ashton Rugby Club, where Darren plays, and a discussion with a marquee-hire company, we agreed to have our wedding reception on the first-team pitch in a marquee, with round tables, fancy gold chairs, and posh portable toilets. We'd both rather spend money on booze, food, and entertainment rather than say we had our wedding at this year's "it" place. It's not like we're out to impress anybody; those days have definitely gone.

We still have arrangements to finalise, like cars, flowers, wedding invitations, and the guest list. If you ever want to guarantee a family row, arrange a wedding or a funeral. Neither of us have seen or spoken to a lot of family members for years, and to be honest, I'd rather not invite some of them, but I can already hear the words flying out of my mother's mouth. "You can't invite Uncle Steve and Auntie Alice without inviting Uncle Ed and Auntie Monica, and don't sit Paul near Jack and Sid. They'll be drunk before the end of the first course; they're a bad influence on one another." Even though my parents are not paying anything towards my wedding—they made that quite clear: "We've done it once, we're not doing it again," like we'd want them to—they still have to have their say.

Darren struggled to choose his best man. He's got three really close friends who have been together since high school, and he didn't want to upset anybody. He eventually asked Marc, his business partner, much to the delight of the other two, who didn't want the speech job; they just wanted to get pissed.

Marc's a good-looking bloke, even though I say it myself. Forty-five, six foot, going grey around the temples, which just adds to his looks. All-year tan, works out regularly with a personal trainer. He has to beat women off with a stick. I love him as a friend, but he's not somebody I'd want to be in a relationship with. I think a man who spends too much time looking after himself is a little strange. Also, he can't be trusted. He's a bit like the male version of Sam (I've lost count of how many times he's slept with her), only he's not married. He divorced two years ago. Cathy, his wife, left him for the bloke who owned the garage where she bought her Mercedes SLK 250 CDI. I say good luck to her. To say Marc was shocked was an understatement, but I don't blame her. All his life he's found it hard to keep the zip up on his pants. It was his pride that was hurt more than Cathy leaving.

I dread to think what his speech is going to be like. I can only imagine it will be filled with tales of rugby tours and lads' holidays from Ibiza to Amsterdam. I just hope my grandma hasn't got any batteries in her hearing aid.

Frankie, Chrissy, Sam, Roxy, Izzy, and me went wedding shopping. It took forever to find a wedding dress. I made appointments for us to visit bridal stores from Alderley Edge to Saddleworth. They were so expensive. I couldn't justify spending a few thousand on a dress that was going to be worn for a few hours and then stored in a bin bag in the loft, waiting for my grandchildren to use it for dressing up.

The biggest problem we had was that every time we visited a new town, we found the pubs and bars kept calling us in for a couple. I lost count of the number of times we had to abandon our wedding-dress search and get taxis home and then go back and collect the cars the next day.

I tried on zillions (slight exaggeration) of wedding dresses, from big frilly ones, just for a laugh, to the slimmest of fitted dresses. I don't know what I was thinking, trying that type on—they haven't made enough Spandex to make me look good in a slim-fitting dress. The last dress I tried on took my breath away. It was in a bridal store near where Chrissy lives in Saddleworth. It was a full-length, off-the-shoulder ivory gown, fitted at the waist, with a slight train, decorated with pearls on the bodice. I knew straight away that that was the one for me. No frilly toilet-roll wedding dress here. My eyes welled up, Roxy and Izzy started to cry, and even Chrissy, who rarely shows any emotion, had a tear in her eye. I couldn't believe even at the age of forty-one I could still feel like a princess. My outfit was topped off with a pearl and diamante tiara, and short veil. I felt amazing, but I really couldn't justify spending that amount of money on a dress. That's when we set about looking on eBay. We found a similar one on there for a fraction of the cost. I felt like I was stealing it off the woman selling it, but secondhand wedding dresses don't hold their value, and after being dry-cleaned, the dress looked as good as new.

Bridesmaid dresses were purchased from Debenhams. The girls all chose different styles of long black evening dresses so that they could wear them again.

Darren begged me—well, sort of, he promised me a top-class spa day with one friend—to let him have City blue as the colour theme to our wedding. After bargaining for four friends, I agreed. We all went to Titanic Spa in Huddersfield, which Michelle so kindly recommended, and split the remaining cost between the lot of us.

Darren and his mates, who are going to be suited and booted in morning wear, arranged to go to Moss Brothers in St. Anne's Square, Manchester, to order their suits. My dad was going to go on another day with Mum. He said he was too old for all that drinking malarkey. He's henpecked, and the hen he's pecked by said he had to go with her. I'm so glad the lads had a nine o'clock appointment on a Saturday morning, because by the time I picked Darren up in the Northern Quarter at five, he was hammered. Pre-stag do, he called it. Not that I can complain—we did exactly the same, only worse.

Darren has arranged to go on an activity weekend in Scotland for his stag do with twenty-three of his mates. They've arranged it for April just in case of any bruises or, God forbid, any broken bones. I can imagine Marc'll have some additional material for his best man's speech.

I'm brought out of my little daydream by Sonia's voice coming over the public-address system, reminding every-body about the Robbie tribute act starting at two.

At the far end of the pool from where we'd set up camp, Chrissy and Michelle came into view, laden with about half a dozen bags each of sexy goodies. Chrissy lifted her right arm up to acknowledge me, and Michelle smiled. I waved back. Soon it would be time for Michelle's first sex les-son, so I wouldn't have to wait too long before I could have a good nosey at what they'd bought. It was gonna be such a laugh. I hoped it wouldn't be too long before Frankie woke up, as she insisted in coming along as well. Chrissy goes into so much detail when talking about sex, and she handles those vibrators with such skill, if she does ever need to add a few extra pounds to her bank balance, she'd make a great Ann Summers rep or sex counsellor.

Sam, looking all refreshed and relaxed from her spa treatments and dressed in an black and white two-piece from Debenhams, plonked herself down on the lounger at the side of me. She ordered a coffee, whipped off her top, which gained a few smiles from the older blokes sitting close by, and promptly closed her eyes before having even one mouthful, but not before informing me she'd had extras with her massage off Jason. She never ever stops.

I was beginning to get rather restless now, lying on my lounger. I wanted to go back into the hotel to see what Chrissy and Michelle were up to. I couldn't sit quietly by and wait any longer for Frankie to wake up. I went into my bag and pulled out a bottle of water. I checked it, it wasn't too cold. I quickly opened the top and poured the lot onto Frankie to wake her up. I didn't want her to get too dehydrated. It was getting hot around the pool. *Killed two birds with one stone.* After Frankie had stopped screaming, I told her Chrissy and Michelle were back, and she better get a move on if she wanted to go and watch the sex lesson. After drying herself down, she slipped on her shorts, and we made our way towards the hotel.

TWENTY-FOUR

"Can we come in? You decent?" Frankie shouted, knocking on Chrissy's door.

"It's open," Chrissy shouted back.

We barged into the room, where we found both beds covered in a variety of sex toys and gadgets. I didn't even know what half of them were for. They also had a few pieces of underwear, not Chrissy's normal choice of designer ones, but cheap and tacky lacy knickers, bras, suspender belts, and stockings. Chrissy and Michelle were taking gulps of vodka, passing the bottle back and forth.

"Starting early, aren't you, Michelle?" I chuckled.

"Michelle needed a bit of Dutch courage," Chrissy answered.

"I need it, Helen…Ellie."

Wow! That was the first time she had ever called me Ellie. The relationship really had changed between us. I was happy we were going to be friends. I wanted Michelle to get to know Roxy and Izzy. Usually when we were in the same company, she'd just blanked them. It was awful. I wasn't bothered about me but my girls, what had they ever done to Michelle. It was going to be such a relief at family parties without that atmosphere anymore. And her posh accent hadn't returned, her Manchester accent was well and truly back. *Darren won't believe it when I tell him what's happened between me and Michelle.*

"You can't possibly intend to use all those toys today." Frankie's eye widened.

"We are not going to be using them all today. Jesus, Frankie, she'd be raw," Chrissy replied seriously. "Michelle can take them home with her to play. I just wanted her to have a look at what products are on offer."

"Couldn't you just have done that in the sex shop?" I asked.

"Oh no, I couldn't do it there—I was too embarrassed. I didn't know where to look. They had a blow-up doll with a removable vagina and arse, it said on the box. What sort of people go in them shops to buy something like that?" Michelle replied, her face going a deep scarlet. Bet she'd never used the word "arse" before.

"Saddos who can't get sex for free," Sam said as she walked in the room. "You can't leave me out of this one."

We watched as Michelle, encouraged by Chrissy, began to open the packets and boxes. The look on her face as she held a latex vibrator was memorable. She shuddered as her hand touched the shaft. Her body language was shouting for the floor to open up and swallow her whole. I looked towards Frankie and Sam, who were struggling to keep straight faces. I put my fist in my mouth to stop myself from laughing. We continued to watch like statues, frozen on our spots, as Michelle opened the packages. There was a penis ring, a selection of vibrators from the solid smooth variety to ribbed ones, and a small Rampant Rabbit with just the ears to tickle the clitoris. Next was something called a Box of Tricks including a small selection of sex toys and included a hand held remote control; I might look into getting one of them for myself. A strap-on? I hoped Chrissy wasn't intending to do the dirty with Michelle. It's no secret she's had sex with women before. I blamed that on her convent upbringing.

There were vibrating knickers, quite pretty actually—all lacy—vibrating nipple clamps, an array of creams and lotions in different flavours, and a selection of condoms. This lot could've kept all of us happy for a year.

"So come on, Dr. Ruth, where you gonna to start?" Sam asked.

"If you're not going to take this seriously, Sam," Frankie said, holding back the laughter, "you're going to have to leave."

"I want Michelle to spend time with the products, and then and only then, we can see what she feels comfortable with and get to work," Chrissy replied.

"If you're not going to use that," Sam said, "I'll leave right now with it." She pointed to the Box of Tricks, which I had my eye on.

"You can take it," Michelle said.

"Thanks, it looks fun. I'll be off, then. I expect a full briefing, girls." Sam blew us each a kiss as she left the room with a big grin on her face.

It wasn't only Michelle who was having a good poke around all this sex stuff. Frankie and I were, too.

"So what do you think, Michelle?" Chrissy asked.

"Chrissy, this is so embarrassing."

"You're amongst friends, Michelle—don't be embarrassed," Chrissy reassured her. "Look, if you wanted to learn how to cook, you'd buy a cookbook. If you wanted to learn to swim, you'd book yourself in for swimming lessons. So what's the problem with learning about sex and self-pleasuring? There are thousands of books and DVDs out there, even sex classes. You should make an appointment for you and Nigel to have a private counselling session. It's the prudes of this world that make sex a dirty word. Sex is the most natural thing in the world. By the time I've finished with you and Nigel, you're going to be begging each other for it."

"I'm really not sure I can do this, you know, put something up...there. Is it safe?"

Frankie couldn't help herself. She grabbed the strap on off the bed and tied it around her waist and held two vibrators on top of her head like horns and started charging around the room like a bull. I chased after her with the biggest black vibrator I've ever seen. I rugby tackled her, and we collapsed on the bed out of breath in fits of laughter.

"Will you two pack it in?" Chrissy threw a box of multifla-voured Durex condoms at us. "Of course it's safe, Michelle. I only purchased the best products. Just pick one."

"It's still a bit embarrassing." Michelle paused for a moment. "OK, then, I'll...try this Rampant Rabbit vibra-tor." Michelle picked it up and turned to me and Frankie. "I'm sorry, Ellie, Frankie, but I can't do it with everybody in the room."

"Right, clear off, you two. Now!"

"Aw, come on, please let us watch," Frankie said. "I'm a doctor."

"No, out." Chrissy playfully shooed us out of the room.

As the door closed behind us, we crouched down like two naughty schoolgirls and listened as events unfolded. First we heard the buzzing of the vibrator, followed by muffled voices.

"Get yourself comfy on the bed...Michelle, you've got to take your knickers off first. Put this gel on," Chrissy directed. "It will make it easier to insert. Have another swig of vodka."

"OK...Don't I need to put a condom on it?" Michelle asked.

I slapped my right hand across Frankie's mouth to stop her screaming out laughing. My left hand was slapped across mine. Did she really just say that?

"Why?" Chrissy asked. "You're not going to catch anything."

"Oh! I thought it, you know…it shot something out of the end, when it climaxed."

"It doesn't climax—it's you who climaxes, Michelle. It's not like one of those Tiny Tears dolls you had as a child, where you put something in one end and it splurted stuff out the other. The only thing you fill this baby with is three AA batteries, sweetie."

"This gel stuff is a bit sticky."

"Just slap it on, Michelle, and slide the vibrator in your vagina."

"Ooh, it's cold."

All went quiet. Frankie and I were still clutching our stomachs, trying to suppress the laughter that was so desperately trying to escape our mouths.

Suddenly the door opened, and we fell backwards into the room. Chrissy and Michelle were standing over us laughing. They had been winding us up.

We quickly picked ourselves up off the floor.

"One, we could hear you giggling. Two, Michelle isn't ready to do it yet. Did you really think I was going to stay in the room with her? We're going to have a chat. We thought it would be more polite to invite you in, instead of you being left outside crouching by the door. Just in case you had something to add." Chrissy smirked.

I was just a tad embarrassed. "Think we'll go back by the pool and catch some sun. Right, Frankie?"

"Sure, Ellie."

"Meet you down there in ten," Chrissy shouted after us as we made our way to the lift.

I took my place back on my sun lounger, still giggling, and took a sip of water. Frankie took one of Faith's cigarettes, lit it, and grabbed a magazine off the table before stretching out on her lounger, making herself comfy.

"How did the orgasm lesson go?" Faith asked.

"Still going on. We got caught out listening at the door. It was just the funniest thing." Frankie laughed. "Shall I order some drinks?"

"Good idea. Get a couple of bottles of Cava," I replied.

I spotted Chrissy coming out of the hotel, wearing a black swimsuit with a multicoloured sarong wrapped around her waist. Tinted aviator sunglasses protected her eyes from the sun. As usual, she turned heads as she made her way to join us. She sat herself down on the end of my lounger. Faith offered her a cigarette. She lit up.

"Where's your apprentice?" Faith asked.

"Hopefully having her first orgasm," Chrissy replied. "She'll be down soon. We had a good talk this morning she's had a bit of a rough life you know."

"What do you mean?" I asked. "She's come from a really nice family."

"Has Darren ever mentioned their Auntie May, their mum's oldest sister? Bit of a bitch, by all accounts."

"No, never."

"I am no therapist, but I think that is where all Michelle's problems stem from..."

Chrissy began to tell us about Michelle and Auntie May. When Michelle was about eight, their mum was being treated for breast cancer. I knew about their mum. Darren had told me that she had had a double mastectomy. Michelle was sent to live with Auntie May in Bury for about six months. Darren, being five years older, stayed at home with their dad. Auntie May had never been married. She was really strict, and nothing Michelle did was ever good enough. Auntie May drained all Michelle's confidence. She was put down at every opportunity and basically treated like a slave. It sounded like hell. Over the six months she lived with Auntie May, she very rarely saw her mum, and when she went back home and her mum found out what had been going on, her mum and Auntie May never spoke again. Auntie May died about ten years ago. Michelle has had problems with relationships ever since. There was loads more that Chrissy didn't want to go into, but that was the overview.

"Wow. I didn't know," I said. I felt sick to my stomach. I had a wonderful childhood. My mum and dad were strict but only to guide me and our Paul.

"She and Nigel haven't had any sexual contact for over ten years. They only sleep in the same bed, because she wants people to think they are a normal, happily married couple," Chrissy continued. "I truly believe she does love Nigel and wants to try and sort their marriage out, and if I can help, I will do. I do know she definitely doesn't want a divorce."

"It's going to take time though, Chrissy," Faith spoke. "Has she never had counselling?"

"Never, she's too proud. I've told her, she needs to like herself first and take it from there. She's a typical Cancerian, tough on the outside, bag of mush on the inside. Her life is just one big act. I feel for her."

I didn't know what to say. The waiter arrived with the two bottles of Cava Frankie had ordered and eight glasses. He popped open the bottles and began to pour as Sarah came back from her shopping trip.

"Did you get Maisy anything nice?" I asked.

"Yeah, I got her a little doll in a Spanish dress, a fan, and just the cutest flamenco dress, all tassels and lacy frills. Ooh…and matching red shoes with one-inch heels. She's gonna love playing dress-up in them. Here, have a look."

Sarah began to pass them around, and we oohed and aahed. They were really cute.

It took me back to when Roxy and Izzy were little, and they used to play dress-up. We couldn't afford to get them dresses from the Disney stores or like the one Sarah had bought for Maisy. They used to wear outfits my mum made for them. My mum wasn't the best seamstress, to be perfectly honest, and they looked more like the clothes Annie wore in the orphanage that Miss Hannigan provided. Mum could never get the tension right on the sewing machine, so the stitches were always pulled, the hems were never straight, and if there was a pattern on the material, it was never lined up, so I used to tell my girls they were playing dress-up in poor Cinderella's clothes.

It was beginning to get really busy around the pool when Michelle stopped by to pick up Chrissy, on her way to the spa to have her brows plucked and to get a much-needed leg and bikini wax. Michelle looked different. She had a spring in her step. Maybe it was the orgasm—nobody actually asked if she'd had one—or it could have been the amount of vodka she'd consumed. Or maybe it was just that she had been able to open up to Chrissy. One thing Chrissy was good at was getting people to talk. I struggled to look Michelle in the eye. I still couldn't believe what Chrissy had told us about their Auntie May, and I wondered what else could have happened to give her such a tough exterior. I'm not sure I wanted to know, but one thing I did know was that I was going to try really hard to build a relationship with Michelle.

The Robbie tribute and quiz was due to start in forty-five minutes. Faith suggested we pack up and meet in reception at two and go see what havoc we could cause in and around the streets of Benidorm. Frankie and I gathered all the magazines together; Sarah, Faith, and Jess picked up the towels from off our sun loungers; and we all made our way back into the hotel.

TWENTY-FIVE

A s usual, Sam and I were the last ones to arrive at reception. Everybody sat amongst the fine arts and cream
decor waiting for us. It was Sam's fault, not mine. As I
opened the door of the room we were sharing, moans
and groans greeted me. She was in the last throes of a
self-induced orgasm accompanied by the bullet vibrator
from the Box of Tricks she took from Chrissy's room earlier.
She slowly moved off the bed, as naked as the day she was
remodelled at the Bridgewater Hospital, Manchester, and
winked at me as she went into the bathroom to shower.

Sam never ceased to amaze me. Any one of the hotel
staff could have walked into the room. She hadn't even
bothered to put the DO NOT DISTURB sign on the door handle
to warn them—or me, for that matter. Not that she'd have
cared much if someone did walk in. It's not like it was the
first time I'd caught Sam self-pleasuring or having sex; in
fact, it's perfectly normal behaviour for Sam. I don't blush
anymore when it happens.

I quickly undressed, throwing my bikini on the pile of
clothes that was growing next the dressing table. I put on a

clean pair of blue denim shorts and an orange vest T-shirt. I gave my hair a quick brush through and tied it up into a knot on the top of my head with a scrunchie. Sam was shouting to me all the time she was showering about the bullet, telling me I'd have to get one. The uneven surface of the shaft felt amazing against her clit, she informed me, and then continued to give me the lowdown on the rest of the products contained in the Box of Tricks. Maybe I'll nip out in the morning and grab one before I went home. Sam kindly offered to lend me hers, but I draw the line at sharing sex toys.

Wrapped in a bath towel, Sam slowly walked towards to the balcony, rubbing her hair dry with a hand towel. She opened the doors, and the outside heat gently snuck into the room, keeping the chill of the air conditioning off me. I told Sam she had to hurry and get dressed, as Faith had gone into mother mode again and wanted us to get something to eat—she had fears we were all going to die of malnutrition or something like that. Sam could sit on the balcony and spy on all the guys when we got back.

We headed off in the direction of the beach, walking swiftly pass the Irish bar. I didn't want to bump into Jerry today. I needed to get all thoughts of him out of my head. Earlier, as I lay on the lounger, my daydreaming consisted of Darren and our wedding for about ten minutes and the rest of the time of Jerry and only Jerry. I went all tingly remembering the heat of his breath on my neck yesterday in the bar as he leant across me, passing out the drinks on the tray he was carrying. Wow...he had a great smile, and his teeth—he could have walked straight out of a toothpaste commercial. I like to see a man who looks after his teeth.

We survived the walk from the hotel to the beach, only getting attacked a handful of times by the mobility-scooter mob. Faith again threatened to slash their tyres if they came anywhere near us.

As we approached Levante Beach, we saw a crowd had gathered along one section. We quickly walked over to find out what the attraction was. The crowd were watching a young Spanish guy creating a sand sculpture. He'd already sculpted a horse, some kind of Greek god, mountains, and mermaids. I looked on in amazement at what he'd achieved with just a pile of sand and a few buckets of water. I struggled when we went to Blackpool with Roxy and Izzy to make a decent sand castle and moat. I never seemed to get the consistency right. That's probably one of the reasons why I can't bake a cake: the consistency.

"Hey, I've got an idea," Frankie said. "Jess, Faith, go over there to that shop and buy some buckets and spades. We're gonna do our own sand sculpture."

"You're mad," Faith replied.

"Go!" Frankie shouted. "Chrissy, Sarah, go buy some beers. It's going to be thirsty work, creating."

The rest of us followed Frankie onto the beach.

"OK, Mrs. Picasso, what do you suggest we make?" Sam asked.

"The biggest penis and balls you have ever seen."

"What did you say?" I said.

"You heard," Frankie replied.

Faith, Sarah, and Chrissy rejoined us with our supplies.

"Guess what we're making," I shouted.

"Go on, shock us," Faith said.

"Penis and balls." Michelle struggled to contain herself.

"I bet you don't see many of them sculptured along here," Chrissy said. "Well, not during the day, you don't. I was down here last night, and there were people having sex all over the place. It was like one big gang bang. Even the pensioners were at it."

"Have you got a model lined up, Frankie, or are we doing it from memory?" Sam asked.

"Sam, we'll go off your memory. I'm sure you've seen more than the rest of us," Frankie replied.

"Oh, and by the way, Chrissy, I heard about you giving some greasy gringo a hand job to get out of paying your taxi fare. Well, hand jobs don't count as sex in the bet. Sex is sex, not hand jobs," Sam informed her.

Frankie organised us into groups and gave instructions as if she was delivering a presentation, and then off we went. Frankie drew the outline of the penis and balls in the sand with the end of a spade, it must have been at least twenty foot in length, and the rest of us started to shape it by filling the buckets with sand and building it up. Jess and Faith took it in turns to go to the sea and fill up buckets with water to help set the sculpture.

It didn't take long before we started to attract a crowd of our own. Chrissy spotted Mike and the rest of the firemen.

"What you making?" one of them shouted.

"Can't you tell? Penis and balls," Chrissy said.

"Do you want me to model for you?" Mike shouted.

"Wouldn't want you to feel inadequate, love, best keep it in your shorts," Faith replied.

"Aren't you going to stick up for me, Chrissy?"

"Do I know you?" She smiled back at him.

"Sarah, aren't you warm? You've had your cardigan on all day," Jess asked.

"No, I'm fine. It's only thin," she replied.

We chatted along whilst Frankie walked up and down, blasting out her instructions, making sure we were getting the right shape, and taking photographs of our little holiday project. Sam and Chrissy ran off to get more beers. It was thirsty work, this creativity.

"I can't wait for my hen party," Jess said, digging the sand and putting it into her bucket.

"Alan's got to leave his wife first and get a divorce before you can get married, Jess," Faith chirped.

"Why do you always have to put a dampener on things, Faith? You're like a dripping tap…annoying. I keep telling you, Alan will be getting a divorce soon, he's waiting till the end of the year when his son will have left college. He doesn't want to upset him during his exams and getting ready for uni. I've told you all this."

"I know…you're like a broken record, going over and over and over the same line…He's taking the piss, Jess. He's not going to leave his wife. He's a wimp."

"He's not a wimp. He's a caring man who wants to leave his wife without causing any upset."

Faith continued. "Jess, wake up, you're wasting your time on him. I just want you to be realistic. You've been with him for how many years now? You need to accept that it's going nowhere. You're not going to have any change in your life for ages yet. I've done your charts."

"Faith, why do you always have to be so negative? Not every relationship is going to end like yours. It will happen one day. Alan loves me. And stop doing my bloody charts! They never come true, anyway."

The sculpture was now beginning to take shape. I bet nobody had ever made a penis and balls like ours before on Levante Beach. The firemen were still watching us, as were the lads from the Oldham rugby club, with pints in their hands. We were all in good spirits. Frankie was now running back and forth to the sea, gathering water with Jess. Faith rushed to an ice cream bar and grabbed a load of straws. She wanted to use them as hairs around the balls, very creative. I noticed some of the girls from Liverpool watching. I waved them over to help, which they did without any hesitation.

"Oh! Oh! Look who's coming," Sarah exclaimed, pointing in the direction of the promenade.

"Who?" I said looking up, taking a quick break from my digging.

"The police are on the way over," Sarah continued.

We looked towards the young officer making his way in our direction.

"Leave 'em alone," one of the bystanders shouted to him.

"Oh shit, how can we get arrested in Spain for this?" I said.

"Don't worry, leave it to me," Sam said. "Keep working, girls."

She stood up and rubbed the sand off her legs as she made her way towards the officer. He smiled as she greeted him like an old friend.

"What's she saying?" Sarah asked.

"No idea, but it's working. They're walking off the beach together," Faith replied.

"I'll go and see what's going on." I quickly walked in their direction, closely followed by Chrissy.

The police car was parked up on the promenade with its blue-and-red lights flashing. We saw Sam and the officer sit in the front seats of the car chatting; suddenly Sam's head disappeared out of sight into his lap, and the car began to shake.

"I can see she has this situation well and truly under control." Chrissy smiled. "Come on, let's go back and finish off. And remind me to tell her that doesn't count in the sex bet, either."

We'd done it. Our sculpture was finished. We took our bows and accepted the rapturous applause from the crowd that had gathered. Even the young Spanish guy who was sculpting next to us came over to have a look. Faith asked Mike to take some pictures of us, just as Sam rushed back in to join us.

"I think that's enough excitement for one afternoon. Can you believe we nearly got arrested? How cool would that have been?" Frankie gushed. "We need to find a bar now. Come on, let's go to the Irish bar and see if that Jerry's around."

"I fancy a walk around here. Anybody coming with me?" I didn't want to go anywhere near Jerry; I didn't think I could trust myself, not after what Sam said.

We split up into two groups. Frankie, Faith, and Sarah set off in the direction of the Irish bar, and the rest of us moved in the opposite direction along the beachfront to have a mooch around. We call into a few of the bars along the front, where people were destroying some of the best songs ever written with karaoke, playing bingo, and taking part in pub quizzes. Some were serving afternoon tea, advertised with real Devon cream.

It was Sam's idea to have a different drink in every bar we came upon. Michelle got right into the swing of things.

We left the promenade and headed down one of the side streets full of even more gift shops and stopped outside a tattoo studio and stared in the window at some of the artwork. It was amazing.

"Who fancies getting a souvenir?" Chrissy asked.

"You don't mean…" I replied.

"Certainly do, sweetie. Come on, who's up for getting a tattoo?"

"I don't think so," Michelle exclaimed.

"I'm up for it," Sam said.

"Me too, come on." Jess led the way.

"Oh, I can't," Michelle repeated.

I followed along, speechless. What would my girls and Darren say if I went back home with another tattoo?

The walls of the studio were full of even more designs. It looked more like an art gallery than a tattoo studio… it was fantastic. It looked pretty clean; I could even smell the disinfectant. It still didn't convince me to have one, though.

"Alright, ladies. Rambo…tattooist. Anything I can do for you today?" he asked in a broad Manchester accent. My eyes were glued to the exposed parts of his skin that were displaying his own works of art, with the designs flowing flawlessly around his body. There were skulls, dragons, women, and snakes, to name but a few.

"Not sure, Rambo. What we having, girls?" Chrissy smirked.

"We haven't really thought this through, Rambo. Sorry." I nervously smiled.

"What about something simple on our bum cheeks?" Sam said, looking over her shoulders and pointing first to her left buttock, then to her right. "How about a pair of bright-red lips?"

"Are we not going to talk about this?" I spoke louder.

"As long as they are not Mick Jagger's lips. I know I've got a big arse"—Jess laughed—"but it's not that big."

"Am I talking to myself?" I spoke louder.

"Elle, shush…I'm concentrating." Sam waved as if dismissing me.

"What about something like this?" Rambo walked behind his desk, took hold of a pencil and paper and drew a set of lips, pouting. Sam watched closely as he doodled away.

"Perfect. What do you say, girls? Elle?" Sam pouted.

They could be her lips; she was always pouting. Just point a camera and pout…that's our Sam. Did I really want Sam's lips on my arse forever? All eyes were on me.

"Oh, what the hell…" I answered.

What was I thinking? I'm just glad I'd had one too many. Hopefully it would help numb the pain a little as the needle, guided skilfully by the tattooist, danced around my bum to create a pair of pouting red lips. Sam climbed on to the couch first and lay face down. She slowly wiggled her shorts and thong down just far enough to expose both her bum cheeks and chatted all the time to Rambo as she was having her tattoo done.

Rambo came from Gorton and had lived in Spain for eight years with his Spanish girlfriend, Ariadna, whom he'd met in Benidorm whilst on a lads' holiday nine years ago. Rambo was a nickname given to him at school because he really enjoyed outdoor activities and bodybuilding. His real name was Rick. He was thirty-five and had gone to

Wright Robbie, where I had met Andy, my ex. I was going to join in the conversation and tell him all this, but every time I tried to speak, my mouth just went drier and drier at the thought of the tattoo.

Sam also had gone to Wright Robbie and enjoyed reminiscing about her school days with him. She never once flinched whilst Rambo left his mark on her. The sound of the buzzing needle was making me feel sick, the kind of sick I only usually have when I'm sitting in the dentist's chair, in anticipation of the needle being thrust into my gum. I stood by an upright fan in the corner of the room and tried to cool myself down. My heart was pounding ten to the dozen.

Rambo slapped a bit of cling film on top of the tattoo when he'd finished and taped it securely in place. I looked at the clock. Was it only fifteen minutes since Sam got on the couch? That was the longest fifteen minutes ever. Chrissy went next, then Jess. I went last, putting it off as long as I could.

"Come on, sweetie, have one. It'll liberate you," Chrissy said to Michelle.

"No, I'll pass, thanks. Shouldn't we get back to the others? They'll be wondering where we are."

"Don't worry, they can survive without us," Chrissy said. "Come on, Michelle, when was the last time you ever did anything spontaneous? I don't mean this morning; that was planned."

"Well, never. I'm not that sort of person."

"Michelle, get your knickers off, get on that table, and do it today. Let Nigel see you're a changed woman." Sam chuckled.

Michelle gave me a look of panic that shouted, "Help me, Ellie!" I shrugged. I couldn't help her with that decision; it was up to her. She would never do it.

"OK, I'll do it," she said. She removed her linen pants, took her knickers off, and climbed on the table.

You could have knocked me down with a feather. "Michelle, don't let them bully you into it. You don't have to," I said feeling a bit guilty I didn't speak up a few minutes ago. "And you didn't have to take your knickers off."

"No, I'll get a tattoo." She started to laugh hysterically. "Come on, Rambo, before I change my mind."

Considering Michelle had never had a tattoo before, she handled it pretty well and didn't even flinch. She's a lot tougher than I give her credit for. As for me, on the other hand, you could have heard me squealing back in Manchester. I'm such a wimp. Sam had to hold my hand the whole time. To me it felt like childbirth all over again. The last tattoo I'd had, of an angel on my wrist, hadn't hurt at all. I used some of the numbing cream they use on children when they give them injections in hospital. Frankie got it for me.

Chrissy somehow managed to use some hypnotic power over Michelle. Michelle was a different person, she was, well, normal, and she was smiling all the time. Her face looked completely different as well, now that she had two eyebrows instead of one, and the red waxing mark had disappeared.

After paying thirty euros each for our newly acquired tattoos, we called into a couple more bars before heading back to our hotel to get geared up for our fancy-dress night of fun in Benidorm. I couldn't wait to see what fun we were gonna have with them handcuffs and truncheons.

TWENTY-SIX

Faith, Frankie, and Sarah had a little picnic going on out on the balcony of Faith's room. Empty Stella bottles graced the table, accompanied by an overflowing ashtray full of cigarette dimps. The floor had a couple of empty packets of Monster Munch Ham & Cheese crisps and a couple of Subway wrappers. Faith had just finished reading Frankie's cards, and before she had a chance to tell us what the future held for her, Sam got her tattoo out to show the girls what they'd been missing. Frankie couldn't believe we'd gone off and had a tattoo without her, so Jess promised she'd take her in the morning to get one. Faith and Sarah decided not to bother. Faith set off in mother mode and began to lecture us all on hygiene standards, which was well too late as we'd already had the tattoos. Chrissy told her so, but it still didn't stop her lecturing.

Time was pressing on, and we'd already agreed earlier to go out around eight. Sarah gathered up her belongings and went back to her room to get some sleep. Michelle said she just had to try out another one of them vibrators and left, followed by Chrissy, who was going to have a nice long soak in the bath.

Sam and I headed back to our room, where Sam went straight to the dressing table and poured out two vodka and Cokes. My face said it all...I couldn't drink it. All I wanted was to drink lots of water and get my head down for a couple of hours before getting ready to go out. Sam walked out onto the balcony, taking both drinks with her.

I lay on my bed, tossing and turning, my mind flitting from one thing to another. Every time I closed my eyes, the bed started spinning, and when I'd open them, thoughts of Jerry came into my mind, followed quickly by Darren. Sam walked back into the room, grabbed the bottle of vodka, and walked out, saying something about going into Faith's with Frankie; they never stopped. This lot would give the lads from *The Hangover* a run for their money.

I woke to hear Sam singing Donna Summer's "Love to Love You, Baby," sound effects included, in the shower. I looked at my watch. Seven o'clock, still warm.

"You having fun in there, Sam?"

"Oh! Sleeping Beauty's finally awake. You don't half snore, you know."

"I never do!" I exclaimed as I walked into the bathroom holding my head.

"You do. I have evidence, just in case I ever need a bit of something to blackmail you with in the future." Sam laughed.

"You gonna be long?" I leant into the shower and turned the tap towards cold.

"You bitch!" Sam screamed. "Not now, I'm not."

"Good." I giggled. "How's your bum?"

"Great, yours?"

"OK." I laughed at the thought of having Sam's lips following me around for the rest of my life.

It was gonna be a good night, I knew it. The party was well underway, and we hadn't even left our hotel rooms yet. All our bedroom doors were wide open, and the drinks were out. Faith had her iPod at full volume, and we were all joining in with the songs along the corridor—a bit of Bryan Adams's "Summer of '69," Bon Jovi's "Living on a Prayer"—and you can't help but dance around to Banarama's "Venus." They're always good songs to get the party started. Jess came bouncing into our room in her full fancy-dress outfit, waving her truncheon around in the air, singing "Let's Get Ready to Rumble" by PJ and Duncan. Faith followed closely behind her. We all joined in.

"Hey, going for the lesbian look, Faith, nice," Sam commented.

Faith ran a hand across her gelled, scraped-back hair. "Lesbian look! Don't you like it? I saw it in a magazine. I thought it looked nice."

"Sorry, I thought as you'd had no luck with blokes in Benidorm, you were gonna be heading to the gay part of town later to try your luck there. An orgasm is an orgasm after all, Faith." Sam laughed.

"Cheeky bitch," Faith replied. "If you'd shut your legs for five minutes, then maybe the rest of us would stand a chance."

"Speak for yourself, Faith. I don't want sex. I've got Alan," Jess said.

"I've got Alan," Faith mimicked her.

I know it's not possible for anybody to change in a day, but Michelle—wow. Me, Faith, Jess, and Sam nearly collapsed when she walked into our room dressed for our night on the town. I had to do a double-take—in fact, a double double-take.

As promised Chrissy had done her makeup, all smoky eyes, false eyelashes, and a Chanel deep-red lipstick. Michelle was persuaded to throw her black-rimmed glasses, which did her face no favours, in the bin and put contact lenses in. She had straightened her shoulder-length frizzy dark hair, and she looked younger and happier by the minute.

Michelle was wearing one of Chrissy's white long-sleeved cotton blouses with the sleeves turned up and tied in a knot around her waist and Sam's black leather skirt and black court shoes. With her newfound confidence, she wasn't shy about showing a bit of cleavage in one of Frankie's Wonderbras. I gave her a pair of fishnet tights, and with the handcuffs and truncheon, she wouldn't have any problems arresting anybody tonight.

A WORK IN PROGRESS sign really needed to be hung around Michelle's neck, as her transformation wasn't going to happen overnight, but she knew that. Chrissy enlightened Michelle with her wisdom and knowledge, informing her she wouldn't get her life back on track until she felt better about herself, and boy, did she look better.

Chrissy was buzzing about the new image she had created for Michelle and couldn't contain the excitement. Michelle, she explained, had tried out yet another one of the newly acquired sex toys—the one with the Rampant Rabbit ears. "She took herself off into the bathroom and was oohing and aahing like I've never heard anybody ooh and aah before." Now we understood why Michelle was smiling so much.

Chrissy had another surprise in store for Michelle. She had convinced her to wear some remote-control vaginal balls whilst we were out. I didn't even know a piece of equipment like that had been invented. I'm glad Darren doesn't know about them. He'd have me jigging about the house wearing them all the time.

The music and our laughter gained the attention of other guests around the hotel. A group of male pensioners stopped by to see what the commotion was. At first they thought we were British policewomen, until they noticed the stockings and suspenders. We invited them to join us in our rooms and offered them a drink, but they refused. One of them blamed a bad heart, and another said he hadn't got a bad heart, but his heart was pumping so fast at the sight of all the stockings and suspenders on display he felt as if he might have a heart attack any moment. Frankie did say she was a doctor and Faith was a nurse, but that still didn't convince them. Before leaving they asked if they could have some photos taken with us, and we duly obliged. Jess just had to get her boobs out. "It's gotta be done!" she shouted.

As Sam was about to put on the last remaining false eyelash to complete my makeup, we heard Frankie screaming at the top of her voice. We turned to look at each other and dashed out of our room, followed quickly by Jess and Faith. Frankie was frozen in the doorway of her bathroom still screaming, arms waving in the air.

"What the fucking hell? Sarah! What the hell are those marks?"

No answer…

"Sarah, don't ignore me, girl. What the fuck?"

"Get out!" Sarah bawled.

"Not a fucking chance—not till you tell me what's going on."

I pushed my way past Frankie and saw what Frankie was screaming about. Sarah's back was covered in bruising and scratches, some old, some new. The only time I had ever come close to seeing anything like this was when my brother Paul came off his motorbike when he'd been scrambling, and he was in agony.

"Get out and leave me alone," Sarah begged.

"Sarah," I said calmly. "Where'd you get those marks from?"

"Hey, what's going on in here? We're having no falling out," Faith said.

"Fuck off!" Sarah screeched. "Get out of my room. It's got nothing to do with you lot. I don't have to tell you anything."

"I beg to differ, our kid," Faith cried as she barged into the bathroom.

Sarah slowly pulled herself up out of the bath, knowing we were all watching her. Marks were now noticeable on her arms and legs as well. She grabbed hold of a large fluffy bath towel and wrapped it around her body as she climbed out.

"Move!" Sarah pushed past us and walked into the bedroom, leaving wet footprints on the bedroom carpet.

"Look at the state of her fucking body. I knew it!" Faith ranted.

"You don't know anything, Faith," I said, trying to calm things down.

"Please, will you just leave me alone?" Sarah said softly.

"Not a fucking chance." Faith slowly walked towards her sister.

"Will you all stop yelling at me? I'm sick of people yelling at me all the time." Sarah raised her voice. She looked Faith straight in the eye. There was so much hate and anger there. "OK, then, Faith, what do you want me to say? Yes, you're right. My bastard husband beats me. There, I've said it." She threw the towel covering her delicate frame to the ground. "Go on, then—have a good look, why don't ya?" With arms outstretched she turned around slowly.

We stood like statues, eyes welling up at the sight of our beautiful, quiet friend, whose husband had been using her body as a punch bag, turning it into a mass of black, blue, brown, and orange. Oh! He'd been very clever not to mark her face and hands; all the marks and bruises were on her body. That's why she'd been covering herself up. Deep down we had known something was going on with her and Jimmy, but I would never have imagined physical abuse. Now I understood why she'd been driving us all away, never letting us go around to her house. I felt terrible, and I knew the other girls were feeling exactly the same as I was.

"Happy now? Had a good look, have you?" Sarah snapped.

"Happy now? Happy—I want to smash the fucking bastard's head in," Faith said.

"Faith, calm down," Sam said.

"Calm down?" Faith started stamping around the room.

"Sarah, we need to talk." I walked over, picked her towel up off the floor, and wrapped it around her tiny frame.

"I want to get ready to go out. I don't want to talk," Sarah protested.

"No fucking way," Faith said.

Chrissy and Michelle entered the room, with no need to ask what all the shouting was about.

"Is this a peep show?" Sarah shouted.

"Why didn't you tell me? I'm your sister. You could have come and talked to me, to any of us. You can't stay with him now. I won't let you." Faith had tears streaming down her face.

"I *can* stay with him. I have got a five-year-old daughter, no job, and no money. What am I supposed to do, live on the streets in a sodding cardboard box?"

"You can stay with me. You know you can," Faith said and put her arms around her sister.

"I can't stay with you, Faith. Your life's a mess. And besides, your Charlie is moving back in with you whilst she has baby number three." Sarah sobbed and pushed Faith away. "He doesn't mean to hurt me. It's just when he gets stressed, he takes it out on me."

"Don't they all." Chrissy sighed. "Well, I for one have heard and seen enough. Sarah, you and Maisy are moving in with me. That's the end of it. And don't you worry about money. If it's an issue for you, I'll employ you if that'll make you happy. You're not going back to Jimmy, and that's final. If I have to kidnap you, I will. You will only be returning to your home to collect Maisy and your belongings. And if he objects, I will have him killed. Don't think I won't."

Sarah sat on the edge of the bed, sobbing.

"Everybody out. I need to examine Sarah. You go and get ready, and we'll meet in the bar in half an hour. Ellie can you stay—I need you to take pictures." Frankie the doctor spoke now, not Frankie the friend.

"I'm going nowhere," Faith said.

"Faith, move." Chrissy took hold of her hand and gently teased her out of the room.

The room emptied as quickly as it had filled.

"I need a drink. Pass me that bottle of vodka, Frankie," I said. "Sarah, want one?"

She shook her head.

"I do." Frankie took a large swig out of the bottle and passed it to me to do the same.

"Sarah." Frankie spoke quietly. "I'm sorry for shouting, I really am. I'm not going to ask you to talk about what's been going on, but if you want to—"

Sarah interrupted with her head in her hands. "Frankie, Ellie, I don't know where to start." She lifted her head and again shook it. "It's been going on for that long now, it's just normal. I've wanted to say something for, oh! I don't know. How could I have let this happen to me, Ellie?"

"It's not your fault, Sarah." I put my arms around her weak body to try and offer some comfort, which to be honest was more for my benefit than hers.

Sarah continued. "It got worse when I was pregnant with Maisy." She slowly released herself from me. "Remember when I was rushed to hospital not long after I found out I was pregnant? Jimmy pushed me down the stairs; he wanted rid of the baby. He didn't want us to have kids. He wanted me all to himself." She quietly sobbed. "Until he realised if I had a child, I'd be tied to the house, and he'd have even more control over me. He wanted us to have another baby. We've been trying for three years—well, he has. I got this last bashing because I couldn't get pregnant. He called me so many names, and when he decided his fist wasn't enough, he took his belt off to me. What he didn't know was I had a coil fitted about two years ago, that's why I haven't been able to get pregnant. Do you think I'm awful, Frankie? But how could I bring another child into the world, when I'm struggling to look after myself and the child I have already? If he ever found out, he'd kill me."

My eyes were releasing tiny tears for my beautiful friend. "Well, it's over now," I said, and I meant it.

"You know I always wanted a big family, Ellie. I feel so sorry for Maisy not having a brother or sister, but I just couldn't get pregnant, not again."

"You did the right thing," Frankie said comfortingly. "Can I examine you, just to make sure you are OK?"

"No, I'm fine, Frankie. Jim hasn't hit me since last Saturday. The physical stuff doesn't bother me—it's the mental stuff I have to take off him. I'm glad it's in the open, though. I actually feel relieved because I know it'll stop now, but I can't leave him and go to Chrissy's. I need to sort this out on my own."

Frankie and I gave each other a puzzled look.

"My heart is breaking for you, Sarah, it really is. You don't deserve this. You know that, don't you? But you have to go with Chrissy," I said.

"Can we talk about this later? I want to get ready to go out."

"Are you sure?" Frankie asked. "I don't mind staying in with you."

"Are you kidding? I've waited years for tonight, and if I don't go out, Jimmy will have won again by ruining this weekend for me. I'm not going to let him spoil another day of my life."

"OK, then, Sarah, if you're sure," I said.

"I'm sure, Ellie. Please, I want to go out."

"OK, I'll leave you both to finish off getting ready." I gave them each a kiss and returned to my room.

All the girls were in my room when I returned, everybody was trying to calm Faith down.

"I'm glad it's out," Faith said, sitting on my bed. "I hate him, and at this moment, I want to kill him, the tosser. I'm so glad we're in Benidorm. If I were at home right now, I'd go round their house and knife him. How could he do that to her? She wouldn't hurt a fly. She even catches spiders in cups and puts them outside. She is the nicest, kindest person you could ever wish to meet."

"Faith, will you give me that vodka?" Sam said. "I want to make a drink."

"Get another—I'm keeping hold of this." She took another swig.

I grabbed it off her. "You've got to calm down, or Jim's won. Look, we need to get ready. Sarah wants to go out," I said simply. "Faith, you need to go back to your room and finish getting ready, and try to leave it now with Sarah. She doesn't want to spoil tonight. Chrissy, it's great she's going to go and stay with you. She's just said she's not, but we'll sort that out before we leave tomorrow."

Chrissy smiled. "Sarah is such a proud lady. That's why she never asked for help. It should never have got to this. Come on, then, let's get this show on the road and see what fun we can attract with these truncheons and hand-cuffs." Chrissy turned to Michelle. "Are you coming? Meet you downstairs in the bar in fifteen minutes."

Sam finished off putting my false eyelashes in place whilst I filled her in with the details of Sarah and her abuse. I didn't get it. How could a person say they love you and want to take care of you for the rest of your life, yet want to harm you and fill your life with so much cruelty?

I had actually envied Sarah when she first told me Jim wanted her to be a stay-at-home mum and that she wasn't going back to work after she'd had her baby. I remember when I went back to work after I had Roxy, then Izzy. I was so tired; most of the time I functioned on autopilot. Every time I put the lottery on, I would pray we would win just enough for me to be able to pack in my job and not go back to work. I think I must have been the only person on the planet who didn't want to win millions; I just wanted to stay at home with my children. Never did I even contemplate that Jim wanted Sarah to become a virtual prisoner in her own home, and all this time, she never said one word to anybody.

"Darren will never speak to Jim again. He's gonna kill him…what a mess."

"What a weekend this is turning into," Sam replied. "What with Michelle's frigging marriage problems, Libby disappearing with Marco the stallion, and now Sarah, I need another drink. Can't be doing with all this personal stuff."

TWENTY-SEVEN

I smiled as I looked in the mirror at the crisp short-sleeved white shirt and black-and-white tie, I was wearing. The tie had an elastic band that went over my head and underneath my collar, just like a child would wear before they learned how to tie a proper tie. A black miniskirt, black stockings, suspenders, and three-inch stiletto heels were topped off with a replica policewoman's hat, plastic handcuffs, and a truncheon purchased from Claire's accessories. I looked so good that maybe I should have joined the police force. I was *so* gonna dress up for Jerry—*What!* I meant Darren—when I got home. It seemed a shame to waste this outfit. God, my mind was all over the place.

All dressed in our police outfits, we lined up in reception to have a group photograph taken by one of the hotel staff. If anybody asked why Libby wasn't in the pictures, we agreed to say she had been the photographer. Hotel guests gathered around us to join in the fun. Sam, Chrissy, Frankie, and Michelle were wearing similar outfits as mine, and the rest of the girls had trousers on. Chrissy brought along the handcuffs that had belonged to the ex-copper she'd dated, and her truncheon for tonight was going to be the big black vibrator Michelle bought this morning, as she'd lent the one she brought for herself to Michelle. One of the ladies staying at the hotel asked if she could have a picture taken with us, and when Chrissy gave her the vibrator to hold, she didn't want to give it back. She had never held one, let alone used one, which made us laugh all the more.

We didn't stop in the hotel for food. We decided to grab a bite whilst we were out. There were so many places to eat, nobody would ever die of hunger in Benidorm, and besides we didn't want to waste any more time in the hotel as we'd only managed to visit a couple of bars last night. So armed with my list of bars and clubs recommended off Trip Advisor and the street map I grabbed off reception, we headed out to find the Star and Garter, Café Benidorm, Sinatra's, Sandra's, the Red Lion, and many more.

We spotted Jerry outside his bar, smoking. He waved to acknowledge us; we noisily waved back and carried on walking in the direction of the Star and Garter.

I'd not seen Jerry today, but he was still heavy on my mind, and seeing him standing there smoking made my body shiver. I wondered if something should have happened between us. I quickly shook the thought from my mind.

As we made our way through the brightly lit streets of Benidorm, we were enticed into a couple of bars with offers of free shots. The first bar we stopped in had a comedian halfway through his routine, getting heckled by the lads from the Oldham rugby club. It only stopped when the comedian called the bouncers over to eject the lads. We walked out with them, laughing as we went. Some people can be so touchy. The next bar we all walked into had a singer on stage by the name of Suzi Gee, who was belting out eighties and nineties tunes, and with that being our era, we quickly joined in with the singing and dancing. When we walked into the third bar, we were immediately lined up on stage by the comedian. He wanted to make us part of his act, but it didn't take him long to ask security to remove us from the bar. I don't think he liked what Chrissy wanted to do to him with her truncheon, as she was trying to get his pants down. When I grabbed the mike off him and started singing "Like a Virgin" acappella, I think that was the final straw. We went down well with the audience, though. Glad to know we still had it. Frankie moaned all the way to the next bar, as she wanted to go back and complain that we never got our free shots.

We finally came to Café Benidorm and were welcomed, as we walked in, by the firemen, dressed in normal attire tonight, I was pleased to note. Mike quickly made his way over to Chrissy and offered to buy her a drink, and the rest of us headed over to the bar and bought fishbowl-size cocktails. The place was a bit dark and dingy and in need of having a few quid spent on it, but it was in full swing, with people from every age group dancing away to music from across the sixties up to the present.

Frankie was approached by a group of German lads on a lads' weekend. One of them kept trying to knock her hat off her, which she wasn't too happy about. The lads from Newcastle, who I hadn't even noticed in the place, went to her rescue, and it looked at first like it might be getting out of hand until the bouncers calmed things down. I waved to the girls we had met the previous night from Ireland, and they dragged us up with them to do the conga when Kylie Minogue started singing "The Locomotion."

Sarah looked so happy, the best I'd seen her in years. She was dancing with some of the firemen and having the time of her life, singing along to "Dancing Queen" by ABBA. Steve caught Frankie's eye, and she went over and spoke to him.

I spied Chrissy, Sam, and Jess huddled in a corner. They were up to something, I knew it. I continued dancing to ABBA as I crossed the dance floor to investigate.

"What's going on?" I asked.

They were having trouble speaking through laughing.

"What you doing?" I asked again.

"Watch Michelle at the bar," Chrissy panted. "We've sent her over to talk to that man, to work on her confidence now she's had a few more drinks."

I turned to see Michelle wiggling about quite awkwardly. Why did she keep crossing her legs in front of each other, as if she needed a pee, trying to make conversation with a bloke in a floral shirt and knee-length denim shorts?

That shirt alone would have made it hard for me to concentrate on a conversation with him.

"What's so funny?" I pleaded.

"Look." Sam lifted up her right hand. "We've got the remote control for them love balls she's wearing. We keep changing the settings. Any minute now, she's gonna be screaming like a banshee."

The people standing on either side of Michelle started to give her strange looks, as she kept banging into them. We could see the concentration on her face as she tried to keep the conversation going.

"Did she know you were going to do it now?" I asked.

"No, but she knew it was going to happen sometime tonight, and now seemed as good a time as any." Chrissy giggled.

"E'are, give us a go, Sam." I put my hand out, and Sam gave me the controls. I looked down at the buttons, first placing it on slow. Michelle gently panted as if trying to catch her breath. Then I moved it up a notch or two for about fifteen seconds and then back down, just so she could catch her breath again. Michelle looked straight at me and giggled. Then I flicked it on full. She started dancing and screaming like a madwoman, all the time looking around. She spotted what she was looking for—the toilet—in the corner. She ran off, quickly followed by Chrissy. The bloke Michelle had been talking to at the bar looked stunned. Sam, Jess, and I collapsed on the floor in helpless laughter, which then turned into hysteria. I finally remembered to put the dial to the off position.

"I'm gonna wet myself." Sam chuckled.

"I already have." Jess was howling. "That was just the funniest thing. I've not even got a spare TENA Lady on me."

"I know what you mean. I think I may have peed, too," I replied.

Faith waved to us from the dance floor; she'd got all cosy with a guy who had had more than a couple to drink and was rubbing his hands up and down her body, as they gyrated to the dance medley from *Dirty Dancing*. When Patrick Swayze put her down, she came over, bent down, and spoke to Sam. Sam nodded and managed to pull herself up off the floor clutching her stomach, still laughing.

"We've been here long enough now. Think we should try to find one of them other bars on your list, Ellie," Faith announced.

"Are you sure, Faith? It looked like you were having a good time with Patrick Swayze there," I replied, tears still streaming down my cheeks.

"No problem," Faith said. "I've got his number. If I can't do any better, I'm gonna meet him for sex later. I've made my mind up. He was getting hard when we were dancing. I could feel it rubbing against my leg. It felt great."

"Well, good for you." Sam smiled. "Tonight may be the night Faith finds her orgasm."

"Let's hope so," Faith said. "Glad you're having a good time, Ellie."

"The best, Faith, the best." I filled her in with the details of Michelle as Jess rounded up the rest of the group. Chrissy was linking Michelle as they walked back to join us. They had both been laughing; tears still graced their faces.

"I won't be having them inside me ever again." Michelle giggled. "If anybody wants them, you only have to ask."

"Michelle, I'm so sorry, but that was one of the funniest things I have ever seen," I said, still laughing.

She smiled as I linked my arm through hers, and we walked out of the bar and onto the next one.

By now the noise outside the bars was as loud as it was inside. It was brighter outside than inside as well, as we were surrounded by neon signs advertising anything and everything. Men and women approached us offering to sell us whistles, flashing bunny ears, and other novelty trinkets usually sold to drunken party people. We were offered some weed, which I pulled my face at. I've never done drugs, but Faith bought a couple of spliffs for later. One of the weirdos she used to go out with when she first got divorced from Pete got her into it when he took her to Glastonbury for a holiday with lots of other weirdos. It became a problem. She began taking time off work because she couldn't function properly. Luckily for her, she realised the guy only wanted her for her money, and she soon dumped him and got help to stop smoking the weed. She only used it occasionally now.

Lads and girls were all around us with tongues down each other's throats. I remarked to Jess about the number of hands wandering up girls' skirts, and nobody was taking the slightest bit of notice—apart from me, that is. Maybe I was getting a bit too old for all this.

"Stop...I've left my papers back in the bar, the ones giving directions to the bars," I announced.

"Don't worry, I've remembered where the bars are," Faith answered.

At the end of the street, two groups of lads were taunting each other with football songs. In about half an hour, with the amount of alcohol being consumed, it was going to end up a full-blown war zone, so I was glad we are getting out of there. There were police on opposite corners watching them from their patrol cars. They waved as we passed on by. I was glad we uniformed-services people liked to stick together.

"Where we going now?" I asked.

"Not far, just around this corner," Faith answered.

"I feel a bit sick," Jess whispered to me.

"You can't be sick. We've got ages yet, Jess."

She gagged.

"Look, if you really want to be sick, do you want me to put my fingers down your throat and force it out?" I said.

"I'll see how I go on."

TWENTY-EIGHT

We made our way down into a basement bar. I didn't catch the name of it, but it was dark with those lights that make white clothes glow. If you were wearing dark clothes over white underwear, it showed through, a bit seedy. Faith spoke to a very pretty dark-haired English girl on the door, and we were shown on through and taken to a plush booth upholstered in black-and-red leather, with black velvet curtains tied back with black rope. Everybody shuffled into the booth with Faith at one end and me at the other.

I became strangely aware that we were the only women in the place. I saw an array of dancing poles. I don't mean people from Poland dancing—I mean the sort that pole dancers use. I said, "Libby would've loved it in here. She'd have been up them poles faster than you could say... Marco D'Acampo."

Two bottles of Taittinger champagne, which is my favourite, were brought over to our table in ice buckets emblazoned with the Taittinger label. *What are the chances of me nicking one of them to take home?* I wondered.

It's miles better than the one I pinched from Brannigans. Eight glasses were positioned on the table, and the waiter opened and poured the champagne perfectly for us, without spilling a drop. What a star!

"Don't you think it's funny, you know, us being the only women in here?" I remarked.

"There's loads of women in here." Sam chuckled. "Drink your champagne!"

"I can't see any other women apart from the ones behind the bar and the ones dancing on the poles."

The music stopped, and the DJ—whom we had named DJ Perve because his silver satin shirt was open to display a thick mass of black chest hair to compensate for the lack of it on his head—introduced Sophie. The only thing he was missing was a big chain and medallion hanging around his neck like they wore in the seventies. The music started up again, to rapturous applause from the customers in the bar, and we joined in with clapping, too. Sophie walked onto the stage to Beyoncé singing "All the Single Ladies" and began to dance. Her hair was up, and she wore a grey fitted suit with a split up the left side, a white blouse, black-rimmed glasses similar to Michelle's that Chrissy had thrown in the bin, black stockings, suspenders, and four-inch stilettos with massive Lucite platforms. I stared open mouthed as Sophie began taking her clothes off in time to the music. We were in a strip club, and my bessies were encouraging Sophie to get 'em off. Chrissy, Sam, and Sarah stood up in the booth, clapping along with the music, and began waving their hands up in the air when Beyoncé told them to and shouting to the men in the club that they should've "put a ring on it."

What were we doing in a strip club? I didn't remember that being on the list. I must have got one of the names wrong. What an idiot! We'd leave after we finished the drinks. Bet the girls thought I was mad, putting this on the list.

Sophie flung her bra in our direction. We clapped louder. Her perfect little boobies and body without an ounce of fat on it started moving around the stage. She was waving her buttocks around in a red lacy thong. She unclipped it at the sides and threw it in the face of a man with his tongue hanging out, who sat at the front of the stage wearing a Columbo mac. I was looking at her, thinking that two of her bum cheeks would make one of mine and that I couldn't honestly remember when my boobs were ever that close to my chin; they touch my belly button now. I bet she just slips her boobs into her bra when she puts it on. Whilst me on the other hand, I have to roll mine up first before I put them in my bra. As the song came to an end, the applause got louder and continued until she'd taken her bow and headed off the stage.

"Girls, I am so sorry. I don't remember anything on Trip Advisor recommending this place. I must have written it down wrong," I said.

"Don't worry about it," Faith said. "We're having a good time, aren't we?"

"Course we are." Sarah laughed, still waving her hands up in the air.

The DJ turned down the background music to announce that Krystal would be on stage in five minutes with a very special guest, to which the audience started clapping and banging their glasses on the table. "So get your drinks in and don't be long about it," he warned the crowd.

Krystal must be a popular dancer getting a response like that, I thought. He turned the music back up high.

"Wonder if they have any women's loos in here. Ellie, I need you to make me sick," Jess said.

"Come on then. I'll find some." I moved out of the way to let Jess out.

"Hey…Don't be long—you heard what DJ Perve said." Frankie chuckled.

"She doesn't feel too good. Don't be horrible," I shouted back.

Two more bottles of champagne had been delivered to our table whilst we were in the loo. Jess and I climbed back into our seats as DJ Perve introduced Krystal, who came onto the stage carrying a small wooden chair, dressed as a policewoman, in attire similar to ours.

I'd know this tune anywhere…"Sisters Are Doing It for Themselves" by Aretha Franklin.

"I love this song!" I shouted above the noise.

Sam sniggered.

What was she sniggering at?

Krystal placed the chair in the middle of the stage and began to dance around it, rubbing her body up and down it, lifting one foot over the back of the chair, placing it on the seat, and moving her bits around as if being stimulated by the back of the chair. This dance move was greeted with loud woo-hoos and clapping from the men in the bar. Her knickers were crotchless. I could see all that she had to offer. She quickly turned in our direction and started to undress. In time with the music she wiggled from side to side as she began unbuttoning her shirt; walking around the stage, she teasingly removed it from her upper body, followed by her skirt, which slowly slid down her legs. She stepped out of it and walked over in the direction of our table.

Krystal now stood before me in a black nippleless bra and crotchless knickers. She offered me her hand; I quickly refused and shook my head. Suddenly, I was being pushed onto the stage by my so-called friends. I'd been set up. I was the special guest. "I'm not taking any of my clothes off, I can tell you that now," I told them.

Krystal led me to the chair in the middle of the stage whilst continuing with her dance routine, as if giving me a private dance—only it wasn't private; there were about one hundred people watching us. I tried to pull down my already short miniskirt, but it moved only about half an inch, just enough to cover the tops of my stockings. The audience went wild. I never thought I'd ever be part of a girl-on-girl show in a strip club. Krystal removed her bra, and she gently rubbed her breasts across my face, her nipples tracing the outline of my lip.

I wanted to die, is what I wanted to do right then. *Sisters are doing it for themselves? I don't think so.* She turned and gently gyrated her buttocks into my lap, and rip…the knickers were off, again to loud screams. Another dancer came onto the stage carrying two canisters of squirty cream. *Please God, no!* The tops were removed, and a canister was placed in each of my hands. Krystal seductively straddled my knees, her breasts facing me, her naked buttocks facing the audience. She encouraged me to squirt a big dollop of cream onto her breasts and lick the cream off them. Actually the cream wasn't too bad. It had been ages since I'd had any, not counting my Irish coffee last night. My face was covered in cream, and my so-called friends were going crazy, screaming, clapping, cheering. I saw a man giving his man part a good tugging on the front row. Dirty sod.

Krystal put her breasts in front of me again, indicating I was to use the cream, and I politely obliged. Krystal took hold of my hands and dropped the canisters onto the stage. She then took hold of my wrists and placed my hands on her cream-covered breasts. Aretha was singing the chorus: "Sisters…are doing it…for themselves." The timing was right, Aretha. Krystal began to move my hands around in slow circular motions, steadily moving them towards her belly button, stopping at the top of her pubic hairs. *Too close*, I thought—and then she pushed them down into her groin as she made the sound of an orgasm.

I'm so glad I've had more than my fair share of booze tonight, I kept telling myself. As the song reached its climax, Krystal turned around, her back towards me, and sat, spread-eagle, across my lap for all on the front row to have a good look up her flue, as if they'd not already seen enough of it.

Everybody stood and applauded. Krystal climbed off me and took my hand, and we took a bow, both of us covered in cream. With legs like jelly, I wobbled off the stage, holding firmly onto Krystal's hand and taking in what had just happened.

As I sat back in my seat, Sam handed me a damp towel and a full glass of my favourite champagne; she had tears streaming down her face. I knocked it back in one.

"Get off." I pushed her away. "I told you I didn't want a stripper."

"You never mentioned a female stripper. You just kept going on about male strippers, their meat and two veg, and covering them in oil."

"Same thing."

"Beg to differ, Missus. One's got a willy, the other's got a flue." Frankie giggled.

Faith passed me another glass of champagne. I couldn't believe she was a part of this, not my sensible Faith.

"Faith, how could you? Thought you were supposed to look after me."

"Sorry, Ellie, but it's your hen party—we had to do something memorable."

DJ Perve asked everybody to give me—and mentioned me by name—another round of applause, and he wished me all the best for my forthcoming marriage to Devon, whoever he might be.

"Are we going now, then? I'm getting some strange looks off them perverts on the front row." I took another drink off the table and poured it down my throat, my heart rate steadily making its way back to normal.

"Are you sure? Bet we could get you and Krystal a regular spot up there," Chrissy said. "You'd have to change your name, though. Helen sounds too nice. Anybody got any ideas?"

"Something with a Belle in it," Frankie suggested.

"What, like Ding-Dong?" Jess laughed.

"No. Trixabelle, that sounds like a stripper's name." Frankie laughed.

"That makes up for the love-ball thing, Ellie. You're forgiven." Michelle smiled.

I lifted my glass up in the air. "Cheers for that, Michelle."

"You've got a bit of cream on your nose, Elle. Can I lick it off?" And before I could answer, Sam was licking at my face.

"Get off me!" I screamed, laughing.

We finished off the champagne and said our good-byes to the strip bar, laughing and giggling as we made our way out into the Benidorm night air. The firemen appeared as if by magic and asked if we wanted to join them. They were heading to Sinatra's. None of us were in any fit state to make a decision on our own, so we followed them. Chrissy and Mike were trailing along behind us deep in conversation, when suddenly Chrissy was by my side, placing her arm through mine and joining in the conversation Frankie and I were having about my first night as a stripper's assistant. I looked around and saw that Mike was nowhere in sight. Chrissy pulled Frankie and me into the nearest bar and ordered a bottle of white wine. We sat a table in the corner and poured the wine.

"What's going on with you, Chrissy? Mike likes you, you know. He's asked me to put a word in for him," I told her.

"I don't go out with married men. Just shag 'em," Chrissy replied, taking a drink of her wine.

"He's not married."

"What's the ring for? Does he think if a woman sees a wedding ring, it's some kind of magnet?"

"Do you not know? His wife died in a car accident two years ago, along with his son. Steve told Jess. He was one of the first firemen to arrive at the scene. He didn't know it was his wife's car until he arrived at the accident. He's hardly ever spoken to another woman, let alone had sex with one. You're the first person he's shown any interest in," I said.

"So he's going for the sympathy vote now," she replied.

"Chrissy, what's wrong with you? It's not like you to be so cruel!" I exclaimed.

"I'm pissed and pissed off. Elle, I'd give anything to have a relationship like yours," Chrissy admitted.

"Me too," Frankie added.

"We're not perfect, ya know."

"You're not far off it. You and Darren are so good together, Elle. When I think about getting involved with another man, I have flashbacks to all the relationships I've ever had. I know men are not all the same, but the ones I meet are. I am sick of being hurt all the time. I'm not doing it again. I'm going for a dance." Chrissy stood and pushed her chair in frustration.

I grabbed her arm. "Chrissy, one day you're not going to be able to keep doing this, going out all the time, grabbing whatever comes along. You're gonna have to change your ways, or you're gonna end up an old and lonely woman living in a house full of smelly cats." I waved my hand in front of my nose. "Even a little ginger one."

"I don't even like cats." Chrissy sat back down. "What a mess."

"Look, I'm not saying Mike's the guy for you, but he's not the type of bloke you normally go for, so it's obvious he's got something, or you wouldn't have spent the weekend with him. How many blokes have you had sex with this weekend? Well, go on—how many?"

"One and the wank, but that doesn't count."

"What happened to shagging around all weekend and your bet with Sam? I'm just saying think about it, give him a chance." I put my arms around her. The B-52's "Love

Shack" intro began. "They're playing our song, girls. Shall we go and show 'em how to move in here?"

"I love you, Ellie." Chrissy leant over and hugged me.

"That's just the booze talking, Chrissy." I laughed and returned the hug.

As we approached the dance floor, Mike walked in with a couple of the other firemen. They ordered drinks and stood at the end of the bar talking. Mike looked in our direction as we showed off our moves. He put his drink down on to the bar, walked over towards us, took Chrissy by the hand, and walked her back to our table. Frankie and I carried on dancing around like there was no tomorrow. Frankie handcuffed herself to a young lad wearing a badge announcing it was his sixteenth birthday. I attached myself to one of his friends, trying very hard to focus and not fall on the floor. I looked over towards our table and around the bar. Chrissy and Mike had left.

After a few more dances with our handcuffed partners, Sam came rushing in, followed by Sarah and a few more of the firemen. Jess was finally getting her wish of a fireman's lift and was being carried in behind them by Steve. He navigated her through the bar, taking care not to fall over the chairs and tables before placing her down on the dance floor; she landed as ladylike as possible. Screaming with laughter, Jess and the others joined in with our dancing.

In all the excitement, Frankie rushed over to the stage and removed the microphone from the DJ's hand and began to sing "I Predict a Riot," to which we all joined in. The DJ quickly found the karaoke words and put them up on the large screen at the back of the stage. We were bouncing around at the front of the stage, waving our arms in the air and singing at the tops of our voices, as if attending a pop concert. After taking her bow and accepting our applause, Frankie walked off stage straight over to Steve and kissed him full on the lips. He pulled her in tight and kissed her back. They were giggling like teenagers as Frankie whispered into his ear. She waved to me as they left.

TWENTY-NINE

It was beginning to feel hot and stuffy in the bar with all the dancing and singing. I needed some air. I walked over to the bar and bought a bottle of water, which cost nearly as much as a bottle of wine, robbing sods. I took myself off outside.

I didn't remember walking in the direction of our hotel, but I stopped when I heard my name being called.

"Hey, Ellie." I recognised Jerry's voice. "You come to arrest me? Put me in handcuffs?"

"Hi." I giggled. "Didn't see you there, Jezza. Had a couple too many, eyes are not as good as they used to be. Seen any of my bessies?"

"Yeah, a couple of them called in earlier, mentioned something about going to a gay bar in the Old Town. Why don't you come over and let me get you a drink?"

"No, ta, I best go and look for the others." My body temperature was rising again, and them silly little butterflies had returned and were fluttering around in my stomach. The voice is my head was screaming at me, *Stop looking and listening to him! Move whilst you still can.* "Come on,

Ellie, just a little one. You're going back to Manchester tomorrow, back to the real world, and we may never meet again…just a little nightcap. It's only a drink, and I promise not to struggle as you put them handcuffs on me."

I giggled. "Well…OK, just a quick one." I felt as if my heart was going to jump out of my throat. I wondered if this was what the contestants felt like waiting to audition for the *X Factor*.

"And besides, you don't really want to be walking around here on your own. You never know who could be out on the prowl, looking for a beautiful English girl from Manchester."

My lungs were now fighting for air. "Stop it!" I blushed.

I stumbled off the edge of the kerb, staggered across the road, and smiled as I walked unsteadily through the door Jerry had opened for me. The DJ was packing up for the night, and the bar was listening to a combination of eighties tracks. I looked around to see if I recognised anybody. I didn't. I didn't know what time it was, but I was sure the nightlife would be coming to an end soon. The girls would be making their way back to the hotel by now—or somebody else's, depending if they got lucky or not.

I pulled up a stool and sat myself down at the far end of the bar. Jerry poured us both a brandy, walked back from behind the bar, and stood beside me. His hand brushed against mine as he passed me my drink. "What shall we drink to?" He stared straight into my eyes. "Shall we drink to you? Me?" He hesitated, leant in, and kissed me gently on the lips. "Or us?"

I couldn't fight it any longer. Eyes closed, I kissed him back, kissing him with so much force, we both fell against the bar. It was hot, passionate…tongues touching all corners of our mouths. The brandy fell out of my hand and smashed on the floor. Jerry wrapped his arms around me and scooped me up. He kicked open a door. It slammed shut behind him. My whole body began to weaken. I opened my eyes and took in the whole area. We were in his office. A large wooden desk stood strong in the middle of the room, surrounded by filing cabinets and shelves full of A4 ring binders. Why was I even interested in what was in the room? My beloved Prada bag slipped off my right shoulder and fell onto the floor. Our mouths hadn't separated since his lips first touched mine.

As I reclosed my eyes, Jerry placed my feet back on the floor whilst pushing his body against mine. *He's hard. Oh my God, he's hard, and it feels massive.*

His kisses began to cover my neck and shoulder whilst his strong hands began descending slowly down my back; they stopped at my bottom, where he took the opportunity to caress my buttocks, slowly but firmly, as if kneading dough. I didn't stop him. The touch of his hands on my skin made my body scream for him. He began to unbutton my shirt to reveal my white lacy bra, where my nipples stood to attention, begging to be taken in his mouth. As if reading my mind, he did as I requested. I groaned with delight. His hands moved swiftly down my body, stopping at my stockings' tops, where his fingers slithered into a strap of my suspender belt. Wetness intensified down below. His fingers found it as he slipped his hand inside my G-string. With a sweep of his left arm, everything on the overcrowded desk was sent crashing to the floor. He roughly forced me upon the hard surface, pulling my skirt up around my waist. The sound of heavy breathing echoed around the room.

With a start, I opened my eyes. *What am I doing?* Darren came into head. *Oh my God! He'd be devastated. I can't ruin everything for this. I can't do it.*

"Stop! Stop!" I gasped.

"What do you mean, stop?" Jerry shouted, clinging onto me with one arm and unzipping his shorts with the other.

"Please get off me…I'm so sorry."

"No…You're not stopping me now. You've been gagging for it ever since you first set eyes on me, falling out of your fancy limo, with your gang of slags." He continued to prepare himself.

"I can't do this. You have to get off me!" I screamed back. I pushed him off me and stumbled off the table.

Jerry lunged towards me and grabbed my arm. "You're not getting away that easily."

With every ounce of strength in my body, I smacked him straight in his groin with my right fist. He released me and doubled up in pain. I grabbed my bag off the floor and rushed out of the office and out of the bar, pulling my skirt down as I ran.

Jerry shouted after me. I didn't stop running until I felt sand beneath my feet. Panting, I stopped to catch my breath and dropped down onto the sand. It felt cool against my skin, the sea making gentle swooshing noises.

I opened my bag and took out my mobile. I selected the photos icon and opened up a picture of Darren. He was smiling. It had been taken on our first holiday together, in Turkey. I touched his face whilst tears streamed down mine. My phone bleeped with an incoming text. It was from Roxy: *hope ur avin a gd time, cnt w8 2 b ur bridesmaid. Lv u x.* I shook my head. "What the fuck have you just done? What the fuck were you thinking? You stupid, stupid bitch!" I shouted at the top of my voice, and dropped my head in my hands. My blouse was open wide; I slowly began to button it back up.

"Is that you, Ellie? Ellie, you OK? It's me, Brian from the Oldham rugby club. Are you crying, sweetheart?" He walked across the sand and put his arms around me whilst I sobbed into his shoulder. "Nobody's hurt you, have they? If they have, I'll smash their fucking face in."

I took a tissue out of my bag to wipe my tears away, then blew my nose. "No, no. I'm having an emotional moment."

"You look like Alice Cooper. You've not got waterproof mascara on, have you?"

"I just thought I'd add it to my fancy dress." I attempted to laugh.

"It suits you, you know, being dressed as a policewoman."

"I hope you're not hitting on me, Brian."

"In my dreams! Only one woman for me, Ellie, and she's snugged up in bed in her Primark PJs back in Oldham, or she better had be. No, I'm just saying if the coppers looked like you in Oldham, I'd get in trouble all the time just so I'd get arrested. Somehow, though, I don't think they'd be allowed to wear stockings and suspenders," Brian said. "Anyway, what you doing down here on your own?"

"Oh...nothing, just wanted to a bit of me time to catch my breath, you know? It's been a bit of a mad one." I couldn't look him in the eye, in case he saw the shame sprawled across my face.

Brian looked down at my phone. "That your fella? He's not bad looking for a City fan."

"I know." I sniffed as I placed my phone back into my bag.

Oh, Brian, if you only knew what I had nearly done, would you still be trying to comfort me? I feel so bad, I just want to go home.

"Can I walk you back to your hotel?" Brian offered me his hand.

I took it. "Thanks." He helped me up, and I brushed the sand off my skirt and legs.

It wasn't long before we came upon the Irish bar. Jerry stood outside smoking with his arms draped around a twentysomething blonde who was in a worse state than I was. I leant into Brian; I didn't want Jerry to see me.

"Are you trying to cop off with me, Ellie? Cos I wouldn't say no, you know. Forget what I said earlier." Brian laughed.

"As you said, Brian, in your dreams." I smiled. "I'm giving you a hug because you've been so nice to me, and you're a real gent, and if I don't hold onto you, I don't think I'll make it back to the hotel."

As we approached our hotel, I kissed Brian on the cheek, thanked him for walking me back, and staggered through reception to the bar. Sam, Michelle, Jess, and Sarah were chatting to the Geordie lads. Sam waved me over. The Alice Cooper eyes had been noticed. Sam got up off her chair and rushed over in my direction.

"Hey, what's up?" Her arms were around me.

"Sam, I nearly made the biggest mistake of my life." I told her everything. "What was I thinking? I just walked past Jerry, and he's already trying to get his grubby little hands into another girl's knickers. Sam, I got caught up in the moment—I'd have been just another conquest for him, but I'd have ruined my life. I wouldn't have been able to look Darren in the eye. Our relationship would have been over."

"I warned you about him, Ellie. I told you…Look, it's over now, come and have a drink with us."

"No, I'm going to go up. I'll get a drink there. I want to ring Darren," I told her.

"Ellie, it's four in the morning."

"I need to speak to Darren."

"Don't say anything stupid." Wow. Sam was giving me advice.

"I just want to hear his voice. I'll meet you back in the room." I kissed Sam on the cheek, waved to the others, and headed towards the lift.

I quickly undressed as I entered our room, letting my clothes drop onto the floor where I stood. I took a hot shower before ringing Darren, scrubbing any trace of Jerry from my body. I stopped when I realised I was gonna have no skin left. I dried and wrapped myself in the thick cotton robe provided by the hotel, made myself a black coffee, and settled down on the bed, suddenly feeling very sober.

A couple of rings, and I heard his sleepy voice.

"Morning, babe." He yawned.

"Night. I've not been to bed yet, so technically it's still night," I whispered.

"You OK? Had a good night?"

"Great, yeah! Just wanted to hear your voice and tell you that I love you and can't wait to marry you. I am so ready to be Mrs. Fletcher."

"Glad to hear it. Love you, too. Hope you've got plenty of gossip for me when you get home. Have Sam and Chrissy been dishing it about?"

"You know I can't tell you anything. It's law."

We continued talking for half an hour about anything and everything. The poker night had gone well. Plenty of alcohol had been consumed, and they'd ordered a takeaway from our favourite Indian, Bollywood. Jim lost about a grand to Darren and four of his mates, so all in all, without Jim knowing, this had been the beginning of the downfall of Jimmy weekend, as Darren had predicted whilst picking Sarah up at hers on Friday morning.

I didn't have the energy to tell Darren about Sarah and Jimmy. I was saving that for Sunday evening at the airport. He kept trying to persuade me to give him even a hint of what we were all getting up to. He loves a bit of gossip; I just hoped he'd never hear about mine.

What on earth had I been thinking? I'd be beating myself up about this for a long time. I made another coffee and climbed back into bed as Sam fell through the open door.

"Everything OK? Speak to Darren?"

"OK." I sipped my coffee.

"It's been a great night, Ellie. In fact the whole weekend has been fantastic. I'm going to have a shower before I get into bed. I feel a bit grubby—I've had sex four times tonight."

"Don't know how you do it, Sam."

"What d'ya mean? You enjoy chocolate, I enjoy sex." She began peeling off her clothes and throwing them on the pile beside her bed.

"I know I enjoy chocolate, but I don't want it all the time."

"That's because you've not found the right one. If you had, you'd want it all the time."

"I'm not arguing with you about sex. I'd be wasting my time. Have you seen much of Chrissy? You know you've won your bet, don't you?"

"Dunno, have I? How do you know?"

"She's been with Mike all weekend."

"Really? So that means I won the bet. Yeah…get in there. I'll get my fiver off her at the airport."

"A fiver, is that it?"

"We only do it for the laugh, not the money." She giggled, walked into the bathroom naked, and climbed in the shower.

"Sam, can you hear that banging?" She didn't—she was too busy singing Right Said Fred's "I'm Too Sexy" at the top of her voice.

I climbed out of bed, wrapped the bed sheet around me, and went out into the corridor. Sarah was banging on her own door. I walked over to her.

"Frankie! Frankie! Are you awake?" Sarah shouted. "I know you're in there. I've lost my key. You better not have anybody in there with you."

The door opened. It was Steve the fireman, as naked as could be, with a huge package on display.

Sarah pushed past him. "Frankie." She shook her shoulder to wake her. I stood at the door, trying not to look at the view. I smiled.

"Ugh…what?"

"Frankie, get him out of here. I'm not sleeping in a room with a man I don't know. I've got enough problems."

"Steve." Frankie moved her arm to nudge him and realised he wasn't there. "Steve, where are you? You've got to go."

"OK, give me a minute."

"No, now." Sarah turned away. "And put some pants on before I throw up."

Steve picked up his pants and put them on. He'd put them on back to front. I tried not to laugh. He grabbed the rest of his things and gave Frankie a kiss and then Sarah. "Night, Sarah." He walked out of the room half-asleep. "Ellie." He smiled at me.

He hobbled along the corridor towards the lift, with his bum hanging out, trying to dress himself.

"Why did you have to bring him back in here?" Sarah snapped.

"The beach was full. Aw…make us a brew, Sarah. My mouth feels like sandpaper."

"Make your own bloody brew. I need my bed."

"I'll leave you to it. Night." I closed the door.

THIRTY

I was wakened by the sound of Faith and Frankie talking outside on the balcony as they had, I could only assume, their first cigarettes of the day. I rubbed my eyes and glanced over at my mobile; it was eight fifteen. Sam was sleeping like a baby, stark naked and curled up in the foetal position on top of the quilt.

It was another beautiful day. The sun was dancing around the bedroom floor as it seeped in through the curtains, which were moving ever so slightly in the breeze, just like yesterday. The sound of sun loungers and chairs being dragged across the paved area below my room informed me that people were already up and about, ready for another day of sunbathing and games.

I quickly dressed, trying not to disturb Sam, and headed off to Sarah's room. I gently knocked on the door and in a soft tone asked, "Sarah, you in there?"

Sarah slowly opened the door, her body wrapped in a hotel bath towel.

"Hey, you."

"Hey, you. Come in." She stood to one side to let me pass.

"Can I make you a coffee? I could do with one."

"Sure, thanks."

I walked over to the kettle and switched it on. "Sarah, I just wanted to check you were OK. We didn't really talk about what happened last night—you know, Jimmy."

She sighed. "Do ya want to know what I've been doing since I got out of bed this morning, Ellie? I've been looking at my reflection in the mirror, wondering how I ever let myself get into such a mess. How did I ever let Jimmy get so far under my skin that I let him beat me regularly and think it was OK, and that the last time would really be the last time? Deep down I knew it wasn't."

"Sarah, you can't blame yourself."

"Who else can I blame, Ellie? Have you seen the state of my hair?" She ran her fingers through it. "And just look at my nails." She put them out in front of her. "When did I stop getting my nails done?"

Her face and body showed a multitude of signs of tension and tiredness. Her frame was weak, her eyes lifeless. It was a complete contrast to last night, when we were happily dancing and drinking in the bars. The reality of what was to come had sunk in. Her secret was out, and there was no going back.

"It's gonna be OK, Sarah," I tried to reassure her.

"Is it, Ellie? Is it really? How can you be so sure? You don't know Jimmy."

"You're right, Sarah. I don't know Jimmy. But one thing I do know is that he will never lay another finger on you. We are going to go to your house tonight to collect Maisy, and you are going to stay with Chrissy until you get your-self sorted, however long that might take."

She sighed. "It all sounds so simple when ya say it, Ellie, but did ya not hear me last night? I have no money, and I have no job. How am I going to look after Maisy? Jesus, I can't even look after myself."

"Sarah, I know it's hard for ya right now, and I'll be honest, I don't know what I can say to reassure ya, but we will all look after ya. I know it's easier said than done, but please try not to worry. Look, let me finish making ya a cof-fee. You'll have to have it black, you've got no milk."

There was a knock at the door. Sarah opened it. Faith walked in. There was genuine sadness in Faith's eyes. It was no secret Sarah and Faith didn't get along, sisters or not; they never had. It could have been the seven-year age dif-ference, who knows? Without speaking, they put their arms around each other, Faith holding onto Sarah as if she was never going to let her go, and they cried like I had never seen them cry before. Faith was full of guilt and pain for her baby sister. I finished making the coffee and left them to talk.

I made my way to the restaurant to grab a piece of toast and cup of coffee. Jess and Michelle were already in there. The conversation was light, catching up on last night's antics. I probably should have filled them all in about me being an absolute idiot with Jerry, but I thought if I didn't say anything I could pretend the whole thing had never happened. Jess was the only one of us who had the energy to eat.

"Chrissy didn't come back last night. Do you think she's all right?" Michelle spoke quietly whilst sipping her black coffee.

"Chrissy'll be fine," I said. "She went off with Mike again. I think he took quite a liking to our Chrissy in her policewoman's outfit."

"With or without her uniform, he's taken a liking to her," Michelle answered, looking sad. "I like Chrissy, Ellie—in fact I like all your friends. You're all really good friends. I've never had that. It's nice."

"Hey, Michelle, hey. Smile, you're part of the gang now. No going back for you. New hair, new clothes—bet you didn't know you had a sex goddess screaming to get out all these years. Nigel's not going to know what's hit him when he sees you."

"Them Cheshire housewives are gonna have to lock up their husbands now. You were never a problem to them before, but you will be now. Good job you've got us as friends, because I can see you're going to be seeing a different side of them now." Jess laughed.

"Thanks, Jess." Michelle smiled.

"Hey, wonder if Chrissy will come back with sand on her shoes again," Jess said as she continued eating her breakfast.

I spotted Chrissy, dodging hotel guests carrying plates loaded up with lots of breakfast goodies, making her way towards us. "Why don't you ask her?" She looked as though she'd just come back from filming the *Walking*

Dead, with her wild hair and smeared makeup. I smiled to myself as she sat beside me.

"Michelle, be a love and get me a coffee," she croaked.

"You do realise you're out in public, Chrissy, and people can see you," I replied. "You've got a stocking missing."

"Have I, sweetie? I hadn't noticed. I am exhausted. For a man of Mike's age, he is amazing. I was struggling to keep up with him. I've never been out with a man in his fifties before. Maybe that's where I have been going wrong. I'm going to start looking for the Richard Geres of this world instead of the Leonardo DiCaprios. Hope there are some spare out there."

"I'll go and get you a coffee," Jess said. "I was going to get myself another one and grab a couple of them sausages. They're ace."

"So where did you end up last night, Ellie? Last time I saw you, you we were in that bar near the strip club," Chrissy asked.

"I...I—" I stuttered. "I ended up talking to Brian, you know, the manager guy from the rugby club. I turned around, and you were all gone. He walked me back to the hotel."

"What a nice man he was. Sarah and I were talking to him earlier in the night. He's got a five-year-old granddaughter. Sarah was telling him about Maisy," Michelle said.

"Jess, how on earth can you eat all that food in a morning, after drinking all night?" Chrissy exclaimed.

"Years of practice. It's great. Do you wanna bite of my sausage?"

"Do I want a sausage? I've had enough sausage for today, nearly nine hours of sausage," Chrissy replied. "I'll just take my coffee from you, thank you."

Sarah and Faith walked arm in arm into the restaurant. I stood and waved them over.

"So, what have you got planned for us today, Faith?" Michelle asked.

"I got something organised for early afternoon. Everybody's free to do their own thing till then. I'm going to chill around the pool this morning," Faith replied.

"I meant to ask. Who organised my stripper experience last night?" I smiled.

"Me. Joseph owns the club." Faith laughed.

"Chrissy, is there any chance we could go shopping—you know, to get me a few bits for when I get home?" Michelle asked.

"Why, what you buying?" Jess giggled. "Like we don't know."

"Sure, give me an hour, and I'll be fine, sweetie." Chrissy yawned as she held her head in her hands. "I need a couple of my pills. How are you feeling, Michelle?"

"In need of a couple of your pills."

After breakfast, we headed back up to our rooms. Sam's bed was empty, and she was nowhere to be seen. She'd probably gone for her morning workout in the gym. I took a nice hot shower, grateful for a bit of quiet time, and slipped on a blue-and-white one-piece. After covering myself in Nivea factor eight, I went down to the pool to join Faith and Sarah.

Jess and Frankie had gone wandering the streets of Benidorm to find the tattoo shop we all went to yesterday, so she could be tagged just like the rest of us.

I stretched out on my sun lounger, grabbed a copy of *Hello*, and carried on from yesterday, catching up on celebrity gossip and seeing who was selling their soul this week just to pass the time away. The last few months of exercising and dieting at Slimming World had done me proud. It was surprising how losing a few pounds could make me look and feel a whole lot better in a bikini, and it was great I didn't have to breathe in all the time, anymore.

Everything was the same as yesterday around the pool. The man who was wearing the Speedos with the elastic gone was wearing them again, and the ladies chatted in their little groups. People relaxed everywhere, drinking, tea, coffee, or whatever they wanted. Everybody looked happy, with not a care in the world apart from which of the hotel's three bars their next drink might come from. They deserved it. They'd worked hard all their lives, and this was payback for them all. Long may they keep coming to Benidorm.

This is the type of life I want when I retire, I thought. *When I get back home, I think I'm going to have a look at my pension and start getting a plan together.*

Michelle and Chrissy stopped by to say hello, arms weighing heavy with loads more bags of goodies, to help with Operation Get Michelle a Life.

At twelve fifteen, Faith announced we had to get our bodies back up to our rooms. We had to pack, check out, and hit the streets of Benidorm one last time. I was so comfy lying in the sun. The heat was really building up now. Part of me was sad, thinking my hen party with my bessies was coming to an end. I didn't know when we were all going to be able to get together again. Work and life really does get in the way of spending time with my friends. The other part of me just wanted to get back to Darren and my girls.

We gathered up all our belongings. Faith went into mother mode, checking to make sure we hadn't forgotten anything. All the magazines were a bit dog-eared, having been read from cover to cover and smeared with different varieties of sun cream. They were fit only for the bin. I tore out articles about Marco to show Libby later and threw the magazines away.

When I arrived at my room, the door was ajar. Sam was lying on the bed, reading a letter. "Where've you been?" I asked.

"One last workout," she replied without lifting her eyes off the page.

"What ya got there?"

"This? It's a job offer."

"E'are, give us a look. You never said you'd applied for a job."

She passed it to me. "I didn't. The manager of the gym I go to near work wants to know if I want to train as a personal trainer. It came in the post Thursday. I forgot I'd put it in my bag, I've only just opened it. I'm seriously thinking about it."

Sam would be an excellent personal trainer. She knows everything there is to know about fitness and healthy eating. And dedicated, nobody could say she wasn't dedicated. Sam's a walking advertisement for fitness—you just had to look at her. She'd make more money, as well, than we make as legal secretaries. It was a no-brainer. I'd have to leave Baxter and Turnbull's; I couldn't work for the bitch on my own. Perhaps this job offer was the push we both needed to get us to leave. We were always talking about leaving. Why not?

"Go for it."

"What about you?"

"I'll go and work for Darren. It'd be less travelling."

"What about Manchester? You'd miss it."

"I know, but maybe we could do with a change. I'd have more money, that's for sure. No more impromptu stop-offs on my way home, into Debenhams buying stuff that I can't afford." I laughed.

"OK, let's do it. I'll ring the gym up tomorrow. Wanna beer to celebrate?"

"Yeah, please."

Sam slid off the bed and walked into the bathroom to get us both a bottle of Bud from the bidet, where we'd kept them all weekend. We were now down to the last two.

"Thanks," I said. "Come on, you need to get dressed. We're going out. We've got to meet the others downstairs for one."

"Hey! You decent in there?" Frankie shouted as she walked in. "Found the tattoo studio." She pulled down her black shorts to reveal her new tattoo, covered with taped-down cling film. "What do you think? He remembered you, Ellie—you left an impression there. He said he's never had anybody scream that much ever."

Everybody else had made it on time to reception and was waiting patiently on the comfy cream sofas for me and Sam. I apologised profusely on behalf of both of us. It fell on deaf ears because they'd heard it all before. Faith began to round us up like sheep. Maybe we should have got her a whistle; then she wouldn't have had to keep shouting at us to move. We followed. It wouldn't be long until we found out what she had planned for us. I wasn't sure if I could take any more surprises. If truth be known, I wouldn't mind sneaking off for one of those cream teas serving real Devon cream advertised on the beachfront.

"Anybody know where we're going?" Jess asked.

"It's a surprise was all I got out of her, something to do with payback," Frankie said.

We continued to follow along like three-year-olds going on our first field trip. I expected Faith to ask us to walk in twos and hold hands. We passed by the Irish bar, but Jerry was nowhere in sight, thank God. We crossed over and headed towards the beach.

"Please don't say you want us to do another sand sculpture," Michelle begged.

Faith kept on walking, not replying.

"I can't believe we're walking past bars. Can't we just stop off for one?" Frankie called out.

"Are we nearly there yet?" Sam and Sarah giggled.

"Nearly there."

"That's what they told me the last time I was in labour. They lied then, and she's lying now." I laughed.

Faith ran off ahead and ran straight into a mobility-scooter shop. We hung around outside, wondering what on earth was going on.

"OK, it's payback time," Faith said as she walked out. "I've booked mobility scooters for the next hour. I decided if we can't beat the old buggers, we may as well join them."

"You're kidding!" I cried.

"Fantastic!" Sarah yelped. "Give me a key."

"Back in a min," Frankie shouted. "Sam, come with me."

Faith handed out keys to everybody. I felt like I'd been given the key to my first car after passing my driving test. This was so exciting. I chose a deep-red one with a shopping basket on the front. Frankie and Sam handed out bottles of Stella. I dreaded to think how many bottles of beer we had drunk this weekend.

"Not sure if we can drink and drive, but these old sods are driving without eyesight, so I'm sure we're able to drive with a bottle of beer in us." Frankie smiled.

"Start your engines, girls," Faith announced.

We placed our keys firmly in the ignitions and turned them. Unfortunately, the scooters didn't have engines, with them being electric, so to compensate, Frankie started making *brum-brum* noises, followed by Faith.

"OK, girls, payback time!" Jess shouted.

Frankie and Faith led the way, the rest moving close behind.

"*Chaaarge*!" Frankie shouted, holding her bottle of Bud in the air. She headed straight for a group of pensioners, who were positioned in a line talking whilst moving slowly on their scooters.

"Move, you bloody idiot!" a man shouted at her.

"Move your bloody self!" she shouted back.

This was great fun, weaving in and out of the pedestrians walking along the promenade. We looked like we were starring in an episode of *Wacky Races*, with us being like the Ant Hill Mob with Faith as our leader. On the other hand, though, Sam did look a bit like Penelope Pitstop, acting all hopeless and forlorn, and Frankie was behaving a bit like Dick Dastardly, doing sneaky little tricks to get past everybody. I should have stopped off at one of them tacky shops and bought her a stuffed dog. Then she could have put Muttley in the basket on the front. People sitting in bars watching us making our way through the streets of Benidorm clapped and cheered us on.

"Get one for us!" yelled a girl in one of the bars. "Bloody nuisances."

I spotted the lads from the Oldham rugby club on the beach having an impromptu game of rugby with the girls from Liverpool. I waved and shouted hi.

What started out as a bit of fun was beginning to become quite competitive between Frankie, Faith, and Sarah.

After a couple more trips up and down the front and again around a few of the side roads, our time as the cast of *Wacky Races* came to an end.

"That was great fun," Michelle said. "I've never done anything like that before."

"No kidding," Sam replied. I gave her one of my looks again, one that said, "Leave her alone, she's trying."

"I think we definitely deserve a drink after that," Frankie suggested. "Come on, now, you can follow me." We headed into the bar next door to the scooter shop to spend the last few hours downing as much alcohol as possible before we had to go back to the hotel and collect our belongings.

"Wonder how Libby's gone on," Jess asked.

"Bet she's red raw," Sam replied. "Lucky bitch."

"Look who's talking." I laughed. "We'll soon find out, can't wait for all the gossip."

"Michelle, have you spoken to Nigel since you've been in Benidorm?" Sarah asked.

"No, we don't really contact each other when we are away from home. I have texted him, though, to ask him to collect me up from the airport and to say that we need to talk. I've arranged for Nigel's mum to come at stay at our house tonight, and I've booked us into the Radisson Blu hotel at the airport. I want to strike while the iron is hot, so to say. You never know. I may be having my first orgasm off my husband tonight. I'm nervous but excited."

"Good for you, sweetie," Chrissy replied. "If you start to struggle, remember how you felt last night when we used the remote control love balls on you."

Sam started laughing. "It was funny, though, Michelle. I thought you were going to burst out and do a full Irish jig."

Chrissy continued. "And don't be afraid to tell Nigel what you want him to do. Men come across as knowing what to do. But believe me, after years of experience I can tell you, they love it when you boss them around and show them you're not scared of your own body. Take hold of his hand, and place it where you want it to be."

"But I don't know where I want it to be," she replied.

"That's a real turn-on, Michelle. Alan loves it when I do that," Jess joined in.

"Get on the Internet and do some research before tonight. Tracey Cox is a good one to look at," Chrissy advised.

"I'm going to have to have a drink to do all this. I'll ring the hotel when we get to the airport and arrange for some wine to be waiting for us in the room," Michelle said.

"Sarah, what about you?" Chrissy asked.

"What about me?" She shrugged.

"You and Maisy coming to stay with me."

"Oh, that. It'll sort itself out."

"Don't think so, Missus." Faith interrupted. "If you don't go with Chrissy tonight, I'm going to go to your house and put every single window through and let everybody on your street know what's been going on."

"Faith, it's not as simple as that." Sarah's eyes started to fill up.

"It is that simple," Faith replied.

"Sarah, we spoke about it this morning, and you agreed to go with Chrissy," Frankie said sympathetically.

"I'm scared…" Tears began streaming down her face.

"I know, Sarah." I put my arms around her. "But we'll be with you every step of the way. You know you can't go back now. We know everything, and we've stood by long enough."

Sarah looked down at the floor. *Perhaps we don't know everything*, I thought. *Maybe Sarah does have more secrets. But what? What can be worse than being used as a punch bag by your scummy husband?*

"Don't look now, fireman approaching at two o'clock, Chrissy," Sam whispered. "Has he got you tagged."

We turned around. Mike was alone. He was dressed really nicely in a pair of stone-coloured chinos and a blue polo shirt. He smiled as he approached us. "Hi, ladies."

"Hi, Mike," Frankie gushed. Chrissy jabbed her in the arm.

"Chrissy, do you have a minute?"

"Sure, back in five," she said. Mike walked towards a table at the back of the bar, Chrissy joined him, and as she said she was back with us —in less than five.

We watched as he walked out of the bar without looking back. Chrissy continued drinking as if nothing had happened. I thought that after our little chat last night, she might have given Mike a break, but it looked like she'd built that tough shell of hers up again. *Will nothing make her crack?* I walked out of the bar and into the gift shop next door and quickly found what I was looking for. I bought a cute little ginger stuffed cat and walked back into the bar.

"Present for you," I said and gave Chrissy the cat.

"'What's this?"

"The first of your collection, only this one doesn't smell."

"Leave it, will you, Ellie?" Chrissy snapped back.

We all continued chatting away when Sarah interrupted our conversation. "You don't know everything," Sarah blurted out. "I'm an idiot."

"What you going on about now, our kid?" Faith asked.

"Me and Jimmy. Err…When we first got together, Jimmy was studying photography, and…I was drunk one night, and like a fool I let him take some, you know, pictures of me. I regretted it the next day and asked him not to develop them. Get rid. He wouldn't. That's why I can't leave him. He's been threatening me with them ever since, saying if I ever leave, he'll put them online for all the world to see. I've searched the house high and low for them pictures I don't know how many times, but I can't find them. That's the reason I can't leave. I would kill myself if they ever got out, and what would happen to Maisy then?"

"He's just scaring you," Frankie said.

"He's not. I know him, he's got them safe somewhere."

"There are laws against that type of behaviour now," Jess advised.

"Jim doesn't care about laws. My life would be over."

"Sarah, I know where they are!" I exclaimed.

"How could you know?"

I began to explain. "About three years ago, Jimmy gave Darren a small package to put in our safe. It was some valuable stuff of his mum's. He said he used to have a safety deposit box but didn't want to keep paying for it, and he didn't think they'd be safe just left in the house. He knew we had a safe and asked Darren if he could keep them there. I bet you any money it's them."

"She didn't have anything valuable when she died. We had to pay for her funeral."

"That's where they are. Let me ring Darren. Give me five minutes." I took my phone out of my bag and rushed off outside to call Darren.

Darren's anger came across loud and clear when I briefly explained about Sarah and Jim. I calmed him down long enough to explain he had to check out the contents of the package in the safe Jimmy gave him—and it turned out that I was right. Darren flicked through the pictures just to check there was nothing else in there and immediately destroyed them and the negatives in the shredder in our office. Darren said he'd call Jim and arrange to go for a drink when Sarah got home, so he wouldn't be in the house whilst she collected some of her and Maisy's stuff. He also promised not to hit him, at least not until Sarah was safely on her way to Chrissy's.

I hurried back into the bar. "Darren destroyed them whilst I was on the phone. Now give me another excuse, Sarah."

"I don't need one. Oh, Ellie thank you." She rushed over and flung her arms around me.

We finished up and made our way back to the hotel.

THIRTY-ONE

We stood outside the hotel reception waiting for our transport to take us back to the airport, suitcases by our sides. I watched Jerry walking out of his bar and tried to hide behind Michelle. He noticed us. "Thanks for this weekend, Sam, especially this morning. Hope we can catch up again soon!" he shouted, looking in my direction.

I couldn't hide the shock spreading across my face. So that's where she had been this morning. Sam looked back at me.

"What? Ellie, sorry. Did I forget to tell you? I couldn't just leave him. He just had to be done. I did warn you about him, though. How do you think I found out what he was like?" Sam paused and turned to face Jerry. "You never know, Jerry, we may be back."

"You might be. I won't," I snapped.

"You can be a real bitch sometimes, Sam," Faith said.

"Why, are you bothered, Ellie?" Sam asked.

"No, I'm not. I can't believe I nearly fell for him." I was shaking.

"You never did," Frankie said.

"Yeah," I answered guiltily. "But don't worry, I didn't do anything."

"Ellie," Jess squealed.

"Jerry told me he has sex at least three times a night in his bar," Sam said. "Girls are easy pickings, especially when they're in Benidorm on hen parties. He just uses women, you know. He's probably responsible for breaking up loads of relationships. It turns out he got hurt about three years ago by an ex. Sound familiar, Chrissy?" Sam turned to Chrissy.

"Leave it out, sweetie," Chrissy replied.

"It's so much better when you're the one in charge. No man will ever get the better of me," Sam continued. "I didn't want to tell you I'd slept with him because I knew you had feelings for him, but if I hadn't have done him, I would have only regretted it."

"Sam, what the fuck has got into you?" Frankie snapped.

"I don't have feelings for him. I was pissed. I wanna forget the whole damn thing." I felt myself choking up as Michelle looked in my direction.

What the hell was going on with Sam? Why was she being such a bitch?

"Cars are here, girls." Faith cut my thoughts short as she pointed to our approaching transport.

Chrissy had ordered a limo for our return journey to Alicante. "We started this weekend in style, and we're going to end it in style."

"I hope there's no more alcohol in there. If I died now because of the amount of alcohol in my body at the moment, I wouldn't even have to be embalmed. I think I already am," Jess said.

The limo came to a halt outside the hotel, and once the driver had placed our bags in the accompanying vehicle, we set off on our journey home.

"Michelle, pass me the champers," Sam demanded and clicked her fingers.

"Chill, baby," Chrissy snapped. "Getting withdrawal symptoms already, Sam?"

"Sorry, didn't mean to do that, Michelle." Sam looked across at me. "Ellie, I'm sorry for what I said."

"Oh, forget it, Sam."

"I'll get the glasses," Sarah said as she crawled across the floor to take the glasses out of the cabinet. "I'm getting nervous. I need a bit of Dutch courage."

"No, you don't," Chrissy said, passing the champagne. "You're going to be fine."

"I hope so, thanks. Ellie, you having one?"

"Do I have to?"

"Yes, you do. You can't stop drinking till we get back to Manchester Airport," Frankie said.

"I'll be dead before we get back to Manchester," I replied.

"Well, you can stop then." Sarah laughed nervously.

"I think we need to have a toast," Sam announced.

"What, another one?" Frankie sighed. "Can't we just drink?"

"No, we're having a toast. Ladies raise your glasses, to friendship and new beginnings."

"Friendships and new beginnings," we chorused.

"Come on, get drinking. We've only got about half an hour before we get to the airport, and we've got all this lot to drink," Sam said.

I sat back in my seat and closed my eyes with a glass of champagne in my hand. I left them all to it, chatting, laughing; my mind drifted. It had been a strange weekend. If you'd have told me three days ago my uptight future sister-in-law, Michelle, would end up friends with Chrissy, I'd never have believed it. And even more so, she was now my friend.

Michelle hangs on Chrissy's every word. When they get back to Manchester, Chrissy is arranging for Michelle to have a proper makeover, new hairstyle, makeup, the works; then they're going to spend some of Nigel's money on a new wardrobe to show off Michelle's fantastic figure. Since yesterday Michelle has had five orgasms and quite proudly tells us. Michelle is desperate to rebuild her relationship with Nigel, and she's got Chrissy's mobile number just in case of emergencies. She's also got newfound confidence and feels ready to tackle Nigel's soon to be ex-mistress and get her out of their lives forever. There is going to be one shocked Nigel when Michelle lands at Manchester Airport. She's wearing a pair of Chrissy's skinny denim jeans, and a pale blue blouse. Chrissy has done her makeup again, and straightened her hair. Michelle has decided not to wear glasses again, and has now got her contacts in. Talk about a new woman; she went to the airport looking like a cast member from *Benefit Street* and now looks like one of the cast of *Made in Chelsea*.

And Darren—any doubts I had about marrying him were well out of the window. At least I knew now I wasn't making a mistake with him. So I looked upon the unfortunate episode with Jerry as a kind of test to see if I was really in love with Darren, and I passed. *Yeah...I'll look at it like that.*

"Hey, Mrs. Daydreamer, pass us your glass over." Sam poured the remaining champagne into my glass. "Drink up. We're nearly at the airport."

THIRTY-TWO

Jess spotted Libby smoking outside the departure entrance, waiting for us to arrive. She opened the window and waved crazily.

"Hiya, Jess!" Libby yelled whilst waving back. "Have you had a good weekend? I have! I'm knackered, and I don't want to see another alcoholic drink for at least six months. I'm still pissed."

"Have you been waiting long?" Faith asked as we began to disembark from the limo.

"About ten minutes. Marco's flight is in a couple of hours, so he arranged a taxi for me. We couldn't risk the chance of arriving together—you never know who's hanging around airports."

"No, you don't," Jess answered. "We'll talk about that when we've checked in, and then you can fill us in with the details of your dirty weekend. We're dying to hear what you've been up to."

"Can you still walk?" Sam asked as she gave Libby a hug. "You don't look too bad for a woman of your age who's been getting slam-dunked all over a villa for a weekend."

"What about you, Sam? Is there anybody left in Benidorm you've not been getting jiggy with?"

"Maybe one or two." Sam laughed. "I'll get them next time, when I come back with Martin. Benidorm is fab, Libby. I'm definitely bringing Martin here. He'll love it."

A blue-and-white minibus pulled up in front of our limo, and the firemen climbed out carrying holdalls.

"Hey, girls," Steve called out as he walked towards us. He took hold of Frankie and pulled her close, grabbing her backside and squeezing it. "You've got a cracking arse, Dr. Frankie."

"Well, you'd know," Frankie replied. "You've been playing with it all weekend."

"Who the hell is he?" Libby asked.

"Quite a lot has happened this weekend, Libby," Frankie explained and planted a kiss on Steve's lips.

"Hi, Chrissy," Mike said.

"Oh, he's a bit of a dish. George Clooney lookalike or what?" Libby whispered.

"That's what I said," Jess whispered back.

"Hello," Chrissy replied, and walked off in the direction of the departure building.

"What is her problem, Ellie? I only asked if we could keep in touch when we got back to Manchester in the bar earlier, and without speaking she just got up and walked back to you lot."

"It's not you, Mike, it's her. She doesn't like to get too close. Please don't take it personal."

"Don't take it personal? I really like her, Ellie."

"I know you do. You've really got to her, too, Mike. Look, I'll see what I can do. Give me your mobile number. I can't promise you, though. Sorry, Mike." I gave him a hug and passed him my phone so he could put in his number.

He followed the rest of the firemen inside the departure building, looking dejected. I'd not really had time to get to know him whilst we were here, but from what Faith and Jess had told me, he appeared to be a really nice guy. He didn't know much about Chrissy apart from she's divorced, owns her own business, and lives in Saddleworth, and it was Jess who told him that; Chrissy refused to tell him anything about herself. I hoped I could play matchmaker because they did look good together.

"Libby, how come you've got three cases? What ya been buying? Are they genuine Louis Vuittons?" Sam asked whilst rubbing her hand up and down them.

"Yes, they're real. Can you believe it? I've not been shopping, though. Marco brought all this stuff with him from Manchester for me. I can't take it home, or Barry will have a fit thinking I've been on a shopping spree all weekend."

"I'm sure he'd have more of a fit if he knew what you'd been up to," Faith said.

"Well, get 'em open, then. Let's have a look and see if we can take anything off your hands before we go through check-in," Frankie said excitedly.

"Chrissy…get back here!" Sam shouted.

Chrissy made her way back to join us, and with the help of Frankie and Sam, Libby began to unzip the cases on the pavement. My eyes nearly popped out of my head. There were candles and toiletries from Jo Malone, numerous items of underwear from Agent Provocateur in a variety of colours, makeup by Chanel, dresses by Victoria Beckham from her new collection—I only know because I read about them in a magazine this morning by the pool—and it didn't surprise me Marco bought dresses from Victoria Beckham. It's common knowledge David Beckham is Marco's all-time footballing legend, along with Georgie Best. Two handbags—no, three handbags—and two pairs of shoes by Jimmy Choo. Oh flip, he'd only gone and bought her a pair of black stiletto Louboutins—I would die for those red-soled shoes. A Miu Miu black leather handbag, two gold necklaces, a watch by Patek Phillippe—never even heard of that make, bet only the rich and famous buy them—a Pandora charm bracelet with two heart charms on it, perfume—Chanel No. 5, couldn't see what the others were—jeans, and T-shirts. The list was endless. "Cuddly toy, cuddly toy," I said to myself. He'd even bought her a cuddly bear with a love heart on the front from Henley's toy store. I felt as though I'd been transported back to the late 70's watching the conveyor belt on *Generation Game*. If all this had passed before my eyes in the final, nothing would have been left behind. Marco must have spent a bomb on Libby. No wonder she was worried about what Barry would say if he saw this lot.

"What am I gonna do? I want to keep it all, but you know I can't. The Louboutins are definitely coming home with me. I wore them all the time, even in bed."

"Shit, I wanted them," I said under my breath.

"Don't you be worrying about all the other stuff, Libby," Sam said. "We'll help you out."

"Yep, don't you be worrying," Frankie added, slavering.

"I knew you would. OK then, I'll take out what I want, and you lot can have the rest," Libby said.

"Unless he got your size wrong and he got you some clothes and underwear in a size eighteen or twenty, I won't be having any of them." Jess laughed. "So I'll be having some of the other stuff. Just a warning, girls, I'll be heading for candles and bags first. And nobody is ever too fat for foundation, so that's mine as well."

Libby knelt and stared at all of the beautiful gifts from her young lover with tears in her eyes whist trying to decide what she'd take home. The rest of us, on the other hand, all looked as if we were about to take part in a shopping-trolley dash. As soon as Libby made a decision about what she wanted, the rest of us were going to be diving in like a pack of shopaholic wolves, and at the end of it there'd be nothing left but empty Louis Vuittons. Slowly she removed her precious Louboutins, her Pandora charm bracelet, a Victoria Beckham cream dress, the Miu Miu leather bag, two basques, three bra-and-knicker sets, the gold necklaces, and the watch. She suddenly stopped and picked out a blue dress by

Victoria Beckham, looked at it carefully, and handed it to Sarah.

"You take this, Sarah," she said. "The colour will really suit you and next time we go out, you're not going to have the excuse you've got nothing to wear. Take these diamante strappy Jimmy Choos and the bag to match. See? Outfit complete."

Sarah's eyes welled up. "Thanks, Libby," she managed to reply. Nobody had had a chance to tell Libby about Sarah and Jimmy yet.

"I don't think I should take any more." Libby sighed. "Oh, the teddy, and I'll keep one of the cases. I'll say Chrissy gave it to me."

"You're right, Libby. You don't wanna be taking any more," Sam said. I dug her in the ribs.

"What? I'm just saying." Sam laughed.

"OK, the rest is yours," Libby declared.

We didn't need telling twice.

"Michelle, get some of that underwear, you need it," Chrissy shouted.

"I've never had a pair of Jimmy Choos," Faith yelled.

"You don't even wear shoes like that," Jess said.

"Never too late to start," Faith replied.

"I'm having some of the Jo Malone things and a Jimmy Choo bag," Jess said, grabbing what she could.

"Get off that Beckham dress, Faith, it won't even fit you. She doesn't make fat sizes." Sam grabbed the dress.

"Fat?" Faith replied. "I'm a fourteen."

"That's what I said!" Sam shouted back. "Now get off it."

"Cheeky cow," Faith replied, keeping hold of the dress.

"Chanel No. 5! My favourite," Michelle said. "Could I take that and the Chanel makeup?"

"Can I have one of them cases? I'll pay the extra for it at check-in," I said.

"Knock yourself out, Ellie." Libby laughed. "Who's having the other one?"

"Me, if that's OK," Jess said. "Oh…and I'll have the Dior makeup kit"

We were all on our hands and knees with a crowd around us wondering what on earth was going on as we rummaged through the cases. I managed to get three T-shirts, a red Jimmy Choo bag, a few pairs of knickers, a few Jo Malone candles, and some toiletries. I was surprised I managed to get all that. Sam kept pushing me out of the way with her elbows like some raving lunatic. I was going to be all bruised tomorrow. Sarah stood watching, clutching her gifts off Libby, tears trickling down her face. I wasn't sure if they were tears of joy or tears of sadness.

"Sarah, what's the matter?" Libby asked.

"I'll tell you later, Libby," I replied as I got up off the floor and walked over to Sarah. I placed my arms around her. "It's going to be OK. You have my word. Jimmy will never lay a finger on you again."

THIRTY-THREE

With all of our new possessions placed firmly in our cases, Faith led the way to check-in, and once we were through security, Faith, flanked by Frankie and Jess, headed for the bar and purchased nine Budweisers.

"Who's going to start?" Libby said as she took a drink of her Bud. "I'm dying to know what you've all been up to."

"I think you should start, Libby. We know what happened in Benidorm, so go on, dish it up. Tell us all about the adventures of Libby and Marco, before we read about it in the papers." The words came out of my mouth without me thinking—because that might just happen.

Libby said they'd driven for about an hour up into some mountains lined with oranges or lemons, she couldn't tell the difference.

"It's easy. Oranges are orange, and lemons are yellow," Frankie said.

"They were yellow," Libby replied. "They must have been lemons." The views had been nice, a bit like the mountains in North Wales but with sun, and probably not as green. They arrived at a cream-and-yellow villa enveloped in high walls with large iron gates with Marco's family emblem on them. Some initials and squiggles, it looked like. The family's housekeepers, a Spanish couple in their midsixties, greeted them. The villa had two floors, and there were five bedrooms, all en suite with baths big enough for two very fat people. She told Jess she'd ask Marco if she and Alan could stay there as she knew they had never been able to have a bath together. Jess threw a beer mat in her direction, but it missed. There was a steam room, a sauna, a bar, a twelve-seater cinema, and a kitchen to die for, with every appliance you could wish for in it. It was a good job they had housekeepers because there was stuff in the kitchen she'd never seen before and didn't know what to do with it.

The grounds were a blaze of colour with their own olive grove, and they walked through them every day. They had sex there twice, up against the trees. And the kidney-shape swimming pool took over nearly all the patio area.

They never left the villa once, and apart from her wearing her Louboutins, they were naked the whole time. She offered to show us her tan lines, just to prove it; she had none. All they had done was eat, drink, and have sex—everywhere in the villa and on the grounds. She'd already given Marco a blow job before they reached the villa, and she'd had an orgasm. "Automatic cars are amazing," she bubbled. "Marco didn't need both hands to drive."

We told her we knew about the blow job, as we had seen her head diving into his lap before they drove out of the airport car park. Libby laughed. Not once had they made love, it was sex all the way—wonderful, fulfilling, exciting, satisfying, screaming, toe-curling sex.

At night they'd snuggle up on the Baltiese bed by the pool, and Marco had traced with his fingers the tiny stretch marks on her stomach. It was so sexy, the way he did it, she said, and then his fingers would wander farther down as if they were being pulled in that direction by a magnet. We were told to leave the rest to our imagination. She didn't want to go into detail as she could feel herself getting excited down below. Marco's body was sculpted like one of them Michelangelo statues in Venice and Florence and Italy. Jess pointed out that Venice and Florence were *in* Italy. Libby smiled and said she knew that.

His skin colour was the colour of a block of Galaxy milk chocolate and just as smooth. "Sex is better than chocolate," she said. "Next time I fancy a Fry's Mint Cream, I'm going to have sex. Not only will I be saving on calories, but I'll be losing weight at the same time."

Sam piped up, "That's why I have sex, but nobody ever listens to me. It isn't just for pleasure. It's part of my exercise and diet regime."

"Sounds heavenly!" Frankie exclaimed.

"It was. I know I shouldn't say it, but I didn't want it to end. I think I may have a bit of a predicament. Marco told me he's in love with me," Libby said. "And I think I'm in love with him. He wants me to move in with him."

"What?" Faith screeched. "But you said—"

Libby interrupted her. "I know, but I have never felt so alive in my life. I don't know what to do."

"Oh, heavens above, Libby. You need to come over to mine tomorrow night. We need an emergency tarot reading. The cards will tell you what to do," Faith said.

"Thanks, Faith, that's what I needed to hear," Libby said.

Did Libby just say that she's in love? And Marco wants her to move in with him? What about the kids? I didn't know what to say; I couldn't think straight. She wasn't thinking straight. It had to be the sun; it did crazy things to people.

"OK, enough from me. What about you lot? Did you leave your mark on Benidorm? Are we allowed to go back, or have we been banned for life?" She laughed.

"First, we need to tell you something," I started. "On Saturday morning a few of us made the front pages of the *Sun*."

"That's fantastic! What did you get up to Friday night, you naughty girls?"

I took out the paper and a couple of articles I'd ripped out of the magazines before I threw them away this morning and showed them to her. Libby quickly read the headline, looked at the picture, and glanced at the articles.

"It's nothing, is it? You can't tell it's me, can ya?" Libby gasped.

"Well, not really, but we just wanted ya to know," Jess said.

"If anybody asks us anything, we'll just say we spotted Marco, and we were waving at him," Frankie tried to reassure her.

"Oh, let's stop worrying. Nothing will come of it. Ya know what journalists are like. So tell me…what did you lot get up to?"

I couldn't believe how calm Libby was being about the stories in the paper and magazines. I was worried sick about Darren ever hearing about my little episode with Jerry, and that had lasted about a minute. She's been with Marco the whole weekend—in fact, the last four months.

Without a care in the world, Libby listened with excitement as tales of our weekend began to unfold. We told her all about Jerry and the Irish bar, Sarah and Jim, the mobility scooters, Sticky Vicky, the firemen from Stockport, the lads from Oldham rugby club, the Geordies, Michelle and Nigel's marriage problems and her discovery of sex toys and orgasms, the sand sculptures, cocktail-making lessons, my girl-on-girl sex act in the strip club, how I had licked squirty cream off a stripper's boobs—she was shown the video evidence on Sarah's mobile phone—and everything else.

Mike and Steve were watching our laughter. Steve brought more drinks over for us whilst we carried on talking. We were so neck-deep in conversation we hadn't noticed our departure gate had been announced. People were beginning to move towards it. Steve came over and told us that if we didn't move, we'd miss our flight to

Manchester. We gathered our belongings and headed off in the direction of the gate.

Sam and I rushed over to the group of lads from Newcastle and got the mobile numbers off a couple of them. Michelle followed us to say bye. Sam promised the lads we'd be up in their part of the world before the year was out, and Michelle said she'd keep practicing their Geordie accent for when they met up again.

Sam, Michelle, and I were running to catch up to the others when Sam abruptly came to a halt in front of me. I nearly went flying.

"What've you stopped for?"

"Ellie, look who's over there." Sam pointed in the direction of our gate. I couldn't believe it. I would've recognised that brown basin cut anywhere. Brenda the bitchy witch stood in line, waiting to get onto our plane, and she was staring at us.

"What the frig is she doing in Spain? I wouldn't take it past her to be spying on us." Sam spoke in a low voice.

"That's you not going off sick tomorrow." I sniggered.

"Bitch…Oh, no. Jess is going over to talk to her," Sam said.

As Jess and Brenda were talking, Brenda kept looking in our direction and smiling. She had known we were coming to Benidorm and had never said a word about her being here at the same time. We smiled back, uttering obscenities towards her in voices only a dog could hear. Jess slowly walked back towards us.

"What the hell is she doing here?" Sam snapped.

"She's been to her brother's wedding in a village on the other side of Benidorm."

"Didn't even know she had a brother, she never said. Wonder what he looks like," I said.

"Take a look, that's him at the side of her in the light-blue Ralph Lauren polo."

A tall, dark, fit man in his late thirties stood by her side with a young Spanish woman who must be his new bride.

"They both came out of the same vagina? Never." I shook my head. "He was adopted. He had to be adopted."

"Obviously all the ugly, malicious, spiteful, evil genes went to Brenda. He is pure sex on legs. Aw, look at the way he's looking at his wife. That's one couple who really do need to get a room, even I'm getting giddy watching them," Sam gushed.

"No, Sam, that's not it. It's because you've spied a bloke you've not had, and you want a go," I replied.

THIRTY-FOUR

Once we were seated on the plane, I fastened my seat belt and turned my full attention to the cabin crew whilst they gave the safety briefing. Then I said a little prayer, asking God to keep us safe on the flight home as per usual.

The seat-belt sign went out, and a beeping noise above my head brought me back from my thoughts.

A member of the cabin crew appeared by my side. "Can I help?" She politely smiled, probably thinking, *The seat-belt sign has only just gone off. Can't these people wait? Have they not had enough to drink?*

"I'd like nine of those half bottles of champagne and glasses," Chrissy requested.

"No more, please," I begged.

"Good call, Chrissy," Frankie, who sat two rows in front with Steve, said.

"Sweetie, we are still on your hen party for the next two and a half hours, and really, when is the next time we are all going to be together again?" Chrissy explained.

"It's gotta be done!" Frankie shouted.

"OK, then, if it's gotta to be done," I moaned.

Michelle lifted her eyes up from the duty-free magazine she was flicking through, looked towards me from her window seat, and smiled. She leant across Chrissy, who sat between us, and gave my left hand a gentle squeeze. "I will never be able to thank you for inviting me this weekend, Ellie. You and your friends have changed my life forever. I have had the best time!"

"You're welcome," I replied. "Are you having some more champers, for a bit of Dutch courage for when you meet Nigel?"

"I don't think there is enough champagne in the world to help me over the next twenty-four hours, but I'll give it a go." She laughed.

"You'll be fine. Just take it slow, the rest'll come naturally."

"I know."

"Sam, what's the chance of a repeat performance of Friday, now we're on our way back to Manchester?" Dave the fireman shouted in her direction.

"Not a chance, think I'll give it a rest for a few hours. Meeting the hubby soon, need to be refreshed for him." Sam mouthed to us, "He was useless."

"I remember you telling us that on the way out." Jess laughed.

It could have been worse. Normally she tells them what she thinks of their sexual performances. At least she spared him that.

Two of the cabin crew arrived with our drinks and handed them out. Corks popped, and we screamed with excitement, laughing as we poured. The captain made an announcement over the public address system, introducing himself and the cabin crew and welcoming us on the flight. He informed us we had about two hours of the flight left until we arrived in Manchester, and yes, it was raining.

As he continued speaking I heard my name, Ellie McDonald, and my ears pricked up. "And on behalf of all the Benidorm Virgins who are flying with us today"—a roaring round of applause and cheering went up in all quarters of the plane—"they would like to thank you for a fantastic weekend on your hen party and would like to wish you and Darren the very best and lots of love for your future."

I smiled, just thinking about Darren and what the future had in store for us. Then my mind turned to Jerry and how my future with Darren would have been over. I wondered just how many people had been to Benidorm—or anywhere else, really—excited about the prospect of getting married, and then with one stupid mistake, they had changed their lives forever. If this weekend had taught me anything, it taught me any doubts I had about marrying Darren were wasted thoughts. Now I realised just how much I love him. I couldn't wait. I lifted up my glass alone and raised a toast to Darren and me for our future together.

Sarah was quiet, her mind slipping into deep thought. I gently reached over the seat in front and placed my hand on her shoulder. She turned around.

"Wanna talk?"

"No, thanks, not sure what to talk about."

"We'll be home soon. It will be fine."

"Of course it will, Sarah," Chrissy joined in. "Everything is arranged."

"It's Maisy I'm worried about now. I don't want her to be upset."

"Maisy will love it. She is going on holiday to stay with Auntie Chrissy. It will be an adventure for her. One step at a time, hey, Sarah," Chrissy comforted her. "Auntie Chrissy can take her over to feed the horses tomorrow whilst my solicitor comes to talk to you, OK? She'll love that."

"Thanks, Chrissy. I'll pay you back."

"Shush. Not another word," Chrissy replied.

The seat-belt sign was illuminated, followed by the announcement we were making our descent into Manchester. Michelle looked out of the window and spotted the Pyramid in Stockport. It wouldn't be long now until we landed.

THIRTY-FIVE

The baggage collection area was manic. It looked as if every plane in the world had just landed at Manchester International Airport, and it took us about forty-five minutes to get through passport control. Jess pointed to the carousel where we had to go to collect our bags. Mike caught my eye, and I smiled in his direction. A smile came right back at me. "I'll try to speak to Chrissy before we leave the airport," I mouthed to him.

We said our good-byes to some of the people we'd met over the last few days. We told the girls from Liverpool we'd keep in touch and arrange a night out in Manchester with them soon. I felt as if I had known some of these people forever. The boys from the rugby club came over and handed out kisses and hugs freely, as did the firemen. Mike walked in Chrissy's direction, but she quickly headed towards the ladies'.

Faith, Sarah, and I were the first to walk through the nothing-to-declare lane and out into the arrivals hall, where we stopped dead in our tracks. People crashed into us and started pushing, shoving, and moaning for us to move out of the way. We moved to let them through. Jess, Frankie, and Libby were the next to come out. Frankie and Libby stopped, too. Jess was too busy talking to notice what was going on.

"Jess…Jess." Libby punched her in the arm. "Jess, shut it, will ya?"

"Oi, what's that for, Libby?"

"Look." Libby pointed to a handmade banner being held up by Alesha and Roxy saying JESS, WILL YOU MARRY ME? in bright-red letters, with hearts in varying sizes placed strategically all around. Alan stood underneath it, wearing a pair of cream chinos and a navy long-sleeved shirt, holding a large bunch of red roses.

"What the…" Jess gasped.

Alan walked nervously towards Jess and gave her the flowers.

"Alan! What ya doing?" Jess looked embarrassed.

"Jess, I want to ask you something." He went down on one knee.

"What's happening?" Sam asked, with Chrissy by her side.

"Looks like Alan's gonna make a prat of himself," Faith replied.

In the arrivals hall, all eyes were now on Alan and Jess.

"Alan, are you drunk?" Jess took hold of his lapels and pulled at them, trying to get him up off the ground. "Alan, get up everybody is staring at you…us."

"No, Jess, I'm not drunk. I have never been more sober in my life," Alan replied.

"Well, go on, then, explain yourself!" Sam shouted out.

"Alan, stop it," Jess snapped. "Get up now, you're going to dirty your trousers."

"No, not until I've asked you to marry me."

"I've told you I am never going to let you ask me to marry you until you tell Stella and get a divorce. Why are you doing this to me, Alan?" Jess's voice was quavering.

"I've done something this weekend, something I should have done a long time ago."

"Oh my God, you've killed your wife!" Faith screeched.

"Don't be stupid," Alan and Jess said in unison.

"No, I haven't," Alan replied as he took hold of Jess's hand, looking her directly in the eye. "I drove to Kent on Saturday morning. I didn't want to go, but I had to. I'd made my mind up on Friday evening I was going to tell Stella about us, and when I arrived, she was in the kitchen, crying."

"She was probably feeling the same way as you," Sam said sarcastically. "Ooooo…Alan's home."

"Please don't interrupt, Sam. You're not helping," Alan said. "I asked Stella what was wrong, and as usual, the answer was 'nothing,' which in women's language means there is something wrong, but I'm not telling you until you've asked me at least a million times. Stella got up off a bar stool and walked into the lounge. I went into the bar and poured myself a large brandy for courage. And it did give me courage, Jess, because I went into the lounge and told Stella about us, and she burst out crying again."

"Oh! Alan. I'm so sorry," Jess replied.

"Should have thought about that before you started your affair," Faith said. "Poor woman."

"Jess, they were tears of joy and relief. And yes, you're right, Sam. She was feeling the same as me. It turned out she, too, has been involved with somebody else for the last eighteen months. Jess, Stella wants a divorce. We went out on Saturday night, we laughed, we cried. It's the best night out I've had with Stella in years. It's all sorted. We're getting a divorce. You can even arrange it if you want to."

Jess's eyes welled up, and tears began slowly rolling down her cheeks.

"I left first thing this morning and drove back up to Manchester. I rang Alesha on the way back to tell her, and we met on King Street this afternoon to do a bit of engagement-ring shopping. It was Alesha's idea to make the banner, and Roxy and Izzy helped. So, Jessica Ann Buckley, please will you do me the honour of being my wife?" He put his hand into his jacket pocket and took out a small black box, opened it, and removed the biggest diamond ring I had ever seen.

"Jess!" I gasped.

"Yes! Yes! Give it to me!" Jess screamed.

Alan proudly placed the ring on her wedding finger, then kissed her hand.

Jess lifted her left hand and looked at the sparkling solitaire diamond ring that now had pride of place on the third finger. "I'm getting married. I'm getting married. Libby, look. Everybody, look." She waved her left hand around for all the world to see. "I'm getting married."

Jess threw her arms around Alan's neck and then planted a kiss smack on his lips. It must have hit him like a sledgehammer, she went at him with such force.

"Ahh, I can't believe it. Oh, Alan. Thank you. I love you."

Rapturous applause and cheering filled the arrivals hall. I looked around and spotted Darren. He smiled and winked. I smiled back and mouthed, "Love you."

"Come on, we've got to go." Alan took hold of Jess's hand. "We've got a plane to catch."

"What are you talking about?" Jess gave Alan a puzzled look.

"We've got to catch a flight to Heathrow. I've been promising you for a long time I would take you to the Maldives. We're flying out tomorrow."

"Alan, are you joking?"

"No, Jess. I'm not joking."

"As much I would love to go, Alan, I've got a mountain of paperwork."

"No, you haven't. I rang Jim Turnbull and told him what I was planning, and he said, with his blessing. You never take any time off, and they would cover you for a week. So shift your backside. I've got a British Airways plane waiting for us. We're going to the Maldives, baby." And he gave her bottom a cheeky slap.

"Mum, I've packed some things for you, and what I've not packed you'll just have to buy." Alesha gave her mum a big hug. "I'm really happy for you, Mum."

"Oh! Alesha, I can't take all this in. Where are you going to stay?" She hugged her daughter tightly.

"I'll stay at Auntie Ellie's. It's all arranged with Darren."

Jess snatched hold of Alan's hand. "Come on, then, let's get moving!" she excitedly shouted as she pulled Alan along. We could do nothing but wave after them.

Brenda and her family walked past us. She sort of smiled. We sort of smiled back. Sam put two fingers up in her direction and waved them at her, whilst sticking out her tongue.

"I can't wait to tell her to stuff her job," Sam said.

"I know, me too. We'll do it Tuesday."

Mike and the rest of the firemen were making their way out of the terminal building. Mike looked back again and caught my eye. He nodded, threw his holdall over his shoulder, and continued walking.

I rushed over to Chrissy. "Why won't you say bye to Mike? You've spent all weekend with him. It's not going to kill you."

"I can't, Ellie."

"Why not?"

"Like an idiot, I've fallen for him, Ellie. I'm trying to keep as much distance between us as I can, so I can get him out of my head, but as Kylie Minogue keeps singing

'*I can't get you out of my head.*' It's bloody hard to forget him. It's been so easy this weekend being around him. Mike has made me feel…well, normal, but I can't get hurt again. No, I'm leaving it."

"Look, if you don't take a chance, you're never going to know if he was the one. You may regret it forever, Chrissy. Look at him. He looks so sad. And you can tell a mile off you like him. Remember the smelly cats, even ginger ones." I laughed.

Chrissy looked towards to exit and saw Mike walking out of the door. "Oh! What the fuck—you're right, sweetie."

"So what are you waiting for? Move." I took hold of Chrissy's hand, running as best I could in my new Jimmy Choos, which were slightly too big for me but they'd fit me fine, once I'd bought some insoles and heel grips.

"Mike!" I shouted, a little out of breath.

He was standing at the rear of their hired minibus, helping to load his colleagues' holdalls into it. He stopped and turned around when he heard me shouting his name.

"Chrissy has something she'd like to say." I thrust her forward.

Chrissy opened her bag and took out one of her business cards. "I'm sorry for the way that I"—she looked towards me for support—"Mike, I have been hurt so many times in my life by men. I didn't want it to happen again. I'll admit, I felt something with you I have never felt before. My tough exterior has started to show signs of cracking, and I'll be honest…I'm scared."

"I'd never hurt you, Chrissy—you're too special. If you'd have taken the time to talk to me over the weekend, you'd know I'm not that kind of person, but you wouldn't talk about personal stuff."

"I know, I never do personal, it gets too...personal." She smiled. "Look Mike, if you want, I'd like to go on a date with you, a proper one. Will you call me tomorrow to talk, please?"

The firemen started cheering for their friend and commanding officer.

Mike retrieved the card from Chrissy's hand and slid it into the back pocket of his jeans. He took hold of Chrissy's face and kissed her tenderly on the lips.

"It will be my pleasure to call you tomorrow, Chrissy. Good night, princess," he replied.

Arm in arm we made our way back into the arrivals hall, Chrissy still unsure if she had done the right thing by agreeing to meet Mike and go on a date. Men who were not as wealthy as Chrissy usually had issues about her money, and it usually drove them away. That was her biggest concern with Mike as she really did like him.

Darren walked towards me and took me in his arms. "You OK, busy lady?"

"Yeah...just had a bit of a mad weekend. Glad I'm home," I replied as we hugged. "It's a good job we were only there for three days. Not sure I could take much more. I'm knackered."

"What you done to our Michelle? She looks amazing."

"That's Chrissy's doing. I'll save that tale for another day."

"Michelle, do you want a lift home?" Darren asked her, as he kissed his sister on the cheek.

"No, you're all right, Darren. Nigel is here to meet me. Oh! There he is." Michelle waved to greet him. He acknowledged Darren with a nod, and Darren nodded back. Nigel's face had a look of surprise on it as he took hold of his wife and softly kissed her on her cheek. He was probably wondering if that fit bird that he was holding was really his wife. "Nigel and I have got a lot of catching up to do." She gave Darren a peck on the cheek. "Ellie's a great woman, Darren. You are one hell of a lucky man."

"Good luck. Call me." Chrissy smiled.

"Will do, and thanks, Chrissy," Michelle replied.

Darren couldn't take his eyes off Michelle as she walked away holding hands with Nigel. I smiled.

Frankie said bye to Steve. Frankie definitely has met her match there. They've already got plans to go out next weekend in Manchester, and he's going to book a room in the Midland Hotel for them both.

"Psst...Libby, Barry's coming towards us," I said. "What's he waving at you—is that a newspaper?"

"Lucky me," she replied. "Back to bloody normal. Anyway, what's he doing here? I thought I was getting a lift with Faith."

Suddenly within the throng of people still waiting in the arrivals hall, bright lights started flashing all around.

They were lights from cameras. Flash…flash…flash…followed by shouting. "Liberty Davies, Liberty Davies."

"Are you Liberty Davies?"

"What the…" said Sam.

"Have you had a nice weekend with Marco, Liberty?" one of the photographers shouted.

"Did you enjoy the villa, Liberty?"

"You've got a cracking body, Liberty. Ever thought about modelling?"

"Liberty, turn around, give us a smile."

Barry grabbed the flustered Libby before giving her a chance to answer and dragged her out of the building, I assume towards a waiting taxi, with the paparazzi shouting after them.

"Faith, I'll see you tomorrow night. Bye, everybody, thanks for a great weekend," Libby shouted without turning around.

"What the fuck was that all about?" Darren asked.

"Shouldn't we go and help her, Ellie?" Faith asked.

"And do what? Barry looked like he had it all under control."

"What's going on? What the hell have ya all been up to?" Darren howled with laughter.

"I'll tell ya later." I didn't know whether to laugh or cry. "We need to get out of here before they come back and start on us."

I wondered how they had found out it was Libby. And why was Barry here? Maybe we were trying to kid ourselves that you couldn't recognise Libby on the front page of the *Sun* in Marco's Jaguar. Shit…what a mess.

Darren walked over to Sarah and put his arm around her. "You OK, kid?"

"I'm not sure I can go through with this, Ellie," Sarah said.

"Sarah, will you stop saying that? I'm sorry, but there's no going back," Faith said. "You know you're going to have to report this, Sarah."

"Please, no. I can't."

"OK, we can talk about that again, but you've got to go with Chrissy, Sarah. Next time, you might not be so lucky. I see people all the time being brought into A and E because of domestic abuse. You've been there, remember? Or have you forgotten? Some are not so lucky; next time you might not be so lucky. I'm sorry to be so blunt, Sarah, but who's going to look after Maisy if anything does happen to you?"

Sarah bowed her head. "Can I do it tomorrow, then, when Jim's in work? He's on earlies. Jim'll go mad if we turn up tonight. I don't want Maisy to get upset. There'll be a lot of shouting and screaming off Jim. Believe me."

"It's all sorted, Sarah, I told you," I explained to her. "Darren's going to take us all back to your house, and he's already arranged to go out with Jim for a pint. We'll get all your stuff together whilst they're out. Chrissy's driver will be close by, and he'll come and collect you and Maisy. Me and Sam are coming, too, and we'll help you get settled.

So there's gonna be no shouting or screaming. You don't need to get upset or stressed. You're not on your own anymore." I put my arm around her shoulder and squeezed. "Once we've got everything together and we're on our way to Chrissy's, I'll give Darren a ring and let him know."

"He won't know what's hit him," Chrissy said.

"If it was up to me I'd beat him black and blue all around Ashton, but I promised Ellie I wouldn't lay a finger on him," Darren said. "Sarah, everything will be OK. I promise. Nothing is going to happen to you, and believe me, you'll get no grief from Jimmy."

"You certainly won't. In the world that I live in, if people upset us or get in our way, we make them disappear. You see, Sarah, money talks. Look what happened to Lord Lucan." Chrissy tried to make light of the situation.

"Thanks, Darren. I know this is hard for you, with Jimmy being one of your mates," Sarah said.

"No mate of mine's a wife beater. I'll get him for this, Sarah, believe me. He'll get used as a punch bag next time we're playing rugby. That's if he ever shows his face up at the club again."

"Darren, let's get going." I could feel him getting wound up. I put my arm through Sarah's, and we began to make our way to the exit, pulling our cases behind us. As the automatic doors opened, the cold Manchester air hit us all, and not one of us was wearing anything appropriate for this kind of temperature.

THIRTY-SIX

"Mummy, mummy." We all stopped and turned around to see Maisy, dressed in a Pink Panther fleece onesie running through the arrivals hall towards Sarah. Jimmy was smiling, dressed casually in dark blue jeans and a T-shirt with a picture of Marilyn Monroe on the front, slowly walking behind her. What the hell were they doing here? A wave of fear spread over my body. I don't like confrontations or arguing. This was going to turn bad. I could feel it.

We turned and walked back inside the arrivals hall. Sarah bent down and hugged her pretty little five-year-old and covered her face in kisses. "I've missed you, Maisy. Have you missed me?" Maisy hugged Sarah back, no answer was needed. This little girl has missed her mummy.

"Course she's missed ya, been bloody moaning since I picked her up from your mum's at six," answered Jimmy. "Thought we'd come and pick ya up—you've been away from me for too long."

Yep…this was going to be awkward. How could we get Sarah away from Jimmy without causing a scene, especially in front of Maisy? I looked around the arrivals area. It was a lot quieter now than when we had first come through the sliding doors to be greeted by Alan and his banner. Most people had made their way out of the arrivals hall now into the waiting cars and taxis. The paparazzi hadn't come back in. They disappeared just as quickly as they arrived. Thank goodness. I couldn't have coped with them as well as Jimmy. I would give Libby a call later from the car to see how she was. I waved Roxy over, gave her a hug, and whispered for her to take Maisy and Alesha to Darren's car and wait for us there. I took the keys off Darren and passed them to her. I said I'd explain later.

I crouched down, so I was on the same level as Maisy. "Hi, Maisy. How are you? You look beautiful in your onesie. You remember Roxy and Alesha, don't you?"

"Hi, Maisy, love your onesie. Wanna come and play?" Roxy said as she took her hand.

"Hello, Roxy. Hello, Alesha, can we play I spy? I'm not very good though. I know *A* is for apple and *B* is for ball. Oh, and *C* is for cat."

Roxy smiled. "Course we can."

Jimmy watched Roxy, Alesha, and Maisy walking out of the building. "Where the bloody hell are they going? We need to get going, Sarah. Some of us have got work in the morning. Not everybody gets the chance to sit around all day and drink tea, or whatever you stay-at-home mums do."

I took a deep breath. I was bubbling inside. I'd never really paid attention to anything Jimmy had said before Benidorm, but every word out of his mouth now was making my blood boil. Who was going to tell Jimmy Sarah wouldn't be going home with him—not today, not ever? I opened my mouth to speak, but Darren beat us all to it. "We know about you and Sarah, Jimmy."

"Know what? What the fuck have you been saying, Sarah?" He looked her straight in the eye.

"She didn't have to say anything, Jimmy. We've seen the bruises," Frankie answered calmly.

"Them fucking bruises. She's always knocking into things, aren't you, silly girl?" Jimmy walked towards Sarah.

I looked at Faith, Chrissy, and then Darren. I put a hand on his arm. *Please don't hit him, Darren*, I pleaded in my head. *The weekend can't end with you being charged with grievous bodily harm. I just want to go home and cuddle up in bed with you.*

Jimmy took hold of Sarah tightly by the arm. "Sarah, move and let's get Maisy. I haven't got time for this."

"Let her go, Jimmy. She's not going anywhere with ya," Darren calmly spoke.

Jimmy released his hold of Sarah. "Darren, Daz, mate." He smirked.

"Don't fucking 'mate' me. Now we can do this two ways, Jimmy. We can discuss what's been going on with you and Sarah here in the arrivals hall, and then I can drag ya kicking and screaming out of the building like the little shit you are, or you can take yourself out of my sight before I kick ten bells of shit out of ya. Your choice, *mate*."

"Look, it's not what you think. Tell 'em Sarah—tell 'em they've got it wrong. We're OK."

"You're OK, you bastard!" Faith screeched and lunged at Jimmy, arms flying. Darren caught hold of her shirt to stop her.

Darren stared Jimmy straight in the eye whilst still holding on to Faith. "If it's a scene you want, *mate*, then it's a scene you'll get, and I'll get them two coppers over there with their guns to referee. Now fuck off, you fucking wimp." Darren was beginning to raise his voice.

Sarah was frozen to the spot, holding on to my hand all the time Darren and Jimmy spoke. I gave her a reassuring squeeze. Frankie, Sam, and Chrissy stood beside us, letting her know we were with her all the way.

"You've not heard the end of this—fucking kidnapping my wife, filling her head with shit. I'll deal with you later, Sarah."

Darren released Faith and smacked Jimmy straight in the face, causing him to lose his footing and stagger back. Jimmy took hold of his face in shock. His nose was bleeding. I think Darren had broken his nose. I looked around; the two police officers were out of sight.

"Don't worry, *mate*. I'm not gonna be wasting another punch on you—you're not fucking worth it. Oh, and for a bit of info, that's the last time you're gonna threaten or touch Sarah. And that valuable stuff of your mum's in our safe. Don't bother asking for it back. I used it to light my wood burner this morning."

Jimmy turned and walked away, still holding his hands over his nose and mouth. Darren told us to go and wait for him outside—he wanted to make sure Jimmy went to his car. I prayed nothing else would happen.

We walked out of the arrivals hall and said bye to Faith and Frankie, who had a taxi waiting for them. I suggested to Chrissy, Sarah, and Sam that they too should take a taxi, just in case Jimmy followed our car, and that Darren and I would take Roxy and Alesha home. Then we'd make our way over to Chrissy's house with Maisy if everything was all right; if not, Maisy could stay at our house and we would bring her over tomorrow morning. Jimmy would find out soon enough where Sarah and Maisy would be staying, but for now, Sarah needed to feel safe. I watched them all climb into their taxis and waved as they passed me by.

Darren ran back to join me, slightly out of breath, and gave me a kiss on the cheek. He told me he'd watched Jimmy pay for his parking, get into his Jag, and head out of the car park. Darren went back into the airport to pay for our parking.

We crossed the road and walked into the short-stay car park. I took hold of Darren's hand and squeezed it. I was so glad to be back. What a weekend. I really did hope Michelle and Nigel would be able to get their marriage back on track, especially with the help of Chrissy. And I had got myself a sister-in-law. Jess got her man. Faith was still Faith; I wasn't really sure what was going to happen to her. Frankie got herself a new boyfriend, Steve, and Chrissy was gonna give it a go with Mike. Sam won her bet with Chrissy for sex. I'll be honest—if I were Sam, I wouldn't be able to walk for a month, let alone a week. And me, I only hoped it wouldn't be too long before I stopped beating myself up about Jerry.

Roxy waved to us as we approached the car and popped open the boot. As I helped Darren load my bags into the car, he pulled me towards him, put his arms around my body, and kissed me slowly. How I'd missed the taste of his breath, the smell of his body. I didn't want to let him go. I walked around to my side of the car and gripped the door handle. Darren made his way around to the driver's side, leant on the roof, and gave me one of his cheeky smiles.

"So go on, then. When we get rid of all the girls, are you gonna dish the dirt on what happened this weekend, or what?"

I laughed. "Darren, you are such an old woman. You'd never believe what I told you, even if I did. And besides, you know I can't do that. As you always say to me when you go away with the lads, 'What goes on tour, stays on tour.'"

THE END

ABOUT THE AUTHOR

Janita Faulkner is originally from Manchester and now lives in West Yorkshire, England with her husband David. Between them, they have four daughters, two sons, two sons-in-law, one granddaughter, and two grandsons. Her family and friends are her world.

Janita enjoys singing, walking on the moors around her home and in the lake district, travelling anywhere and everywhere (has spent a lot of time in China) and has a bucket list that grows and grows all the time. She has quite a few guilty pleasures ... one being drinking Champagne in a warm bubble bath while reading a great book—her idea of pure heaven!